SUCCESS STORY

TIM PAULSON

Ⓢ

A SIGNET BOOK

NEW AMERICAN LIBRARY

PUBLISHER'S NOTE

This novel is a work of fiction. Names, characters, places, and incidents either are the product of the author's imagination or are used fictitiously, and any resemblance to actual persons, living or dead, events, or locales is entirely coincidental.

Copyright © 1985 by Tim Paulson

This is an authorized reprint of a hardcover edition published by St. Martin's/Marek.

SIGNET TRADEMARK REG. U.S. PAT. OFF. AND FOREIGN COUNTRIES
REGISTERED TRADEMARK—MARCA REGISTRADA
HECHO EN CHICAGO, U.S.A.

SIGNET, SIGNET CLASSIC, MENTOR, PLUME, MERIDIAN AND NAL BOOKS are published by New American Library, 1633 Broadway, New York, New York 10019

First Signet Printing, May, 1986

1 2 3 4 5 6 7 8 9

PRINTED IN THE UNITED STATES OF AMERICA

FIRST INSTALLMENT

Diane was slightly dizzy from the champagne, but her head cleared when John Bradley kissed her. His kiss was neither awkward nor egotistical, neither aloof nor passionate. His kiss asserted competence. It risked little. It told her that he was proposing a game. The next move was hers.

"I'd like you to spend the night," he said. Then he said, "Is anything wrong?"

"I'd like to get carried away," she said. "But I can tell I'm not going to."

"That's okay," he smiled amiably. "If you were passionate, I'd probably be intimidated."

"I didn't say I wasn't passionate."

"Can't you settle for excitement?" He put his arms around her and, as he kissed her, they sank slowly down onto the carpet . . .

. . . and Diane began to learn what having it all was all about. . . .

SUCCESS STORY

To Jane Hughes Paulson

PART ONE

PART ONE

one

Diane Yaeger believed in great things for herself, but she had not expected the magazine interview with John E. Bradley, Jr., to end with a dinner invitation. It was not an interview you took the subway home from. The brilliant late March afternoon was fading to cold twilight as she headed down Lexington Avenue to the cash machine she had passed earlier, running, late for the meeting.

The line was long but Diane had plenty to think about until it was her turn to step up to the screen. The program asked whether she wanted to conduct her transaction in English or Spanish. She did not speak Spanish, but after what she had pulled off that afternoon she could do anything. Things progressed smoothly until the computer refused to give her the seventy-five dollars she requested. She switched to English. The screen apologized for not being able to help her. She asked for her balance. Eighteen dollars and thirty-two cents. With a sinking feeling, she remembered the check written earlier that week for the white silk blouse she was wearing. The smallest figure under the withdrawal category was twenty dollars. She picked up the service phone.

"I've got eighteen dollars in my account," she told the customer service representative, "and I'd like to withdraw it." The woman explained in an impersonal monotone that the cash machine could not give less than twenty dollars. She would have to wait until Monday and present a check for that amount at her branch of the bank.

"But there's money in the account." Diane lowered her voice. The vestibule fell silent as the people in line watched her and listened. "I want it now."

The representative apologized and hung up. Diane slammed the receiver down and headed out into the street to hail a cab.

"The promenade in Brooklyn Heights," she told the driver, "or eight dollars, whichever comes first."

"You'll never make it, lady."

"Let's see how far we get."

Traffic was light for rush hour, and the cab moved steadily through side streets to the F.D.R. Drive. The sky over the East River reflected sunset. Though it was windy, individual clouds hung stationary in the east, a flotilla of rose-colored dirigibles at anchor.

"It sure don't feel like spring," the driver remarked.

"But the sun's still up," she said, "and it's almost six."

Diane was relieved that the cab driver did not continue the conversation. Blocking out the sound of the meter, she settled comfortably into her pleasant thoughts. She saw Bradley again waiting for her at the doorway to his apartment, handsome but surly-looking with his high, furrowed forehead, a day's growth of beard, his muscular, softly hairy forearms.

Diane was exhausted. Bradley, best-selling author of *The Great Thaw*, evidently prided himself on being a difficult interview. He had been alternately arrogant, haughty, evasive, hostile, and sarcastic as she attempted to draw him out. She had been up until six that morning trying to finish his book, and then worked feverishly all morning at *The New York Times* to get the "Company News" column to press. But never in her life had fatigue been accompanied by such a satisfying sense of accomplishment. Bradley had found many of her questions superficial and others annoyed him, but something about the interview had piqued his curiosity about her.

It had taken Diane a long time to decide what she wanted to do with her life. In college, she held out as a poet when students were turning from revolution to MBA programs. After graduation, she attempted short-story writing, but when a year and a half of Sunday afternoons consecrated to writing failed to get a story in *The New Yorker,* she turned to magazine articles. She had had better luck as a journalist, progressing from the hand-to-mouth existence of a freelance writer to a part-time job at the *Times.* The freelance article on Bradley for *Rolling Stone* stemmed from a decision to write about movies. Her future, beyond meeting moviemakers, had the sublime sketchiness of an impressionist painting. But she was moving quickly in the right direction, she reflected in a moment of uncharacteristic self-satisfaction. Bradley was the real thing. He would know the right people.

From the Brooklyn Bridge, the western sky was a dark purple. The lights of lower Manhattan were so clear and star-like that the skyline might have been viewed from a telescope. The meter read five dollars and fifty cents. She would make it across the bridge. Things were clicking. The singing stopped under the taxi's wheels. They were in Brooklyn.

"If you stop here," she told the driver as he turned off the Cadman Plaza exit, "I can give you a ninety-cent tip." He turned the meter off, but did not stop.

"Where on the promenade?"

"You can let me off here, really."

"As long as I had to leave Manhattan, what's a few more minutes?"

"Thanks." She directed him to her apartment. She wanted to shake his hand, or kiss him, she was so pleased for herself, but she confined herself to a cheerful goodnight.

Diane was too excited to go inside, especially to an apartment as dirty as hers had become during her current working binge. Instead, she almost ran down the sidewalk to the promenade, where she leaned against the railing and gazed out beyond docked ships to Manhattan, shimmering across the harbor. She had moved to Brooklyn Heights for this view. She meditated upon it almost daily. No matter how frustrated she became, no matter how close she came to giving up hope in her dreams, this view invariably revived her. It was somehow appropriate, too, that she studied this objectification of her ambitions from someplace so different from Manhattan. She was as much a foreigner in Brooklyn as she was across the East River in Manhattan.

Diane was not dressed for the icy wind blowing off the harbor. She turned back to the tree-lined streets and walked past a row of restored Victorian brownstones to Alan Jennings's apartment.

Diane knew Alan from his days as a pre-medical student at Northwestern a year ahead of her. She was instrumental in convincing him to switch from medicine—a career path he had chosen out of deference to his father, a successful orthopedist from a North Shore Chicago suburb from which his son commuted to school—to photography, an avocation that gradually grew into an obsession. He was now one of the highest-paid industrial photographers in New York.

Diane climbed the steps to the entrance of the imposing townhouse where Alan occupied the fifth floor.

"Yeah?" His voice exploded over the intercom. Diane wondered if the volume could be adjusted. Alan was undoubtedly in the middle of a project.

"It's Diane," she called. The buzzer let her in. Using the heavy walnut handrail, she vaulted herself up the stairs two at a time.

"What are you doing all dressed up?" He peered down at her through the bannister as she climbed. It was rare for Alan to notice her appearance. She was pleased that his eyes registered the trouble she had taken for the interview: the curling iron used on wavy brown hair, makeup accentuating the blue of her eyes, the dressy blouse, and long, straight, navy-blue skirt.

"An interview," she said, out of breath. "What happened to you?" She grimaced, dodging his friendly kiss. The tall, bearded young man waiting for her in the paneled hallway was covered with mud. It had begun to dry on his hair and beard and was flaking off in patches from his sweater and jeans. Mud on his black engineer's boots had been trailed up the red carpet on the stairway.

"You look like you've been shooting an ad for a grave diggers' association," she said.

"Weirder than that." His smile chipped a scale of mud off his face. His brown-green eyes, surrounded by the mud, sparkled like a coal miner's. She followed him into the apartment and shut the door. They walked through a sparsely furnished living room into a back room. "Here. I just finished the contacts."

"Rats." Diane shivered as she moved the magnifying glass from frame to frame. From thirty-six angles, a rat gnawed voraciously at a pile of pellets. "Where did you take these?"

"In the sewer under the reservoir in Central Park—the place where they filmed *Marathon Man*. If you think those are bad," he went on breathlessly, "wait until you see these." He entered a darkroom and returned with a dripping contact sheet.

"Amazing." Diane shook her head. A pretty blonde woman whom Diane saw occasionally in a bathroom disinfectant commercial knelt in a pair of short shorts and a halter top to spoon poison onto a sewer drain.

"How did you get a model down there?"

"She got double time," he laughed, "the same rate she gets for wet T-shirt shots."

"I'd prefer semi-nudity," Diane said, smiling.

"You wouldn't believe this poison." His incredulity was boyish as he put the two contact sheets side by side on a drawing board. "They explode inside. It's so strong it can't be sold to the public. The rats down there are as big as cats. We had to wait forty-five minutes for one to come up to the trap."

"How long have you been home?"

"A couple of hours. I had to see the contacts. The lighting was real tricky with the water and the artificial light on the wet walls. It couldn't be too bright, either, or the rats wouldn't come."

Alan Jennings was a fanatic about detail. He would have worked until midnight without a shower. He had probably forgotten he was dirty until Diane arrived.

"I can't believe a client expects you to get that dirty."

"My own parents would probably roll around in mud for four hours for fifteen hundred dollars," he laughed.

"Not with rats gnawing at their toes."

"That's true," Alan conceded. "My mother's afraid of mice."

Though just thirty, there were crow's feet around Alan's eyes when he laughed. He had been everywhere—above ground, below ground, under water, in deserts and mountains. He got amazing assignments.

"Let's go get Chinese food," she said.

"Which province should we do tonight?" Alan called from the bathroom, where he had begun running water.

"I feel like something hot. Let's do Szechuan."

"Maybe I'll shop for the week."

"I can't believe you really like cold Chinese food," she said. Alan would often bring five or six entrees home from a Chinese restaurant, and have a smorgasbord of Chinese dishes for dinner the rest of the week. It saved trips to the supermarket, he insisted.

"I heat it up," Alan defended himself. "Sometimes."

"You heat it when I come over for a midnight snack."

Diane heard him turn the shower on. She had assumed that he would be free for dinner. He was much too wrapped up in his work for a steady relationship with a woman. He thrived on sudden assignments, trips around the world, and all-night deadlines before fifteen-projector multi-media shows. He kept even odder hours than she did. He was likely to be awake if she tired of reading at three in the morning and wanted someone to bounce a reaction off of. He didn't mind hearing about the men she went out with, either, though with an inexplicable tact she withheld physical details. They shared a sense that being from the Midwest, their openness to things unusual or bizarre made them unique. They were determined, independent, ambitious people. Diane felt that if Alan was more successful, at least materially, this was because he had taken the trouble to understand the needs of the business world, while she found people who lived less structured lives more interesting. However, to Alan's credit, he had become, if anything, more of an individual as he became more successful.

"Guess who I'm having dinner with tomorrow night?" Diane walked into the steam-filled bathroom and sat down on a hamper next to the tub.

"Who?" He called, invisible behind the faded brown shower curtain.

"The guy who wrote *The Great Thaw*."

"John Bradley?"

"Yeah. I interviewed him for *Rolling Stone* this afternoon."

"He asked you out for tomorrow?"

"He asked me out for tonight," she corrected him proudly. "I told him I had a date."

"Couldn't you cancel it?"

"It's with you."

"I can't believe you turned down a date with a celebrity," he laughed. His voice was muffled by water streaming down his face.

"I can't believe it either. My heart was pounding almost out of my chest and my voice cracked when I told him I had plans for tonight. It was the biggest gamble I've ever taken."

"Why'd you do it?" Alan's voice carried over the steam.

"Ever play five-card stud?" she asked.

"I don't like poker."

"The way we play it in Minnesota, you need a pair of jacks or better to open. Accepting a date the first time he asked would have been like opening without a pair. I wanted to keep the stakes high enough to interest him in a second round."

"You're lucky it worked."

"I'm a good poker player."

"You might have lost the hand."

"I thought I had at first. I would never have done it if I hadn't been half drunk."

"You drank during an interview?" There was disapproval in Alan's surprise.

"He was two or three Scotches ahead of me. He practically insisted."

"I'm surprised he didn't invite you to his bedroom to look at etchings."

"Actually, he invited me back to look at shrunken heads. He got them sailing his boat down to the Amazon."

"I hear he's really crazy," Alan laughed. "And super rich."

"How do you know?"

"Someone I know has a friend who hangs out with him at Coco's. They went across the Arctic together on a Ski-doo." Alan had inside sources of information on everything. "Supposedly he spends a fortune on cocaine."

"He doesn't act like someone who does a lot of coke." The idea of Bradley using an excessive amount of drugs did not conform to Diane's image of the man.

"Maybe he's reformed."

"Do you know anything about the book?" she asked.

"I read a review. Said it was pretty good for a thriller."

"They're making it into a movie. Bradley's going to Hollywood in a couple of weeks."

"Congratulations." A large, dripping hand, dark hair plastered against its wrist, reached from behind the curtain to shake hers. "Hollywood, here you come."

"He's not taking me with him." She took his hand in both of hers and bit it—playfully, but with enough pressure to make him cry out. It retreated behind the curtain.

"Would you get my robe?" he asked. "It's probably on the floor by the bed."

The pipes groaned as he turned the water off. Diane found the green terrycloth bathrobe, damp from a previous shower, in a pile of discarded clothing, and threw it in to Alan. The bedroom had high ceilings, original woodwork, a view of a pleasant garden. She sat down on the unmade platform bed. The only other furniture was a drawing board covered with contact sheets, and a ponderous dresser they had found at the Salvation Army which squatted in a corner like an uninvited great aunt. The room appeared to belong to a man with little concern for material things. However, the front room was filled with thousands of dollars worth of photographic equipment.

Alan was addicted to technology. His special-effects lenses would fill a catalog. He developed all his pictures, despite the time and expense. His work was his hobby; he took more photographs in his spare time. All his profits went into new equipment. He was as fickle with each new lens or filter as Don Juan was with his lovers, but he could never bring himself to part with his former favorites. Diane respected him for his compulsions. She liked a man with passions.

"So what made Bradley give you a second chance?" Alan entered the room wearing his robe.

"I don't know." Diane frowned. "He wasn't mad when I said I had plans, but I don't think he believed me. He cut the interview short right after that because he had to meet a friend. I couldn't tell if he stopped because I said no or because I insulted him. Having a drink was not a good idea, but I didn't want him to feel inhibited. I was going to just let it sit on the table, but it was such a pleasant afternoon. There was sunlight coming through these tremendous windows and a big fire in the fireplace. Before I knew it, I'd finished two drinks."

"How did you insult him?"

"Well, he has a real complex about his father. Bradley Senior is a critic, biographer, and novelist. I read a book of his on Tennyson when I was in college. That was another thing I shouldn't have told Bradley. He said such awful things about his father, I said it sounded to me like his father had worked at making himself a hard act to follow."

Alan smiled at her effrontery.

"When I think about it"—Diane reflected with dreamy contentment, kicking her shoes off and looking up at the ceiling—"it really is amazing that he wants to see me again. We got off to a terrible start. I was fifteen minutes late for the interview and he made a crack about it."

Alan shook his head as he searched for clean clothes in the top dresser drawer.

"You're going to miss something important one day." Alan disapproved of her chronic lack of punctuality.

"Bradley said that being late is an act of egotism. It's a way of telling him that my time is more valuable than his."

"He's right."

"Then he started telling me how he didn't want to do the interview in the first place. His publisher made him do it."

"Sounds like a nice easy interview." Alan began blow-drying his hair.

"It got worse." She sat up, pulled her skirt up over her knees and crossed her legs yoga fashion on the bed. "We started talking about how the movie will be different from the book. Well, I was up all night reading the book, but I didn't have time to finish. I skimmed the last chapter on the subway this morning, but he asked me a specific question about what happens to one of the main characters and I went blank. I did a creditable job of double talk, but

I was blushing and I'm not sure he believes I read the book. It was awful. For a while, I wasn't sure that I had the physical strength to get through the interview. But somehow I stood up to him. I've never had such a strong sense of acting a role. But my performance must have been convincing because he started taking my questions seriously. I love that feeling of hitting my stride as an interviewer. I like being in control."

"Why did he write the book?" Alan asked.

Diane smiled, and brought her hand to her forehead as if to brush away an unpleasant memory. "I thought I remembered reading in the *Times* magazine that Bradley had written the book for money. He said that was my middle-class projection of his motive. According to Bradley, he did it just to see if he could write a bestseller. And to prove something to his father."

"I can understand wanting to prove yourself to your father," Alan said. "I never really wanted to be a doctor. But I wanted my father to respect me."

"And he does now, doesn't he?" Diane's claim was made with the pride of a woman who has altered a man's destiny. "You never get a father's respect, doing what you think he wants."

"I would have given up medicine anyway." Alan pulled on clean blue jeans, then shed his robe. "You have to want to be a doctor more than anything. I had too many hobbies. I thought too much about what I would do with the money I'd make."

"You smoked too much dope for a med student," Diane laughed. "Everyone should smoke dope now and then—except the surgeon who operates on me and the pilot flying the plane I'm on."

"Where did he get the idea for the book?" Alan asked.

"Bradley was telling a friend about a trip he'd made to buy Eskimo art in the Yukon. The friend described an article he'd read about the earth's ozone layer being depleted. Apparently, enough solar energy is getting through to melt the polar ice caps."

"Other scientists think just the opposite is happening." Alan often turned mentions of scientific fact into digressions. "They say pollution is blocking the sun's rays and that another ice age is coming."

"Bradley said it was as good an idea as an earthquake or a burning skyscraper," Diane laughed. "He wrote the book in three months. Just like that." Diane nodded her head approvingly. "Six months later he was on the best-seller list."

"What did his father think of the book?"

"I asked him the same thing." Diane brightened. The fact that they often arrived at the same question independently added a deeper dimension to their friendship.

"And?"

"Bradley went crazy. You should have heard him. I'll play it on the tape."

Alan turned off the blow-dryer and watched her cross over to the briefcase she had tossed onto the drawing board. She took out a tape recorder, starting and stopping it several times before she found the right place in the interview. *"What did your father think?"* she asked on the tape. Diane felt the usual disappointment at hearing her recorded voice, which to her sounded high-pitched and insubstantial.

"Who gives a damn what my father thinks?" In person, Bradley's response had startled her, making the pores of her arms and legs prickly. Without his unblinking glare and his impatience, Bradley did not sound so formidable.

"You're right, I suppose." Diane had been shaken.

"If you want to interview my father, go interview my father."

His overbearing manner had annoyed her suddenly. *"Don't you think you're overreacting a little?"* she had challenged him.

Alan nodded proudly at her audacity. They exchanged smiles. *"Possibly."* They heard Bradley's anger soften into amusement.

"One more question about you-know-who?"

"You-know-who?" Alan smiled at her.

"I'd had two Scotches."

"I know your father reviews books. Did he review yours?"

"Unfortunately, no one would let him."

"Unfortunate for whom?"

"For him. My father's generation has literary spleens. He missed a chance to vent his."

"Wasn't he pleased for you?"

Bradley had seemed puzzled by her sincerity. The question intrigued him; it appeared to strike him as novel.

"You should have seen my father the first time I got an editorial published in Northwestern's paper," she said.

"My father believes in taste with a capital T," Bradley answered. _"He'd have made mince meat of the book"._

"You really don't like him at all."

Diane stopped the tape. "Do you think that observation was indiscreet?" she asked Alan.

"No. But let's hear how Bradley reacted."

She turned the tape recorder back on.

"That's like asking if I like tides," Bradley said.

"I don't get the analogy." Diane experienced again the relief she had felt as his annoyance dissipated.

"My father is a force I work around," Bradley said. _"In a way, he's my superego. I see everything I do the way he would see it. I wasted a lot of time fighting his influence when I was younger. Now I just ignore him when I can, and accept the fact that his opinion matters when I can't. I must say it got to him, though"_ — Bradley chuckled — _"my making so much money on the book. That's not for the record, incidentally."_

Diane switched the tape recorder off. Something about hearing Bradley's voice in Alan's bedroom set her on edge. It was not so much a violation of Bradley's privacy that made her turn the tape off as a sudden inexplicable unwillingness to share the personal experience of the interview with Alan. It was easier to shape his perception of the meeting if he heard about it indirectly, from her.

"You still haven't explained what inspired Bradley to give you a second chance." Alan pulled on a freshly laundered T-shirt over a hairy chest.

She smiled, remembering. "I was really upset when he said he had to leave. There were a hundred questions I hadn't asked yet." She laughed. "I can't believe I drank enough to call after him when he went to get my coat that I wished he didn't have to run off like that. He gave me the most wicked grin and said it was a shame I had plans for the evening. His smile said he hadn't believed me, but that he respected me enough to know I wouldn't change my story. I asked him if I could call him if I had any other questions, but he hates telephone interviews. He had his hand on my elbow, light but forceful, edging me out to the elevator, ignoring my really sweet 'please's.' Just as the bell rang, he said I could ask my questions at dinner tomorrow night. At eight-thirty. I smiled so hard my face hurt. I barely had time to tell him okay before the doors closed.''

"This is your big break, Diane." His serious remark first thrilled, then annoyed her.

"Don't make too much of it." Instinctively she knew it would make her nervous to dwell on the importance of her second meeting with Bradley.

"It's going to be interesting to see how we handle success." Diane plumbed the self-mockery in Alan's eyes and found seriousness lurking beneath.

"Will I be able to keep the link between the med student of ten years ago and the photographer of rats today?" He tucked a red flannel shirt into his jeans and hunted in the top drawer for socks.

"Yes . . ." Diane considered. She lay back on the bed and studied the intricately carved molding along the ceiling. "You've stayed unique. Have I? Or have I changed much since I gave up poetry?"

"You never change." He sat down beside her and pulled on thick white cotton running socks. "You've always been restless. Up to something. Measuring people against some internal standard. In college, you went from person to person like a browser in a bookstore, thumbing through book after book. You didn't read long unless the story caught your interest. Then your friendship was urgent. You couldn't just send in a poem to the literary journal. You had to move in with the editor."

"I slept on Marjorie's floor for a week." Diane smiled, remembering. "I wanted to sit up all night and smoke cigarettes and drink coffee, and talk about Roethke and Yeats. The poor girl had to beg me to go home finally so she could get some sleep."

"A week later you were racing up and down Sheridan Road in an Austin-Healey with that bore from Detroit. You thought he was fascinating until you found out he wasn't really related to the Fords."

"He *said* he was."

"Then there was the valedictorian from the University of Chicago."

"We stayed up every night the two weeks before Christmas finals senior year. I got a four-point average that semester. Who was next?" Diane enjoyed the fondness with which he reminisced.

"Mike. Mike what's-his-name. You drank a pitcher of beer with him at a different South Side bar every night for a week. You lost interest when you found out his friendship with his roommate was platonic."

"I was fascinated by gay men," she admitted. "My high-school sweetheart ended up with a gay man. I was relieved it wasn't another woman. I think I thought if I could win a gay man over, we'd be even somehow."

"You went through people quickly," Alan mused. "They had a hard time sustaining your interest."

"That's not true." Diane found his allegation threatening. "It's true that life was a big library to me then. I wanted to read everyone's story, but there were so many, there wasn't time to study each book closely."

"If you'll allow me to extend the analogy—"

"Metaphor."

"You *were* a tough critic."

"I hope I still am." She smiled. "Now that I'm pushing thirty, I've only got time for the classics."

"Is Bradley a classic?"

"I don't know yet. But the jacket copy is sure interesting."

"The thing I've always liked about you, Diane, is how much you expect from life."

"I want it to be interesting," she said, "for me."

"Has it been, so far?" Tiny pearls of water were woven into his beard.

"There's room for improvement," she admitted. "But at least I'm moving in the right direction. Bradley will have friends."

"What if writing about Hollywood bores you?"

It thrilled her that he was in earnest. She laughed off his remark, asking, "You assume I'll make it?"

"What's the proverb about 'Beware of what you want because you will surely get it'? I have a feeling it's true."

"I'm not afraid of getting what I want." It bothered her

that Alan was attaching more importance to her dinner with Bradley than she was.

"Be careful, Diane." Alan was serious.

"You sound like the big brother I never had." She was impatient with his caution.

"John Bradley runs in a fast crowd. They can afford to make mistakes you and I can't."

"Maybe I just don't know my place." Diane was sarcastic.

"They invite you to spend a month in St. Tropez. It never occurs to anyone to wonder how you'll pay the rent in New York or keep your job while you play."

She laughed. "No one's invited me anywhere yet."

"When they do," Alan said, "you'll go. You like calculated risks."

It was true. Once she and Alan made a thrilling jump on to a train pulling out of Penn Station. When she found out from a passenger that they were on the right train, she felt the familiar satisfaction of a gamble having paid off.

"I'm not reckless though," Diane defended herself.

He considered her words. "True. Your self-preservation instincts are all in working order."

"You know, in your own way you're pretty damned conservative," she told Alan. "Let's go eat." She sprang up from the bed.

Alan put on a leather jacket with a rabbit fur collar.

"Can you cash a check for eighteen dollars?" she asked.

"Sure." He took a wallet out of his back pocket and handed her a twenty-dollar bill. "I don't have any change now."

Alan knew her too well to protest that she could pay him back later. Diane scribbled out a check and slapped it decisively on his dresser, informing him on their way downstairs that to celebrate the upcoming article, dinner was her treat.

two

It was a different apartment at night. Firelight glowed in the floor-to-ceiling leaded French windows, the chandeliers, the crystal. Her shoes echoed on the black-and-white marble tiles of the foyer as she entered.

"You look beautiful." His eyes—large, with too much white in them—admired her as he took her coat. He was not as tall as she remembered, perhaps three inches taller than Diane in heels. She noticed that a receding hairline was responsible for his high forehead. She knew from the publisher's bio that he was in his late thirties.

"Thank you." Her smile acknowledged the compliment. Diane wore a black dress with tiny red dots, red piping around the neck, and a diagonal slash of red halfway down the front. Cinched at the waist with a thin red belt, the dress came almost to her ankles.

She handed him a bottle of Dom Perignon. "I wasn't sure what we were having."

"Always appropriate. Shall we drink some by the fire?"

"It isn't very cold."

"I'll take care of that." He went into the kitchen.

Diane was pleased by her reflection in a mirror. She was filled with a sense of being as physically attractive that evening as it was in her power to be. She was satisfied. A cork went off in the kitchen.

Bradley descended stairs from a formal dining room to join her by the fireplace in the sunken living room.

He carried champagne in an ice bucket and two crystal glasses.

"I like your hair up." Diane resisted an impulse to put her hand to the carefully curled strands she allowed to escape from tortoise-shell combs. He poured two glasses and handed one to her.

"This *is* a coffee table, isn't it?" She set her glass on a chrome and glass box that might as easily have been a modern sculpture. He nodded, smiling, and sat down beside her.

"To a successful article on a fascinating subject." His glass touched hers.

"Cheers." Their eyes met as they sipped. He looked as if he knew something secret about her. It made her laugh nervously and look away.

On the marble fireplace mantle she saw a statue of a squatting Eskimo woman and a photograph of Bradley on skis, in midair, a ski jump and a steep mountain in the background. The walls were decorated with a painting of an Aztec god, a giant rainbow in neon, turned on, and a wall-sized abstract painting that derived its inspiration from the American flag.

"Did you get very far into the article today?"

"I didn't start. I wanted to see if I got any new insights tonight."

"Did I tell you I was a *sous-chef* once, in a one-star restaurant in Cassis? I told the *patron* at *Chez Gilbert* that Mother was Parisian, that she met my father, who was a British aristocrat, vacationing nearby, and that we came back every year. I convinced him he remembered my mother."

"I've always wanted to live under an assumed name," she laughed.

"I used my own."

Diane had never had such good champagne. It was partly its dry, almost bitter purity that made it so special, partly the instantaneous sensation of well-being it produced within her. She had a sense of being on a movie set, of watching herself with Bradley through a camera. She felt elegant, not herself. Bradley's black cashmere turtleneck, khaki slacks, and cordovan tassel loafers looked perfectly comfortable. The room was out of a glossy magazine. Diane's ambition was clear: to live a life with absolutely no false notes, a life like a good movie, like this moment in Bradley's apartment.

"Come keep me company while I finish supper." He stood up suddenly. "Bring your glass with you."

Bradley took his glass and the bottle. They entered a kitchen that was all oak—cabinets, floors, counters. The apron Bradley put on had the words *Le Chef* silk-screened on it.

"Aunt Martha would be right at home here," Diane said, smiling.

"Who taught you to say 'aunt' with a British accent?"

"That's Minnesota English."

"My parents say it that way, too. I say 'aunt' like the insect just to get on their nerves."

Antique copper pots and pans hung from oak beams in the ceiling. The table and chairs had been built in Virginia three hundred years earlier, he told her.

"This is the one room I redid when I inherited the apartment from my grandmother," he said. "I don't cook often, but when I do, I like to do it right."

"Are you doing it right tonight?"

"You have that good fortune."

"I hope you've got the maid lined up for tomorrow. I've never seen so many dirty pots and pans."

"It's a sign of genius," he laughed, filling her glass.

"What are we having?" Diane asked.

"Pâté de campagne. Crudités. Filet de sole meunière."

"Formidable." Diane spoke with her best French accent.

"Vous parlez français?" His accent was determinedly British, charmingly affected.

"I spent junior year in Paris."

"How long ago was that?"

"You mean, how old am I?"

"You don't look old enough to mind my asking."

"It's been eight years. What's for dessert? I'm starving. I worked so hard today I forgot to eat."

"I've never worked *that* hard in my entire life."

"Spring cleaning. My mother would have been proud of me. I turned the rug and washed slipcovers and cleaned the oven. I hadn't cleaned the oven in two years. I stored winter clothes in boxes and threw out a closetful of magazines and old clothes. I love throwing things out. For me it's almost a religious experience, like fasting before Easter. It's cathartic."

"What did it purge you of?"

"My fear of traveling too heavy."

"The dessert's in the refrigerator. *Mousse au chocolat à la mode de Bradley.*"

"Can I peek?" Without waiting for permission, she opened the door and looked in.

"Would you mind getting out the vegetables while you're in there? You can start on the crudités while I work on the sauce for the fish."

"Slicing the vegetables is the worst part." She protested playfully, though she believed it was true.

"The food processor is in the corner."

"I don't know how to use one." She exaggerated her helplessness. "Maybe I should do something else."

He poured the rest of the champagne into their glasses. "Do it by hand, then." Bradley was authoritarian in his kitchen. "Here's a cutting board. I'll make dressing for the salad." He watched her work on the vegetables. "I've got a great recipe for vinaigrette with Dijon mustard."

"It sounds good. Is this enough carrots?"

"Unless you can eat more than half of them. Could you stir this for me?"

The champagne went quickly to Diane's head. She felt carefree.

"I like to get the guest involved in the preparations," Bradley said. "I don't like them just watching my performance." The fact that Diane heard a double entendre in the comment made her wonder if she was drinking too fast.

The phone rang. Bradley ignored it.

"The answering service will get it," he said. "I left strict orders not to be disturbed tonight." He smiled at her meaningfully, then rubbed his hands together and surveyed the kitchen. "The fish is ready to go under the broiler. How are you coming with the vegetables?"

"Almost finished." She was slicing the last plump mushrooms.

"Would you rather eat in the dining room, or in front of the fireplace?"

"The fire would be nice."

"My choice, too." He clapped his hands together. "Now, you take out the silverware, the napkins, the baguette, and the pâté. I'll bring the liquid refreshment and the 'crudities.' " His anglicism amused him.

She was spreading her second piece of bread with pâté when he joined her with the vegetables and a bottle of champagne.

She started to remark that she thought they had finished the bottle when she noticed that it was unopened. "I don't believe it." She could hear herself too amused that they had selected the same champagne, but it must mean something, she thought.

"Great minds . . ." Bradley said. There was an explosion; vapor hovered over the bottle, like the ghost of the vanished cork. "How does it go?" The champagne fizzed madly, with a sound like surf over sand, and welled up to the brim of their glasses.

"Don't *you* know?" she laughed. "I always say 'great minds,' and the other person knows I mean 'think alike' or 'run in the same channels' without my saying it."

"Let's look it up in *Bartlett's*." Bradley jumped up and retreated down the darkened hallway past the kitchen.

"You tell me what it says," she called after him. "I'll stay here and guard the pâté."

One of the charms of the champagne was that it sharpened her appetite and increased the sensitivity of her taste. The pâté was sweet and buttery, the vegetables icy fresh, surprisingly crisp for being so finely sliced. If Paris could be epitomized in a food, it was in the taste of the bread. Diane ate without inhibition.

Her host's search for the author of "great minds" proved futile. They could not find it in the index under "great minds," "all great minds," or any variation.

"My father will know." Bradley sat down on the thick carpet. Diane did not know if the intricate geometric designs on its deep blue background were Chinese or Persian.

"Where is he?"

"He left my mother with friends in London, and is hiking in the Lake District. He's doing an article on Wordsworth."

"It sounds peaceful." Diane sighed. "I walk a lot in the

city, but it's been a while since it had any entertainment value.''

''I've never seen a place as beautiful in bad weather.''

''Were you ever married?''

''No.'' Bradley snapped a carrot between his teeth. ''Why?''

''You have such beautiful silverware and crystal.''

''It was *meant* for a married man.'' He smiled wistfully. ''It came with the apartment, which my grandmother left me and my fiancée. Luckily, Nana died before Claire and I split up. It would have broken her heart. Though they were so close I sometimes think Claire and I would still be together if the old lady were alive.''

It appeared difficult for Bradley to talk about his engagement, but he seemed to want to.

''How long ago was that?''

''Twelve years.'' He put down the bread he had been about to bite into. ''It amazes me, how vividly I still remember the night we broke up. I'm on the phone. Claire is crying. She can't explain why she is going to marry the doctor who treated her after the skiing accident we had together.''

''No warning?'' Diane regretted the pall that descended over the dinner. Bradley did not seem to mind.

''Absolutely none.''

''Twelve years is a long time.''

''I'm conservative about grief. It seems disloyal to get over it. It's also a way of getting back at the rest of the female race for giving me the potential to hurt so much. I may have more in common with my father than I realize.''

''Maybe she's sorry now.''

''I don't know. I have managed not to see her since. I understand she adopted two children and that her husband still practices in New York. That's all I know. My sister insisted it was for the best, I was too young to get married. It didn't help.''

''Is your sister older or younger?''

''Older.'' He was distracted.

Diane spread pâté on another piece of bread. She was bingeing, but decided not to fight it.

''What does she do?''

''She sends her three sons to boarding school, so she

has enough time for her hospital boards. That's called charity. Amelia's a pre-menopausal daddy's girl. Her ambition is for her sons to be the son Bradley Senior never had. She may well succeed. J.B.'s exceptionally priggish for a sixteen-year-old.''

"Another John Bradley?"

"His first and middle name."

"What kind of father imposes his name on a son?" The question struck Diane as profound. "A self-confident man, who sees in himself something worth preserving, or an insecure man who fears his mortality?"

"Let's tackle that one in the kitchen. I want to put the fish on."

"Or let's go a step farther—" She followed him. "What would make a junior name a third?"

"That's like a servant wanting a servant." Bradley removed the fish from the sauce it was marinating in and put it under the broiler. "I get angry talking about my father. His envy has been such a corrosive force in my life."

"Envy?"

"He envies the money I've made on the book, for instance."

"I would think he'd like knowing that you aren't waiting in the wings for an inheritance," she suggested.

"It isn't even his money," Bradley said scornfully. "It was my mother's. The Newport Bradleys' fortune was spread pretty thin by the time it got to John E. Bradley, Sr. So he distinguished himself as an intellectual and married my mother for money. He envies me too for my freedom. My father doesn't like women. Nature designed him to be a bachelor. He never forgave my mother because he had to give up his independence for her money. He has enough of a conscience to feel guilty about his diffidence, but not enough not to resent my mother because he feels guilty. He's witty and well-read, but he is too self-centered to make a good husband."

"Or father?"

Bradley straightened up and cast a sideways glance at Diane.

"Are you a reporter or a psychiatrist?" He spoke jokingly, but his tone did not hide the fact that he was annoyed at himself for talking too much. Diane laughed, almost gaily, at the intimation of honesty.

"Let's talk about something else," he said. "What's it like growing up in the Midwest?" He poured water off a pan of steaming potatoes.

"It's driving five hundred miles three days in a row to see the ocean for the first time when you're sixteen. It's taking your aunt out to Fire Island after graduation to get a bottle of salt water for the guys who stayed home to milk the cows."

Bradley smiled. "I wouldn't have picked you for a farm girl." He sprinkled parsley on buttered potatoes and checked the sole under the broiler.

"My mother was the farm girl. My father was a city kid. I grew up in Minneapolis. Dad was one of the top producers in the state."

"So your interest in film comes naturally."

"Producer's an insurance company euphemism for sales-man," she laughed. "He worked for a large agency. He loved people. Meetings. Rotary Club luncheons, precinct committees, golf or duck hunting on weekends. In the winter it was dark when he went to work and dark when he got home, but that never seemed to bother him. He loved selling. He filled out forms and wrote reports after dinner until sleep caught him in his tracks. Me"—she sipped champagne thoughtfully—"the idea of spending the best hours of the next thirty-five years making a living depresses me profoundly."

"Do what your mother did." The suggestion was offered for the sake of argument.

"Find a man to take care of me? It's occurred to me." She assumed it occurred to most single women. "My father joined the Navy and saw the world. He won a sales contest once and got a trip to Lloyd's of London. He went to his agency's home offices in Chicago and New York several times a year. My mother had my father, me, my younger sister—that was it. I'd rather work."

"You're certainly full of contradictions."

Bradley no longer gave her undivided attention. Like the plate twirlers she had watched on television variety shows as a child, the chef had six dishes going at once. He dried lettuce leaves, beat vinaigrette with a whisk, basted the

fish. With Teutonic abhorrence, Diane tried to ignore the
mess he made—the water dripping on the floor, the dressing sloshed over the edge of the bowl, the melted butter
splashed on the counter. Everything was timed perfectly,
and there was a note of triumph in his voice when Bradley
announced that dinner was served.

"My compliments to the chef." Diane stared at the
supper with undisguised appetite, glad to leave the disaster
area that his kitchen had become. They carried the dishes
to the coffee table in front of the fireplace. Bradley poured
more champagne. She said she wasn't sure that was a good
idea, but was pleased that Bradley detected the insincerity
in her protest. Diane laughed at everything he said, not so
much from drunkenness as exhilaration. She was preternaturally aware of the objects around her—the fork she ate
with, heavy silver, the firelight in the crystal glasses, the
nubbiness of starched linen napkins. There were lighted
candles on the table, and a new log on the fire.

"This is exquisite." Diane sighed. The fish was perfectly moist and flaky. The butter sauce on the potatoes
was inspired simplicity, the salad dressing light and spicy.
As they ate, Bradley described the preparation of each
dish. He was vain about his cooking. Diane listened politely, but told him she didn't like to cook.

"I *can* cook," she elaborated. "Anybody who can read
can cook. But I don't improvise or experiment. No matter
how good the finished product tastes, it takes too long to
fix and it's gone too quickly."

"Cooking is the foreplay to the meal," he explained,
without being suggestive. "Besides, this dinner only took
an hour."

"Oh, it's always worth it when someone else does the
cooking."

"What would you make if you reciprocate?"

"Grandma Lindstrom's sauerbraten, potato dumplings,
and sauerkraut."

"Sounds delicious. But how did you keep such a nice
figure with food like that?"

"Why do you think I left Minnesota?" Diane smiled,
changing the subject to Bradley's book. "What's the most
interesting interview you've done on the book?"

"Besides the obvious?"

She lowered her eyes in enjoyment of the compliment.

"I was on a radio station in Cleveland last week that broadcasts in twenty-seven languages. Next week I'm going to be on the 'Tonight Show.' " Irony and self-satisfaction competed in his grin.

"Does that make you a certifiable celebrity?"

"Only the interviewee is allowed to be ironic."

"What question do they ask most?"

"Could the great thaw really happen?"

"Could it?"

"Not you, too."

"It was your suggestion," she laughed. She took a sip of her drink and shivered. "Could it?"

"Not in our lifetime."

"Why do people like disaster movies?" It seemed like a good question.

"The same reason they get excited about thunderstorms and blizzards. Disasters call existence into question. It's a pleasant sensation."

"Do you think San Francisco will have another earthquake?"

He nodded.

"Are you nervous when you go there?"

"I don't have time to dread catastrophes," he answered. "They take up enough time when they happen."

"You sail a lot, don't you?" The champagne numbed her lips and tongue. She imagined a phosphorescent trail of warmth to her stomach. Her satisfaction at seeing Bradley a second time glowed within her like the wine's secret fire.

"I've sailed around the world," he noted, not without a trace of pride in his voice.

"I'd like to sail around the world some day," Diane thought out loud.

"You should."

"It would take a lot of five-hundred-dollar interviews to do it the way I want to do it."

"How's that?"

"Probably pretty much the way you did it."

He looked amused. "Five hundred isn't bad for a couple of hours."

"I'll be working on the article every spare minute for

the next couple of weeks. Not that I'm complaining—it's going to get me transferred to the 'Arts and Leisure' section at the *Times*. They like the work I'm doing for the business section. All I need is a good freelance article on someone in the entertainment field.''

"Glad to be of service." Bradley smiled. "I imagine it must be deadly, interviewing businessmen.''

"Actually, I like businessmen. They're direct. They know exactly what they want.''

"Money.''

"At least they're honest about it. Interviewing businessmen isn't taxing. They leave me time for my own creativity.''

"Am I taxing?''

She could tell that he wanted to be, but her nodding was not flattery. His constant banter exhausted her.

"What makes me so difficult?" He looked at her through the glass he drank from. She wondered why he wanted to be considered difficult.

"You can't relax when you interview an artist." She had chosen the last word deliberately. He liked it.

"Have you interviewed many?''

"A few." She was relieved he did not press her for names.

"It seems masochistic, subjecting yourself to difficult people.''

"I want to meet people who make movies.''

"Why?''

"I don't know. I feel the same way about Hollywood that Marx felt about the workers' paradise. I have no idea what to expect, but I know I'll like it when I get there.''

Laughing, Bradley got up to put another log on the fire.

"And now here you are with someone making a movie.''

"It's taken a long time." Diane regretted her self-satisfied tone immediately.

"It only took me two weeks to finish an outline, sample chapter, and have a contract for the book," Bradley said, standing at the fireplace. His face was soft in the firelight.

"Things seem to come easily to you.''

"Is that admiration or resentment?''

"A little of both.''

"You disapprove of easy success?''

"I'm ambivalent," she clarified. "I like it. But my father always said it was better to do things the hard way. He never took a two-week vacation in his life. I can't imagine not needing to get away—often. I need variety."

"Me too."

"I would imagine that access to variety is one of the primary advantages of having money." Her speculation sounded dreamy to her. "Do you ever get bored?"

"All the time."

"Does it bother you?"

"Immensely."

"What do you do about it?"

"When things get really bad, I invite ingenue reporters to dinner."

Against her will, Diane smiled. She had left herself wide open.

"You were involved in the London theater for a while, weren't you?" she asked.

"About ten years ago, just after my confused Paris period."

"I had one of those." She brightened.

"Mine wasn't a junior year abroad." His arrogance stung her.

"My father knew several producers in London," he was saying. "One of them gave me a job as stage manager."

"Did your father encourage you to pursue a career in the theater?"

"No. In fact, when he heard I'd shown my employer an outline for a musical comedy, he accused me of abusing his contacts. My father knew I could write, even before I started publishing magazine articles. But he never encouraged it. He prefers me underdeveloped and dissipated.

"Is that how you see yourself?"

"Sometimes."

"But you work, don't you?" she asked. "You're an art consultant."

"Sotheby's pays me a hundred dollars an hour to make sure the Eskimo artifacts they auction aren't fake. But no one takes that very seriously."

"Not even you?"

"It's just a hobby I took up to spite the old man."

"What difference does it make to your father what kind of art you like?"

"A sensible Midwestern perspective. You would have to have experienced the infuriating brunt of my father's blind anglophilia to understand. To him it was a tragic blight to be born American. So I like pop art and disco."

"Would it be fair to say that your father has stunted your psychological growth?"

Diane thrilled with the sense of "getting even," though she could not have said for what. The question caught him off balance. He formulated a response with the plodding consideration a man gives the solution to a problem after several drinks.

"Is that your assessment?" Bradley frowned, then stood up. Now I've done it, she thought. He did not speak right away. Instead, he walked over to a window and stood by a floor lamp. Brown hair covered the collar of his shirt. Hands in pockets, face tan, not from beaches but from outdoor activity, Bradley was silhouetted by the light beyond him. The only thing tempering Diane's frank admiration of his profile was her fear that he struck the pose intentionally, as if to demonstrate that physically at least his development had been exemplary.

"What I meant was—" Her tone was conciliatory as he turned to face her. "What I meant to say was, do you think your father has done much damage?"

"Did yours?"

"I'm sure he did. But I can live with the result."

"So can I. But I resent having to. I resent having a father who's maintained—my whole life, in a thousand ways—that he's smarter than I am. It's been a real struggle—with my mother caught in the middle."

"Who does she side with?" Diane forgot to wonder if she was being too personal.

"When I was younger, I think my mother hated him for his egomania and pomposity and the way he kept me down. Now that I'm older, and I've proved that I can write—and make a better living at it than he ever has—she figures the rotten relationship is partly my fault. In the meantime, my father's become the mellow patriarch with his guest lectureships and his three grandsons. As he gets more absentminded, he's even begun to think that he's been happily married for the past forty-five years. Now my mother wants a golden anniversary and I'm the biggest obstacle. I'm bad for the old man's blood pressure. We can't be in the same room together for more than five minutes."

"That's too bad." Diane was sincere.

"You obviously have never experienced a parent not having your best interests at heart," he said bitterly.

"I can't imagine it."

"It's gotten so bad lately that the steady topic of conversation when we get together is why I haven't married. It's outrageous that a man with my father's contempt for marriage would try to foist the institution off on me. His latest kick is his son's immorality. He accused me last week of suffering from satyriasis. Do you know what that is?"

Diane thought that she did, but did not dare define it for him. "It's one of those words I would never be confident I was pronouncing correctly." She laughed uneasily.

"But do you know what it is?" He pressed her. His eyes were teasing; his upper lip lifted in a sneer of amusement.

"Tell me." She looked at him straight on, forcing herself not to feel intimidated.

"Excessive, uncontrollable sexual desire in a man."

"Maybe you should follow his advice. My mother has always said there's something suspect about a man who isn't married by the time he's thirty-five." It must be the champagne, she thought, enjoying the courage to counter his flirtation—or whatever it was.

Bradley's smile might have said "touché."

"What did you say to your father?" she asked.

"I simply pointed out that he was not in a position to discuss sexual desire, never having experienced it—toward a woman."

"What an awful thing to say." She was not sure why she laughed. "Is your father homosexual?"

"Isn't every English intellectual—at least intellectually? It's part of the Anglophile trip."

"How old is your father?" Diane asked.

"Seventy-five."

"You don't have long to work this thing out."

"Irreconcilable differences."

"Your mother's right," she said defiantly. "You ought to try harder, now that you have the upper hand."

"But that's just the point." Bradley's eyes appealed to her in frustration. "Time and money haven't given me the upper hand. My father is still capable of reducing me to the level of a child. I realized twenty years ago, when the black belt didn't do any good, that nothing short of death would."

"I don't understand."

"I got a black belt in karate when I was in high school. I had so many fantasies about killing my father, I thought maybe if I could really do it—if I could really murder my father with my bare hands—it might break his power over me."

"Did it?"

"Of course not. Anyone can murder someone. But my father's attitude toward the black belt was the same as you feel for a mugger on the street. You're afraid of him, but you don't believe he's morally or intellectually superior to you just because he can beat you up."

"Your ego must be at least as big as your father's."

"Possibly. But it's less abrasive."

"Have you ever done anything pleasant together?" Diane was curious how he would react to the question.

"My parents came to visit in Paris once. I brought the most weather-beaten number in Pigalle to dinner with us at the *Tour d'Argent*. I thought my father would be pissed. But I forgot how much he likes showing off his French. He found her delightful company. We spent the evening in a café, listening to stories about the famous men she had known. My father used it in his only novel."

"The supreme compliment?"

"I always thought of it as a rip-off, but maybe you have a point," Bradley acknowledged.

Unable to grasp the question that floated outside her mind's ken, Diane noticed that she had finished another glass.

"Do you ever worry about doing the right thing with your money?" It had not been the question she was looking for, but it would do.

" 'Right'?" He inhaled thoughtfully as he sat back down. "What do you mean 'right'? Morally right?"

She shook her head. "Nothing that profound. Maybe I mean esthetically right. Say I have a hundred dollars. I can buy a new dress, or go to the Hamptons for the weekend. But not both. I have to decide. Sometimes it's hard to know the right choice."

"I've always had enough money for the right things and the wrong things." Bradley smiled. "And now with the book, there's even more."

"The rich get richer," Diane mused, almost to herself.

"I don't squander money deliberately," he added. "But if something doesn't turn out the way I expected, I can do it another way."

Bradley poured them more champagne.

"Could you have lunch with the Prince of Wales?" She felt playful.

"You read too many magazines."

"It's an occupational hazard." She repressed a laugh.

"A big formal affair maybe. Nothing intimate."

"Have you ever hopped on the Concorde to have croissants and a café crème for breakfast in Paris?"

"It gets there in the evening. But money's not the important thing—"

"But it sure beats whatever comes in second place." Her laugh approached a giggle. "My father used to say that."

"Your father is quite a wit." His sarcasm blasted her sense of security.

"My father died two years ago." She wanted to embarrass him, to make him sorry for his flippancy, but Bradley would not be affected by the remark. He looked at her disdainfully, as if she had told a joke in poor taste, and went on:

"Money is nothing without time," he said. "Hopefully, you wouldn't change places with a rich octogenarian." His bitterness was gone as quickly as it had come.

"Still . . ." She worked to formulate her idea. "When I think about the opportunities you have for enriching the quality of your time—it boggles the middle-class imagination."

"Is that how you see yourself?" Bradley turned the question on her.

"In my lucid moments."

"Money can work against you," he pointed out. "You can have such a good time with it you forget about time. You can wake up forty years old one day and realize you haven't done a damned thing that's really important."

"It's worth the risk."

"I can't remember the last time I met a woman so unabashedly ambitious." Diane flushed with pleasure. It did not occur to her until later that his observation might not be a compliment.

Bradley began clearing the dishes from the table. Thinking about her father made her pensive and quietly sad. She did not offer to help, but watched the fire in silence until Bradley returned with cheese, apples, pears, and nectarines.

"How did your mother get from the farm to Minneapolis?" Bradley asked, sitting down across from her on the floor.

"She went to junior college in the Cities and got a job afterwards as a legal secretary. She worked in the office where my father's brother was a clerk, and met Dad over the phone."

"Why did she leave the farm?"

"Aunt Martha says she was running away from a suitor who wouldn't take no for an answer."

"Does she miss the farm?"

"No, she loves Minneapolis like it's an adopted child. Being 'from Minneapolis' is one of the central facts of her self-image. She sees the rest of the world in relation to Minneapolis. New York is five times bigger than Minneapolis. The winter here is twenty degrees warmer than in Minneapolis. She gets a peculiar pleasure out of having known a neighbor since I was a kid. My sister's the same way. Even her boyfriend is a childhood sweetheart."

"How long have you been away?" Bradley looked at her over his champagne glass as he drank.

"It's been ten years since my father kissed me goodbye in my dorm at Northwestern." She smiled almost to herself. "He liked having a daughter to visit when he came in to the home offices. He loved letting me show him the restaurants I could never afford when he wasn't in town. We shared a special secret during those dinners together."

"What was that?" Bradley's curiosity was good-humored.

"He taught me that security is an illusion."

"Not the lesson one would expect from a crackerjack salesman."

"No, but once you accept the fact, you stop wasting time worrying about what you have no control over."

"That makes sense." Bradley smiled, but a momentary somberness descended on Diane's mood.

"My father knew that life makes as little sense in Minneapolis as it does anywhere else," Diane said bitterly. "My mother and my sister believe in the sense of security, even though Mom's very ill."

"I'm sorry to hear that." Bradley's smile faded.

"I still don't believe it—not really—but her doctors say she's dying. It's a shame, really, she and Dad couldn't have exchanged illnesses. Dad died suddenly, probably before he knew what was happening. If he had had Mom's illness, he would have talked a blue streak, sharing all the ideas and opinions milling around in his head whether you wanted to hear them or not. He would have balanced books and organized records and set things straight. Cancer gives you time, but my mother isn't much of a talker."

"You should go home if your mother's so sick."

"Just drop everything and go?"

He nodded.

"That strikes me as a strange suggestion, especially after all the terrible things you've said about your father."

"I suppose," he laughed. "But I've always imagined I'd turn into the dutiful son in that situation. If nothing else"—he grinned wickedly—"I'd finally have the upper hand. It would drive him crazy.

"I knew when I left home that my mother would die sooner or later." Diane finished her glass of champagne. She felt clearheaded as she spoke, but a storm of emotions rumbled beneath her calm exterior. "If I follow your line of reasoning, I should never have left in the first place."

"But it's different once you know," Bradley said.

"We all know. Your mother will die someday."

"Time goes quickly."

"Not everyone can call 'time out' when someone they love is dying." Diane controlled the tremor in her voice.

"Perhaps they ought to."

"Some of us have to work for a living." Her bitterness flashed, consumed itself quickly.

''You have a chip on your shoulder.''

''I don't expect someone like you to understand.''

''Someone like me?'' Bradley's supercilious expression distanced him from her. He poured more champagne. ''What do you mean by 'someone like me'?''

It annoyed her the way he sat back expectantly, as if waiting to be entertained.

''You're above classification, really. You transcend groups.'' She understood what she meant.

Bradley's eyebrows were raised, his eyes uncomprehending as he peeled a large green apple and cut it into slices with a delicacy that epitomized everything Diane was trying to say about his background.

''My father was your classic 'good provider,' '' she explained. ''We have a beautiful home. I went to the best public high school in the city. My parents sent me away to college. I got my regulation junior year abroad. That's pretty good when you consider my great-grandparents were immigrants.''

''To the American Dream.'' Bradley lifted his glass, touched hers, sipped champagne.

''But ignoring the two-thirds of the world who will go to bed hungry tonight . . .'' Her logic was dogged.

''Not us.'' The crunch of the apple Bradley bit into underlined his assertion.

''You can get claustrophobia''—Diane ignored his joke— ''even in a comfortable space. Suppose my father had gotten up one morning and decided he was tired of working. It's unthinkable. Imagine being thirty years old and knowing that except for two weeks a year you have to spend the best part of your life doing what somebody else wants you to do.''

''Is *that* what all of you have to do?'' Bradley was teasing her, but Diane was literal-minded.

''I work the way I gave up smoking,'' she said. ''One day at a time.''

''I still think your mother had the better deal.''

''I don't know how she stood thirty years in that house. She didn't even learn how to drive until after Lynn was born. Except for church work once in a while—''

''What church?'' Bradley offered his guest a slice of pear, which she took from his hand.

"Lutheran. Low Lutheran."

"Sounds depraved," he said, smiling.

"She really believes. My father went to church to set a good example. My mother goes to church the way you go to a travel agent—to plan a trip."

"Ready for dessert?"

It irritated Diane that he had not been listening. Bradley went into the kitchen and returned with dessert. The mousse was of the same order of excellence as the champagne. Diane's voice was thick with slightly bitter chocolate when she complimented him on it. He acknowledged with modest pleasure that the mousse was better than usual.

They talked about desserts, favorite bakeries. Then Diane asked him more questions about the book: "Do you care what they do to the book?"

"I'm curious," he answered. "But essentially, I see the book as a commodity."

"Are you writing another book?"

"Not yet. I'd like to try a serious one when I do."

"Do you have a favorite writer?"

"Myself."

"Seriously."

"Henry James."

"You're just saying that to prove you're serious." Diane was surprised to hear herself teasing him.

"What was the last book *you* read?" he asked.

"I finished *The Great Thaw* at six yesterday morning."

"Before that."

"*Middlemarch*."

"That's a book."

"I'm funny about reading," she said. "I'll go out every night for two weeks, and suddenly I'm starved for books. I stop everything, stay home. I live and breathe the world of the book I'm reading. I need all those different worlds."

"I like a woman who bores easily." Bradley was smiling.

Diane was alarmed that she heard a sexual innuendo in the comment.

"But not a woman you bore?" The question was not as witty as she had intended.

"It's a chastening experience to bore a woman," he said. "I haven't bored you, have I?"

She felt herself straighten up. "No." She shook her

head too energetically. The way he looked at her made her nervous. She hurried to ask another question.

"Is it true what I read about your going on location to Greenland?"

"It looks now like they're going to film it in Alaska. It's closer to California."

"Will the movie stick pretty closely to the book?"

"As you know, the book has an unhappy ending." Had he believed she read the book? Was he helping her out? "The scientists can't figure out how to keep the polar ice cap from melting, and Pittsburgh and Atlanta end up the two largest ports on the east coast. In the movie, Dr. Martin will probably figure out how to preserve the stratosphere and save London, Paris, and New York from the fate of Atlantis."

"Probably?" Diane was the reporter again.

"We still disagree on some details," he answered. "That's why I'm going to Los Angeles in a couple of weeks."

"Is writing a screenplay different from writing a novel?"

"It's easier," he said. "A novelist has to read minds. On the screen, you just show what characters do and say. Screenplay writing is like reporting." His irony took a playful turn. "It doesn't require much creativity."

Diane smiled. His tone flattered her.

Bradley got up to close a window rattling in a gust of wind, and the talk turned to spring, to Bradley's impatience to get his boat out. Diane told him that she had never been sailing. He invited her to see the boat the next morning. She accepted enthusiastically. It was only with a delayed reaction that it occurred to her he might think she had been fishing for the invitation to sail.

Diane's nose was numb when she inhaled during a pause in their conversation, a sure sign that she had drunk too much. But it was a lucid drunkenness, and she worked at feeling a sense of control as she contemplated the slow, deliberate speed of her reactions.

They finished dessert. Bradley built the fire up and Diane began scrubbing pots.

I didn't load dishes because I couldn't figure out how to get the dishwasher open," she explained when he came into the kitchen.

"You really *are* a farm girl."

"Are you kidding?" It was her turn to laugh. "My aunts on the farm have every electric kitchen convenience known to modern woman. They're all into microwave lately."

"Some of these pots are going to have to soak," Bradley told her.

"I'm not going to let you get away with that excuse," she said, continuing to scrub a saucepan in which chocolate had been melted. She admired the efficiency with which he loaded the machine.

"You're awfully well coordinated for someone who just drank a bottle of champagne." She realized that she had been defensive, pointing out that he had drunk more than she had. But she didn't care. Everything about him amused her.

"Think how nice it'll be, not to have to do them in the morning." She felt a nervous twinge in her stomach. Why did Bradley think she was there? Why *was* she there?

They drank coffee and brandy in front of the fireplace and were silent. Normally Diane did not like brandy, but tonight it went with the overall tone of the evening. Diane lost track of time. She was daydreaming. She preserved the peacefulness of the moment by refusing to consider it.

"What are you thinking?" Bradley sat up to take a sip of his coffee. He had slipped off his shoes.

"How rare it is to feel this peaceful in New York."

"I rarely feel this peaceful anywhere."

"Your dinner was delicious. It's been a very pleasant evening."

"It isn't over." The comment was vaguely aggressive. She remembered what Alan had said about his reputation. "More brandy?"

"No thanks."

"Just a little." He smiled as if she had been insincere. Perhaps she had been insincere. He paused.

They fell silent again, but there was an edge to the silence.

"What are you thinking now?" He was making conversation. His lapse from naturalness banished serenity for the night.

"I was thinking how most men look good in a black turtleneck."

"You think so?" He moved perceptibly closer. He was smiling when he kissed her. She stiffened, interpreting his kiss. It was neither awkward nor egotistical, neither aloof nor passionate. His kiss asserted competence. It risked little. It told her that he was proposing a game. The next move was hers. Though Diane had expected Bradley's kiss, it still surprised her. She did not respond. She was afraid of him.

Bradley drew away. They looked into each other's eyes. The irony in his smile did not threaten her now. It protected him, as her lack of response protected her. This close, his mouth was full, sensual. But a reservation neutralized this physical attraction. She contemplated his size and his black belt, and became aware of her defenselessness. The stranger who had just kissed her could hurt her. Diane was sorry she had come. She realized with sudden panic that of course he had assumed all along that she was there to make love with him. There was no time to decide if that was indeed why she had come. She needed desperately to say something, but nothing came out when she opened her mouth.

Bradley came to her rescue. "What are you thinking?" he whispered.

"I'm thinking that's the third time you've asked that question. What are *you* thinking?"

"I'd like you to spend the night."

"Oh." Her temporizing exclamation expressed many levels of emotion—anger with herself, fear, surprise at what was happening to her, perhaps on the deepest level an excitement easily confused with dread. It would have been easier not to have come.

"Is anything wrong?"

"No." She paused, reconsidered. "Yes. We have to talk."

"A woman should know when to quit talking." He started to kiss her. She backed away.

"I'd like to get carried away," she said. "But I can tell I'm not going to."

"That's okay." He smiled amiably. "If you were passionate, I'd probably be intimidated."

"I didn't say I wasn't passionate."

"Could you settle for excitement?" He put his arm around her and as he kissed her, they sank slowly down onto the carpet. His kiss was friendly, good-natured. Diane felt a peculiar passivity invading her limbs. She realized suddenly that the occasion—her subconscious would not profane the moment by thinking of it as an opportunity—called for courage and the ability to take a risk. She was not sure that she could tell him she had not come for this. She was too old to play that kind of game with a man. In her confused perception of the moment, she was convinced that she had gone too far to back out. This decision would not have been possible if she sensed any attempt on his part to overpower her, psychologically or physically. But seeing from his look of detached amusement that he would make no protest if she left, it became impossible for her to leave. She could not bear the prospect of his scorn. Still, there were practical considerations.

"What's the matter?" His breath smelled of chocolate and champagne.

"You couldn't respect a woman who brought her diaphragm along on a first date, could you?"

"This should be our second date," he pointed out, then admitted, "I suppose that would be considered vampy in the Midwest."

Laughter dispelled the tension building up between them. He kissed her again, leisurely. For the first time, Diane realized that she might be able to give in to the excitement of the situation. John Bradley, Jr., best-selling author and millionaire, was kissing her. It was hard to believe, but it seemed perfectly natural at the same time. His hands were large and smooth on her bare arms. His shoulders were broad, his back strong. She liked big men.

"What if I told you I was sterile," he whispered.

"I've been waiting for that line a long time," she laughed.

"How about Russian roulette?"

"I love to win." She drew away from him and sat up. "But I hate to lose. Do *you* have anything around the house?"

"I thought those went out with slicked-back hair and '57 Chevys." He sat up, reached for a log propped against the chimney, and began to build up the fire. The comment embarassed Diane first and then annoyed her. She stood up and walked over to the living room window, where she studied the neon signs across the street.

"I don't think the question is unreasonable," she said finally. The moment was slipping away from them. She watched the passersby on the sidewalk below, tense in her ambivalence, trying to determine whether relief or disappointment would prevail if Bradley chose not to save the evening. It was his move.

"I'm sorry, Diane." She saw his face in the window as he came up behind her and kissed her shoulder.

"It's all right," she murmured, uneasy in the thrill of his contrition.

"See the drugstore on the corner?"

She nodded. His lips brushed the nape of her neck. She shivered.

"It's open until midnight. Let's go for a walk."

She turned, smiled, put her arms around his neck and kissed him.

_____ *three*

There was no clock in Bradley's bedroom, but it felt early. Diane awoke surprisingly clear-headed, with a sense of life taking a new direction. She sat up, careful not to disturb Bradley, asleep under the navy-blue comforter. His face was smooth, his day's growth of beard a soft brown, the irony dormant behind closed eyelids. His hair was definitely thin, but Diane doubted he would ever be bald. She turned her face into the shoulder of the white cotton T-shirt he had given her for a nightgown. She was too excited to go back to sleep.

Diane slipped out of the king-size bed and tiptoed across thick white carpet to the mahogany dresser. She slowly opened the top drawer and froze when one of the brass handles clinked. There was nothing but underwear inside. She closed it gently and opened the second. A pistol sat like a paperweight on a pile of neatly folded sport shirts. The gun looked too small to be real, but judging from the way it sank into the shirts, it was heavy.

"Looking for something?"

Startled, she pushed the drawer shut. Her eyes met Bradley's in the mirror over the dresser. He sat up.

"Yes." She turned to face him, frankly embarrassed. "Is the gun real?"

He looked puzzled. "Why would I have a toy gun in my drawer? What were you looking for?" He was not angry, but neither was he amused.

"The shrunken heads."

He did not understand at first. "Did I tell you—"

"You know damn well you did." She walked toward the bed.

"It wasn't true." His laughter was deliberately eccentric, as if pretending he was crazier than he was.

"You've got a weird sense of humor." She sat down next to him. Somehow knowing he had played a joke on her made them even; she was less embarrassed about having been snooping. She kissed him, mildly aggressive. They made love, fast, almost impersonally. Bradley clung to the remnants of his dreams, Diane to her excitement. When it was over, they were awake, pleased to be together in the bright light that filled the room.

"It's a good thing I bought a twelve-pack."

"I told you not to underestimate my charms."

Diane got out of bed and walked over to one of the French windows. She was disappointed that it was raining. When she opened the window and put her hand out, the rain beading on her palm was warm. At least it was spring rain.

She was as detached from the events of the night before as if she had seen them in a movie. She was not sure what they meant. She had always been a careful person. She liked to *cause* things, to control them. This morning she was comfortable where she was.

She was not casual about lovemaking. She had had only one one-night stand; the parting had been awkward, with a strong sense of having given more than she got.

"What's it doing outside?" Bradley squinted against the glare.

"Raining."

"I can smell the ocean."

"I'm hungry," she announced.

"I bought bagels and cream cheese and lox in case I had company this morning."

"Don't tell me last night was premeditated." She looked at him with pretended dismay.

"Since Friday afternoon."

"What did you think your chances were?" Diane meant the question as a joke, but saw there was no right answer.

"You journalists are a pretty loose crowd."

She stuck her tongue out at him. He rolled out of bed.

"Let's make coffee." Bradley found a bathrobe and put it on. He handed Diane a plaid robe and she followed him into the kitchen.

"We won't be able to go sailing if the rain keeps up." He measured coffee into a filter.

"Too bad." She made no effort to hide her disappointment.

"Let's drive out to my parents' place anyway. If it clears up, we can take the boat out in the afternoon."

"Will your parents be there?" She hoped not.

"They're in England." She had forgotten. "What kind of bagel do you want—sesame, onion, or raisin?"

"Sesame."

"What kind of jam?"

"What have you got?"

"Name it."

"Strawberry."

"Orange juice or half a grapefruit?"

"Both." Bradley handed her a glass of juice and took a grapefruit out of the refrigerator.

"I won't be much of a crew," she said.

"The boathouse watchman knows what he's doing."

They sat down at the kitchen table, and he poured her coffee. She spread cream cheese and jam on her bagel, and took too big a bite.

"These bagels are so fresh," she spoke with her mouth full, nodding with approval.

"Have some lox?"

She shook her head.

"It's from Murray's."

She had never heard of Murray's, but she was not interested.

"No thank you. I don't like lox. We weren't big on seafood in the Midwest."

"Have you ever tasted it?"

"No."

"Try it."

"I'd rather not," she said firmly.

She was surprised to see that he was annoyed.

"There's nothing worse than a woman without a sense of adventure," he said.

"Except a bully."

"One bite. At least then you could say you tried it."

"Do you always get your way?" She was sardonic.

"It's called wearing the opponent down." There was anticipated triumph in his smile.

"In order not to spoil the day"—her voice had a sarcastic edge—"I will taste the lox."

She picked up a pink strip of fish and brought it to her mouth.

"No, don't." Bradley grabbed it from her. "You're right. I've been a bully." He pulled the plate of salmon away from her.

"No, I *want* to now," she insisted. "You've made me curious. It must be awfully good to merit such enthusiasm."

Diane cut a piece and put it into her mouth. She refused to give in to her impulse to gag. She chewed deliberately, forcing herself to consider the salty, fishy flavor. Bradley waited for her response.

"It's not as bad as I expected," she lied, swallowing.

"I'm sorry. Want another cup of coffee?"

She nodded, and bit into her bagel. The strawberry and cream cheese and bread dispelled the fishy taste in her mouth.

"Do you want to stop by your place to change before we head out to the Island?"

"I'm fine with what I wore last night. I've got a pair of sandals in my bag."

"What for?"

"I couldn't *walk* in the shoes I wore last night. They're strictly ornamental."

"Where did you change into them?"

"In front of your building."

"Women are amazing." He smiled.

"I wish I had a toothbrush, though."

"I've got a couple of extras in the bathroom."

"A true man of the world."

"I'm going to shave while you finish," he said. "want to take a shower?" She was not sure if he meant alone, so she declined.

The false note over the lox dissolved without a trace. Freshness and originality imbued every object in Bradley's kitchen. It was a rare morning. Diane had the satisfaction of recognizing it. How far she would be admitted—or would care to enter—into Bradley's world, she did not know. But drinking coffee at his kitchen table, she had crossed the threshold.

When she walked into the bedroom, Bradley was on the phone instructing someone to have his car ready. He handed her a toothbrush. The cold water she splashed on her face brought color to her cheeks. She decided against makeup. After pinning her hair up and brushing her teeth, she was ready to go.

The car was waiting in front of the building when they got downstairs. If the doorman was surprised to see her, he did not let on.

"Nice car," she observed as the doorman shut her in. Bradley started the engine; its hum was deep, authoritative.

"Thanks." He accepted the compliment simply, aware of the merits of the machine.

"It feels like a car I should recognize," she said.

"It's a Morgan."

"Does it bother you that I didn't know?"

"No."

"I love the smell of leather upholstery." She inhaled deeply. "It feels like you should light up a pipe."

"It's a shame we can't put the roof down."

It had begun to rain more heavily. Traffic moved slowly on the 59th Street Bridge. Viewed from Bradley's sportscar, the Manhattan skyline looked like a movie set—romantic, unreal.

"What are you thinking?" He spoke absently, the best part of his energy devoted to weaving in and out of traffic.

"About the languages you speak that I don't."

"I thought you spent a year in France."

"I did. But you speak cars, too, and sailing."

"Cars are my weakness," Bradley admitted complacently.

"I went through a stage in eighth grade when my father would point to a Plymouth or Ford and I'd tell him the year and the model. But I was tired of the game by the time fins disappeared. Now I don't know a Morgan from a Studebaker. And the only boat I ever navigated was a canoe at girl scout camp."

"Anyone can learn to sail," he told her.

"With enough time, and a boat." Again, she was thinking out loud.

"I'll teach you."

"I wasn't fishing," she laughed. "At least, I don't think I was."

"You romanticize sailing," he said. "Everybody's into it."

"Not the way you are."

"I sail some nice boats." He smiled a connoisseur's smile.

The windshield wipers made a pleasant music as they sped east on the Long Island Expressway. Once on the open road, Bradley was reckless. He changed lanes compulsively, tailgated slow cars and passed them much too fast after he intimidated them into moving over. Bradley enjoyed her nervousness. He laughed when she reached behind her seat and pulled the seatbelt over her shoulder.

"Were you a race-car driver too?" she asked with annoyance after he slammed on the brakes suddenly to avoid hitting the car in front of them.

"I always wanted to be," he said, smiling, slowing down imperceptibly in deference to her uneasiness.

It was cool outside the city, and the heater was on, insulating them from the rain that fell on middle-class Queens. Row houses gradually gave way to semi-detached houses. Beyond the city limits, the backyards got bigger, the homes farther apart. They were beyond the suburbs before Bradley turned off the expressway.

The road they followed wound along the North Shore, and Long Island Sound was often visible beyond the estates they passed. The countryside was surprisingly unspoiled.

"It's hard to believe we're only an hour from New York." Diane watched a flock of seagulls wheeling above the rocks along a cove. The air was damp and salty. "What a different world here. It's beautiful."

Bradley nodded. "This is robber baron country," he said. "Our grandfathers did a lot of dirty work to leave us all this."

"I'm glad they did." Diane studied an estate on a hill beyond the hedge they drove along.

"Me too." They drove for about half an hour before

Bradley turned suddenly, driving past an ivy-covered gate-house that appeared unoccupied.

"Here we are," he announced.

The gravel road ended in a circular driveway about two hundred yards from the gate. Bradley parked in front of a mansion that she recognized from a magazine article and got out to open her door. It had been a long time since a man had extended her that courtesy. Diane liked it. There was an element of playacting in the gesture.

"I feel like we're on the movie set for *The Great Gatsby*," she laughed. She was glad she had not changed into a casual outfit.

"Welcome to East Egg." He helped her out of the car.

The house was a turn-of-the-century American version of French provincial, set in an English garden. The eclectic outbuildings did not match the mansion's motif. Diane half expected a butler to greet them at the front door, but they were past the foyer and standing in a bright, comfortably furnished living room before an older woman came out of the kitchen, drying her hands on her apron.

"Good morning, Mrs. Robinson." Bradley kissed her with affection that was genuine for all its condescension.

"What a surprise," she beamed. "And what a shame your parents aren't here."

Bradley was on the verge of contradicting her, but introduced his companion instead.

"This is Diane Yaeger. She's writing a magazine article about me because of the book."

The woman nodded. Diane shook a hand moist from dishwater.

"I started to read the book after Mr. Robinson finished it. But it's too frightening."

There was a trace of Irish or Scottish—Diane could not tell which—in the woman's accent.

"You'll have to see the movie then." Bradley clapped her around the shoulder.

"Are they making a movie of it?" She was proud, but not particularly surprised.

"I'm going to Hollywood in a week."

"He's going to be on the 'Tonight Show.' " Diane eyed him playfully.

"Are you?" The housekeeper nodded. "You must write

the time down for me. Mr. Robinson will never be able to stay awake that late, but I'll be sure to watch. I don't need much sleep, you know.''

"What are our chances of getting lunch on such short notice?''

"I can put something together for you.'' She started back toward the kitchen.

"In the meantime, I'll give Miss Yaeger a tour.''

The house was large, but not formidable. It had high ceilings and spacious rooms, furnished with simple elegance. Her favorite rooms were a sitting room à la Duncan Phyfe, a Victorian library with rare books lining glass cabinets, and a Fifties den, where Bradley and his sister had listened to rock'n' roll records with friends. The living room was traditional and lived in. There were family portraits in the old-fashioned rooms, modern art—Diane recognized a Picasso, a Miro, several early Jackson Pollocks—in the contemporary rooms, New England seascapes in the guest rooms.

"It's a beautiful home,'' she told him as they climbed the stairs to the second floor.

"I'll show you my room.''

As faithfully preserved as Pompeii by Vesuvius, Bradley's room was a monument to a preppy East Coast teenager—Ivy League football team pennants on the walls, *The Catcher in the Rye* on a nightstand by the bed, 45 RPM records piled by an old hi-fi.

"The scene of my earliest—solitary—sexual experiences.'' He patted the bed affectionately as he sat down on it.

Diane smiled. Her gaze was arrested by the vista out the window. "What a beautiful garden. And the Sound's so wide here. Is that Connecticut?''

"Straight ahead.'' He leaned into a window seat and opened a window.

"It's beautiful.'' Diane's heart swelled at the idea of a child's life flowering in such surroundings.

"This brings back some good memories.'' His complacency returned. "I remember as a teenager thinking I was unique because I liked living here. My friends all wanted to be screwed up. But I always loved this room, and the thoughts I thought here.''

"What kind of thoughts?" Sitting down on the window seat, Diane watched rain flatten the surf.

"I used to invent countries," he said. "I'd draw a map of an undiscovered territory—usually an island. I was fascinated by islands. Then I'd write a history—who discovered and settled it, how they won their independence. I mapped out the country's regions and kept demographics. Sometimes religious movements would spring up on the island and I thought up the religions."

"The fledgling writer," Diane suggested.

"I never told anyone about the game," he went on. "I was afraid of finding out I was the only person in the world who played them."

"I invented a sister," Diane laughed.

"What was *her* name?" The way Bradley asked, they might have been discussing a real sister.

"Diane." She was surprised to feel herself blushing. "Her dream was to grow up to be just like her big sister. My mother got pregnant about the time I was getting tired of the game. Unfortunately, Lynn was never as exciting as the make-believe Diane."

"You haven't changed much."

"What do you mean?"

She followed Bradley out of the room and they headed down the stairs.

"The life you lead isn't as satisfying as the life you imagine leading."

"Has *your* life lived up to all your expectations?" she asked.

"I'm not a malcontent."

"Neither am I." It irritated her that he would make such a serious interpretation of her revelation. "I hope I don't come across that way." The observation was a plea that he not criticize her. They stepped out onto a semicircular porch overlooking the garden.

"Your expectations may be too high," he suggested.

"Why lower them unless I have to?"

"Good point." Bradley took her hand and led her down a flight of marble steps into an unstructured expanse of lawn, more park than garden. They walked down a brick path lined with hedges. Diane inhaled deeply.

"I love the way boxwoods smell after it rains."

Bradley had brought an umbrella, which he opened over them.

"I shouldn't judge you when we've known each other such a short time," he said. "I'm just talking impressions."

"The only poetry my father knew was a paraphrase of the line about a man's reach exceeding his grasp," she explained. "He always said it so matter-of-factly I assumed that was the way everyone felt. I have a hard time with limitations. I want everything."

"What do you mean, 'everything'?"

"Time. Money. Places. Things. Isn't that what everyone wants?"

"Not everyone," Bradley answered. "Most people don't have the courage to want."

"I should get a purple heart."

"You're young to have such a highly developed sense of time passing. How old are you?"

"I already told you."

"No, you ducked the question."

The accusation confused her. "Twenty-eight."

"I envy you your sense of direction. I was aimless at your age."

"At my age," she mocked him. "You have to have goals when you don't have what you want." She smiled. "If I had your time and money, I'd probably drift along as contentedly as you have."

"Do I seem content?" Bradley frowned.

"You called me malcontent."

"Here, let's get out of the rain." They directed their steps into a small gazebo midway between house and water. "It's not fun drifting," he said. They sat down on a wooden bench.

"It's tough being rich." Diane's teasing had an edge to it.

"You've really got a chip on your shoulder."

She dismissed the criticism impatiently. "The fact is, there aren't that many people I'd change places with. I had my secret islands too. Only mine didn't go away when I grew up."

Bradley was silent, reluctant to disturb her train of thought by encouraging her to go on. But Diane intended to share her secret.

"I've always believed that I was special."

"In what way?" His tone respected her honesty.

"It's never mattered how."

"You still believe it?"

She nodded. "It's a hard thing to say. It sounds so conceited."

"And you would be able to realize your specialness with enough time and money?"

"It isn't as easy as that," she answered. "Having advantages doesn't mean that you use them wisely."

"Amen."

"I might not make the right decisions."

"You would."

Diane flushed.

"You're the kind of woman who time and money would improve."

"That may be the strangest compliment I've ever had." She glowed inside with the peculiar pleasure she felt when someone recognized the fact that she was special.

"I want to show you something." He took a wallet from his jacket and handed her a piece of folded paper. It was a check for fifty thousand dollars, made out by Hartley-Bennett Publishers to John E. Bradley, Jr. "It's the advance for my second book."

"What's it about?"

"I haven't the slightest idea. They trust me to come up with something."

"That's a big advance." She handed the check back to him.

He took a pen from his jacket and wrote on the back of the check, "Pay to the order of Diane Yaeger," and signed his name.

"What's the 'E' stand for?" It did not yet mean anything that he had written her name and his name on the check.

"Edmund."

"I like that. It's aristocratic."

"I want you to have this." Bradley handed her the check.

"I don't understand." Diane was confused.

"You keep talking about opportunities. I'd like to see what you do with this one."

"Are you serious?" Blood rushed burning to her face. Anger and embarrassment welled up in her throat. She strode out of the gazebo and started up the path to the house. He forgot the umbrella in his haste to follow her.

"Wait, Diane, what's wrong?" Bradley's genuine puzzlement caught her off guard. A tremendous relief flooded over her as she realized that Bradley had not been making fun of her.

"Have you ever done anything like that before?" She brushed damp hair away from her face as she watched him.

"Come back out of the rain, Diane. You'll catch cold."

She refused the hand he offered her, but returned with him to the gazebo.

"I don't understand." She shook her head as she sat down. "You spend the night with a woman and offer her fifty thousand dollars the next day."

Bradley looked at her with wounded dignity. "You've got a problem more serious than a chip on your shoulder if you think there's any connection between the two."

"What exactly are you proposing?"

"I want you to put my money where your mouth is," he said, smiling. "You feel you're exceptional. I challenge you to prove it."

"You'd give me fifty thousand dollars just to see what I'd do with it?" Diane shook her head at the strange idea. "Could you really give away that much money on a whim?"

"This is more than a whim. Besides, the money isn't real to me yet. I haven't worked for it."

"Why, John?" She was too baffled by his gesture to remain defensive or angry.

"I like the idea of improving your life."

"Do you think fifty thousand dollars would do that?"

"I don't. But you do. I'd like to see if you're right."

"I've got a great idea for your next book," she said. "A bored Long Island aristocrat stalks the city, offering large sums of money to single women. It's the only way he can *affect* the people he meets. We could call it *Pygmalion II*. Or maybe you need a more contemporary title. How about *Makeover Man*?"

"You misrepresent my motives." Bradley's brow knit in irritation.

"I don't like your game," Diane said.

"It isn't a game."

"Your experiment, then."

"Look—" He broke away. "It was just an idea. I'm sorry I brought it up."

His apology defused her anger. Why *did* she always take things so seriously? Her sense of adventure was chronically mistimed.

"What do you get out of it?" Diane eyed him warily.

"I'm a writer. I might learn something."

"About what?"

"Life. You have unusually high standards. I think it would be worth the money to remove the obstacles to your ambitions and see where life leads you."

"If you're crazy enough to give fifty thousand dollars to a woman you've known forty-eight hours"—she laughed nervously, but was careful not to let her tone imply that she would reconsider—"then maybe I'm crazy not to take it."

"Take it," Bradley urged.

She shook her head. "I've never even taken cabfare from a date."

"Think of the opportunity for me to exercise my sense of noblesse oblige. You confirm your middle-class status by not taking the check."

"I can't." Diane realized that her protest had enough weakness in it to make him think that she might give in. "I couldn't."

"Be exceptional," he coaxed. "It's a pleasant experience, having money. Buy a dress at Bendel's *and* go to a party. Buy a diamond watch and leave it on your nightstand. Forget about time. Tell me in a week what it's like to have done things you always said you'd do if you had the time and money. You can get a week off from work, can't you?"

Silhouetted against the garden and gray sky, gray rain, and gray ocean, Bradley's face was the only thing in focus. Diane swallowed. Her pulse quickened. Her stomach tingled. She had never in a year earned half the money he was offering. Though Bradley found the money unreal, the check was quickly losing its abstractness for Diane. His offer might tempt her if it weren't for his detachment. She was silent, watching fine droplets of water bead halo-like on Bradley's hair.

"Why?" she asked again.

She was not afraid of his impatience. The possibilities before her were thrilling and terrifying, but once she was certain she could have them, it was no longer necessary. To have been able to have was as satisfying as having—and safer. She waited.

"I would like to see my freedom through your eyes."

She liked his answer. "When do you leave for California?" she asked.

"A week from today."

"I'll take the money on one condition: You spend the week with me."

He tried unsuccessfully to hide his surprise. Diane realized suddenly that he had not expected her to accept his offer, but this amused rather than upset her. It served him right.

"That makes the proposition riskier," he hedged. "I prefer the sidelines."

"I don't want a director." She returned his smile.

"It could get complicated."

"You're free to reconsider." She was perfectly sincere. It was in his hands now. Diane could not have said what outcome she hoped for, until he said "All right." Then she realized that she had been hoping he would not take her up on her dare. If she had imagined the scene between them, there would have been laughter and a romantic embrace after he agreed. Instead, they spent the walk back to the house setting out the conditions for the experiment. She would spend the money by the following Sunday. It was not to be invested or used to buy a permanent asset such as a Mercedes. Diane had to use the money to *live*, to do things she had never done, see things she had never seen.

When they fell silent Diane thought about the complicated arrangements involved in getting a week off and finishing the article. She felt an intellectual certainty that she would take the risk. There was a sense of obligation, almost, in her decision. She was not sure whether it would be fun to spend an entire week with a man she hardly knew, however attractive, but it was up to Bradley to call the thing off. She suspected that he was as reluctant to make himself look foolish by reneging on his wager as she was to appear intimidated by it.

They ate hot roast beef sandwiches in an elegant Victorian dining room. For dessert, Mrs. Robinson served chocolate chip cookies, the chips still molten from the oven, with glass cups of cappucino. After lunch they locked themselves in the library and looked at the books behind the glass cabinets. Diane was delighted with the illustrations in a first edition of *David Copperfield*. Bradley was surprised how many of Dickens's novels she had read. He thought of her more as a Bronte type. He showed her his own childhood favorites—*The Three Musketeers* and a translation of *Les Misérables*. He had never heard of Paul Bunyan, so Diane entertained him with stories of skaters greasing giant pans with slabs of bacon tied to their feet. She had not read *The Canterbury Tales* in middle English. His reading of the "Prologue" failed to convince her that it was easier than it looked.

They were comfortable talking about books, though they did not consider themselves intellectuals. They read to escape from themselves, not to know themselves better.

They sat on a thick carpet sipping brandy in front of an easygoing fire.

"Are those your parents?" Diane nodded toward two portraits over the fireplace.

"None other."

"I suppose it's lucky you don't look like your father," Diane said, "though he's a nice enough looking guy."

Bradley laughed. "It changes my perception of the old man to hear you call him a 'guy.' "

John E. Bradley, Sr., was thinner than his son, with more hair—thick, white, and brushed back off a furrowed brow—and a pencil-thin moustache etched over lips compressed almost to nonexistence. His face had more strength than his son's, but the price of this character was a rigidity of expression that hinted to Diane that Bradley might not be the only one to find his father unlikeable.

"Everyone says I have my mother's eyes," he added. Mrs. Bradley's large brown eyes were warm and intelligent. Bradley also had her full sensuous mouth, though their resemblance was not striking.

"Is there a picture of your sister around?" Diane asked.

"She would never have a portrait done," Bradley explained. "It's really too bad she and I couldn't have switched genes. She looks just like Dad. She's got the same stiff carriage, the same thin, dry face, and she's had white hair as long as I can remember. I was prettier as a kid."

The observation put Diane off. There was something precociously decadent about a young boy considering himself prettier than his older sister. However, her displeasure faded as her limbs warmed and her hair dried in front of the fire.

Diane lay back, closed her eyes, and allowed herself to be hypnotized by the music of rain slapped by sea breezes against the windowpanes, wood lapped by flames, muffled footsteps in a distant part of the house. Bradley's kiss was tender but urgent. They made love on the carpet. Their haste, the fear of discovery (Diane could not remember if he had locked the door), the sacrilege of being naked in front of his parents' portraits, in a room consecrated to learning, gave their lovemaking a novelistic quality.

They lay silent afterwards, gazing dreamily at the beamed ceiling, her head on his shoulder. Diane was the first to speak. "Do you ever have motifs in the background when you make love?"

"All the time." They shared the joy of recognition.

"What was yours, just now?"

"I was Julien Sorel, taking Mathilde in the library, with her father in the next room. It was all very swashbuckling."

"I felt very"—she sought the right word, and decided on—"literary. The heroines in these books were watching me. Comparing notes. Emma Bovary approved. Emma Woodhouse was scandalized."

"Did you mind their watching?"

"No." She sat up to kiss him. "We were worthy of the company."

It was dark by the time they left for New York. The rain had stopped—seemingly for good. Through their open windows they smelled the wet tree trunks and waterlogged earth. They made good time back to the city. When the

Manhattan skyline came into view, it hovered above the East River like an elongated cloud of pulsating stars. The lights outlining the bridges reminded Diane of circus tents, roller coasters, artificial mountains. Everything was too beautiful to be real.

But it was. Making love in the library, Diane had finally been overcome by the reality of Bradley's offer.

Now, with all of New York spread before her like a banquet at which she and Bradley were free to sample whatever struck their fancy, finally Diane was excited. But the intensity of the sense of possibilities was also enervating. Bradley suggested dinner out, but Diane was tired.

"Let's get some deli food and go home," she suggested. "The prospect of extravagance has worn me out."

They went to Zabar's. It was chaos inside. Shoppers waited six deep to check out. Long lines of customers, tickets in hand, stood at counters for meat, fish, cheese, coffee.

"I'm starving." Bradley took a shopping cart; Diane wheeled her own behind him.

"I'm going to buy everything I ever wanted," she whispered huskily, suddenly hungry.

At the meat counter, she tried to assimilate the information she heard about the different styles of ham and veal and wurst and corned beef, but the variety exceeded the scope of her memory and she ended up asking the counter man for recommendations.

"John," she called over to him as he stood in line to buy lox, "come try this salami and tell me what you think. It's called Roumanian Sibiu." When he nodded his approval, she ordered a half-pound. "And what about pork? Should we get the Texas barbeque or roast loin Chinese style?"

"That's a tough decision."

"We'll take a half-pound of each, then," she said decisively. Bradley's number was called at the fish counter.

The butcher offered her samples of duck French style, stuffed with fruit, ham smoked with applewood, long, sweet Lebanon bologna, and roast veal stuffed with fontina, ham and spices. She took a little of each. She attracted attention, filling her shopping cart. She pushed it over to Bradley.

"They've got Matjes herring filets today." He spoke with appetite. "And Western Nova."

"I'm glad for you. I'll see you in condiments." She waved.

When Bradley joined her, she was weighing the merits of heather honey, New Zealand buttercup honey, and wild flower honey.

"I like the wild flower." He read the label, which was in French, like poetry. "*Miel de fleurs sauvages.* Beautiful." She put the honey into her cart.

"This grapefruit marmalade looks good," he observed.

"I already got some," she pointed out. "Here's my favorite though." She held up a bottle in which two full-size oranges were suspended in golden liquid. "They're called harlequin oranges. They're stuffed with cherries and prunes."

She put two jars into the cart.

There were several things she bought on principle: pickled walnuts, which she suspected she would not like, hazelnut oil (strictly a whim), and a bottle of Provence vinegar in which a bouquet of spices was embalmed. At the cookie shelf she took a box of each Bahlsen brand— Mesino, Waldersee, Susse Last Azora, Cortez, Bella Minta, Butter Keks. She liked the names.

Bradley had four pieces of imported cheese in his cart when he met her in the coffee and tea department.

"I'd never heard of *Fromage explorateur* before"—he showed her the package—"but I couldn't resist 'explorer cheese' tonight."

Diane bought Souchong tea and a pound of Vienna roast coffee.

"Look, espresso's on sale," she pointed out to Bradley. "Want some?"

"Sounds good."

"We'll have a pound of espresso," she told the clerk, who ground the beans. "What's the best espresso machine you've got?"

"The Caffarex is good. It's on sale this week. Marked down from a thousand dollars."

"A bargain," Bradley said. Irony did not cover up his inability to look nonplussed.

"Do you think it will fit in the car?" she asked him.

"With the other ten bags?"

"Could someone help us get this out to the car?" She admired the machine. A clerk volunteered.

"Get some bread at the checkout stand," she called to Bradley as she followed the clerk to the front of the store, "and buy me some Bacci's."

"Some what?"

"Bacci's. Italian chocolate kisses."

When she rejoined him at the cash register, Bradley was waiting for the manager to approve his purchase. The bill came to just under a thousand dollars.

"Two percent of my budget for the week," she said cheerfully. "I'll write you a check after yours clears."

She held the door for Bradley as he struggled out to the car with the first two bags of groceries.

"You're my guest for the week. I insist on it," Diane told Bradley. The point had come up at the end of the picnic spread on the floor of Diane's living room. She was adamant about her right to spend her money any way she wanted to.

"I'm expensive," he warned her.

"The coach turns into a pumpkin when the meter hits fifty thousand," she said. They had assembled the espresso machine without any problem, and were sitting on her couch in candlelight, drinking the bitter coffee as they watched the ships docked at the harbor below.

"How many kinds of cookies were on that plate?" he asked.

"Twelve. I had at least one of each."

"What will we do this week?" He put his arm around her.

"I've got *Vogue*. Let's look at clothes."

"I won't go shopping with you."

"I hate shopping, too," she laughed. "You can have tomorrow afternoon off. I'm going to do Fifth Avenue like a Texas tycoon."

There was a knock at the door. It was Alan. Anyone else would have announced himself through the intercom in the lobby. She turned a lamp on, went to the door.

"Who is it?" she asked, to be sure.

"Alan."

She opened the door. "Hi. I've got company," she told him as he entered. "Alan, this is John Bradley. John, Alan Jennings." Bradley stood up to meet him. He was taller than Alan. They shook hands.

"I'm really enjoying your book," Alan said enthusiastically.

"Thank you." Bradley did not appear surprised that Diane's friend was among his readers.

Diane was surprised. Alan never read fiction. If she had not had such a strong sense of the acceleration of events, she might have stopped for more than a fleeting second to wonder why he was reading the book.

"I've got something to show you," she told him.

Alan followed her into the kitchen, where Diane turned on a light and posed with a new owner's pride beside the coffee machine.

"You finally did it," Alan said, beaming. Bradley joined them.

"Want a cup?" He nodded.

Diane and Bradley sat on the couch together when they returned to the living room with more coffee, but no other gesture or words betrayed the change that had taken place in their relationship since Diane had last seen Alan.

"I got some new machinery myself." Sitting in an easy chair, Alan reached over to set his cup on the coffee table.

"What did you get?" She was glad to see him.

"A three-hundred-and-sixty-degree camera. I've had my eye on one for a long time," he told Bradley. "It's beautiful."

"How do you keep yourself out of the picture?" Bradley smiled. "Aim and duck?"

"Or hide behind something."

"You wouldn't believe all Alan's gadgets," Diane told Bradley. "He has lenses that can do just about anything you can imagine."

"Is photography what you do for a living?" Bradley asked.

"That's how I started. I still shoot about half the year."

"Alan's one of the top industrial photographers in the country." She was eager to display her loyalty to a friend. She wanted Bradley to understand that she was not defensive about being a business reporter. "How many Fortune 500 companies do you do annual reports for?"

"Twenty, maybe." He dismissed her enthusiasm with a modest shake of his head.

"Alan just got back from two weeks in the Seychelle Islands shooting a brochure for Air France."

"They're beautiful, aren't they?" Bradley said.

"They seemed pretty nice," Alan replied. "I didn't have much time for sightseeing."

" 'They seemed pretty nice.' " Diane repeated his words with practiced exasperation, conveying by her tone that she and Alan had had this discussion before. "Alan gets trips to Alexandria or Kyoto to shoot pyramids or geisha girls and I ask him how it was and all he ever says is they seemed pretty nice. I suppose I could give up the sightseeing, too, for the kind of money they pay you. He got a thousand dollars the other day for shooting rats in a sewer."

"Not bad." Bradley was sincere.

A thousand dollars a day *wasn't* bad, she thought. "Alan's company does unbelievable multi-media presentations for advertising agencies," Diane told him. "Quadraphonic disco music. Slides with letters that pulsate. Film and video and slides all interspliced. How many slide projectors did you use on that Thompson presentation last month?"

"Just nine."

"*Just* nine?" Bradley laughed.

"For three screens. That's a pretty standard show." Alan qualified her praise.

"The client was pushing a new deodorant," Diane told Bradley. "The presentation practically had me out in the streets afterwards selling the stuff."

"Commercials are more entertaining than the programs nowadays." Bradley's observation was perfunctory, but polite.

"Alan doesn't do commercials."

"Film and video production houses produce the commercials," Alan explained. "My audience is business people. It's amazing how much money they spend making presentations interesting. Amazing."

"Did you work today?" Diane asked.

"I just fooled around with the new camera. But it's hard to find a place in New York that looks good all the way around. Would you two like to come over and see the camera?"

"Can I do it tomorrow night?" Diane asked, forgetting that Bradley might be with her.

"I'll be in Cleveland taking pictures of a machine that molds plastic car fenders."

"Bring it over when you get back, then," Diane told him. "I'd like to go over tonight, but John and I have to finish the interview."

"All right." He stood up tenuously, waiting to see if Diane would detain him. Her loyalty was not as strong as her desire to be alone with Bradley, though, and she let him say goodnight.

"Before you go . . ." Diane beckoned to him to follow her into the kitchen.

"I don't believe all this food," he gasped when she opened the refrigerator. "Are you expecting another Depression?" She began filling a shopping bag.

"Maybe you can freeze the Chinese food and work on this stuff for a while."

"I never tried freezing it before."

"I've seen frozen Chinese vegetables in the grocery store. It'll work," she assured him.

Alan waved goodbye to Bradley from the front door, signaling that he didn't have to get up. Diane kissed him goodnight casually, like a friend. They did not kiss often, bu tonight she was grateful that he had had the sensitivity to leave.

"Nice guy," Bradley observed when she sat down next to him on the couch.

"Alan and I have known each other since college. We have an unusual relationship. We care for each other a lot."

"What's unusual about that?"

"It's hard to explain. We're not in love. But it's more than friendship. Much more."

"That can get complicated." Bradley smiled.

"We don't talk about it," she said. "Alan says we'll spoil it by talking about it."

"That must frustrate an analyzer like you."

She shook her head. "I prefer it that way. We're as free as we need to be to get where we're going. But we're backup for each other if things get out of hand."

"Does he go out with anyone else?"

"He doesn't go *out* with me," Diane elucidated. "Women don't fit into Alan's schedule. Which is one of the reasons I like him. Sometimes it seems weak for a man to need women. In certain moods, I like a man self-sufficient. But when I need him, Alan's a point of reference—as solid and predictable as the machines he photographs. No matter how crazy things get, I know he'll be too busy to notice. And if something isn't bad enough for Alan to notice, it probably isn't as bad as it seems.

"Let's have more espresso—in bed," she suggested.

"As long as you don't expect me to sleep." He smiled suggestively. "This is my third cup."

"There's plenty to talk about," she called from the stereo, which she was tuning to an all-jazz radio station.

"There's one thing I don't understand about your friendship with Alan"—Bradley's voice preceded him from the kitchen—"and that's how you get a sense of security from a guy who's only half there."

"He cares for me," Diane answered as she arranged her bed. "That really matters when I'm depressed."

"I can't imagine you depressed." Bradley set their cups on an end table.

"On my birthday last summer, we sat on Alan's roof and got drunk on gin and tonics. I started crying because I should have married a guy I'd broken up with the year before and I'd never find the right guy with all the competition in New York. Alan told me to take it easy, he'd marry me if it came to that. He would, too. That's what I mean about backup. I don't expect to marry Alan, but it's relaxing, having such a close friend."

"What will you tell your ace in the hole about us?" Bradley smiled.

"I don't know." Diane was not sure why the question disturbed her. "I'll have to wait and see what there is to tell him first. Which reminds me"—Diane reached for a note pad next to the telephone on the night table—"I've got to call the magazine in the morning and get a week's extension on the deadline."

"Tell them I offered you a hundred times the going rate not to write the story."

"Are you kidding?" she laughed. "I'll tell them I've got a chance for an inside story."

They had bought the Sunday *Times* before coming home. Bradley began going through it.

"Do you always check the paper at the newsstand to make sure they haven't left anything out?" He scanned the front page.

"The only time I didn't, the 'Arts and Leisure' section was missing," Diane answered. "I was pissed. What's your favorite section?"

"The sports section."

"I don't believe you."

"I love basketball. I got interested to spite my father. If I'm ever a father, one of my cardinal precepts will be 'Don't take your five-year-old to the Met.' I still have a hard time with opera and ballet."

"I like ballet."

"I never believe people who tell me that," he said. "What kind of pleasure do you get out of it?"

"Physical, mainly. It doesn't take me as deep into my feelings as music does, though."

"Do you like painting?"

"I could go the rest of my life and not set foot inside a museum," she confessed.

"Museums are the wrong place for good paintings."

"I might as well admit it, since I saw a lot of modern painting at your place and at your parents'—I have the standard, middle-American bias against modern art. Deep down, I think I could do a lot of it better myself."

He laughed.

"Do you keep up with the New York visual arts scene?" Diane asked.

"Sporadically."

"Take me to an opening this week." Diane brightened.

"A good friend just opened an exhibition at the Reyn Gallery," he told her. "We could have a look at his stuff and then visit him in his studio."

"I'd like that."

"What about dinner tomorrow night at Lutece?"

Diane shook her head. "I want to go someplace I haven't been."

"Have you been to Coco's yet?" Coco's, the latest "in" discotheque, was built in an abandoned theater.

"I was always afraid they wouldn't let me in," she

said, "and I don't have the energy for a discrimination suit."

"God, you're scrappy."

"I am not."

"There you go again. Don't you think someone's filed a suit by now?"

"Probably not. The people I know who haven't gotten in knew before they got in line that they wouldn't. They blame themselves. It never occurs to them that it's the management that's not cool and not the people they won't let in."

"If you told them all that," Bradley laughed, "you'd wear them down and they'd let you in without a struggle."

"I'd like to say screw 'em, they don't deserve me," she said, smiling. "But I'm a great believer in using connections. If you can get me in, you've got a date. I hope you're giving dancing lessons first, though."

"Most of us still dance apart," he told her.

"You mean I can twist?"

"That you'll have to do by yourself. Twisting gives me a side ache."

"I'm really excited about this week." She was serious. "So am I."

He put his arm around her shoulder and kissed her. She drew back to look into his eyes.

"It's really going to happen, isn't it?"

They lay down on the bed as they embraced.

"I left something in my coat pocket." He sat up and set the newspaper on the floor.

"It's my turn and I've already taken care of it." She smiled at the pleasure in his face.

"What a surprise."

"Stick around," Diane whispered, grazing his ear with her lips as she reached over and turned off the bedside lamp. "I'm full of surprises."

_____ *five*

Arranging a week off was not as easy as Diane had expected. She told her boss that she had to go home because her mother was seriously ill. He grumbled, so that Diane was first indignant at his lack of sympathy and then afraid that she had sounded insincere. She felt a pang of superstitious guilt using her mother's illness as an excuse.

Putting the *Rolling Stone* article off a week ran right up to the magazine's deadline. Only the promise of a candid second interview with Bradley—Diane's discreet description of the upcoming week—convinced the editor that it was worth holding space for an untested freelancer.

Bradley was gone in the morning, his note said, to work on the new novel. He had taken the liberty of looking at the checkbook in her purse, would transfer the money into her account, and would see her at seven.

For the first time in her life, Diane was looking forward to shopping. She got an appointment for a haircut at Michael's of Fifth Avenue, and practiced in the bathroom mirror looking as if a hundred-dollar-plus haircut was an everyday occurrence. While sipping coffee, she searched the Manhattan yellow pages for a club near Michael's where she could get a massage and sauna. When the appointments were made, she changed into jeans and her white silk blouse and headed outside.

Jonquils were blooming in the flower beds along the promenade. On Montague Street, a communal sense of renewal was rampant in the midday crowd. People loosened collars, took off hats, unbuttoned sweaters, and smiled at one another for the premature warmth.

Diane was open to new experiences, she thought, climbing into a cab outside the bank (where she now had a balance of $50,018), but she had never thought that she could let another human being massage her body or paint her toenails. Today she would overcome both inhibitions. The sauna was a good start. Except for halfhearted attempts to learn tennis or start jogging, Diane Yaeger rarely perspired. But in the cedar-fragrant steam, it felt good to sweat. A winter staleness floated to the surface of her skin and was washed away in a cool, purifying shower.

Diane confessed outright to her masseuse that this was her first time. "I feel awkward," she said. "This massage is a gift," she added, as if apologizing. The attractive, middle-aged Scandinavian woman smiled, assuring Diane that she had encountered this reticence before.

"Concentrate on how you feel," she told Diane. It was good advice. There had been a thin line between excitement and tension in her first encounters with Bradley and the massage hurt at first, but after the pain came a relaxation she could not have imagined. The only thing that came close was sleep after making love; the massage was possibly the more pleasant sensation. She felt wonderful.

After dressing, she made an appointment with the masseuse for the same day the following week. Even spending her own money, it would be worth it.

Michael, on the other hand, was a pain. Five minutes into his performance, Diane resolved for the tenth time to find a woman hairdresser. The man's egotism exasperated her. Her hair was the artist's raw material.

"Whatever you think," was her response to a long lecture on why he wanted to cut most of her hair off. Because *Vogue* had given him a rave review, she submitted.

Michael's work of art was radical. When he presented it to her in the white light of a makeup mirror, too sure of his talent to ask an opinion, she gasped.

You made my head look like a mushroom cap, she wanted to cry. But instead she mumbled, "You really *did* cut off a lot." It was not the first time she had choked back disappointment and told a hairdresser that his cut was "interesting."

As the manicurist led her away to do all twenty nails, Diane felt wind in her ears and a draft on her bare neck. She was too preoccupied with her haircut to enjoy the sensation of cream being massaged into her skin, and pumice being smoothed into the pads her Dr. Scholl shoes had worn on the balls of her feet. Michael's *visagiste,* as his makeup artist termed herself, told Diane about the dermatologists and cosmetologists she had studied with in France and compared the merits of American and French makeup as she applied lotions from the latter country to Diane's face.

Outside, Diane plunged into the crowd, a river of humanity flowing up Fifth Avenue. She was uncomfortable. The makeup blocked the sun; her skin could not breathe. In the ladies' room at Bergdorf's, washing off fifty dollars worth of makeup, she remembered Bertha, the family sheepdog. She and her father had wrestled the dog into the bathtub each spring, only to have her roll in the dirt afterwards. With brisk brush strokes, Diane deflated Michael's mushroom. The haircut was short, but not unflattering. She had not had bangs since high school. They made her look younger. She could not decide if that was good or bad.

A saleslady intercepted Diane as she headed through the sportswear department on her way to the street.

"May I help you?"

"What would you wear to lunch at the Plaza?"

"Which dining room?"

"The Palm Court."

The saleslady showed her a sleeveless white cotton dress with tiny green dots. Diane bought a silk slip to go with it.

It was after two when she sat down to lunch. She sipped a Campari and soda and watched the comings and goings of guests in the lobby. As she ate seafood salad and drank a glass of white wine, she thought about Bradley: his strong, elegant hands, the perfume of Scotch on his breath, his smooth back, cool to the touch under his shirt. He was mature. Diane liked that. It had been a long time since she had been physically attracted to a man. Her capacity for sensuality was like that of a desert flower—bursts of spec-

tacular beauty blooming after long dry spells. The awaken-
ings were special, because unexpected, but dormancy had
its restrained pleasures, too, and none of the intrinsic
sadness of flowering. An awakening was only a moment,
after all, not something to be prolonged. Not in "real
life." Diane had always believed in "real life." Now she
would have to discover a new universe, where it made
sense to be offered fifty thousand dollars from a stranger,
and to take it. The spree she planned by the splashing
fountain as she ate raspberries and cream did not fit into
the general scheme of things. There was no precedent for
such pure selfishness. She was going to enjoy it thoroughly.

In the department stores on Fifth Avenue, Diane bought
a black sheath evening dress for the gallery opening and
French designer jeans for the boat. She chose a shimmery
navy-blue dress that flared out for dancing because it
matched a bag she liked. Consulting *Vogue* like a tourist
referring to her Michelin guide, Diane pointed to dresses
and sweaters and designer shoes. She bought a frilly panty
slip. She was as gullible to the flattery of obsequious
saleswomen as the Emperor in the "Emperor's New
Clothes." She made them work for their commissions,
though, helping her take things off and put things on. She
spent forty-five minutes at a cosmetics bar, sampling per-
fumes. She bought an entire line of her favorite beauty
products, from cleansing regime to the latest spring colors,
and two pair of sunglasses. The afternoon passed quickly.
It was exhilarating—and exhausting.

Diane decided to have a drink at the Cafe Carlyle before
heading home. The sun was setting behind Central Park as
her cab crossed side streets on its way uptown. In the
twilight, the galleries and dress shops of Madison Avenue
had the flair of Rome. A world of material things beckoned to her, and she responded.

Alone in the dark, uncrowded bar, Diane felt both safe
and vulnerable. She was glad to sit down. She ordered
Dewar's and soda and slipped her feet out of her shoes
under the table. The Art Deco murals in the windowless
bar were soothing. Sipping her drink, she wished she still
smoked. She was tempted to ask the man two tables away
for a cigarette, but did not have the energy for conversation.

Diane thought about shopping. It was hard work. Her

mother had done it dutifully, but had often said she didn't
see how a woman did it for entertainment. An unavoidable
invitation for lunch downtown and an afternoon at Day-
ton's was accepted almost grimly. But what, really, had
her mother enjoyed? Diane tried to recall her mother's
laugh, but could not hear it. Perhaps the stereotype of the
taciturn Scandinavian was valid.

"May I buy you a drink?"

The man from two tables over stood beside her. He was
tan, with a pencil-thin moustache and dark, wavy hair. He
had a foreign accent.

"No, but you could lend me a cigarette."

"Will you give it back?" He was pleased with himself,
as if he had demonstrated subtle mastery of English with
the joke. Diane decided he was Brazilian.

"I'll buy *you* a drink," she proposed.

"May I sit down?" What he meant was, where could he
sit down. The chair opposite Diane and the bench on either
side were covered with shopping bags.

"Hand me those." She pointed to the chair. "What will
you have?"

"White rum on the rocks." He would have sounded less
foreign saying "with ice." Diane ordered another Scotch
and soda. She nodded thanks when the man lit the cigarette she took from him, and then his own.

"You look like a—how do they call it—a 'bag woman'
from Fifth Avenue." He smiled too eagerly. "How have
you carried all these things?"

"It took a little organizing." The cigarette smoke made
her dizzy. She repressed a cough. When the waiter returned with their drinks, the man attempted to pay.

"It's against the rules for you to buy me a drink." She
handed the waiter a ten-dollar bill. "I'm someone's
mistress."

"How interesting." He smiled amiably, before the information registered.

"But I am sure your master would not mind." His
English was good enough for her to feel something sinister
in his innuendo. It was nice to know that she never had to
see this man again, but it made her angry that she could
not have a drink alone without the suggestion of danger
from a man. As a high-school girl in Minnesota, she had

often enjoyed walks along deserted lake shores, late at night, when the sky was jammed with stars. Now she knew more, and the violence of life, everywhere, made her afraid to seek this longed-for solitude without the company of a man. At times she resented this need for the safe man almost as much as her fear of the dangerous one. But at this moment, the only thing she wanted was to be home with Bradley.

"I have to go now. Please don't get up." She called a waiter to help with the packages so that the Brazilian would not accompany her to the taxi stand.

Bradley was sitting on the couch pouring himself a drink when she walked into her apartment.

"Hi. How did you get in?"

"The super gave me a key. I said I was your brother."

Diane smiled at the idea as she dropped the packages on the floor of the front hall.

"You look nice," she said. He was wearing a tuxedo.

"So do you." His kiss was friendly. "I like the haircut."

"I'm still in shock," she laughed. There was something comfortably domestic about his greeting. She could imagine them married. They would have a drink together, and she would fix pork chops. The tuxedo was the only detail that did not fit.

"Why the tux?" She called from the bedroom, where she began unpacking on the bed. He did not hear her.

"Want a drink?"

"Why not. It'll be my third. Come see all my loot." She took the drink when he entered and showed him the bed, covered with blouses, skirts, pants, and dresses.

"What'll you wear tonight?" Bradley fingered a velvet jacket with an oriental floral print.

"Where are you taking me?" She put her arm in his affectionately.

"I was thinking of '21.' "

"You really *are* old-fashioned," she laughed. "Every other CEO I interview takes me there. Let's go to the River Cafe. The service is slow, but the view is magnificent."

"Is that the restaurant under the Brooklyn Bridge?"

She nodded. "We can walk from here. It's right on the river."

"Will I be overdressed?"

"You'll look like one of the waiters."

"I'll take you to Coco's afterwards if you'll wear this."
He held up a three-quarters-length black satin evening
dress.

"What about my disco dress?"

"Slinky is better."

"I'll wear it if you're sure you can get me in."

"I'm certifiably cool."

"You make the reservations while I get ready."

Diane locked herself in the bedroom with her new dress,
shoes, stockings, and cosmetics.

"I got reservations for nine-thirty." Muffled by the
closed door, his voice was sexy. She heard the ice clinking
in his drink.

"I'll probably need that long. I'm exhausted." She
stood by the door. "Now I know how Jacqueline Kennedy
Onassis must feel after an afternoon's shopping. I may
never be able to shop again."

Diane decided to take a bath. She turned the hot water
on all the way and poured in twice the recommended
amount of bubble bath. The fragrant soapy warmth was
exquisitely sensual. Every pore, muscle, and bone in her
body relaxed as she lay suspended, dreamily, at peace with
herself and the world. Mounds of suds, white as the skin
on the inside of her thighs, cottony as summer clouds,
floated over her small, round breasts. Bradley had called
them "renaissance" the first night. Through half-closed
lids, she watched her toes, wriggling them among the
bubbles. They seemed a long way off. She drew her knees
up almost to her chest, and, massaging her feet, sank
slowly down until the water was over her ears. In this
silent world, she listened to her breathing, her heartbeat.

Diane washed and dried her hair and turned it with a
curling iron into a series of tight waves. With an artist's
confidence, she applied shadow and liners that accentuated
the deep blue of her large eyes. She calculated that she had
been putting on eye makeup for half her life, and disguised
her fleeting sadness at the thought with a subtle blush
along her high cheekbones and a dab of powder along a
nose she decided had been passed down from an unfortunate Frankish maiden abducted from Normandy by one of

Diane's more ruthless Viking ancestors. The mouth she applied lipstick to was old-fashioned—small and bowed. She might have modeled for Vuillard or Munch, until she stepped into the tightfitting black dress, slit past her knees on each side, and the black *peau de soie* pumps.

Diane had never experienced such pleasure in *things*. She was overcome with sensations—the touch of the silk camisole, the fragrance of imported powder, the rustle of satin, the taste of fiery red lipstick, the gleam of matching polish on her finger and toenails.

She made her entrance into the living room.

"What do you think?" She remembered the excitement as a girl, playing dress up in her mother's clothes, her mother's amusement, her father's flirtatious admiration.

"Turn around." He spoke with a designer's imperiousness. She strode model-like across the room and turned for him.

"That dress does great things for your shape."

"You think?" To diffuse her pleasure, she picked up the drink she had left on an end table.

"You look like Jean Harlow from the rear."

"Let's get going, Professor Higgins, or we'll be late for dinner." She retrieved a new mink wrap from the bedroom.

"I didn't dress you," he defended himself as he put on his Chesterfield. "It's your good taste."

He made a motion to help arrange the wrap.

"I'm sorry, John." She transferred several objects from her canvas shoulder bag to a small black clutch. "I'm glad you like the way I look. I'm self-conscious, that's all."

By the water under the Brooklyn Bridge, they stood on a pier for a long time despite the cold. Boats and barges glided by, traffic sped a hundred feet above them. The cables from which the bridge was suspended formed geometric patterns as awe-inspiring in their ordered intricacy as the constellations obscured by the lights of lower Manhattan. The imagery of life, of organisms, came to mind as Diane watched the city. Traffic circulated, boats swam against the current, lights pulsated, the bridge hummed. Like the city, Diane was alive, too, that moment, vibrant and beautiful.

Few places in the city rivaled the café for atmosphere.

Boats seemed almost to touch the picture window beside their table.

They hardly noticed the food, they were so involved in a heated discussion about appearances and reality. He insisted that because she looked and felt different, she *was* different. She said he put too much emphasis on style. He countered that she had middle-class insecurities about the continuity of her personality. She ought to be able to enjoy becoming a different person for different occasions. Diane preferred being herself. Bradley accused her of being too serious. She accused him of being too superficial.

They had not argued exactly, but they had little to say to each other in the cab on the way to Coco's. Diane admitted to herself that there was something attractive about people for whom life was a series of roles. But she had given up acting when she lost the lead in her high school's production of *My Fair Lady*. Diane Yaeger was Diane Yaeger. A week with John Bradley, Jr., was not going to change that. She wondered if this seriousness, this insistence on being herself would be an obstacle in life, but she could not say what it might be an obstacle to.

"What are you thinking?" Bradley put his arm around her as they progressed up the FDR Drive.

"I was wondering if you were going to kiss me."

They kissed long and tenderly, oblivious to the cab's route, until the flashing white lights of Coco's marquee recalled them.

Diane had an insider's skepticism about the media, but had to admit that Coco's lived up to its hype.

She could not decide if she was impressed or appalled by the familiarity of the doorman who ushered Bradley past the throngs of people standing in limbo outside. Diane identified with the crowd. The businessmen might have been friends of her father, on a lark during a trip to the home office. The tourists who wandered by after a Broadway show for the chance glimpse of a starlet might have gone to high school with her. The man dressed in the ape costume watched as a limousine discharged two women in shimmery sequined evening gowns, on each arm of a young man in tight jeans and a black "Brooklyn" T-shirt. Kids who had probably learned the latest steps in Brooklyn discotheques and had long since traded black T-shirts for white disco suits watched the trio pass fearlessly through the barricades. No one protested. It was as if each on-looker suspected deep down that he or she was not worthy to enter into the mysteries of this kinky paradise. On Bradley's arm, Diane had the sense of "passing." She dared not look back for fear that one of the preterit would catch her eye and cry out, "Hey wait, you can't let *her* in, she's one of us."

Ridiculous as it was, her heart was pounding as Bradley helped her out of her wrap and gave it to the coat-check girl. It was only when she saw her reflection in one of the hundred mirrors, which gave a trompe l'oeil effect that made her step cautiously into the main room, that she realized her disguise was perfect. And at Coco's, she was quick to observe, you were your disguise.

The club was immense. This converted Broadway the-ater assaulted the claustrophobic New Yorker with a cubic city block of open space—the ultimate opulence in New York. The light was blinding, as if all the lights in Times Square had been channeled into the cavernous room. The music was deafening, alternately bisexual rock 'n' roll and relentlessly repetitive disco. Lights flashed, music thun-dered from every direction, obliterating the world beyond this one. A gargantuan neon collage descended to the dance floor from five stories up in the ceiling, followed by four glittering pillars lowered into the crowd like the fuel rods of a nuclear reactor.

The most enticing area of the club was the balcony, where row upon row of plush velvet seats ascended at forty-five-degree angles into the ceiling. From the last rows, the stage and the dance floor were a distant mirage, white hot desert sun seen from a mountaintop.

Diane and Bradley sat down on a couch near the dance floor and ordered drinks from a waiter wearing only bikini running shorts.

"I love it," Diane shouted. They had two options for conversation—shouting, or whispering into each other's ear, which made the alcove where they sat intimate despite the shrill music.

"I'm glad." She read the words on his lips.

Several people stopped to say hello to Bradley, but the music was too loud for introductions. They surrendered to silence, to the natural desire to watch the human comedy performed by the club's patrons. She had never seen such an odd assortment of social climbers: perennial boys, with slicked-back hair and sleeveless jean vests over skinny naked chests; foxy women, glitter sprinkled on their faces and bare in unexpected places—a hip, or the inside of a thigh; the very rich and the furthest left on the sexual spectrum. Everyone on the dance floor shared a communal sense of mutual self-esteem, a self-conscious pleasure in being among the elect. They had another drink. Diane was pleasantly drunk by the time they made their way to the crowded dance floor.

Bradley was a good dancer. His style was contemporary. He executed his steps somewhat mechanically, but it was obvious his instructor knew the latest dances. As Bradley had predicted, almost everyone danced freestyle. Physical communication was as rare on the dance floor as conversation. Partners seldom touched. Narcissism was rampant. The dancers were caught up in their personal rhythms. The enthusiasm of some dancers verged on masturbation. The songs melted indistinguishably into one another. The music would not stop. Diane was dancing harder and harder. It was as if a roller coaster operator had abandoned them on the ride, leaving them to go up and down, peak after peak, five minutes, ten, a half an hour. She spun dizzily with the music. She hardly noticed Bradley, she was so absorbed in her own feelings. No brakes, no steering wheel—just flashing lights, the machine-gun pounding of drums, the heat of the dancers' bodies, communal ecstasy. Diane's consciousness shot out of her body like a rocket. There was a scream inside her, then nothing. She thought she might faint. She wondered if she had the energy to get to a seat. Bradley did not want to follow her, but it was impossible to keep dancing.

The darkness and the relative quiet upstairs was soothing. The flicker of the strobe lights on the dance floor looked like lightning below them, as if seen from an airplane. "I like the way you dance," she said.

"I like your rhythm," he returned the compliment. "You get it inside, not from the music."

Two women were climbing the stairs toward them.

"Hello, Brad." A tall woman dressed in white silk trousers and blazer spoke first.

"Susan—" His greeting was not natural. "Diane, I'd like you to meet Susan Aldrich. Susan, this is Diane Yaeger. She's doing a story on me."

"I thought you weren't doing any more interviews." Her tone made it apparent that they had spoken recently.

"My agent prevailed—luckily." He was not apologizing for his inconsistency.

"This is Catherine Bevington." Susan completed the introductions. Bradley nodded. Diane shook her hand.

Susan Aldrich had 1940's "classy" good looks: a fine, straight nose, prominent but delicate; high cheekbones; large, dark eyes, and dark, wavy hair. She was poised, something Diane rarely noticed in a woman. Diane found the confidence in her smile attractive and intimidating.

"We missed you at the opening last night," Susan said. The observation was perfectly polite.

"You know I can't stand crowds," he said, possibly ironic, and then to Diane: "Susan's a photographer. She just opened a one-woman-show at the Light Gallery. New England fences, isn't it?"

She nodded.

"Can I get anyone a drink?" he asked.

"No, but you can ask me to dance." Catherine Bevington kept time to the music with her foot. She was not as pretty as Susan, but her red dress was cut low in front and back, and the exposed bosom was impressive. Diane thought she detected relief in the haste with which Bradley obliged Susan's friend. He put a hand on Catherine's elbow and they headed downstairs. "Haven't we met before?" Diane heard him say, and then their voices were lost in the music.

"Would you like to sit down?" Diane motioned to the aisle seat next to hers. It was difficult to take her eyes off Susan Aldrich. Her sense of superiority was so deeply ingrained that it hardly offended Diane, who was determined to ignore it and to concentrate on background for her story. Objectivity as defense mechanism, she mused.

"In search of rock 'n' roll climax." Susan said as she sat down and watched her friends' progress down the stairs.

"Have you known John a long time?" Diane asked, objectively.

"Our families are old friends. My brother used to sail with Brad. I was broken-hearted when he left for Yale. I was eight."

Diane calculated that she and Susan were the same age.

Tilting her head to one side, Susan studied Diane's face. "Would you like some cocaine?"

"I've been waiting since I got here for someone to offer," Diane laughed. "Though I have to say, I think it's overrated."

"This will make a believer of you." Bradley's friend sprinkled white powder onto a compact mirror. She minced it with a tiny knife, then rolled up a ten-dollar bill and inserted it into one nostril, pressing the other closed. She inhaled and repeated the process with the other. Diane was fumbling in her purse for a bill when Susan handed her the tube. Diane did not want to appear too fastidious, but she had not taken cocaine often enough to know the etiquette. Reasoning that putting the moist end to the cocaine would make it stick to the bill, she put the same end into her nostril, trying not to touch the sides, and snorted. The numbness, and the acrid dripping in the back of her throat, were unpleasant at first. But the opportunity to talk to Bradley's friend was worth it.

"Feel anything yet?" Susan smiled conspiratorially.

"Wide awake."

They laughed.

"Want to go dance?" Diane wondered with a start if the photographer meant with her. Susan's worldliness seemed suddenly formidable.

"I don't think so." Diane's reply was as nonchalant as possible.

"Been here before?"

Diane shook her head.

"Like it?"

Diane felt herself grinning foolishly, but she no longer cared what Susan thought of her.

"I love it." She felt enormous contentment at having met Bradley, being inside Coco's, talking to such an attractive woman. She was more relaxed, more comfortable with herself than she had been after the massage that morning. Diane had never felt so interesting, so unique. Susan Aldrich, on the other hand, was fast becoming a type, a representative of a class of people Diane had just been introduced to, and wanted to know better.

"Tell me about your photography," Diane said.

"I photograph things."

"As opposed to—"

"People. I don't like to photograph people."

"Why not?"

"They move around too much." Feeling a sudden fear of being patronized, Diane put her defenses on alert.

"Have you been a photographer long?"

"Let's talk about something else," Susan said. "I'm bored with photography just now. I only do it to appear creative."

"Appear?"

"I take pictures of things no one else thinks of, and people say I'm creative." She tossed the comment off. "At least I don't get relegated to patroness status with my artist friends."

Susan seemed to drop into an interview mode; she chose her words self-consciously. "The amazing thing is how much people pay for them."

"I would think you'd find that extremely gratifying," Diane said.

"Lots of artists need the money more than I do." There was a hint of pride in the assertion.

"You'll take it, though, right?"

"Life isn't fair, is it?"

"Not all the time," Diane agreed. "It's interesting, though. John Bradley feels the same way about the novel."

"It's different with Brad. A well-to-do woman can earn a living if she wants to, but no one expects it. But being a wealthy man is like being a respected abstract painter. People expect him to know the basics of realism, even if he decides not to use them. And they expect the well-to-do man to know how to earn a living, even if he doesn't need to. I must say I was pleased for Brad when he published the book. It's made a man of him—literally."

Susan's easy intimacy, her use of the nickname "Brad," made Diane want to hint at their own relationship. She knew that was not a good sign, but there she was.

"He seems to have grown up in his father's shadow." Diane tried to draw Susan out.

"Brad will be two of that man the day he quits caring what his father thinks." The observation made vast claims of personal acquaintanceship.

"Maybe he'll die." Diane was recklessly lucid.

"No." Susan dismissed the possibility. "He's the Bertrand Russell type. He'll be around another twenty years, getting progressively more attached to his prejudices."

Susan knew them too well. It was too early for Diane to feel this jealous. The only way not to think about it was to talk about something else.

For the first time, it occurred to Diane that she had been impetuous. Her conversation with Susan Aldrich reminded Diane that she knew nothing about Bradley, but she was certain that Bradley and Susan had a special relationship. They seemed well matched. Like Bradley, Susan was a creature from another world. Diane found Susan's looks more striking than her own. But it was more the spirit that animated the young woman's finely chiseled features that made her so imposing. Like Bradley, her face glowed with freedom taken for granted, freedom put to good use. Her eyes sparkled with the knowledge that she could have what she wanted. Her smile broadcast the amiability one reserves for an unarmed opponent. Diane would almost have preferred arrogance to the young woman's easy familiarity.

"Where do you live?" Diane changed the subject.

Susan did not hear the question. Bradley and her friend were climbing toward them with several other couples. He was smiling and out of breath.

"We've been invited to a party at Andy Warhol's," he told them. "There's going to be an all-night screening of *Sleep*."

"The film where you watch someone sleep for eight hours?" Diane asked.

"It's fantastic," said a young man in the group. "I've seen it three times."

"I'm so tired, at this point I'd rather experience sleep firsthand."

"A lot of movie people are going to be there," Bradley tempted her.

"I thought you were feeling wide-awake." Susan's sincerity surprised Diane. Nothing so far had indicated that she found Diane interesting.

"I think I'll pass." Diane made herself smile agreeably, but she was tired of music and lights and new faces and wanted to be outside. She did not have the energy required to be interesting to these people.

"Really?" Susan looked at her as if she were abstaining for effect.

"Are you sure?" Bradley's voice was partly concerned, partly annoyed. He wanted to go to the party. He enlisted his friends' aid in talking her into it, but she was desperate for fresh air. It depressed her to realize she was jealous of Susan.

"Let's go then." Bradley was not bluffing, but his heart was not in the offer. Reluctant to make a scene, Diane waited until they were at the coat-check counter before insisting he did not have to take her home.

"Please stay. Just help me get a cab" She stopped short of telling him that she would prefer to be alone.

"You want to meet moviemakers, and you pass up a chance like this." He was disdainful.

She was tired, stoned, a little drunk. Her mind was racing. Trying to be natural with Bradley was taking its toll.

"They like new faces at these parties," he coaxed.

"This won't be their only chance to meet me." The remark was more bitter than she had intended.

On the street, the crowd sized them up to see how they were cooler, and whether they were worth telling friends about.

"This is John Bradley, Jr.," Diane told a Japanese businessman who appeared not to understand her. "He wrote *The Great Thaw*." Several onlookers applauded. A man shook his hand. Diane surged ahead and climbed into a cab that had responded to Bradley's impatient signal.

Parting was awkward. Dismayed by her earlier jealously, she now resented Bradley. He was unable to come up with a diplomatic way of asking if he should come to her apartment later.

"Good night." He gave her an exploratory kiss. She did not respond.

"Could we meet for lunch at noon tomorrow at the

Sherry-Netherland?'' She was aware of his uneasiness and displeasure; her question did not presume acceptance.

''Sure. Are you all right?''

''I'm fine.''

''Good night then.'' He slammed the door decisively and went back into the club.

During the trip back to Brooklyn, Diane's thoughts revolved on a short tether around Bradley and his childhood friend. Susan Aldrich could do anything. She could make Diane like her—in spite of her jealousy. She could probably make Bradley marry her. Somehow Bradley's self-assurance was less threatening than Susan's. Of course there was nothing to resolve so early in the game. Diane was embarked on Bradley's experiment, and she had enough confidence in herself not to turn back.

Diane sat a long time in bed at home, resting her chin on her knees, hugging her legs, watching the distant point of light that was the Statue of Liberty. She could not sleep, but she did not mind being awake. It was soothing to be alone. She thought of Alan, asleep in a motel in Cleveland. She thought of her mother, advancing with each night's sleep closer to death. But mostly she thought about Bradley and Susan. Her eyes remained fixed on the statue's torch, and her thoughts circled their incredible freedom, the only wealth, it seemed to her so late in the night, that really mattered. She had six more days to experience it firsthand.

six

Diane's head ached. Though she had slept late, her eyes stung. She was not sure she would be able to keep her lunch date with Bradley. It was not a hangover: Her anxiety was rooted in a sense of not using her time well.

Soaking in a warm bath for half an hour with her eyes closed helped. A bowl of shredded wheat and a glass of orange juice vanquished her queasy stomach. Fresh air and the sun at her window revived her spirits. The harbor was bustling.

She watched children running along the promenade. She was not going to be sick. She had not been as excessive the night before as she had feared. That she could ignore the meter in the taxi on the way to the Sherry-Netherland improved her mood further.

But she was not ready to see Bradley when she got out on Fifth Avenue. She had to pay too close attention to what he said. Her guard was permanently up. He made her superficial, made her say things for effect. They did not know each other well enough for periods of sustained silence, but Diane was too tired for a complicated balancing act. Today she would have to be herself, whether Bradley liked it or not.

Bradley sat in a mirrored corner, drinking coffee and reading the *Times*. Grand Army Plaza was visible through the window behind. He looked up and smiled when she entered the elegant, cheerful room. It was just after noon, but the café was not crowded.

"How was the party?" She sat down across the table from him, indicating with a shake of her head that he did not have to give up the bench against the wall, that the chair was fine. They did not touch.

"It was okay." He dismissed the question. "I'm sorry about last night, Diane. I should have taken you home. I didn't realize you'd been doing cocaine, either."

It angered her that he might attribute her behavior to the drug. She rebelled at the idea of being discussed with Susan Aldrich. She ordered mineral water without ice when the waiter came.

"How was Andy Warhol?"

"He didn't show up, of course," Bradley laughed. "I ran into one of the producers of *The Great Thaw*, though. We had a long discussion about whether the happy ending is going to improve the movie or ruin it."

"What did you decide?"

"That it didn't matter."

Bradley ordered a hamburger, french fries, and a beer. Diane had a poached egg on dry toast and coffee. She was beginning to feel normal again, and found renewed energy for answering Bradley's question about how they should spend the day.

"Have you ever taken a ride on the Circle Line?" she asked.

"Not since I was a kid."

"Let's do that, then."

"Are you planning any new experiences?" He eyed her sardonically.

"There's something almost luxurious about restraint when it's self-imposed—and optional. But since you're hell-bent on my spending money, I'll buy a painting tonight from your friend in Soho if I like one. Or is that too permanent an asset under the terms of our agreement?"

"Of course not. Half the charm of having money is changing the rules as you go along."

On the deck of the excursion boat an hour later, the sunlight did not dispel the arctic air. The small band of sightseers, hardly enough to ride around Manhattan, stayed inside the passenger cabin. But Bradley lent Diane his

Irish fisherman's sweater and they sat outside. They put on sunglasses as they watched the New Jersey shore. Gulls careened playfully above the boat. A large passenger liner was docked along the pier where the tour began.

"Have you ever traveled on a boat like that?" she asked him.

"My mother and I took the Queen Elizabeth to England once."

"Did you enjoy it?"

"The first day or so. Then I got bored."

"I'd like to spend about a week on a ship," Diane said.

"Let's take a cruise to the Caribbean," Bradley proposed.

"We don't have enough time."

"You mean we don't get to see each other after Sunday?"

"The experiment will be over. You'll be in California. I have an article to write."

"It bothered you, didn't it, skipping work on such short notice?"

"Sometimes life feels like a big degree I'm working toward. This week is independent study. I get credit for it."

"When do you graduate?"

"I don't know. I haven't even finished the required courses."

"Such as?"

"Career success. Marriage and children."

"What makes you so sure you'll get married?"

"It's about time." Diane had the sense of flirting as she returned his smile. "I'll probably be married within two years."

"Have you ever come close?"

"I went out with an editor at a big publishing house. We got along well, liked a lot of the same things—reading on the beach, drinking too much, staying up too late. But there was something wrong. It took me a year to realize that what I didn't like about our relationship was that we called each other by our first names too often. We were too considerate of each other's personal space. Do you know what I mean?"

Bradley nodded.

"I was the only woman he was seeing, but it wasn't enough. I wanted a man who was going to try to take me over and make me struggle to stay myself. I wanted the relationship to snowball, to catch me up in it and carry me downhill. Scott and I skipped the honeymoon and went straight to being comfortable with each other. It wasn't enough. I need fireworks.''

Bradley was amused. "Maybe you expect too much.''

"Haven't we already had this conversation?'' She gave him an obstinate smile. The Statue of Liberty was on their right, the skyscrapers of downtown Manhattan on their left. The wind was brisk, chilly. Bradley put his arm around her.

"My father had an Aunt Nora,'' Diane continued. "She was a beauty in her day. But according to my grandmother, no one was good enough for great Aunt Nora. The guy had dirt under his fingernails or had been seen with the town tart. The most serious suitor was eventually disqualified because he didn't manage his farm well. Nora's sisters married and had children and they all assumed their sister regretted her perfectionism. But I asked her once, a couple of years before she died, and she said to me, 'What's the use of marrying the wrong man?' She made it seem so obvious.''

"But perfectionism is a good rationalization for a person who's afraid to try,'' Bradley pointed out.

"Is that your excuse?''

The shadow of the Brooklyn Bridge passed slowly over the boat. Diane pointed out her apartment building, and the River Cafe, where they had eaten the night before.

Bradley pondered her question. "I'm selfish,'' he answered after a while. "I like to do things when I want to. I've met several women who appear willing to put up with my selfishness, but they bore me. It's a paradox: I don't like a lot of demands, but I'm not attracted to women who aren't demanding.'' Diane found it significant that he did not mention his former fiancée.

"Have you asked a woman to marry you since your broken engagement?''

"No.''

"Are you and Susan Aldrich lovers?'' Diane was surprised by her sudden impulse, but not sorry she asked.

"Did she tell you we were?''

"No.''

"She thought you were quite attractive."

"She can afford to be generous."

"We're not lovers."

"You're a lot alike," Diane ventured.

"Maybe too much. Susan's the closest I've come to a younger sister."

"Does she feel the same way?"

"I'm not sure." Bradley frowned, knit his brows. "I got the impression last night she'd try marriage."

"You make it sound like the latest rage."

"She's tired of the lunatic fringe. She's an old-fashioned rich girl at heart, and she's nostalgic for innocence. She likes remembering the schoolgirl crush she had on me. I'm a little like your friend Alan—a point of reference."

"Does she take you for granted?"

"Susan takes everything for granted. The earth rotates around its current axis because Susan finds a twenty-four-hour day convenient."

"And now it's time to marry," Diane mused, surprised at the objectivity with which she asked: "Are there other contenders?"

"For Susan?" She nodded. "Several. I'm not sure how she feels about them, though. She's developed into quite an independent, talented person. It's impressive."

"And she's ready to give it all up to get married?"

"The beauty of marriage with a person like Susan is she wouldn't give up anything. She'll always be herself."

"She *would* marry you." Diane spoke decisively.

"My mother thinks so," Bradley thought out loud. "And my father likes her so much, he would probably be disappointed."

"Disappointed?"

"I'm not sure he would wish me a happy marriage."

"He's envious if you're not married, and envious if you are. You can't win."

"The immigrant's standard ambition was for his children to have it better than he did," Bradley said. "But I'm not sure a father ever *really* wants his son to surpass him. I think I'd get a kick out of seeing my own son become president of Chase Manhattan or write the greatest book since *Moby Dick*. But watching my own father, maybe I'm deluding myself."

"I don't think so. It's a source of pride to most parents to have their children transcend them."

"You make my father even more disappointing."

"At least he keeps you young."

"What do you mean?" Bradley's frown indicated that he suspected her drift.

"Your problems with your father make you seem younger than you are. At a certain point, you have to write off your parents' bad debts, declare psychological bankruptcy, and start over."

"I paid a professional ten thousand dollars one year to tell me that," Bradley laughed.

"That was a bargain. This amateur's advice is costing you fifty."

"I never got to put my arm around the shrink." He leaned over and kissed her ear. "I like you, Diane," he whispered. "A lot."

Kissing him in the open air reminded her of college football games, sweater pressed against sweater against the cold. When she closed her eyes, Diane imagined hundreds of people watching them from the bridges and high-rise buildings of Manhattan. A symphony of afternoon city sounds played in the background—the traffic on the 59th Street Bridge, a barge plowing against the tide up the East River, a horn somewhere, children in a Roosevelt Island playground. There was only sound and temperature and touch, as peaceful as if she were meditating.

"I wish this were a passenger liner," he sighed. "I'd invite you to my cabin."

"Let's get a room at the Pierre when we get back," Diane whispered.

Bradley looked at his watch. "That's more than an hour, I can't wait that long."

"Let's row ashore." Diane nibbled his ear. The remark had been facetious, but Bradley began looking around. He jumped up suddenly, took her hand, and led her into the sitting room.

"Where is the captain?" he called to the hot-dog vendor, who pointed to the bow of the boat. They went up and down several metal staircases until Bradley was knocking at a door marked PRIVATE: DO NOT ENTER.

"Impossible," was the captain's reply to his polite inquiry about calling on the ship's radio for a boat to pick them up.

Bradley offered him a hundred dollars. The captain told him to "forget it." At two hundred dollars, he protested that he'd have to stop the boat. At three hundred, he pointed out that the other passengers would see them, that he could get into a lot of trouble. At four hundred, he wondered what he'd tell his superiors if they ever found out. Bradley swore that he would lie about a medical emergency if there was ever a hearing. For five hundred dollars, the captain radioed a nearby tugboat.

"Will you take a check?" Diane asked the pilot.

"It's on me," Bradley said, counting out five one-hundred-dollar bills from his wallet.

The day was turning windy. The water was choppy and the boats ground dangerously against each other as Bradley first and then Diane descended the swaying rope ladder into the tugboat. The boat bucked and heaved as it made its way over the rough water to the helicopter pad near the 59th Street Bridge.

"This is crazy." Diane's shout was inaudible over the wind and the splashing water. Terror and exhilaration competed within her. Her life had never seemed more unreal, but she had never felt more alive.

A guard at the helicopter pad tried to prevent them from debarking, but Bradley clung to his story of medical emergency.

"Pierre Hotel," he told the cabdriver, who responded to his urgent gesticulations.

There were no vacancies at the hotel, but Bradley uttered a name that had a magical effect on the clerk. Within minutes they were in a suite with a double bed. Bradley pulled the window shade. Diane leapt onto the soft mattress, kicked off her shoes, and slipped out of her clothes. For the first time, they made love unselfconsciously. Diane imagined herself naked, riding a horse bareback, galloping through woods, across streams, grasping the horse's mane tighter and tighter, wind and sun in her face, the earth blurring under her. Bradley told her afterwards that he had had a horse motif, too. They were flushed and out of breath, and lay still in the dark room. She laid her ear against his naked chest, listening to the pounding of his heart and the deceleration of his breathing.

Later, waiting for room service, Diane looked around the rooms. They were small, with furniture that was not aging well. The windows looked across a flat roof to another building.

"So perfectly New York," she murmured, kissing one of his nipples, then the other, grazing each circle of soft brown hair with her lips.

"I liked New York better when it was on the brink of disaster," he said. "At least then you could get a decent hotel room at the last moment."

"There's something quaint and European about the room," she said in its defense.

"A euphemism for faded and run down," he laughed.

"I can't think of anyplace I'd rather be." She put her arms around Bradley and kissed him. A knock interrupted this renewal of embraces. When the champagne was open, they fed each other melon and strawberries.

"I love getting drunk in the afternoon," she sighed at one point. "It makes me feel sophisticated."

"Spending the afternoon in bed makes me feel that way," he said.

"Me too." She kissed him drunkenly. The radiator was off, but their lovemaking steamed the windows up, blocking out the afternoon sun and the cold wind. His skin tasted of salt. The faintly acrid fragrance of their bodies had an aphrodisiac effect on Diane. She pressed her face into his shoulder and neck; Bradley buried his in her breasts, in her armpit. She was ticklish now. Her laughter in his ear sent a wave of goose bumps like falling dominoes down his arm. They were spilling champagne on the sheets. Bradley crushed a raspberry against her breasts and licked her skin white again. Diane drank champagne from his navel. Though Bradley assured her that Dom Perignon did not usually have such a salutary effect on his potency, they made love again. It went on and on this time, but they were not in a hurry. The world outside the fogged, shaded window vanished. The world inside grew dark. Diane's body had never felt such a perfect physical sympathy with a man's touch. When Bradley moved faster within her, she moved faster around him. She must be hurting him, the way she clutched at his back, but he responded as if to pleasure. She lay suspended, aching, almost angry with impatience, until his climax caught her up and overwhelmed her, and she felt like a surfer carried far into shore on a perfect wave. The sense that words would spoil the moment was strong in them. They surrendered luxuriously to their fatigue. To preserve this moment, Diane thought, her head on Bradley's shoulder as unconsciousness overtook them, but already she could feel it slipping away.

It was dark when they woke up. Traffic outside was stopping and starting, too mobile for rush hour.

"Where's your watch?" Diane whispered, hoarsely tired.

He rolled over sleepily and kissed her. Out of bed, opening the window shade, she saw his face in the light from a nearby building. The heat had come on in the room, and she opened a window. "Why do we always have to know what time it is when we wake up?" he wondered.

"My kingdom for a toothbrush," Diane said.

"Pull the shade, I'm going to turn the lamp on." He was dialing the telephone. "Want some coffee?"

"Yes, please." She went into the bathroom to splash water on her face. She was still sleepy—her eyes stung—but she was relaxed.

"Two toothbrushes, please—Oral B if you can get them—a tube of toothpaste. And a pot of coffee for two. Oh, and what time is it? Thanks." He hung up and was dialing another number. "It's seven forty-five," he called to her.

"Thanks," Diane called back. When she saw a complimentary bottle of shampoo on the sink, she decided to take a shower.

"Hello, Donald," she heard him saying, and then he made arrangements for them to drop by at ten o'clock. Diane was stepping into the shower as he hung up the phone. She was startled when he opened the bathroom door.

"Mind if I join you?"

"No." She felt herself flushed.

"You're sure?"

"Not at all."

Bradley's body was still so new to her. It had been one thing to feel it against her in the dark, and another to stand before him naked. He did not seem so large, so imposing without his clothes on. He began smoothing soap all over her and she rubbed soap all over him and they held each other in a slippery embrace. She lathered the hair on his chest into spirals. She had not expected his penis between her soapy thighs, and gasped when he pinned her against the cold tiles. The extremes of cold porcelain and his warm body were almost unbearably pleasurable. They kissed with the shower roaring over them like a waterfall. Bradley heard the muffled knocking on the door.

"Our toothpaste." He stepped out of the shower, wrapped a towel around himself, and went to answer while she rinsed off.

"I love breaking in a new toothbrush," she said. She turned off the water and began drying off.

"Then this has been quite a week for you."

They studied each other's tooth-brushing technique in the mirror.

"We have different styles." He spoke through a mouthful of foam.

"You do it wrong." She pushed him aside with her elbow to get a better look at herself in the mirror. "You're supposed to brush down from the top and up from the bottom."

"Have you ever had your teeth brushed?" His reflected image looked her in the eyes.

"Sure."

"I mean by a lover."

"That's a little kinky for me." She was joking, but hoped he understood she *did* think it was offbeat.

"It feels nice."

Was he serious? His smile reminded her that they were still strangers.

"I'm sure it does, for some people." She rinsed her mouth out and put the toothbrush aside, as if to change the subject.

"I'll do it the way you showed me," he whispered.

"I'm finished." She dried her lips and started to leave the bathroom.

"You're afraid. Where's your sense of adventure?" He appeared baffled.

"It doesn't extend to tooth fetishists."

"You're missing a really sensual experience."

"I'll survive."

"Just the molars."

"Cut it out."

"Please."

"You're not kidding, are you?"

"I've never been more serious."

"All right then." She bared her teeth.

"You have to open your mouth so I can get the backs and tops."

It *was* a funny sensation. He missed the spots where her nerves expected the brush. The brush tickled. But something made her repress her laughter and she watched him warily as he worked on her teeth. Suddenly he began laughing.

"What's so funny?" she asked icily. She turned away from him, flushing crimson. With a stab of panic, she realized that Bradley had compromised her.

"You've never done this before," she said coolly.

He broke into renewed laughter. "It was a joke. You were great."

She was embarrassed, then angry. With as much dignity as she could muster, she went into the bedroom and began dressing hurriedly.

"Where are you going?" He stopped laughing abruptly.

"I don't like this."

"I was kidding."

"It isn't funny."

"I'm sorry." He tried to kiss her, but she turned away.

"It's a stupid joke." She sulked.

"If it's any consolation"—he saw with relief that she was not going to leave—"it must be as weird to want to brush someone's teeth as it is to let him do it."

"No. It's weirder to let someone do it."

"Have your teeth ever bumped into someone else's when you were kissing?"

"I don't like the feeling." She was not ready to forgive him.

"I do." He kissed her with his mouth open, so that their teeth clinked.

"You're weird, John," she said, giving in.

"You have beautiful teeth. Want a cup of coffee?"

"All right."

"How do you like it?"

"You don't remember?"

"How many times have we drunk coffee together?" he defended himself.

"I know how *you* like yours."

"Women remember those things."

"Sexist. I take milk."

"Where shall we eat dinner?" He had already changed, and was sipping coffee as he watched her put makeup on.

"It feels like a winter morning," she said. "Where could we get hot oatmeal and bacon and eggs and whole-wheat toast?"

"How about a diner?"

"Where?"

"There's one near the Lincoln Tunnel. It's like a truck stop. At four in the morning, half the cabbies in New York are having coffee there."

"Perfect."

"We're supposed to drop by Donald Kaufman's at ten o'clock."

"Donald Kaufman?"

"Do you know him?"

"Didn't he do the poster for the City Opera last fall?"

"Yes."

"I hate it."

"He's the artist I promised to introduce you to."

"I hope I wake up by then."

"Let's go eat."

"You should have had room service bring up a hair dryer, too." Diane shivered as they waited for a cab on Fifth Avenue. She draped the jacket Bradley offered her over her shoulders. Their cabdriver was a character. Diane and Bradley were in a mood to be entertained. By the time they got to the diner, they had heard his opinions on the dishonesty of politicians, the inevitability of inflation, and the price of real estate in Sheepshead Bay.

In the diner, it felt like the middle of the night. Diane ordered ham, scrambled eggs, biscuits with butter and honey, oatmeal, two glasses of orange juice, and coffee. Bradley had steak and eggs. They split an order of pancakes. It was like breakfast on the farm, she told him.

"Of course, they work hard for it."

"So did we," he countered. They smiled at each other.

"I miss Minnesota tonight."

"No one gets homesick like a Midwesterner." He smiled. "It's charming."

"I like New York, too," she added. "But living in New York is like having a parent who's rich but too severe: You have advantages, but you miss the tenderness. You'd like Minnesota."

"Why did you come east?" They reached toward each other with forks to share the pancakes between them.

"Because my father expected me to, I guess."

"How long did it take you to transplant?"

"I never have, really. It's six years since I came here and I still don't feel at home." She speared a last piece of sausage and put it into her mouth. "I'd like to do a study of how it affects your world view, watching network news at six-thirty and the 'Tonight Show' at ten-thirty."

"You go to bed earlier in the Middle West," Bradley laughed. "Maybe that's what keeps you so innocent."

The waitress stopped to refill their coffee cups.

"I'll take a check, please," Bradley told her.

"No, I will," Diane said, suddenly remembering their agreement. "I owe you for the Pierre too. But let's have dessert before settling up."

"The pancakes were sweet enough for me," he protested.

"Who ever heard of eating at a diner without a piece of pie? Can we see the menu again, please?"

The menu listed every American dessert imaginable. It was hard to decide, but blueberry pie a la mode won out. Bradley ordered a hot fudge sundae when Diane promised to help him eat it.

It was almost ten-thirty when they left for Donald Kaufman's loft. The gradual renovation spreading south from Greenwich Village—the spacious galleries, trendy bars, attractive lofts—had not reached the street in Soho where the artist lived in a dilapidated warehouse.

Passing a row of garbage cans overwhelmed with trash, they entered a narrow, dimly lit hallway. Bradley rang a bell.

The room into which they stepped when they got off the elevator on the eighth floor was cavernous, with ceilings twice Bradley's height and a polished hardwood floor twice the size of Diane's apartment. White walls, intensely lit with track lights, were covered with enormous paintings of cartoon-like faces. The space was a permanent collection of Kaufman's work. It occurred to Diane that perhaps if the article on Bradley was well received, she could do one on Donald Kaufman.

The artist was older than Bradley. He had short hair, a wide, serious mouth. He looked nervously around the room when Diane shook his hand. In his eyes, she saw the combination of egotism and insecurity that invariably got on her nerves.

Bradley introduced her as a friend. It appeared that he was not familiar enough with Kaufman to visit without a pretext. Bradley explained that Diane was starting a collection, and wanted to see some of his paintings.

"Do you know my work?" Kaufman asked her. She wanted to say yes, for fear of appearing ignorant, but she hoped admitting that she didn't would deflate his pretentious question.

She shook her head. "That's why I'm here."

"Why don't you look around for a bit?" His meekness was insincere. His humorlessness irritated her. The paintings, on wall-sized canvases, portrayed people—a dancer, an athlete, a woman reclining on a couch. Their faces were two-dimensional, on a spectrum between naive and pop art. She thought it must be depressing, living in one's own gallery.

"Would you like tea?" She had finished the tour without a question. She and Bradley accepted this invitation, and followed their host into a smaller gallery, with walls covered with smaller paintings.

"Have you always painted in this style?" she asked Kaufman when they were seated around a low table. Even with Bradley's sweater on, she was cold. Their voices echoed in the room.

"What do you mean by style?" The question made her want to be sarcastic. She controlled the urge.

"What these pictures have in common."

"I like that." So did she, but it was too late for him to win her over. "In the Fifties and early Sixties I painted simple objects in primary colors. Never realistic, though. Realism doesn't interest me."

"Why not?"

"If you want realism, buy photography."

"That still doesn't explain *why* you don't like realism."

"Realism is on the street outside. I prefer life under the surface."

His pretention to depth was pompous. She could imagine their conversation so far on a talk show. The audience would like Kaufman because he was easy to understand.

"You've got no use for a vase of Corot's flowers, then?" She was pleased with herself at having remembered Corot. Bradley seemed impressed, too.

"Not personally, no."

It was hopeless, talking further. Everything he said annoyed her. Diane signaled to Bradley with her eyes that she wanted to leave. Though abrupt, their goodbyes were not awkward. They accepted implicitly that the "right people" were permitted sudden, unexplained entrances and exits. Donald Kaufman thanked them politely for coming. If he cared about Diane's calculated indifference to his painting, he did not show it. She graciously accepted his invitation to his latest exhibition and they said goodnight.

She and Bradley were silent in the elevator on the way downstairs, waiting by unspoken agreement until they were two or three warehouses down the deserted street before exchanging impressions. She put her arm in his.

"You really didn't like him, did you?" he said.

"I don't care if it is bourgeois," she answered. "I *could* do better stuff than that. Give me one month of drawing lessons, and I'll prove it."

"I've got one of his paintings in my den," Bradley said in Kaufman's defense.

"If you like interior decorating, I'm sure it's fine."

"It's funny how little art I do like," he mused, not interested in her bias. "I can walk through a whole room at the Met without seeing a painting that really excites me."

"How many books in a library would you enjoy reading?"

"Good point."

"Where are we going?"

"Let's have a drink at Puffy's."

"Where's that?"

"Around the corner."

The bar was crowded. A John Philip Sousa march was playing on the jukebox. The room was long and narrow, with high tin ceilings, an ornate antique bar, and a counter running parallel to the bar along the windows where people sat on high stools. The crowd was more literarily avant garde than Coco's. The half wearing blue jeans, flannel shirts, turtleneck sweaters, and boots were probably discussing books or painting. The other patrons were too old to be taking rock 'n' roll music as seriously as their tight jeans, leather jackets, and slicked-back or crew-cut hair suggested.

Diane had never listened to such an eclectic juke box. For two quarters she played Mahler's First Symphony, Billie Holliday's "Georgia on My Mind," Ellington's "Take the A Train," and David Bowie's "A Couple of Kooks."

"Why didn't you like him?" he asked, when they were seated at the bar. The Czech beer they ordered was warm.

"I can't stand a man with a porcelain ego."

"Don *is* a nervous type."

"Do you think he suspects he's not very good?"

"I do." Bradley laughed. "What I love about Don is a certain distrust I see in his face when people overpraise his work. In his defense, his painting is good enough for what it is—better than a lot of pop art. He's picked a style and has kept cranking it out until people think he invented it. He is smart."

"I interviewed the wife of a board chairman of a Fortune 500 company once who lived in fear that a burglar would steal a work of art she'd commissioned and paid thousands for. It was a piece of jagged bent wire sticking out of a white wall. Her husband thought this was funny because the little sculpture had no meaning, and no value, outside the context of their own wall, but she insisted the burglar wouldn't know that."

"He'd have to be a pretty sophisticated art thief."

"People don't discriminate anymore." Diane was reluctant to step down off her soapbox. "Every opinion carries equal weight."

"*That* doesn't sound very middle class."

"People don't work hard enough for things nowadays."

"*That's* more like it," he said, smiling.

"What does one of those comic strip portraits cost?"

"A couple of thousand."

"That's outrageous." She sipped her beer.

"You're hard. There's much worse stuff going for higher prices."

"That doesn't excuse it. Why can't Kaufman take an objective look at his work?"

"Can you?"

"I think I see myself the way I am," she answered.

"I spent a year once trying to see myself the way I am."

"What did you find out?"

"That the sense of knowing yourself is nature's defense against the pain of being unable to know yourself at all."

They nursed their beers in silence for a while, watching the crowd.

"Can you believe that woman with the crew-cut bangs and the long straggling hair in the back?" Diane whispered.

"The leather pants are so tight they look painful."

"When you've gone too far to one end of the spectrum, is there a person in the middle you come back to?" she asked.

"I think of my movements more as being on a tether. I cover more territory going in circles." He laughed. "What about you? Do you feel different yet?"

"Why? Have you slipped LSD into my beer?"

"This isn't supposed to be a normal week in the life of Diane Yaeger."

"Is it business as usual for you?" Nothing about him annoyed her as much as this disinterestedness.

"I think you know what I mean." She was surprised to hear the edge in his voice.

"Why do *I* have to do all the changing?"

"You don't *have* to," he countered. "In fact, you seem determined not to. You know"—he paused, finished his beer—"you'd be much more attractive without the armor."

"What's underneath is worth protecting."

"We could ruin everything with our defenses." He was earnest. She was too tired to point out the advantages of defenses.

"We may," she conceded, yawning wearily. "Let's go home. I'm tired."

They went to Bradley's apartment, built a fire, made sleepy love on the carpet. Diane did not remember falling asleep. She was not sure when she woke in the middle of the night whether they had made love. The fire had burned down, and a full moon shone into the cold room. She had been sitting on a log in a moonlit forest, kissing Bradley.

I'm in love with John, she thought. She closed her eyes. The dream's afterglow was already fading. Diane was left with the simple words "I love John." It did not matter that it had happened so quickly, because it had not happened in everyday time. It did not even matter—yet—whether Bradley loved her. Her feeling had intrinsic beauty and worth. She could decide later whether to share it with Bradley or keep it to herself. Diane huddled against him under the comforter, and drifted back to sleep.

The apartment smelled of fresh-brewed coffee when Diane woke up in the morning. Bradley was humming in the kitchen. She stretched luxuriously on the comforter, basking in the heat of the fire burning in the fireplace like a sunbather in the tropics. She was perfectly happy. She had no idea what it meant to be in love with Bradley, but freedom that morning meant not having to decide.

"Good morning." His greeting was energetic. "Did you sleep all right on the floor?"

"I only woke up once." She sat up smiling. "The moon was shining in my face."

"I slipped downstairs and got some fresh croissants."

"They smell terrific. What a beautiful breakfast." She admired the tray he set down in front of the fire.

"I squeezed the oranges myself," he called from the kitchen, where he had gone to get his own tray.

They had croissants and apricot jam, brioche and hard sweet butter, juice and espresso. Her dream invested Bradley with kinder manners, a more handsome face. In every way he appeared worthy of her emotion. Her feelings were those of a woman taking a drug for the first time: She waited expectantly to see how it was going to alter her perception of the world. Every sensation was heightened. The fire was brighter, the jam sweeter, the coffee's fragrance wonderfully nutty. She knew that she would laugh if he asked her why she was so happy, and that he would want to be let in on the joke.

"What's it like outside?" Talking about the weather contained her joy.

"Cold. Getting cloudy. There may be snow flurries this afternoon. Want to buy a fur coat?"

Her smile faded.

"Is anything wrong?"

"The idea of your buying me a fur coat bothers me, for some reason."

"But I didn't say I'd buy it. I said you could buy one."

"It's still your money," she said.

"No it isn't. I gave it to you. It's yours." He smiled at her qualms.

"Well, even if it is mine"—Diane's shrug accepted her unavoidable seriousness—"you don't know me well enough for me to buy a fur with money that used to be yours."

"Better give me a list before Christmas." The idea of their being together for Christmas cheered her.

"Lingerie's a good example," she went on. "I might have to be married to a man before I could let him give me lingerie."

"I'll put my Frederick's of Hollywood catalogue away then."

"If it's going to snow, I'll buy a flannel shirt."

"I'd rather buy you a sexy French T-shirt. Somewhere warm. Let's go to Martinique for a couple of days."

"I like the end of winter." She bit into a croissant covered with jam.

"You *are* perverse."

"When I woke up this morning, I had a fantasy we were snowed in miles from civilization."

"We've got a cottage near Booth Bay Harbor," he said. "Want to fly up to Maine?"

"Let's do." She brightened. "I'm tired of the city. Do you know how to cross-country ski?"

"More or less."

To exchange on a whim a villa in Martinique for a cottage in Maine—this was freedom. To be in love was almost too much happiness. She urged Bradley to make the arrangements right away.

There was a flight at two. They would rent a car in Portland and drive to the house. The caretaker promised to have it ready by six.

"Let's walk across the park," she suggested as they loaded breakfast dishes into the dishwasher. "I know a place to buy hiking boots and a flannel shirt. If I were ever reincarnated as an article of clothing, it would be a flannel shirt."

"Comfortable and colorful," Bradley said, smiling. "What would I be?"

"Corduroy pants. Wide-wale. A size too big."

"Cotton?"

"We're both cotton."

"You make it sound like an astrological sign. I made reservations for lunch at Trattoria da Alfredo. We can leave from there for the airport."

They walked across Central Park to the West Side. A blustery wind shook water droplets on them when they passed under a tree laden with winged buds, as if a swarm of moths were perched on its bare branches. The walkways in the park were dry now, and low, dark clouds appeared to have spent their moisture. Crossing a soggy baseball field studded with young grass, they stopped to watch a solitary kite flyer bump his kite against the clouds.

"I love the idea that a man is flying a kite in Central Park while millions of people work in those offices." Diane looked south at the midtown skyline. She thought of her own desk, the lamp turned off, unopened press releases and magazines piling up. "What kind of man flies a kite on a Wednesday morning?"

They said good morning, but the man turned out to be a crank. Diane resented the fact that he did not share her happiness. At an ingenious playground on 86th Street that incorporated a child's best playtime fantasies into one sand-covered space, they watched children playing on tires, swinging on a rope over a sand pit, jumping on platforms that vibrated on steel coils, crawling into pyramids to explore, sliding down a twenty-foot slide. The children's laughter echoed the music within her.

"Remember what it was like to be happy without a reason?" she asked Bradley as they sat down on a bench.

"If only we could have stored up all that excess happiness in a psychological battery." He was thoughtful.

"Do you envy them?"

"No." He was solemn. "It's going to take them years

to learn that they can't be this happy again, even longer to
discover that they wouldn't want to be.''

"Why wouldn't they?"

"It's too hard losing it."

"Is there any age you'd go back to?"

He shook his head, looking at his feet, in loafers,
stretched out before him. He looked tall, slouching on the
bench. "It's been damned hard getting as far as I have."

"But there must be some age near the end when people
want to turn back," she speculated.

Again Bradley shook his head. "Most people die when
they want to," he said. "That's what makes fatal acci-
dents so shocking. People are deprived of their choice."

"I don't believe that," she answered. "When I went
into my father's office to pack his things up, I found a
calendar on his desk. It was filled in for months ahead. He
wasn't ready. Neither is my mother." Her tone conveyed
to Bradley that she did not expect an apology for the
remark.

They walked down 86th Street to Broadway. Diane
marveled at the number of people on the street at eleven-
fifteen on a weekday morning. Stooped, white-haired ladies journeyed from market to market, unrecognized actors
and dancers hurried to rehearsals and auditions, panhan-
dlers plied their trade, derelicts sorted through garbage
cans or took their rest on the benches on Broadway's
traffic islands.

"It reminds me of Swift's London," Bradley said.

"Shabby and chic." She smiled.

Diane bought a designer's variation on army surplus
pants, glossy red lace-up boots that came past her knees, a
quilted jacket lined with lamb's fleece, and a hunting cap
with mink ear muffs. The long underwear she chose was
cherry red. She bought a gray turtleneck sweater, a tweed
jacket, and black leather gloves lined with rabbit fur.
Bradley bought khaki pants, hiking boots, and a hand-knit
sweater with reindeer on it and a matching stocking cap.
They selected a canvas duffel bag, and packed for their
trip at the check-out counter. They didn't realize until they
were in a cab that they had forgotten to buy flannel shirts.

Diane had never been to Alfredo's, and was charmed by
the intimate simplicity of its hanging plants and white

tablecloths. Gabriella Brickman, whose socially committed plays from the 1940s and recent autobiography Diane greatly admired, sat with a group of friends near the door. She caught Bradley's eye as they entered.

"It's John, too, isn't it?" A cigarette dangled from her mouth as she spoke. Bradley nodded, shook her hand.

"How *is* your father? Any improvement?" They smiled complicitously at her sarcasm.

"The same as ever."

"I haven't read your book." There was something in her tone that implied she never would. "But congratulations."

Bradley thanked her and sat down. He apologized for not introducing her, but Diane assured him she didn't believe in unnecessary introductions.

"If I had had anything interesting to say, I would have introduced myself."

"She despises my father," he whispered after the patrons in the tiny room had gone back to their lunches. "He kept his nose clean during the witchhunts. To his credit, he never testified against anyone, but he never defended anyone either. Brickman can't forgive his lukewarmness. He's not crazy about her either. As he's gotten older, my father's dropped the liberal pretense that he doesn't believe in the Jewish literary conspiracy. Mention the Holocaust and you get a canned dissertation on the evils of Stalinism. My father was one of the first Thirties intellectuals to give up communism."

Greenwich Village had never seemed so interesting to Diane. There were strange and wonderful stories about every passerby who looked in at them from the street. A black limousine pulled up and the mayor got out. According to Bradley, he was a regular patron there. The mayor spoke to the aged playwright. An expression of annoyance clouded Bradley's face.

"I worked on his election committee before she ever knew who he was."

"Maybe he doesn't see you."

"He sees me. And my face looks familiar. He probably figures it's better to pretend he doesn't see me than to admit he doesn't recognize me. And the fact is, he's right."

They laughed. It didn't matter, they knew. The fact that it didn't matter delighted them.

They could have driven to the cottage from New York as fast as they got there by air, Bradley grumbled. They had changed planes in Boston, and the Portland flight had been delayed because of traffic at Logan Airport. Driving north, they had missed the turn-off for Booth Bay Harbor and had driven half an hour out of their way. It had been dark for several hours by the time they reached the old stone house.

The house was worth the trouble, she assured him the minute they were in the front door. It was more charming than she had imagined. The central room was of nineteenth-century brick and had a massive stone hearth. A fire had been started in the fireplace and the room was warm. There were log beams for a ceiling. A platform had been built over half the rafters. The furniture was antique, early American. Through a door at one end was a corridor leading to several bedrooms. At the other end of the room, a large window reflecting the cozy room offered Diane no clue as to what lay beyond. Across a butcher-block counter was a brick country kitchen with lace-curtained windows looking out in three directions.

"What's outside?" Diane pressed her face against the glass, but saw only her reflection. Bradley came up from behind, put his arms around her, and kissed the back of her neck.

"Wait and see."

"Let's go for a walk."

"Aren't you hungry?"

"Not really. Let's go outside."

"Let me find a flashlight first."

"Don't you remember your way around?"

"It's been twenty years."

"How does it feel to be back?"

"I only came in the summer." He found a flashlight in a cupboard and tested it. It worked. "We're both seeing winter here for the first time. I wish the moon was out."

"Not me. I want to see stars. I miss stars in New York."

When they were outside, she asked him to turn the light off.

"It's so beautiful in the dark."

"We'll break our necks." Holding the flashlight he refused to extinguish in one hand, her hand in the other, he led her down a slippery path that wound between pines and denuded deciduous trees. A native might have recognized signs of spring: It was not bitter cold, nor was the snow deep. But to the two New Yorkers, it was winter again.

Fifty yards from the cottage, the trees and shrubs ended abruptly. They were on ice.

"I don't think this is a good idea." She pulled on his hand, but did not let go when he kept walking.

"It sounds solid enough."

"How can ice 'sound' solid?"

"I don't hear any cracking."

She let his hand go and stopped. "That's not very scientific."

"It's okay. The caretaker told me it's still a foot thick."

"Are you sure?"

"Do you think *I* want to fall through? This water is so cold we'd freeze to death in three minutes."

"A pleasant thought." She took his hand again.

"I'm going to turn the light off now. There's nothing to bump into out here."

There was shallow snow on the ice. Occasionally, one of them slipped, but they held on to each other and kept their balance.

"How wide is the lake?" she asked. They had been walking five minutes.

"A mile maybe. The lake was an ice farm in the early nineteen hundreds. They shipped the ice as far south as Washington."

"How did they keep it from melting?"

"They buried it."

"Did they put it in drinks then?"

"Maybe it was just for ice boxes and ice cream parlors."

"How deep is the lake?"

"No one knows."

"Let's turn around."

"It's not as far down as it is up," Bradley said. "Look."

Diane had never seen such an infinitude of stars. The brighter stars flickered like sequins on the shimmering veil that covered the dark dome of the sky. The overwhelming significance of the stars made them silent. To Diane, they were a truth that had to be confronted individually. She let go of Bradley's hand. Suspended between the bottomless cold darkness of the lake and the chilling endlessness of sky, her first emotion before these legion stars was a sense of insignificance. But this paralyzing humility was fleeting. It gave way to a delight in her consciousness. She contained all these stars. She could *think* about them, *feel* them, contemplate their distance. This consciousness was important. It made her superior to ice and sky and trees and stars.

Her eyes filled with tears suddenly. Everything made sense. Only people mattered. They were more intricate and wonderful than the stars. She took Bradley's hand, grateful for his complex superiority.

"You were right when you said I should be with my mother," she said. "I'll go home after this weekend."

He put his arm around her. "I understand."

Her solemn mood had dissipated by the time they reached shore, and Diane dared him to find his way up the bank without the flashlight.

"I've never seen it so dark."

"Doesn't it scare you?"

"Yes, but it's constructive fear."

"Constructive fear sounds pretty low Lutheran."

"Where are you?" She groped for and found his hand. "It really *is* dark. Maybe we should—"

Bradley lost his balance and slid down the hill, knocking Diane off her feet. She landed on top of him and clung to his jacket. The darkness rushed past her like wind in her ears. She screamed giddily as they spilled onto the ice.

"That would have been more fun on a sled." He was annoyed.

"I'm sorry." Shaking with laughter that was partly relief, her apology rang insincere. "Are you all right?"

"Just a broken rib and a couple of teeth missing." She heard him brush himself off. "Help me find the flashlight."

She searched on all fours and found it in a snow bank.

"Let's try it again," he said, grimly turning on the light. They regained the hill and hurried into the cottage.

"Let me have a look." Diane examined his face in front of the fire. He had an eye threatening to blacken. "I *am* sorry. Let me get you something."

While she surveyed the contents of the kitchen cabinets, he added several logs to the fire.

"How about some hot chocolate?" she called.

"How about some brandy?" he called back.

"I'm on the wagon for the night," she informed him. "Where's the liquor?"

"Over the refrigerator."

Diane made enough hot chocolate to twice fill the biggest mug she could find, and poured Bradley half a snifter of brandy. She also improvised a cold pack with ice cubes and a dish towel. He nursed his sore eye, watching with the other while Diane roasted marshmallows over the fire.

"I don't know how you can eat those."

"They remind me of girl scout camp."

"There's definitely something Midwestern about a marshmallow."

"I love them," she spoke through a mouthful. "Probably the only food that brings back more memories for me is peanut butter."

"I've never tasted peanut butter." He looked disdainfully away from the singed glob of sugar she was blowing on.

"I don't believe you."

He raised his hand. "Scout's honor."

"That's affected."

"Frankly," he defied her, "I've always thought it sounded terrible."

"How continental."

"Your middle-class roots are showing."

She went into the kitchen and poured a second mug of cocoa. "You're in luck," she called to him. Diane heard the spit of burning wood as he arranged a log on the fire. "They've got crunchy peanut butter. I never could figure out why mothers always bought creamy. Crunchy is better."

Diane made two sandwiches, cut them into quarters, and put them on a tray with her cocoa and two apples. In her absence, Bradley had spread a patchwork quilt on the rug in front of the fireplace. Diane sat down next to him with the tray and unlaced her boots.

"They're still pretty stiff." She wiggled her stockinged feet at the fire. "Are you sure you're not hungry?" She eyed him playfully.

"I am, but not for peanut butter."

"You've got to be open to new experiences, John."

He sipped his brandy without comment.

"I'll make a deal with you," she said. "For each bite of sandwich, I'll take something off."

"What have you got on under the sweater?"

"A thermal T-shirt."

"Both socks count as one?"

"Okay."

Bradley bit into a sandwich quarter and tasted it thoughtfully. Diane took off her socks. He chewed his second bite with more appetite. She pulled her sweater off over her head. By the time he started the second quarter, he was chewing heartily. Diane slipped out of her blue jeans, T-shirt, and underwear. Bradley's cheeks bulged as he surveyed her naked body.

"What do you think?" She smiled.

"Not bad." His mouth was too full to speak distinctly.

"I knew you'd like it."

"I mean you." He washed the sandwich down with the rest of his brandy. "You're very beautiful."

Bradley drew her to him and kissed her. The taste of brandy and peanut butter was not a felicitous combination, but it would be unfair to protest under the circumstances. The contrast between her nakedness and his heavy winter clothing made her feel voluptuous, the way the women must have felt in *Dejeuner sur l'herbe*. Her skin glowed with the fire, her face and neck burned with the wool from his sweater and the heat of his breath. He alluded in an urgent whisper to precautions, but it was late enough in the month for spontaneity, and his sensitivity made it exquisite to be able to tell him that it didn't matter. She unzipped his pants in a single smooth motion and he made love to her with his clothes on. The letting down of a physical barrier between them added a thrilling psychological dimension to Diane's pleasure. With the possibility of new life, however remote, conjunction became union. Though Bradley might not know it, they had reached a new level.

They slept in the loft. Diane helped Bradley get his boots off. They lay in the dark, spent, content, awake but silent, watching the fire reflected on the underboards of the roof. A wind had risen outside, and it whistled through the bare trees. From time to time, a strong gust tapped a branch against the house. The only other nonhuman sound was an occasional pop from the fireplace. Diane listened to Bradley fall asleep. She resisted the soporific effect of his heavy breathing because she wanted to stay awake to savor the feeling of her head cradled against his shoulder. His body was familiar already. They slept well together.

She could sense snow the next morning before she opened her eyes. The world outside was muffled, preternaturally quiet. From the kitchen window, she saw the desert of the lake's surface under several inches of new snow. It was still snowing heavily. You want snow, you go get it, she laughed to herself. Bradley's life seemed charmed.

Despite Diane's having grown up in Minnesota, snow still filled her with a holiday spirit. She put water on for coffee, studied a biscuit recipe, boiled oatmeal, broiled bacon, thawed a cylinder of orange concentrate in a pitcher of spring water, and scrambled eggs. The breakfast organized itself like clockwork. Bradley came climbing down the ladder from the loft just as Diane took the biscuits out of the oven and brought them to the table.

"It's snowing," she said, smiling.

"So I see." He kissed her. She felt grown up. Spending the night with Bradley was a mature pleasure. She felt as if she might have been someone else.

"Want some coffee?"

He nodded. "Nice breakfast."

"Can you believe the folks on the farm eat like this every morning?"

"You say they earn it."

"The men do. The women cook all day, and end up heavy."

"Maybe the men like them that way."

"I've never heard anyone complain. How did you sleep?"

"Like a log. I like sleeping with you."

"That's nice." She leaned across the table and kissed him. "What is it about snow that's so exciting?" She looked out the window.

"It's the Nordic blood stirring in you. Do you like being Scandinavian?" He poured himself coffee and got up to put the pot back on the stove.

"It was interesting, once I got out of Minnesota. But I've often thought a little Jewish angst or Irish Catholic guilt might have made me more interesting."

"You couldn't get much more serious," he laughed.

"It worries me that I might become boring."

"You don't have to worry about that until you quit worrying about it." He laughed again.

"Do you get bored?" she asked.

"You asked me that once before."

"I forgot what you said."

"Yes. There's a lot of time to fill. But it's going quickly. Today is going much too quickly."

"Let's go for a long walk," she suggested. Bradley agreed.

Outside, the wind had died down and only a few snow-flakes straggled to the ground. The clouds were thin, likely to shred in places. They chose a path through the woods around the lake. They were warmly dressed, so it did not seem cold enough for snow. In fact, snow was already sliding off branches and turning tree trunks a slippery black as it melted. Before they were half a mile from the cottage, the sun broke through the clouds.

The snow was wet. It clung to their boots, which made hiking arduous at first. Diane was exuberantly out of breath. The air was moist and cool on her face. It felt good to be "earning" their breakfast, good to be out of New York.

They walked miles. Diane abandoned herself to an orgy of nature worship. She jumped brooks, trailed rabbits, ploughed doggedly through fields still knee-deep in snow. They saw a deer, had a snowball fight. The wind uncovered a gloriously blue sky and the sun beat warmly on their backs. They wandered through the small harbor town in search of lobster, but decided instead to have Mulligan stew for dinner. The few townspeople out regarded them with idle curiosity and the two out-of-season tourists had the streets of Booth Bay Harbor mostly to themselves. They talked to a fisherman mending lobster pots on a dock. The harbor was filled with chunks of ice, so the seals on the rocks offshore looked right at home.

In a graveyard beside a white clapboard church, they took turns speculating on the lives and deaths of the people named on the tombstones. Diane tried to piece together the story of the Pritchard twins, Anna and Sarah, who died within a month of each other the winter they were thirty-one. Their father had been minister of the church next to the cemetery. His wife had died, Diane calculated, giving birth to the twins. The Reverend Pritchard survived his daughters by twenty years. Why hadn't the girls married? How had the minister adjusted to life without his women? Could he really accept the truth graven on his daughters' tombstones, that the Lord giveth and the Lord taketh away?

Bradley was interested in Jonathan Stanton, who had died at Bradley's age, a fisherman drowned in winter seas, a shocking, mercifully quick death. Had he thought of Hannah and their three sons, of this peaceful town, in the moment before death? Was it really luxuriously long, that last minute before death by drowning, as many said?

Diane told him about the grove of trees on the crest of a hill above a Minnesota corn field. Her father was buried there, her mother would be.

"I may be, too." She was solemn, but not morbid. "Sometimes when my rootlessness gets to me, I find it reassuring to imagine myself buried there."

"What difference does it make?"

"What a callous thing to say." She was serious.

"Cremation makes much more sense ecologically."

"It's too quick, too definite. What if I wasn't dead yet?"

"I don't really believe that I'm going to die." He was smiling, but serious.

"Neither do I."

"Remember the character in *Alice in Wonderland* who said 'ouch' before she pricked her finger?"

Diane shook her head.

"I suppose it would be impossible to get through life if we really *knew* ahead of time that we were going to die."

Diane was struck with the unoriginal truth of his observation. Yet in the nine months since her mother's illness had been diagnosed, death had become as real to her as the winter cloud that had just passed over the sun. A chill shook her. The exhilaration powering her steps revealed itself as illusion. She was tired.

"Let's go get some tea," she said.

When they were seated in a nearby restaurant, warming hands around hot drinks, she said, "I'm sorry I got so serious just now."

"I know what you mean." Bradley said, smiling. "I went to two weddings last year, and three funerals."

They were silent a while. He eavesdropped on two elderly ladies at the next table. She fought to make sense of her confused thoughts. She was annoyed at herself for having fallen in love so quickly. She knew herself well enough to be sure that she had not conjured up the emotion to assuage her insecurities. She had not even pretended not to be looking for love, as many of her friends did on the principle that you never found love while actively pursuing it. Bradley had taken her by surprise. She had known him seven days, and she could already imagine herself married to him, having their son or daughter. She could imagine them old together, could imagine him at her funeral or her at his. There was nothing in Bradley's behavior that corresponded to these fantasies. He was affectionate, but he could afford to be affectionate. When Bradley wanted something, he got it, even if it cost fifty thousand dollars.

Diane had to hide her newly discovered feelings. If she told him now, he would be suspicious. There was no reason to rush things. She believed that a good relationship would keep. But she worried that her fear of his finding out would make her self-conscious, so that the fear became a self-fulfilling prophecy. I must not scare him off with my happiness, she thought, and suddenly realized how dangerous it was for them to remain alone together in such isolation. They needed diversion if she was going to keep her secret.

"What are you thinking?" He sensed that something was on her mind.

"I'd like to go to Paris for the weekend," she said. "On the Concorde. Do you think we could leave in the morning?"

Bradley liked the idea. The waitress directed him to a public telephone. Returning after several calls, he told her the plan. "We leave at five in the morning, take a seven o'clock flight to Boston, the eight o'clock shuttle to LaGuardia. That leaves us an hour to get to Kennedy. The Concorde leaves at ten o'clock. It'll be tight."

"We'll be in Paris"—she stopped to calculate—"in time for dinner at *Le Grand Vefour*."

"I didn't make reservations there."

"You'll get us in." She smiled.

With the prospect of renewing their fling the next day, Diane could trust herself for one evening with the pleasure of being alone with Bradley.

They walked the three miles to the cottage. A row of pines cast a long rectangular shadow across the last field they crossed on their way home. Their house was the only sign of civilization on the lake, and it seemed in an otherworldly twilight to assert the triumph of humanity in a frozen expanse. They were relieved to get inside and lock out the winter night.

"Why do men always build the fires?" She pulled sweater and boots off and warmed her feet in front of the fire he worked on.

"Maybe they wanted to get warm first."

"Move over." Diane pushed him aside.

Their evening together was more pleasant even than the day. They drank hot buttered rum toddies and made Mulligan stew in a cast-iron pot. Diane baked bran muffins for the morning trip to the airport and taught Bradley how to make ice cream from snow. Bradley worked on an outline at the dining room table, wadding a sheet of paper into a ball every so often and tossing it into the fire. Diane found a copy of *Portrait of a Lady* on a bookshelf in one of the bedrooms. She sat by the fireplace, sipping coffee, interrupting Bradley occasionally to suggest how the story could be made into a screenplay.

The wind in the trees enhanced the coziness of the cottage. They were tired from walking and fresh air. At ten o'clock, they climbed into the loft and set two alarm clocks. They made love with the same theme—the sensation of walking miles through snow, without being cold.

eight

It was ten to nine when Bradley told the cab driver "Kennedy Airport." They had just pulled away when Diane remembered their passports. When the cabdriver heard where they lived, he advised them to split up. Diane stayed in the cab.

"I'll meet you on the plane," Bradley called, jumping into the cab behind her. "Ten o'clock."

Her taxi negotiated the Brooklyn-Queens Expressway at a breathtaking speed. Potholes almost wrenched the cab apart. Once, a bump knocked Diane's head against the roof of the cab. It was like a chase scene in a detective movie. She followed Bradley mentally as she rode, seeing him at the Triborough Bridge as she passed under the Williamsburg Bridge, imagining him on the F.D.R. Drive as her cab raced off the Brooklyn Bridge exit. It seemed providential that she had cleaned: She had seen her passport in a battered transfile.

In the lobby, Diane hurriedly opened her mailbox. The only things that caught her attention were the too-thin telephone bill she recognized from experience as a disconnect notice and a letter from her mother. The telephone was ringing as she burst into her apartment. She set the mail on the kitchen table and picked up the phone.

"You've got forty-five minutes," Bradley said.

"I'm closer than you are," she said giddily, confident they would make it. As she was leaving, she saw the note

Alan had slipped under the door. He was back from Cleveland, wanted her to see the new camera. She had locked her door before she remembered her mother's letter. Bad news would not come in the mail, not from her mother. She raced down the stairs to the waiting cab.

In an act of faith, Diane boarded the plane without Bradley. He burst through the entryway at nine fifty-seven, just as a flight attendant was edging toward the door. Diane stood up, waved. They embraced, victorious. He struggled to catch his breath as the plane taxied down the runway.

"What a ride," she gasped. "The driver missed the Air France terminal and we had to circle back. I almost started crying."

"We hit traffic on the Van Wyck Expressway," he told her. "I told the guy I'd double his fare if we made it."

"What time do we arrive?" Diane asked the flight attendant, who was checking to make sure their seats were upright.

"A little before seven o'clock."

"We'll only get five hours of sunlight today," he complained.

"But we'll get to go to bed earlier. I don't get up at five in the morning that often. Here we go." Bradley took her hand. The take-off was thrilling. The plane shuddered with the force of ascent and climbed steeply, with a different rhythm from the jets they were used to. But once in the air, they lost the sense of traveling faster than usual.

By eleven o'clock, they had finished their second champagne toast sixty thousand feet above the Atlantic. A feast followed that Diane would not have thought possible in such a compact airliner. With an attention to detail worthy of the best restaurant she had eaten at in New York, the flight attendant served them stuffed mushrooms and fresh shredded vegetables, onion soup and French bread, filet mignon and asparagus with hollandaise sauce. They drank a bottle of excellent Burgundy with the meal. Afterwards there was green salad, cheese and apples, pastries and chocolate mousse, coffee and brandy. Bradley observed to the flight attendant with tolerant amusement that they would probably have been capable of entertaining themselves for three hours without something in their mouths the whole time. He and Diane were having a second coffee with brandy when a voice over the intercom announced preparations for their landing in Paris.

"So fast," Diane gasped, drunkenly.

"Did you notice the sun setting?"

"I was too busy eating," she giggled. "I hope you cancel our reservations at *Le Grand Vefour* tonight."

"I may still be full tomorrow night."

"I'll make you walk it off. I can't believe we'll be in Paris. Do you think they'll let me into the Ritz with these dirty boots on?"

"They'd better. My grandfather knew Charles personally."

"You tell 'em," she laughed. "Can we get a room that looks out on Place Vendôme?"

He shook his head. "You'll be glad I got a room on the garden when you see it."

The jet roared into Charles de Gaulle Airport.

"The air smells like Europe," she said when they were outside, which meant, she explained, a mixture of rain and diesel exhaust. It was night. The air was warm, decidedly springlike. The roads glistened, a solid band of reflected light along the expressway into Paris.

"I can't believe I'm back." She was glad it was too dark in the cab for Bradley to see that she was on the verge of crying.

"How do you say 'through'?" she asked Bradley.

"Like finished?"

"No, like 'through the city.' I can say 'to the city' and in and from it, but I forget 'through.'"

"A *travers*."

"A *travers Paris*," she said to the driver. "I want to see everything," she told Bradley.

As they drove past the Porte de Clignancourt flea market, ghostly, deserted for the night, Diane reminisced about student shopping sprees. In the winding, crowded streets of Montmartre, she looked for restaurants that had served three-course meals for ten francs, *with* wine. Passing the brightly lit Opéra, she described cash-flow crises and anxious hours waiting at the American Express office.

Diane marveled at how Bradley transcended wrinkled corduroys and a sweater with a twig still clinging to the back. His imperturbable self-assurance commanded un-questioning respect from the hotel clerk who signed them in and the man who led them to their room.

The room was a masterpiece of simple elegance. Soft green walls and furnishings were restrained by standards of a culture capable of Versailles. Floor-to-ceiling windows looked out on a garden insulated from Parisian traffic. They might have been in a villa near the Mediterranean.

"I feel like I ought to start unpacking and putting things away." She peered into an antique armoire. "But I don't have anything to hang up."

"We'll take care of that in the morning."

"A room with a bath." She surveyed the bathroom's high ceiling, deep tub, anique fixtures. "This is a first for me in a French hotel."

"Let's order champagne."

"And take a bath. Help me get my boots off."

She pulled her sweater off. He picked up the phone. She put one foot, then the other, up on the bed, and he pulled. He ordered champagne, then asked her, "How do you say 'bubble bath'?"

"You speak better French than I do."

"Where's your dictionary?" It was hard to believe it had only been six hours since she had grabbed the paper-back from the bookshelf in her apartment.

"No bubble bath. Just bubble. It's *'bulle.'* "

"Oui monsieur, c'est bon," Bradley answered the man. *"Et où est—"* He covered the receiver. *"Le* or *la?"*

"La bulle."

"And soap for making bubbles in the bathtub," he told room service, translating literally. Diane was impressed at the fluency with which he insisted that there had always been bubble bath in his room before when he had stayed at the hotel.

"What a quaint improvisation," she teased him after he hung up. "A French woman would find it charming."

"What's it do to an American woman?" He pulled her down on the bed and rolled on top of her, kissing her neck and ears affectionately.

"Pretty much the same thing—especially at such close range."

They began undressing each other, languidly, between

and during kisses. They were naked from the waist up and covering each other's nipples with kisses when they heard a tap at their door. Bradley's face and neck were flushed. He pulled a shirt on and answered the door. Diane retreated into the bathroom, where she finished undressing, and began filling the tub. There was a muffled explosion in the bedroom. Bradley joined her in the tub with two crystal glasses, a magnum of champagne, and a large green plastic bottle of Vitabath.

"This isn't very bubbly," she complained.

"It smells good, though. Sort of like the Maine woods."

They were up to their chests in warm water, facing each other in a thin layer of bubbles. They drank the whole bottle of champagne. Flushed, immersed in fragrant steam, the champagne made them garrulous. They tripped over each other's words, interrupted each other, lost, regained, or embarked on new trains of thought. The discovery that they had been in Paris at the same time eight years earlier launched them on a quest for the moment when they might have crossed paths. Diane suggested Sundays, when the Louvre was free, but Bradley hated crowds. He asked eagerly about her café habits, but she had frequented *Le Sélect* and he had been a habitué at *Café de Flores*.

As if the wine bottle were a lamp running low on oil, their conversation became more subdued as they finished the champagne. They had turned off the bathroom light, and only faint illumination came through the half-open bathroom door. The bubbles were gone. Diane sat with her back to Bradley, leaning against his chest, head on his shoulder, his lips on her neck. They were quiet, motionless. There was no awkwardness in the silence, only a pleasant tension between them. She could hear herself swallowing; she heard him swallow. His penis grew warm and hard against her back.

"I feel like one of the lobsters we didn't eat last night." Her whispered joke dispelled the intensity of her longing for him.

"Was that last night?" The deepness of his voice gave away his own longing. They got out of the tub, dried each other off, tiptoed into the bedroom. Diane turned off the lamp beside the bed. Bradley turned out the overhead light. They lay down and embraced.

"I want to kiss you—everywhere," he murmured.

She burned with exquisite passivity as he traced a path down her body with kisses as delicate as the brush of a flower against her skin. She shivered. He kissed the inside of her thighs, the tender spot scalloped between tendons that were now taut. As excitement became frustration, his lips brushed the curls of her pubic hair. She relaxed. He kissed her as sweetly as he had been kissing her lips earlier. His lips, his tongue, his fingertips, the cold enamel of his teeth—each had its own touch, each elicited its own music from her body. His tongue thrust deep into her, and she held her legs apart, as if in childbirth, simultaneously opening herself up to and giving birth to her passion. Beneath closed lids, she saw the Maine sky again, crowded with stars. Her muscles gathered in upon themselves, contracted. The universe trembled, exploded outward into billions of stars. Bradley was inside her, coming with her. They were humbled by their pleasure.

There was perspiration where their bodies touched. Bradley shivered as they came apart.

For the first time, they talked about making love. Caressing his thighs, Diane admitted that she sometimes wondered what it would be like to have a penis. He laughed gently and shook his head when she asked him if he ever personified his. Bradley wondered if a language existed that could enable them to ascertain whether they felt the same pleasure during orgasm. They fell silent, contemplating in the dim light the chasm of physical difference that separated their feelings.

"What do I taste like?" Diane asked. The question excited him.

"Salt, the ocean, the earth—yourself."

"I want to taste myself."

Diane took his penis into her mouth, massaging with one hand, stroking his back with the other. Intent on distinguishing her taste from his, she did not feel him coming. He took her in his arms and kissed her and the distillate of his passion was on their lips.

It was almost midnight when they left the hotel. The streets were wet, the air cool and damp. They were hungry. Bradley headed instinctively toward *Les Halles*, already gone in Diane's student days. He reminisced about streetwalkers and bargaining for produce at dawn as they wound their way through the maze of dead-end streets and new construction that replaced the famous market.

"It feels so natural to be back." She inhaled the fresh night air.

He agreed. "Paris is like a friend you can start where you left off with, no matter how long it's been since you saw him."

"I can't believe I'm back."

"Why did you wait so long?" He took her hand and squeezed it.

"When I left Paris, I made up my mind I wouldn't come back until it could be as special as the first time. I was free here. For a whole year. I had time for everything. I could sit up all night reading Flaubert or Sartre and sleep all morning. I could go skiing in the Alps at Christmas or sit on a beach in Spain. It didn't take a lot of money. Movies and museums were half price. Dinner at the university cafeteria was fifty cents. And no one took attendance at school. If I didn't feel like a history lecture, I hopped on a train for Chartres. I thought about coming back after college, but my father convinced me a junior year abroad was a once-in-a-lifetime experience and that I would only be postponing reality. I believed him. The next thing I knew, I was wrapped up in my hand-to-mouth journalism career in New York and there was no question of going back. I knew I'd never come on a two-week vacation. It would be too much like a furlough, and would remind me of what I had lost."

"Lost?" He turned aside to look at her.

"I say 'lost,' " she explained, "but deep down I've always suspected that I gave up my freedom without a fight."

"It was definitely low Lutheran of you not to come back."

"Life is hard work." She played at ponderousness.

"It is."

"Even free?"

"Especially free."

They stopped to admire fresh shellfish in bushel baskets outside a restaurant. It was too cool for tables on the sidewalk. Inside it was crowded. They took a table by a window upstairs.

"This is the kind of tourist trap that makes me enjoy being a tourist," he said.

Diane ordered onion soup and Perrier water. Bradley had *choucroute garnie* and a bottle of Kanterbrau beer.

"I grew up on sauerbraten and potato dumplings," she laughed. "But I don't think I could handle sauerkraut and sausage after midnight, especially on top of champagne."

"It's dinner time *chez nous*," he reminded her.

"It feels like breakfast time timorrow." She stifled a yawn. "I guess you still get jet lag even on the Concorde."

The waiter brought their drinks. Diane asked for a pitcher of "natural" water as well. Two men in black dinner jackets—a tall man with a guitar and a short man with an accordion—approached their table.

"Bonsoir, messieurs," Bradley greeted them pleasantly. Diane dreaded a serenade in full view of the other patrons. The tall man had not heard Bradley's greeting, and addressed them in English.

"Are monsieur and madame enjoying their visit?" the guitarist asked.

"We miss *Les Halles*." She was determined to demonstrate that they were not the establishment's typical tourists.

"Ah yes, it is a pity." He pronounced "pity" with the accent on the second syllable.

"May we play a song for madame?"

"What would you like to hear?" Bradley turned to her.

"You pick." She had no idea what to ask for.

"La Vie en Rose."

Diane did not know the song by its title, but she recognized the melody. It was quintessentially Parisian. She could not understand the words, but the sentimental music filled her with a sadness that was more universal than the sum of all the moments of her life that had not measured up. The musicians saw tears in her eyes and backed away apologetically. It was only with difficulty that Bradley prevailed upon them to take his ten-franc note.

"I guess I picked the wrong song." He reached across the table and took her hand. She liked the fact that her crying did not make him uncomfortable.

The waiter brought her soup and Bradley's plate to the table.

"The song made me think of my mother," she said. "All the things she might have done. Somehow the music made it all a little less sad." She sipped a spoonful of soup. Its warm salty taste was soothing. He bit into a piece of sausage. They were quiet, listening to the musicians, who had found less sensitive tourists downstairs.

Diane and Bradley became aware of their exhaustion almost simultaneously. The hours of traveling and the afterglow of their lovemaking had advanced their biological clocks to local time—two in the morning.

They took a taxi back to the hotel. Diane was too tired to change into the flannel nightgown she had bought for Maine. They were both asleep before their heads touched the bolster.

Bradley's tossing and turning woke Diane up Saturday morning.

"Goddamn these French pillows," he was muttering.

"Bolsters," she murmured.

"You can't hug them because they snake across the bed, and you can't put them over your head because they're wrapped up in the end of the sheet. It's like sleeping on a log."

"Maybe that's where the expression 'sawing wood' comes from." She squinted to read the clock on the mantel. It was ten o'clock. For the first time that week, Diane felt rested. Sunshine streaming into the room elated her. She felt a momentary disappointment when Bradley pulled on corduroy pants and a turtleneck.

"What a beautiful day." She surveyed the room cheerfully.

He was pulling on boots.

"I want to get out as soon as possible," he said. "You can't trust Paris weather this early in spring."

"Let's have breakfast outside."

"My thought exactly."

They had breakfast in the garden and walked afterwards to Rue St. Honoré to look for clothes. Diane bought a white shirtwaist dress covered with tiny green flowers, similar to the new dress left behind in her hurry to get to the airport. She also chose a green cardigan she draped over her shoulders, a pair of brown leather sandals, and some heels for that evening. She was not sure how much credit was left on her MasterCard and was relieved they did not verify her balance. She let Bradley buy her a string of pearls. He bought himself a pair of close-fitting beige slacks, a collarless striped shirt, and a French version of his tweed jacket, which he changed into, and had a blue oxford cloth shirt and tie delivered to the hotel.

They did not need a map. The city was familiar to them. They walked along the Seine, browsing in the garden shops facing the river among cages crammed with rabbits and chickens, birds and puppies. Trays of seedling tomatoes and perennial flowers—parcels of spring—sold for a franc. Saturday shoppers thronged into *La Samaritaine* to shed winter browns and grays for summer pastels.

Bradley and Diane shared the crowd's sense of well-being as they reminisced about their days in Paris. Bradley had been out of college already, too old, he insisted, for the Left Bank. He had had an apartment in the Marais, next door to Victor Hugo's residence. On principle, he had not yet been inside the Pompidou Art Center.

"You're as bad a Tory as your father," she laughed. They were standing in the sun, watching the tip of Isle de la Cité and Notre Dame across the Seine.

"I knew an odd assortment of people," he told her, "a crazy old Russian countess with fire-engine-red hair who'd had the hots for Gertrude Stein, a man who'd already been old in Joyce's company who gave a reading of Baudelaire's poetry at the poet's tomb—"

"My hotel was right across from Montparnasse Cemetery."

"I was an honorary member of the Huysmann Society. I think one of the by-laws of the group was you had to have known the author personally. There wasn't a guy who met afternoons at *La Coupole* who was under eighty."

"I don't know Huysmanns," she said.

"Neither did I. He sounded like an Oscar Wilde type, but I had a hard time understanding their garbled French translations of Swinburne."

"Strange friends."

"Those were my father's introductions. I also got in

with a group of silly French aristocrats on my own. We
hung out at discotheques and raced sportscars in the Bois
de Boulogne in the middle of the night and ran off to St.
Tropez on the spur of the moment. I used to take out
beautiful women from good old families for dinner and
dancing, and then drop them home with a polite kiss, the
perfect gentleman. Then I'd race down to Rue St. Denis.
There was block after block of female flesh for sale there.
I was a big spender."

"I can't imagine you with a prostitute. You seem too
fastidious."

They stood at the west end of the plaza in front of Notre
Dame. Hundreds of visitors milled around the cathedral. A
busload of Japanese tourists stormed the entrance. Diane
didn't want to go in.

"The last time I was inside it was Good Friday," she
explained. "I can still hear the choir chanting the *Pange
Lingua*. Mom almost lost me to the papists. I don't want to
go in as a tourist."

The sun shone through the scabbed white branches of
the sycamore trees along the Left Bank, throwing a web of
shadow on the bookstands. There were songbirds in the
trees. A man in a trenchcoat and beret stood in the shade
of a bridge, fishing along the edge of the river, undisturbed by the boatload of tourists that floated past him.

The sun had a phototropic effect on the people of Paris.
The streets of the Latin Quarter were clogged with cars,
jammed with people. At a sidewalk café, they watched the
passersby. Diane's student days took on a universal quality; she was overwhelmed by a sense of privilege at having
been able to participate in the great tradition of French
studenthood. She was enjoying memories of total immersion in history and literature. She described friends made
in crowded lecture halls, which led to a heated debate on
the Parisian temperament. She maintained that Parisians
were not nasty if you made the effort to know them. He
countered that she had only gotten to the first level of
intimacy, and that deeper down, it was every man for
himself. Diane, aglow with love of France, could only
sigh: "Why wasn't I born French?"

"It would have deprived you of one of life's sweetest

emotions," Bradley was saying as they entered the Garden of Luxembourg. "Francophilia."

"I don't know why I left."

The park was suffused in a liquid, almost palpable light. There were themes there for a gallery of impressionist paintings on this perfect afternoon. Lovers embraced, nannies rocked babies in carriages, nattily dressed boys sailed boats from the edge of the fountain. Winter was vanquished. Though the short cropped trees were leafless, huge wooden boxes holding gnarled palm trees had been wheeled from the greenhouse like octogenarians enjoying the first warm weather.

"You left"—Bradley surveyed the park with appreciation, but without longing—"because you are as American as chain link fence. You're as out of your element here as that skyscraper is"—he pointed west—"in Montparnasse."

"I resent that."

"If you knew me better, you'd realize it's a compliment," he said. "I've outgrown my inferiority complex about Europe. You don't need Europe, Diane. You're good enough on your own."

Anywhere except the Garden of Luxembourg, she might have been mollified. It seemed that moment the very essence of the civilization she aspired to.

They sat on a bench overlooking the fountain and the palace. Diane took out a red Michelin guide and searched the index for the three-star restaurants of Paris. They already had reservations at *Le Grand Vefour*, but could always change their mind.

Their discussion of restaurants was interrupted by a heated argument between two schoolboys, perhaps eight years old. The boys had been playing marbles on the gravel. One of the marbles had overshot the verge separating walkway from lawn, and lay nestled in the grass beyond their reach. The youngsters searched the well-manicured park in vain for a stick they could use to roll the marble back to the gravel. The owner wanted the marble back, but neither boy had the courage to defy the sign that prohibited walking on the grass.

"What's the French word for 'marble'?" she whispered.

"I was going to say '*marbre*,' but I think that's what you make statues out of. Try '*bille*.' "

Diane walked over to ask the boys in halting French if they would like her to get the marble for them. Their eyes were ambivalent. They wanted the marble, but were shocked by her disregard for the law. She stepped onto the grass, retrieved the marble, and handed it to them. She expected gratitude. Instead, the boys accepted the marble grudgingly, as they might have taken coins from a pickpocket, too intimidated to condone the thief's audacity.

"They would have left the marble there." Diane shook her head with amusement as she rejoined Bradley.

"The French never let us help until they're against the wall," Bradley laughed, "and then they're mad at themselves—and at us—when they do."

They stopped to see what the current attraction was at the puppet theater. Snow White.

"Have you ever seen a show here?"

He had not.

"I have to have children just so I can dress them up and bring them here on a Sunday afternoon. You should see the children. The boys dress in little blue suits and the girls wear smocked dresses with puffed sleeves. They sit perfectly still through the whole performance. I wasn't that good in high school."

They stopped to look at the beehives behind the Apiary Society's picket fence.

"Even the beehives are different here," Bradley pointed out.

"Where do you suppose bees get pollen this time of year?" Diane wondered.

"Maybe they hibernate."

They asked a florist on Rue de Fleurus, but were not surprised that he didn't know. It was possible that he had not understood the question, since they could not remember the word for "pollen."

When they got to Montparnasse, Diane led Bradley down a back street, past pastry shops and Vietnamese and Brittanese and American restaurants to a sign advertising public baths. They turned into a secluded courtyard and entered the unoccupied lobby of a modest but neatly kept hotel.

"Everything's exactly the same." Diane was hoarse with excitement. She rang a counter bell, and a short, plain-faced woman with gray hair knotted behind her bustled into the lobby.

"Oui, monsieurdame?"

The woman recognized Diane before the question was off her lips.

"Jacques, come here, this minute," she called to her husband in French. "Mademoiselle Yaeger"—her valiant attempt to pronounce Diane's last name approximated the French word for yogurt—"she has come back."

A short, middle-aged man—bald, with a big stomach and a day's growth of whitish stubble—joined them from the back room. Their welcome was enthusiastic, though they did not touch Diane. They acted as if visits from former guests were a regular and pleasant part of being good proprietors.

Diane introduced Bradley in French and they shook hands. Madame wanted to know if he was her husband.

"I don't have that distinction," he answered in French. Diane did not like Bradley as well in French. There was something vaguely effeminate and affected about the way he spoke. He might have been mistaken for English. Diane told them about Bradley's book, and the movie that would be out in six to eight months. Though impressed, it was apparent they had not heard of the book. Had Diane become an actress?

"A journalist," she told them, adding in correct French: "Sometimes it's the same thing."

They laughed. *"Monsieurdame"* were fine. Their daughter, who had been an adolescent when Diane lived there, was married to a truck driver, and expecting her first child. Business was good. The hotel was full that night, unfortunately. Repressing a desire to tell them where she was staying, Diane assured them they were visiting friends. She would like to show Monsieur Bradley her former room, if that was possible. Madame informed her that the old lady who had now been living in the room for five years was out. She was English, the landlady told them. An old Frenchman paid her bill. If they heard her coming, which would not be difficult because she had a severe case of asthma and stopped on each landing to catch her breath, they were to leave immediately.

"They call it the sixth floor"—Diane was breathless

with anticipation and five steep flights of stairs—"but it's really a seven-floor walk-up."

"It's one way to keep in shape." Bradley puffed a flight behind.

The light in the hallway went out. Diane pushed a button and, when the light came back on, unlocked an insubstantial door at the end of the corridor. The room was dirty, and though it had no kitchen, it was cluttered with food. There were unwashed dishes in a bathroom sink, dirty clothes on the floor, cheap mementoes of European travels on a night table. But Diane hardly noticed evidence of a new occupant. She went to the single window, which opened out over Montparnasse cemetery. The setting sun cast long shadows in the city of the dead, with its thoroughfares and side streets, its graves and mausoleums like the houses and temples of an ancient Roman city, patiently awaiting the last judgment.

"You should see it when the trees have leaves." She took his hand when he came up beside her. "It's beautiful. I used to look out on the cemetery when the sun was going down, like now, or there was a full moon overhead, and it made me appreciate being young, seeing all the dead. I guess that seems morbid."

Bradley shook his head and smiled. "It's reassuring that all our struggling ends so peacefully."

"I read *Père Goriot* and *The Red and the Black* in that chair. I drank a quart of wine a day at that table." She sat on the bed and tested it with several bounces. "This is where I made love for the first time." Bradley sat down beside her, without touching her, reluctant to interfere with her stream of memories.

"A Frenchman?"

"An American graduate student counting conjunctions in avant-garde French novels. He was an expatriate at heart. I've been expecting all day to run into him."

"Would he recognize you?"

"Right away. I haven't changed."

"Is that good or bad?"

"Good. You have to be consistent to be successful. David didn't give a damn about success. Whatever he's doing here, I'm sure he's doing a mediocre job."

There were footsteps on the stairway. Diane straightened the bed hastily and they left the room. On the fourth floor, they passed a shabbily dressed woman gasping for breath.

"May we help you?" Diane asked in French.

"Leave me alone," the woman snapped, in English, her voice quavering with suspicion. Diane was seized by a visceral aversion for the current occupant of "her" room. Sordidness threatened to cloud fond memories. The woman was an incarnate reminder that happiness was fleeting. Diane shivered and hurried downstairs.

They stopped in the office to say goodbye and there were cordial farewells all around. Diane would see them again.

In the cab back to the hotel, Bradley calculated that they had walked four miles. Though it was only half the distance they had two days earlier, their feet were sore. They slipped their shoes off under the table in the Ritz bar, and Bradley took her tired feet in his lap and massaged them as they sipped Scotch and Perrier. He decided to rent a tuxedo. On their way back to soak in the tub, they stopped to give the desk clerk Bradley's measurements. That Bradley knew them in centimeters secured in Diane's eyes his claim to be a man of the world.

After supper at *Le Grand Vefour*, sipping brandy and looking out on the dark arcade behind the *Petit Palais*, they analyzed the meal, describing respective highlights. Diane wanted to know how much it had cost.

"Let me see," she asked when the waiter brought the check. "My menu didn't have any prices."

"Don't put a price tag on a beautiful experience," he teased her.

"It's part of my education." She took the bill from him. "My God." The meal cost as much as she would get for the article on Bradley.

"That's with service," he reminded her.

"Twenty dollars for asparagus. My mother would die."

"Remember the hollandaise."

She laughed when she realized that the experience had been worth it.

"Let's order more champagne," she said.

"That's the spirit."

Afterwards they took a taxi to Montmartre and sat high

and chilly on the steps of Sacre Coeur with the City of Light spread below. When the night air was too cold to sit out any longer, they went into a nightclub down the hill to get warm. They drank more champagne and watched a parody of cancan with an audience of foreign businessmen.

Their walk took them through a red-light district. Prostitutes formed a reception line along both sides of the street, welcoming them to a celebration of female flesh. Bradley was propositioned repeatedly despite the companion on his arm.

"Maybe they think we're in the market for a *ménage à trois*," Diane whispered. She could not take her eyes off the wall of breasts and legs. The women were not threatening like the prostitutes in New York. Here she could imagine a man enjoying himself.

"Were these the kind of women you visited?" Diane asked.

"This is the place. But that was a long time ago."

"Why did you do it?"

"I had a vague notion of writing a book about the experience. At least that was my rationalization."

"What was it like?"

"I learned every nuance of whore and prostitute and call girl, French and foreign. I spent hours and nights and days with African women and Caribbean women and Japanese women and Vietnamese women and women from every country in Europe." He looked at her significantly. "I tried everything."

Diane was confused. Her feelings alternated between admiration and resentment.

"What did you learn?" She affected nonchalance.

"How difficult it is to know a woman."

"What did you expect—communion for twenty dollars an hour?"

"Men are sentimental."

His answer amused her. "I can imagine commiting an act of prostitution," she said.

He laughed.

"I might have despised you," she told him.

"Some of them did."

"Sometimes the desires of men frighten me."

"They frighten me, too. That's what I was going to

write about. I bought stories along with bodies. I was
going to call the book *One Hundred Women*.''

"You and Henry Miller." She disliked the idea intensely.

"I didn't get very far," Bradley said. "In real life, the
women were fascinating, but on the page they were stereo-
types. Then the student revolution came along. What might
once have been path-breaking became exploitation,"

"I didn't realize you were so sensitive to other people's
opinions."

They could not stop walking. They crept into the darkened courtyards of landmark mansions. They sat on a wall
on the edge of Isle St. Louis and watched the moon rise.
Paris was surprisingly quiet at night compared to New
York, and they played in its empty streets like two Hollywood drunks who had stumbled onto a deserted movie set.
It was their city. They rattled the gates of parks closed for
the night, demanding to be let in. They wove through
narrow streets, talking in boisterous stage whispers, spiral-
ing into helpless laughter at silly jokes.

Daylight caught them by surprise. Their energy deserted
them all at once. Diane remembered dinner and offered
Bradley a check. He insisted they could settle later. The
sky had become overcast, and with morning, a fine mist
began to drift over the city. They sat in the Tuileries,
uninspired by the birds whose singing defied the gloom.
Diane's head ached. Croissants and café crème in a nearby
cafe did not restore the spirit of the night. They were tired.
Dull with fatigue, they walked through the mist shrouding
the city back to the hotel.

nine

Watching the rain in the garden the next morning, Diane tried to project her relationship with Bradley beyond their week together. Her imagination failed her. He was off to California to write his screenplay. She was back at work. He was too polite to drop her all at once, of course, but he had seldom used the future tense in their conversations.

Diane was surprised to see by her reflection in the window that she looked rested. She faced her feelings squarely. She was in love. She could happily spend her life with Bradley. Which meant marriage and children. She might as well play out the whole scenario. Without preconceived notions about how long it ought to take to fall in love, she did not question the validity of her feelings. He knew her better in a week than any man ever had. She had gotten to know him, too. But for him to admit that was to give up a lot of his freedom.

Diane thought about Bradley as she packed perfume and toothpaste and bath powder into the knapsack. She had learned while sampling his kind of freedom how difficult it would be to give it up. What could she offer in its place? He had certainly spent a more pleasant week with her than he would have spent alone, but prolonged indefinitely, the experience might lose its charm. However, the ephemeral nature of their relationship, which enhanced the experience for Bradley, spoiled it for Diane. She was packed, and depressed, by the time he woke up as church bells tolled eleven.

"Good morning." He sat up cheerfully, but his smile faded when he saw her staring absently at the rain. He yawned.

"Hello." Her greeting was flat. No feminine altruism could compel her to save for him the week that had been ruined for her.

"It's cold in here."

"It's raining." She could not take her eyes off the rain. It objectified her mood.

Bradley took her to brunch at the *Café de Flores*. It was smoky and crowded in the high-ceilinged café. The Welsh rarebit and *café crème* might have cheered her if Bradley's false cheer had not convinced her that all her fears were justified. He was intent on ignoring her mood and did not see the effect his talk of California had on her. He didn't like California. It was an artificial world. The only interesting people there were from the East Coast. Had she seen *The New Yorker* cartoon about being bi-coastal? Diane could not be interested in his unoriginal observations. She was aware of blowing the week, but she was powerless against her mood. The more he talked about movie-making and script-writing, the frenetic hours and crazy people he was looking forward to, the more she envied his freedom. His life would continue to be fascinating. Diane hated his life.

Bradley debated whether he should continue straight on from Kennedy Airport to Los Angeles, or spend the night in New York. He was nervous about his television appearance the next evening.

"I'd rather spend the night with you," he said, smiling. The suggestion did not seem so much insincere as clumsy. She tried to convey to him with her eyes how irrevocably their situation had changed, but he would not notice. She was angry. Sensing that this anger would be incomprehensible, was possibly even unjustified, made her angrier. She confined herself to pointing out that it would be risky to wait until morning to leave.

"Are you all right?" he asked in the cab on the way to the airport.

She was evasive.

"What are you thinking?" That he had picked up on her bad mood, finally, improved it infinitesimally.

"Nothing," she said.

"What are you thinking?" he asked again when they were waiting to take off.

"The immigration officials didn't stamp my passport coming or going. Someday I'll wonder if these couple of days really happened."

He laughed and watched the plane taxi down the runway.

She declined the flight attendant's offer of beer, wine, or cocktails.

"I'm sick of drinking," she told Bradley. "First-class stewardesses never leave you alone," she grumbled. The flight attendant brought Bradley a double Jack Daniels on the rocks. Diane was tired of his good mood. He lifted his drink to her glass of club soda and lime.

"To our week together."

"Cheers." Her tone belied the celebratory gesture. She touched his glass with hers.

"I really had a good time." He tried to make eye contact, though she avoided his gaze.

"I'm glad." Her voice sounded far away to her. There was a clutching sensation in her throat.

"Did you?" His tone was naive. It almost touched her.

"I had a wonderful time."

By his silence, she feared that he suspected irony in her reply. But she could not think of a way to tell him she intended no ambiguity. He was disappointed, and puzzled, by her mood.

"I'll never make it to midnight in these glass slippers." Diane eased her shoes off under the seat in front of her. Bradley's smile told her that he would not let her mood ruin his. She turned away from him and looked at the sky. The jet had broken through the clouds. She was glad to see the sun. Bradley respected her silence.

She tallied up how much she had spent that week. Ironically, Bradley had picked up much of the tab. She had spent five thousand dollars at most. Diane debated borrowing money from her mother to pay him back. The question Diane turned over and over in her mind, aware of Bradley's eyes on her, affectionate and mellow as he sipped whiskey, was whether she had compromised herself. She had never spent the night with a man so quickly, so—she flinched at the word—"casually." Whatever her confused feelings, they were not casual. The French word *bouleverser* came to mind. Bradley had bowled her over. If he had asked her that moment what she was thinking, she might have had the courage to tell him that she wished the week could go on indefinitely.

They knew each other well. That was why they could not go on together. Their relationship had gained momentum so quickly that not to see each other steadily now would be a painful regression. He was by nature free. Freedom was what made him attractive. They *did* belong in different spheres. The familiar bitterness returned, the very bitterness, perhaps, that had piqued his curiosity a week earlier. It caught in her throat. Swallowing made her eyes water, but she was not in danger of crying. She lay back, closed her eyes, and tried to see herself from Bradley's point of view. A pretty, plucky Midwestern girl with a different perspective on things, liberated enough for a fling. Seen through his eyes, her onrush of feeling was frightening. My God, she could imagine him thinking, sleep with a woman for a week and she wants to marry you. Another nice girl in search of Mr. Right. That she might appear insecure, or uncritically impressed, lumped her with the other desperate women in his life—and she assumed there had been others. It was better to hide her feelings, or smother them, than to have them misinterpreted.

"Was the experiment a success?" Her voice startled him.

"You have to answer that question." The remark struck her as pompous.

"I don't want to write the article now," she said.

"You'll waste all your insights into freedom."

"I'm not happy."

"Who said freedom would make you happy?"

"May I quote you?"

The flight attendant came to take their order for dinner.

"I'm not hungry," she told the woman, and then said to Bradley: "All we've done all week is eat."

Bradley ate, and while he ate, he wondered out loud

what his book would be like as a movie. He was unable to control his mounting excitement.

"Maybe they'll be showing it this time next year on the flight from Paris," Diane said.

Her depression deepened as it began to grow dark. Bradley stopped trying to cheer her up and watched the movie. Diane put on the mask provided for sleeping, and lay back. She had never been able to sleep in a moving vehicle, and surrendered instead to an unfruitful half-waking state in which insights followed one another too rapidly to be remembered. The plane traveled at the same speed as the sunset, which gave Diane a sense of being suspended in time.

The plane landed late. The airport was crowded, customs thorough. Bradley missed a connection to Los Angeles and decided to wait the two hours until the next flight.

They did not talk much. She could not think of anything to say. It was dark—after one in the morning Paris time—when they stood in line for a taxi. The air was balmy, the fragrance of jet exhaust and salt marsh suggesting faraway places. Diane felt the dread she often had on Sunday evenings, not anxiety at going back to work so much as regret for all the things not accomplished during her freedom.

Their parting lacked style. Diane was devoid of grace or eloquence. She wanted to throw her arms around Bradley and burst into tears. The best he could do was to talk about what they would do when he got back to New York. That he had picked up on her insecurities depressed her more.

"I'll call tomorrow. I'm staying at the Beverly Hills Hotel." He put his arm on her shoulder and kissed her. A cab drove up in front of them.

"Good luck tomorrow night," she said.

"You'll watch?"

"Of course." Diane kissed him offhandedly. She wanted him to understand that she was deliberately holding back on the kiss, but he took its casualness at face value. He did not want to know what was wrong.

"I'll miss you." He kissed her one more time before opening the door for her.

It was necessary to look away from him as she climbed into the cab. I must not cry, she thought. Every muscle in her face was clenched as she looked out the window and waved goodbye. By the time the cab was a safe distance from where Bradley watched her on the curb, her tears had been absorbed into her body, poisoning her with the autotoxic by-products of her unhappiness.

Diane was not confused. She knew exactly what she wanted. She would not do better than Bradley. This was not a case for cleverness or feminine wiles. He knew just about everything there was to know about her. There was no situation she could set up to bring him around. It would have to be his own choice. She was not optimistic.

As her cab sped along the Van Wyck Expressway, heading toward the same city lights that had shimmered like a mirage from Bradley's car a week earlier, it occurred to Diane that her feelings proved her unworthy of a free man.

She was exhausted. She looked forward to a long night in her own bed, undisturbed by Bradley's active sleep. She unplugged the telephone and filled the bathtub with hot water. Stretched full length in the tub, she would not have traded her well-being even for the bathtub at the Ritz. It was good to be alone. It would be wonderful to sleep. She could even anticipate the satisfied exhaustion of the next night, when the article was finished. Rising out of the scented bathwater, she decided to put Bradley out of her mind for the rest of the night. She wrapped herself in a blue silk kimono, a souvenir from Alan's trip to photograph high-speed trains in Japan, and went into the kitchen to make a cup of tea. There was a knock at the front door.

ten

Diane left the kettle whistling on the stove and ran to the door.

"Who is it?" She could not dissemble the tension within her. Her heart pounded, her stomach churned, her throat was dry.

"Alan." Her disappointment was fierce. She closed her eyes, pressed clenched fists against the door. She was stunned. She wanted to cry. When he knocked again and called her name, his voice was far away, as if he was down the hall.

Diane could not bring herself to be face to face with someone besides Bradley. She sank down onto the floor and buried her face against her knees. She wanted Alan to go away, but she did not have the voice to tell him so. She longed for unconsciousness, but the kettle screamed and Alan pounded. Diane forced herself to stand up and open the door.

"Hi." She was too exhausted for emotion, no longer even sorry he wasn't Bradley.

"What's wrong?" His eyes showed her how bad she must look. "What happened?" He grabbed her by both arms, but she broke away to take the kettle off the burner.

"Nothing."

"Where have you been? I've been calling since Tuesday night." He followed her into the kitchen. His reproach was imperious enough to catch her attention.

"In Paris."

"With John Bradley?" The jealousy in his question did not seem related to them.

She nodded. "Want some tea?"

"Diane, you look terrible. What happened?"

"Nothing. I went to Paris with Bradley, that's all."

She poured boiling water over a tea bag, went in the living room, and sat on the couch.

"You're not reckless, Diane." He sat down beside her.

If he had been a different kind of man, the week with Bradley might not have happened. Somehow it was all Alan's fault.

"Are you all right?" His eyes were so concerned that she felt her own eyes blur, melt into tears.

"Quit asking me that. Obviously I'm not all right. You've been a lousy friend," she sobbed. He looked confused, puzzled, injured.

"I don't understand."

"No," she said, "you wouldn't. You're like every other man I've ever met—too wrapped up in yourself to give a damn what's going on in someone else's life. Look—it's late." She got up and walked to the front door. "Let's talk about this another time."

Diane watched comprehension kindle in his face. "You're in love with him."

You are so fucking stupid, she wanted to shout. But she was too exasperated for words. In the same instant, her perception of her impatience with him struck her with the force of revelation. Never before had she understood what she wanted from Alan all along. Now it was too late.

"What difference does it make?" she asked.

"It makes a hell of a lot of difference to me."

"It's too late."

"Oh, God—" Alan faltered. Diane closed the door when he indicated with a shake of his head that he wouldn't get up. "I never thought it would happen so fast. I always thought there'd be plenty of warning."

She shook her head. "No woman wants to be predictable."

"You had such high standards," he said. "No one ever measured up. I figured I'd win by default."

"I'm a romantic, Alan. Haven't you noticed?" She spoke wearily. "You can't talk process of elimination."

"Are you going to marry Bradley?"

"No."

"Will you marry me, then?"

"You don't have to do that, Alan." She smiled, touched by his effort to save her from despair. "I'll be all right—really."

"You don't understand, Diane. I love you. I always have." He looked at her earnestly. "You can't marry Bradley."

"What do you know about Bradley?"

"I can see he doesn't make you happy."

"You've got a point there." She was grateful for Alan's loyalty and concern. His face was so close that she could feel his breath. Diane had never studied his eyes so carefully. They were a beautiful forest green. They told her more than his words that he knew her better than anyone, better than Bradley, better than her mother or sister, who would have been frightened by the scope of her transformation into adulthood.

Diane's eyes filled with tears of gratitude and relief at being back home and having survived Bradley's dangerous game. It was comforting to know that in the vast, senseless universe she had contemplated on the lake in Maine, she mattered to someone. It was a miracle that a man could know her as well as Alan did and love her for what she was.

It was not confusing, kissing Alan. His beard felt perfectly natural on her face, softer than she had imagined. It surprised her that she had never touched it before. The soothing motion of his large hands on her back and shoulders filled an enormous void that had existed in her life up to that moment. She sniffled, smiled, touched his beard with both her hands as she studied his eyes. Alan kissed her throat. Her kimono had fallen open and his beard grazed her breasts. She unbuttoned one of the buttons of his shirt, barely conscious of what she was doing, as if weaving her fingers into the hair on his chest was an involuntary reflex to his caresses. With almost ethereal detachment, she noticed that his body was harder, more compact than Bradley's. What was happening was happening to another woman, and yet it was happening to her. Diane joyously embraced this onrushing of events. To accept what Alan said, and what he was doing, was to assert the freedom she had been so eager to give up, but Diane Yaeger was not afraid to contradict herself.

They made love, and to Diane, their lovemaking was a celebration of the unexpected. Alan's impetuosity was infectious. His intensity and heat were different from Bradley's, but to her surprise, she was quickly immersed in Alan's unexpected passion. When they were still, half off the couch, half clothed, out of breath, Diane could not help smiling. She had *never* expected this.

"What are you smiling about?" Alan looked down as they lay together.

"You. Me. Life. Everything."

"Will you take me seriously, Diane?"

"Oh yes. Very seriously."

He sat up beside her and kissed her exposed shoulder.

"I'm going to Minnesota Tuesday," she said.

"Is your mother worse?"

"I don't know. But I have to be with her. For a long time." Diane was trembling with exhaustion. "Alan, you should go now. I have to sleep." It did not occur to her that he would want to spend the night. Too much had happened in too short a time. She was not sorry about the change in their relationship, but she was incapable of absorbing its meaning.

"All right." He kissed her tenderly and moved away. "Are you going to see Bradley again?"

"Not for a while." She looked away. He stood up to go. She wondered if she would see Bradley again.

"Are you sure you're all right?"

"I'm fine, Alan. Just tired."

"Good night. I'll call you in the morning." He leaned over to kiss her, and then he was gone.

More than the concern in his words, his tenderness was unexpected. She had never done justice to Alan emotionally, she realized, closing the door behind him.

Despite the ending of one relationship and the beginning of another, there would be no lying awake thinking that night. She had reached an emotional saturation point. That she and Alan had made love made as much sense as the fact that Bradley was gone. Everything was what it seemed.

She opened a bedroom window. The breeze smelled of salt water. Drifting to sleep, Diane remembered the sun setting over the ocean. It seemed days earlier.

eleven

Diane went out at noon Monday to buy a *Post*. She wanted to read "Dear Abby." Invariably, anticipating the columnist's answers reaffirmed Diane's faith in her own common sense.

Dear Abby, she composed mentally as she walked in the warm sunshine down Montague Street, I met A, the man of my dreams, ten days ago. He's handsome, successful, well-to-do. We hit it off right away. After a torrid week, he left on a six-month business trip, friendly, but without any indication that I'll see him in the near future. B, a guy I've been "just friends" with since college, got wind of the affair. Now he's decided we've been more than friends all these years and wants to marry me. I'm tempted. Meanwhile, my mother's extremely ill in Minneapolis. What should I do? "Baffled in Brooklyn."

Dear Baffled, Diane answered her own question, go home.

On the way back to her apartment, Diane stopped at the cash machine. She had almost forty-three thousand dollars in her checking account, but there was no comfort in the extra digits. She wondered how she would repay Bradley. She would have to pay him for the hotel and airplane ticket too.

Back in her apartment, Diane made a reservation for a flight the next morning to Minneapolis. While she brewed a cup of coffee, she called home. Her sister answered.

"Hi." Lynn greeted her with deference. "I called Saturday night, but you weren't home."

"I was in Paris." Diane was so used to overwhelming her sister that her offhandedness was unconscious. "Was anything wrong?"

"Mom's worse. She was in the hospital last week."

"Why didn't you call?" Diane was angry and guilty at the same time.

"Mom said not to. She says you'll know when to come."

"I'm on the nine forty-five flight from New York tomorrow morning," Diane said. "Why was Mom in the hospital?"

"An operation to make her more comfortable. You know they never tell me anything." She hesitated, then said almost shyly, "I'm glad you're coming home, Diane."

"I can hardly wait." Diane's voice caught with emotion.

They said goodbye. Diane was too agitated to eat breakfast. Instead, she wrote Bradley. The note was deceptively difficult. It took four drafts to produce the simple message.

Dear John, she wrote. *Here's a check for the money I didn't spend. I'll send the rest as soon as I can. Good luck on the film.*

Diane wrote out a check for forty thousand dollars. She did not have the energy to balance her checkbook, and left enough money in the account for the checks she had given him in France and the trip to Minneapolis.

She put the check in an envelope with her note and went out to mail it. It seemed forever before she was back. She was exhausted. The simplest activity required excruciating effort. She could not imagine where she was going to get the energy to write the article on Bradley.

The afternoon sun filled the apartment. It was golden on the harbor, churning with commerce. Diane sat on the couch by an open window, leafing listlessly through the *Post*. Every sense, every cell in her body, sprang immediately alert when her eyes fell on the "Last Night in New York" page. There was a photograph of Bradley dancing with Susan Aldrich at Coco's the night before. They were having a good time, although the paper reported that the "socialite turned photographer" had smashed the reporter's camera and denounced journalists as "parasites" on real life. The caption heralded the couple as exemplars of the "new romanticism" and reported rumors of a fall wedding.

Susan Aldrich's comment about journalists irritated her more than the fact that Bradley had lied about going on to California. Bradley's act had a "just-like-a-man" weakness to it, while his photographer friend's observation was a distillation of her arrogance. Diane could hear the disdain in her voice; it made her face and neck tingle, as if she had been slapped.

Diane told herself that it wasn't the possibility of their marriage that hurt, though she knew she was jealous. She contemplated Susan Aldrich's beauty and elegance with numbing envy. They were well-matched. Facing the image of them together, Diane was left only with her anger. It terrified her that Bradley might have lied. She knew rationally that things might have come up to prevent his going on to California, but the idea of a prearranged meeting with Susan tormented her.

Like the clouds in the past week's skies, her emotions underwent rapid transformations as she stared out her window. Her anger was short-lived; it gave way to an overwhelming relief that she had not told Bradley she loved him. She had been right to hold it back. Things could have been worse. How could she be sure, anyway? She had distrusted the voice within that had urged her to share her ecstasy that first night in Paris; the forces of caution appeared admirably vindicated three days later.

Reason had a place too in the pageant of feelings that crisscrossed her troubled mind. She believed in giving people the benefit of the doubt. In the eye of the emotional storm, it occurred to her that he might have a number of logical excuses for having stayed in New York. Diane knew that she could not have flown another six hours to Los Angeles. She imagined him falling into bed at home, reluctantly awakened by Susan Aldrich's telephone call. Perhaps it had been easier to drag himself out of bed than to explain why he could not go out. Perhaps Bradley had wanted to tell Susan about their week together. She examined the photograph at close range. No. Susan Aldrich was having too good a time. Still, Diane did not believe they were engaged. It was plausible gossip, but Diane was

too good a judge of character to believe that Bradley had
lied.

Diane laughed when she considered her anger against
the backdrop of what had happened with Alan. He had
called first thing that morning, glowing in his new role of
lover. What would Bradley think? Diane imagined him
amused, above jealousy. She would not dwell on the
question of whether he would care. It was all too confusing. Events were disconnected. The world of "Last Night
in New York" had made way for the real world, the world
in which her mother was sick and Alan Jennings had
become her lover.

Who was John Bradley, Jr.? She knew nothing about
him. Diane did justice to this lack of knowledge. She was
not afraid of his separateness, his apartness. She knew the
feeling of suddenly being afraid of a man, but she was not
afraid of Bradley.

Sucker. Diane laughed out loud when the word popped
into her mind. She could not shake it. She had gambled.
She might be the tenth, she might be the fiftieth woman to
rally to Bradley's cry of "live dangerously." She thought
about the expression "to be had." It was ugly. It was
depersonalizing. It reduced her to the level of wine and
song. Diane winced at how easily she had given in to his
advances. All the insecurities acquired in her experience as
a woman came welling up from deep within, and she
wished sincerely that they had never met.

It was still light out when the telephone rang. She let it
ring. She had asked Alan not to call again. She knew it
was Bradley and was not sure she would be able to talk to
him. Panic shot through her limbs; her fingers and toes
tingled painfully as if they had been asleep.

"Diane?" Bradley's voice was thousands of miles away.

"Yes?" It was difficult for her to breathe.

"Have you recovered from last week?" His cheerfulness made her throat ache.

"Not really." She tried to swallow.

"I was too tired to go on last night. I flew out this
morning."

"I know."

"You know?"

"There was a picture of you and Susan Aldrich in the *Post*."

"Amazing. Susan made mince meat of that camera."

"They mentioned that."

"The good old *Post*." He was as much amused as upset. "What else did it say?"

"That you and Susan are getting married in the fall." Diane succeeded in keeping her voice emotionless.

"Mrs. Aldrich must have loved that."

Instead of being relieved at the absence of guilt in Bradley's voice, Diane fell prey to a sinking fear that Bradley might succumb to a double sexual standard when it came time to marry. He could make the mood vanish by saying that he missed her, but his own mood was obdurately cheerful.

"I wish you could come out to California and play" was the best he could manage.

"Me too." She chose to be literal-minded. "But I'm leaving for home in the morning."

"What's your number in Minneapolis?"

She gave it to him.

"Are you all set for the interview?"

"I'm at the studio. We're taping in half an hour."

"Are you nervous?"

"Yes." Just enough, she thought bitterly, to make him sparkle.

"When do you start on the movie?"

"Wednesday."

Diane caught her breath. Her pulse quickened. She was going to tell him that she would miss him.

"John—"

"Yes?" He had picked up on her tone, but his question pretended ignorance. The moment came and went. She would not go on without encouragement.

"I enjoyed last week very much," she said.

"So did I." He accepted the remark without dwelling on it. "I'll wink at you tonight." He was playful. "I'll put my right foot on my left knee and wink into the camera."

"I'll be watching." The promise was mechanical. "Good luck."

He said goodbye amiably and she hung up.

Sucker. She imagined an elfin, smirking old man whispering the taunt into her ear. The word reminded her of Popeye cartoons.

The question that came next to mind, a question she could not answer, was why she, any more than Bradley, should feel damaged by their fling. They were both consenting adults. They were both free to have a good time. Diane stopped at this thought. That was just their difference: Bradley was free, but she was not. It was not a question of money. Diane had lied to herself from the start about her ability to remain objective about Bradley's experiment. Underlying her sense of adventure was a false bravado and an insurmountable conservatism. It was going to take a supreme act of will to invoke the detachment she would need to write the article. A lot was at stake. Time was running out.

The sun was going down beyond the Statue of Liberty. With the sweet spring twilight coming in the open window, she tried to remember details about her week with Bradley. But her mother's illness distracted her like the tick of a noisy clock.

Diane got up, turned on a light, made up her mind that the article would be finished before Bradley's appearance on the "Tonight Show." She unplugged the phone, which made the apartment oppressively quiet. Her body begged for sleep. Her muscles shivered with fatigue. She made a pot of coffee and forced herself to eat half a container of blueberry yogurt.

There was an element of heroism in her single-minded determination to collect her thoughts and write an impartial, entertaining feature on Bradley. The author, always bluntly honest about her motives, would have been the first to point out that she had compromised herself enough without blowing an opportunity as important as this article. Something good had to come out of her gamble.

"There's something almost physically appealing about his arrogance," she began writing. "His self-assurance can be intimidating. He sees life as a game—a game he plays well. Yet John E. Bradley, Jr. is afraid of failure."

Diane did not want to hear Bradley's voice, so she wrote the article without listening to the tape-recorded interview. Once the introduction was on paper, the rest came easily. She wove a spell of objectivity with her words. The man she described bore little resemblance to the man she had spent the week with.

The article painted a sympathetic portrait of Bradley's relationship with his father. She wrote glowingly of Bradley's freedom. She recorded his standard apprehensions about his first extended trip to California. Finally, "this writer" predicted that more serious books would come from the novelist.

It was good. Diane typed it almost without revisions from her first handwritten draft. She was hungry after she finished, and ate a Swiss cheese sandwich and a MacIntosh apple in her bedroom while she packed.

The line-up that night would never make "The Best of the Tonight Show" series, which did not disappoint Diane. A comedian she had never seen before did imitations of the President. A country rock musician played a song she had never heard. An absurd Brazilian woman, apparently a singer, tried to make the audience laugh by mispronouncing words and transposing their order. The genius of the talk-show host was his ability to take each guest on his or her own level and enjoy them for who they were.

By the time Bradley was introduced, the commercials were coming every three minutes. He looked tired and ill-at-ease. It was strange, watching his conversation with the host, to realize that she was really watching a tape, an image of a conversation, no more real than the photograph in the newspaper that afternoon, hardly more real than the image of him she had just completed in her article. Diane laughed, but Bradley did not crack a smile when the Brazilian singer told him coyly that his book was "frightful."

The host protected his guests and audience from Bradley's haughtiness by taking the offensive against him. He described briefly, without insulting the intelligence of the viewers, what Bradley's father had done, and then asked a question that amounted to "What was it like to grow up in the shadow of a distinguished intellectual?" Bradley could not contain his annoyance.

"I would hardly call my father's name a household word," he said testily.

"What did your father think of the book?"

Bradley looked on the verge of asking what difference it made, but said instead, "I doubt if he read it."

"I understand you got more than half a million dollars for the screen rights."

"That's correct," he answered, and then looked irritated for having given out the information.

"What are you going to do with all that money?" Before anyone could find out, they broke for dogfood and floor wax commercials.

Bradley did a miserable job. Diane felt sorry for his publicist as he missed one opportunity after another to plug the book. He came across as a prig. She was not sorry for his poor performance.

Bradley was the last guest. The host got off on his timing and the program ended abruptly. Diane turned the television off. She had forgotten to watch for his wink, but was fairly sure she would have seen it if he had remembered. She wondered what he had said to the Brazilian singer after the show. Maybe they were having dinner together.

Diane's senses were glutted with thinking of Bradley. It exhausted her. The only thing that mattered to her that moment was that she had written a damned good article. Though she did not believe that the end necessarily justified the means, the article had a certain salvage value.

Deeply satisfied with the evening's work, she turned off the lights, took her clothes off, and lay in bed. Work made her peaceful for the first time that day. In the warm spring night, Diane surrendered to memories of childhood, of first love, of the simple life before Bradley and Alan.

PART TWO

_____ *twelve*

With her long, straight blonde hair, Lynn Yaeger looked right at home waving across the waiting room filled with German- and Scandinavian-Americans. The sisters embraced. Diane, certain of Lynn's pleasure at seeing her, was magnanimous in her affection, like a celebrity returning home of her own free will. Diane had never been so happy to see her.

"How long are you staying?" Lynn asked, as they headed to the baggage-claim area.

"As long as you need me. I took leave without pay from the paper."

"The doctor says Mom doesn't have long. It's hard to believe, though. She looks more beautiful than ever, like her eyes are getting their light from the inside."

Lynn's fiancé, Mark, was waiting for them in the car. Diane stood on tiptoes to kiss him when the thick-featured, dark-haired young man got out to put her suitcase in the trunk of his old Impala. The streets on the way home were wet but clear; the snow on the houses and lawns was patchy, week-old. Spring was further away here, but there was a hint of it in the noonday sun.

"Is there still snow in New York?" Lynn was proud of the snow. It belonged to her town.

"We haven't had snow for a month. And the jonquils were out in Paris."

"Diane was in Paris last week." She touched Mark's

165

arm and he glanced sideways. Her look indicated that that
sort of trip was not at all uncommon for her sister. Diane
could never resist Lynn's ready awe.

The Yaegers' was a large Victorian house, all white
wood. The ivy-covered house had a sprawling front porch,
and was shaded in summer by several magnificent oak
trees. Never, as an unnoticing child, or later, with the
strained status of houseguest, had the house seemed more
beautiful to Diane than at that moment. It had an animate,
almost human air as if it were a friendly soul, and the
Yaegers were but one in a succession of bodies to give it
life. It had been a privilege to share in the spirit of this
house.

"It's so nice to be back." Diane turned to Lynn on the
walkway to the front porch. They linked arms.

"Mom's staying on the sunporch now," she whispered
to Diane. "She has trouble with the stairs."

Diane found her mother sitting on a daybed in the
glassed-in porch, surrounded by potted plants and flowers.
She hugged her tightly, buried her face on her shoulder,
and swallowed her tears. Her mother held her with a
rocking motion and patted her elder daughter on the back.
When she heard Lynn whisper to Mark to take her suitcase
up to the guest room, Diane leaned back to look into her
mother's eyes. They had become an almost transparent
blue. They radiated joy at seeing Diane.

"I'm so glad to see you, Mom," Diane said.

"I'm glad you're here." Her mother squeezed her.

"I should have come sooner."

"I wanted to call two weeks ago." Lynn ignored a
warning glance from her mother.

"What happened?"

"You'll have to ask the doctor," her mother dismissed
the question. "I've lost track at this point. Something was
blocked. Liver, pancreas. I forget. I felt better for a couple
of days after the operation."

"You look good." Diane sat back on the bed and
examined her. Emma Yaeger had always been thin. Diane
estimated that she had lost fifteen pounds since Christmas.
She did not look ill, but her face was gaunt. With gray hair
pulled behind her head, she looked older than fifty-nine.
Her deep blue eyes had grown to dominate the Scandina-

vian features of her handsome face. "You could be the heroine in a Bergman movie," Diane laughed.

"But his movies are depressing," Lynn said.

"Not all of them."

"It doesn't matter," her mother said. "I'm just glad you're home." She kissed Diane. Her breath smelled metallic. Her skin was cold.

"Mark and I have a one o'clock class," Lynn said. "We have to get back to school."

"Diane can babysit." Mrs. Yaeger smiled. "Why don't you two take the evening off? Mark, take Lynn somewhere nice for dinner. It'll be my treat. My purse is over behind the chair."

"That's okay, Mrs. Yaeger, we can eat at my folks'."

Lynn kissed her mother and sister goodbye.

"Are you hungry?" Mrs. Yaeger asked. Mark's car started up in the driveway.

"Starving. What can I make you for lunch?"

"Just a cup of tea." She followed her daughter into the kitchen. Large and sunny, it combined character with convenience. "The tea is in the cabinet over the sink."

"I didn't know there was such a thing as decaffeinated tea." Diane studied the label on the box.

"Cancer's robbed me of my last vice."

"How do you feel?"

"Pretty bad, most of the time. Today I feel fine, though." She walked up behind her daughter, put her arms around her waist, and gave her a hug.

"Are you taking any painkillers?"

"Only when it gets really bad."

"I don't believe this refrigerator," Diane said as she peered in. "It reminds me of summer vacations during college."

"I was trying to bribe you into coming home," her mother said, smiling, seating herself carefully at the kitchen table. She wore a full-length navy-blue flannel robe.

Diane took out roast beef and ham, Swiss and Wisconsin cheddar cheese, pumpernickel and rye bread, pickles, cole slaw, potato salad, tomatoes, lettuce, mustard, an apple, and a half gallon of whole milk (no one in Minnesota drank skim milk) and built two sandwiches side by side.

"I'm hungry."

"So I see."

Diane filled the tea pot with water and set it on the stove. Electric burners struck her as Midwestern.

"Can I fix you something?" Diane asked.

"No thanks. I'm fine."

"Are you still doing chemotherapy?"

"Oh no, I quit that before Christmas. I felt awful. The doctor wanted me to keep going. But I don't think it was doing much good or he would have put up more of a fight."

"Is it any better, since you quit?"

"I felt much better, until recently. Dr. Harris wants me back in the hospital. But I have a feeling the next time I go in will be the last. I feel like Lady Dracula as it is, going in for my weekly transfusion."

"When did that start?"

"January."

"No one said anything." Diane poured hot water over a teabag in her mother's cup, added milk, brought the tea and her sandwiches over to the table.

"I feel guilty eating in front of you."

"Don't." Mrs. Yaeger reached over and put her hand on her daughter's. "This may sound funny, but I've loved watching you and Lynn eat ever since you were babies. When your father and I used to watch documentaries on the war on Sunday afternoons, what haunted me most about the idea of being a refugee was seeing your children hungry. I would have killed first."

Diane was surprised by her mother's vehemence.

"The house looks great." Diane spoke with a mouthful of sandwich.

"Lynn's been so good. She's done the housecleaning, the shopping, the chauffeuring, and the nursing."

"I should have come sooner. I'm sorry." Diane's sudden dejection prompted her mother to assuage her guilt.

"Nonsense. Lynn lives here. You've got your life in New York."

"I should have come, though." Exonerated, she could indulge in her guilt.

"You have to do what you have to do," her mother said. "I stay home. You want to be a famous journalist.

Lynn loves helping people. The only thing that nags at me about Lynn is I wonder if I conditioned her to be dutiful before she was old enough to know better.''

"Lynn was born with a sweet disposition. Luckily, she's so far beyond me in generosity, I've never felt guilty about it.''

Her mother's laughter faded abruptly. "Lynn's had a hard time the last couple of months."

"Are you afraid?"

Mrs. Yaeger nodded. "Yes. But it's manageable. It reminds me of the way I felt when I was pregnant with you. I was afraid then, too. But I remember looking at myself in the mirror one day—I was big—and thinking to myself, Emma, you're going to have to go through with this. I felt panicky at first, but once I realized there was no turning back, I relaxed. I wasn't afraid anymore. I was even a little curious about what it would be like. When I went into labor, my impulse was like Christ's in the Garden of Gethsemane, you know, Lord let this cup be removed from my lips. But once the hard work started, I forgot all about being afraid. The anticipation is the worst part. Having you, I discovered a strength within me I never suspected. I still have it.''

The analogy of pregnancy and cancer revolted Diane. She rebelled angrily against her mother's acceptance.

Only this time, you won't survive the delivery, she thought, staring at her plate.

"It isn't fair," Diane said.

"Everything means something to God," Mrs. Yaeger declared.

"You believe that?" Diane asked impatiently. Reconsidering, she squeezed her mother's hand. Mrs. Yaeger looked tired. She had not touched her tea. "Want some milk?" she asked her mother.

"If you're having some."

"Go sit on the couch and I'll bring it in."

Her mother lifted herself up from the table with painful deliberateness. She looked old.

"There are some chocolate chip cookies in the cookie jar," her mother called. Diane piled cookies on a plate and brought them out with glasses of milk. Religion had always been for people who could not face life the way it was. This revelation of her mother's strength was unsettling.

"Are you happy about Lynn and Mark's engagement?" Diane sat beside her mother on the bed. The sun porch had three walls of windows with a view of the wooded backyard, where an archipelago of muddy islands dotted melting snow.

"He's so nice. And he loves Lynn. I'm sure they'll have a good marriage. They're going to live in the house."

"I'm glad," Diane said reflectively.

"She loves the house the way I do. Of course if there's anything you want—china, the furniture, maybe—"

Diane smiled. "If I ever live in a house, I'd like Dad's desk." From childhood, Diane had loved the pigeonholes, the rollback cover, the tilted writing surface, the ubiquitous drawers. "What's the date of the wedding?"

"June sixth. But I don't know how they'll get anything done with me around. It took me three hours yesterday afternoon to make those cookies. It's discouraging."

That she had worked so hard touched Diane.

"We'll have a lot of fun, planning," Diane said.

"I want everything to be perfect for her," Mrs. Yaeger said. "I worry more about her being happy."

"Have you given up on me?" The associations in the taste of the cookie Diane bit into were comforting.

"I don't think it matters much to you whether or not you're happy." Mrs. Yaeger sipped her milk.

"No one wants to be unhappy."

"No, but you wouldn't let it interfere with your game plan."

"You make me sound callous." Diane was too vulnerable for criticism from her mother. "Just because you keep going doesn't mean you don't suffer."

"Your father never suffered."

"You make too much of our similarities." Diane's protest had an edge to it. Mrs. Yaeger was occasionally prone to self-pity, an emotion her daughter would not tolerate. "Dad didn't believe in your Satan. He organized evil out of existence. He was too busy for it."

"Sometimes I think he had the right idea," her mother sighed.

"I can't admire a man who blinds himself."

"You *are* deeper than your father. But you have his fearlessness. You won't live your life the way I have, afraid of everything."

"I'm sorry I've depressed you." Reaching for another cookie, Diane felt that her apology sounded insincere.

"I'm the one who should feel guilty," her mother said, "unburdening myself on you like this. But it feels wonderful. I'm sure Lynn would let me talk, but I can't get over wanting to protect her. I know it's selfish on my part to want to prolong her innocence—"

"Not so much selfish as useless. Lynn is an adult."

"Take care of her, Diane. She has as hard a time expressing herself as you or I do, but she needs you."

"She'll be fine. Look how well she's done here."

"You hate to see your children suffer." Mrs. Yaeger's eyes were bright with tears. "Especially when it's your fault."

"It's okay, Mom." Diane put an arm around her. "She'll have a spectacular wedding."

"I'm afraid I'll spoil it for her," Mrs. Yaeger spoke sadly.

"You're tired, Mom." Diane massaged her mother's shoulder. "You need some rest."

"I was so excited about your coming home, I couldn't sleep last night."

"Why don't you eat something?"

"How were the cookies?" Her mother rubbed the back of her pale hand wearily over her eyes.

"Great."

"Maybe I'll try one."

Diane held the plate for her.

"These *are* good," Mrs. Yaeger chewed the cookie, settling back against a pillow. "what have you been doing in New York?"

"The most amazing thing happened last week." Diane had not expected to tell her mother about the interview with Bradley, but before she knew it, she was giving a bowdlerized account of her first date with Bradley and his subsequent proposition. Mrs. Yaeger's smile faded at the mention of her having taken the money, but curiosity overcame disapproval.

"Tell me all about it." Her illness was forgotten.

Diane searched her mother's burning eyes and saw that she was sincere. She took care to capture the past with words. Once she admitted that she had fallen in love with

Bradley, her mother heaved a sigh of relief and fell totally under the spell of the story.

"I wish you'd called to tell us to watch the 'Tonight Show,' " her mother said when the narrative had been brought up to date. "When will you see him again?"

"I'm not sure." Diane hesitated. "He's in California making the movie."

Mrs. Yaeger frowned at her daughter's evasiveness.

"Does he know how you feel?"

Her accusatory tone made Diane flinch.

"Diane—"

"Well—"

"You didn't tell him?" The lines in her mother's face aligned themselves to communicate concern.

"You can't tell a man you've only known a week you love him." Her mother's eyes were too intense. Diane looked away.

"Why not, if it's true?"

"Not if he doesn't want to hear."

"You can take fifty thousand dollars from him, but you can't tell him how you feel." She shook her head. "You talked so much about honesty when you were in college."

"You think I blew it?" Diane swallowed uncomfortably.

"Everything moves so fast nowadays," her mother reflected. "I made your father wait for two years because deep down he wanted a nice girl. Then the war came along and we lost six of our best years. I've often wondered if waiting was the right thing. I was thirty when we got married."

"I'll be thirty pretty soon."

"I thought you'd never fall in love." Her mother smiled.

"I've been in love before."

"Not with anyone who's challenged you."

"I'm not sure anything will come of it"—Diane was suddenly tired of talking about Bradley—"except maybe indirectly. Alan Jennings proposed."

"Finally." Mrs. Yaeger had met Diane's friend twice: at Diane's graduation from college and once later on an assignment in Minneapolis. "Are you interested?"

"I don't think I could marry a friend."

"There's a lot to be said for it. Lynn and Mark were friends and look how comfortable they are. I was more like you. I wanted the opposite of myself. In some ways, Bill was a stranger to me his whole life. There were mysteries he wouldn't share.''

''Alan can be a stranger that way, too,'' Diane said. ''For all the years we've been friends, he gets into moods— there's one crazy laugh in particular—when it makes me nervous to be alone with him.''

''I like Alan. He would leave you room to be yourself.''

''I'm not sure I don't want to be made over.'' Her mother nodded. She understood. ''I want love to change me, to make me better—deeper, less selfish, more beautiful—something.''

''That's not too much to ask.''

''Would it be better to marry a friend than not to marry at all?'' Diane was not sure how her mother would answer the question.

Her mother frowned, cleared her throat, watched a bird dancing on a shrub outside. ''I can't tell you categorically not to compromise. Look at Trudy—'' Diane's aunt, her father's older sister, a divorcee in her early seventies. ''She married Jack Swensen for love.''

''Wasn't he involved in some crooked real-estate dealings?''

Mrs. Yaeger nodded. ''It was just before the war. The poor man never even stood trial for the scam, but Trudy couldn't forgive him for not living up to her standards. He was basically a good man, but Trudy gave up the chance to have a family rather than accept his moment of weakness. I've always thought Trudy made a big mistake. Never trust a woman who tells you marriage and children aren't important.''

''But Trudy's enjoyed herself.''

''Trudy's read too many magazines and seen too many movies. I used to plead with your father when you were little not to leave you alone with her, but he said you'd get exposed to people with unrealistic expectations sooner or later.''

''But as long as Trudy isn't sorry for not having compromised—''

''Your aunt has the Yaeger knack for bending the facts to suit her own point of view. She's quite pleased with her life. In fact, I'm not sure she doesn't prefer keeping house for a widower brother to having made her marriage work.''

"What happened to Jack Swensen?"

"He married again to a very nice woman. One of his daughters goes to school with Lynn.''

"I have to put these cookies away." Diane put down her fifth cookie after a bite. "More tea?" Diane raised her voice in the kitchen.

"No, I'll finish this milk.''

Diane put the kettle on for herself.

"You have to see John Bradley again." Mrs. Yaeger was decisive. "Does he know how to reach you here?"

"Yes." She stood at the kitchen doorway. "But he won't call. It would be too personal.''

"Can you be any more personal than you've already been?"

"Yes.''

"Could you drift apart then?"

"It happens. Maybe he'll call when he's back in New York.''

"A good man is worth going after.''

"You sound like Trudy.''

"This must be love," Mrs. Yaeger said. "I've never seen anyone shake your self-confidence so completely.''

"I'll be honest. I *do* care. A lot. But there's such a thing as self-defense. I've gone halfway.''

"I'd say you've gone 'all the way,' " her mother said, smiling.

They talked all afternoon, mother and daughter: about family—aunts and uncles and cousins; about the farm—new combines and a burned-down barn, the bad winter and federal crop subsidies. About Lynn, the wedding, her chances of getting into veterinary school. Diane gave her mother's update the rapt attention a Victorian reader might have given the latest installment of a Dickens novel. In Minnesota, the real world was still a meaningful concept.

Diane regretted the life she had given up. It seemed to her, that afternoon, that she had exchanged authenticity for illusion. Even her mother's illness had an honesty lacking in any aspect of her relationship with Bradley. When she contemplated her mother's condition, her first reaction had been panic. Time had run out. She had waited too long to come home. Her mother was dying, and her daughter yearned to be a tape recorder, capturing every word of this flood of past and present in their conversation.

Diane was ashamed when she realized that there had always been a trace of condescension in her love for her mother, an intellectual superiority to her piety, her sense of place, her enthusiastic housewifery. As the afternoon wore on, this was supplanted by a surge of pride at being Emma Yaeger's daughter. Her mother had never looked more beautiful than in this sun-filled room. Her pale porcelain skin, fine silver hair, and deep, wise eyes set in dark circles made her look dignified.

Diane's sense of time passing too quickly subsided. She felt herself relaxing. She entered a universe in which there would be enough time to study every beautiful detail of her mother's face, enough time to ask the questions she had always wanted to ask and the ones she had never thought about asking until now.

Emma Yaeger had stepped into the same universe. Their appreciation, one for the other, was complete. That Diane would not have time, or remember to tell her mother, would not matter, because her mother accepted everything in advance. A barrier came down between them, and Diane came face to face with the sheer animal intensity of the mother-daughter relationship, the impossibility of their not loving each other. This maternal love was both frightening and exhilarating. The only thing that diminished Diane's joy was the sense that she could not requite her mother's love in equal strength. Her mother had been conscious of the bond so much earlier; her experience of it was undiluted by the self-centeredness of childhood. But the essence of her mother's love was its gratuity, and Diane drank it in like a plant that had barely survived a season of drought.

Mrs. Yaeger lost strength as the sun grew low and disappeared behind a neighbor's roof. She was barely visible by the time they fell silent. Diane was exhausted. Her mother closed her eyes, dreamily, it seemed to her daughter, and leaned against the wall. When she opened them, it was as if she remembered something unpleasant. Even in the dim room, Diane saw the color drain from her face. Mrs. Yaeger got to her feet and started unsteadily to the bathroom. She was sick to her stomach. Diane's impulse was to help, but an instinctive delicacy held her back. Her mother was so discreet; she dreaded imposing. Diane was shocked by the violence of the nausea that racked her. She overcame reticence and crossed the front hall to the bathroom door.

"Damn this body," she heard her mother whisper, between seizures.

"Mom." Diane tapped at the door.

"I'll be out in a minute, dear."

"Can I help?" The door was locked.

"I'll be right out."

"Please, Mother."

Mrs. Yaeger unlocked the door without getting up from where she sat on the carpeted floor, her legs collapsed beneath her, her face resting on an arm draped along the toilet bowl. Beads of perspiration stood out on her forehead and temples. Diane could not tell if she was shivering or crying, but the nausea appeared to have subsided. Diane was frightened. The sickness had come so suddenly, had been so absolute.

"Are you okay?"

Her mother did not look up.

"Let me help you back to bed."

"I can't get up," Mrs. Yaeger said. She buried her face in her arm. It was impossible to lift the ill woman without her cooperation.

Diane urged her gently: "Stand up."

Her mother's arm over her shoulder was cold and trembling. Straining with exertion, they did not speak until Mrs. Yaeger was back in bed.

"Does that happen often?" Diane covered the older woman with a blanket.

"Only when I eat." She smiled weakly.

"Is there some medicine for it?"

"Yes." Mrs. Yaeger spoke like a nondrinker who was going to make an exception because company had come. "There's a bottle of pills on top of the refrigerator. I'll take two with some water."

"What caused that?" Diane asked. Her mother tossed her head back and swallowed the pills.

"You'll have to ask the doctor for details," she said.

"He'll be by in the morning. I think my system is gradually being poisoned by something. Normally it has a deadening effect. But sometimes there's nausea. It feels wonderful when it's gone. Heaven can't possibly be any better than the way I feel when the pain stops. When it gets bad, I believe a person can be possessed by the devil. Sometimes I beg God to let me die, it hurts so much. Then it goes away and one of my African violets has bloomed or Lynn gets a B plus in organic chemistry or you get an article published. Then I want to fight to stay alive and I'm afraid of dying again."

"I was scared for you." In the dark room, Diane recovered from a child's fear.

"The nice thing about pain is, the Lord doesn't give you more than you can bear."

Suffering would never lead Diane to faith.

Mrs. Yaeger soon slept a drugged sleep—shallow, even, unrestorative.

Diane went upstairs to her old room—the guest room now. The obverse of Shakespeare's "All's well that ends well" struck her. The serenity of the communion of mother and daughter was shattered by the image of the woman huddled abjectly on the bathroom floor. Diane was drained of nostalgia.

Mrs. Yaeger had not allowed the room to remain a museum of Diane's childhood. Dolls, stuffed animals, the posters, had been methodically packed, labeled, and consigned to the attic. Her suitcase laid on the only trace of the former occupant, a four-poster bed. Even the sketches of horses done during a teenaged summer on the farm had been replaced by hand-painted Victorian illustrations of plants and flowers.

Lynn's bedroom was intact. Turning on the light, Diane surveyed a room into which an entire lifetime had been crammed with charming disorder. Toys and books were piled on a footlocker sent generations before from Sweden, stenciled with their great-grandmother's name and the address St. Paul, North America. There was evidence of a more protracted horse stage, possibly not yet outgrown, and an interest in spectator sports indicated by a wall covered with pennants. Heaped upon these inchoate fossils of a young girl's life were the textbooks accumulated during four years of college. Diane wondered what idea a future archaeologist would form about modern civilization from the relics in her sister's room.

Diane turned off the lights and lay on her bed, too tired to sleep. Her mind raced. Her body shivered with exhaustion. She lapsed into a semi-conscious state. Thoughts flashed through her mind like shooting stars, obliterating themselves as quickly as they flared up. Insights flowed past her and disappeared, a waterfall into a vast abyss. When she heard Lynn and Mark downstairs, she was relieved to be rescued from her sterile reverie.

"What time is it?" Diane squinted on the stairway.

"Eight-thirty," Mark answered.

"Were you asleep?" Lynn asked.

Diane shook her head.

"How was Mom?"

"Fine all afternoon. Then about six she got sick. She said it was the cookies we were eating."

"She's hardly eaten anything the past week." Lynn looked concerned.

"She felt better after she took a couple of the pills on top of the refrigerator.

"A couple? She must have really felt bad." Lynn's face fell.

The sisters peeked into their mother's room. She was sleeping peacefully. Her face was untroubled. Diane felt close to her sister.

They made coffee and drank it in the room Lynn called the den, because they watched television there. Their mother called it the study, because of the massive desk at which Bill Yaeger had paid bills each month for thirty-five years. Diane called it the library, because the walls were lined with bookshelves. Mark built a fire.

"Could you be ready to get married on Saturday?" The question surprised Lynn and Mark.

"It's only two months until June," Lynn protested.

Diane was surprised, too, but a plan was taking shape in her mind. "Mom's really sick." Diane considered telling Lynn that their mother would not live two months, but said instead: "She thinks she'll spoil it. She can't trust herself. Worrying will only make it worse."

"Three days from now?" Mark sounded incredulous.

"Uncle Bob can swing the paperwork," Diane dismissed the objection. Their father's older brother was a lawyer.

"We have to meet with the minister, reserve the church. What if someone's already got it?" The excitement kindling in Lynn's eyes belied her reservations.

"Church? I think we should have the ceremony at home," Diane said. "Pastor Schulze would let you."

"Mark?" It was apparent that Lynn could be persuaded.

"My parents were going away this weekend." He paused, thinking about Saturday. "I've got a midterm Monday."

"Your parents will understand," Diane said.

"You can get out of the exam if you tell him why." Lynn's cheerfulness faded from her lips as she turned to her sister. "What about Mom, if we move the date up?"

"It's worse for her not knowing how she'll be in June."

Lynn jumped up, went over to the rolltop desk, and returned to the table with paper and pen. "Diane, help me make a list of what we have to do."

The two sisters would tell their mother in the morning. Diane would: see their uncle in the morning to implement the legalities; invite the Yaegers' relatives; contact Pastor Schulze; get their mother's wedding gown to a tailor for rehabilitation; find gowns for the bridesmaids—their cousin Sue and Diane. Diane was also in charge of organizing a rehearsal dinner for Friday evening. A minimum of nine people would be down from the Pine City farms, so Diane would book rooms at a nearby motel.

The prospective newlyweds were to execute the duties most directly related to their union: blood tests, license, announcement list, honeymoon plans.

"What do you think of light blue dresses for the bridesmaids?" She turned to Diane. "Mark, you take care of the tuxes." It amused Diane to see the couple so animated. At eleven o'clock, Mark left, promising to tell his parents that evening. Lynn walked him to the door. She struck Diane that moment as a woman ready for life, comfortable with the future. Diane had never noticed this confidence in her sister.

"You're lucky" Diane said when Lynn returned. "Even at four years old, you were comfortable." Diane pointed to a family photo on the desk. "I wish I knew your secret."

"You just have to be stupid, I guess."

"I wish I knew you better." Diane was not sidetracked by Lynn's self-deprecating joke.

"I've always felt like I knew you," Lynn said. "You left a lot of yourself behind."

"Not nearly enough." Diane smiled ruefully and sat down on the couch beside her sister. "Today I feel like I made a terrible mistake."

"You had to leave," Lynn said. "You're like our great-grandparents, a pioneer looking for a better life. I'm the type that never would have left the Old World."

Diane inhaled with emotion. "I had a vision of myself this morning at the airport dragging my roots with me in suitcases or slinging them over my arm like my suitbag."

"You can always come here." Diane heard pride and tenderness in her sister's voice. "I'm not going anywhere."

"I've been such a lousy big sister."

"That's not true."

"Has it been hard since Dad died?" Diane asked abruptly.

"Not until Mom got sick. When she dies, I don't know what I'll do."

"You've already accepted it, haven't you?" Diane realized that the question was reproachful.

Her sister nodded. "I don't want it to last, either. It hurts to see her suffer."

Diane rebelled at talking as if their mother was already dead. "You talk like Mom's a sick animal you could put to sleep," Diane said angrily.

"I'm sorry. It's just that she's always been the one to protect us from all the awful things. It's been hard, for both of us, having the tables turned. Do you think I'm too young to get married?"

"No." Diane did not hesitate. "You were never meant to live alone."

"A chicken." Lynn smiled.

"No, a woman who needs to live for other people. Mark is worth living for."

"So are you, Diane. When you need us, we'll always be here."

"Thanks."

Lynn kissed her sister and went upstairs.

Before going to bed, Diane looked in on her mother. There was enough moonlight to illuminate Mrs. Yaeger's face. Her eyes were open wide. She appeared to concentrate on her breathing.

"How do you feel?" Diane whispered.

"I have two states, sleeping and aching. What time is it?"

"Almost midnight."

"What have you and Lynn been talking about?"

"The wedding. She's decided to get married Saturday."

"That's wonderful." The flatness in her mother's tone made the reaction sound ironic. Diane remembered from childhood the disappointment she felt when her mother was not as excited as she had expected.

"We'll have the wedding in the living room. What do you think?"

"The house hasn't been cleaned properly in months. Lynn does the best she can, but how can a student who works as hard as she does find time to scrub woodwork and wash windows?" There was a hint of peevishness in the observation.

"I've got nothing to do for the next three days except plan a small wedding," Diane said cheerfully.

"Thank you, Diane." Her mother was falling asleep. The disproportion between the content of her words and the monotone in which she spoke them was eerie. Smoothing the gray hair on her mother's forehead, she squeezed her hand. The older woman was asleep when she leaned over to kiss her good night.

thirteen

Diane saw her Uncle Bob the next morning. He got up from his desk and came forward to embrace her. There was something almost sinister in his physical resemblance to her father. Certain mannerisms—a half wink following a humorous remark, a sniffle before a serious observation, a vigorous nod as he listened—invariably renewed her sense of the loss of her father.

"When did you get home?"

"Yesterday."

"How's Emma?"

"The doctor wants to put her back in the hospital. Mom says there's nothing they can do for her. And she won't go now. Lynn's going to be married Saturday. Will you give her away?"

He was torn between pleasure and concern for his sister-in-law. "The wedding so soon?"

"The doctor thinks Saturday is a good idea. Mom isn't eating."

He stiffened formally and took a deep breath. Through the window behind him the dome of the state capitol glowed golden in the sunlight. "Of course I'll give her away—and if there's anything else I can do—"

As she had expected, he agreed to host a rehearsal dinner on Friday evening. Diane would take care of the invitations, he would stock the bar, and Aunt Trudy would make the dinner.

Diane took careful notes on the legal paperwork preceding marriage. The doctor had taken blood samples at the house that morning. Bob Yaeger assured her that all the papers could be ready by Saturday. They called Trudy on the speakerphone.

"Trudy, Bob here." The greeting struck Diane as clipped, Germanic.

"You sound like you're calling long distance." Trudy had the raspy voice of a heavy smoker.

"I'm on the squawk box. Diane's here."

"Diane—" The old woman was pleased. Of her two nieces, Diane interested her more. It was understood between them that they were "women of the world." Trudy was the only relative who had visited Diane in Paris. The aunt firmly believed that her favored niece had as much to gain from her experience as she had to gain from Diane's.

"What brings you out to the hinterlands?" It did not occur to Trudy that the visit might be connected to her mother's health.

"Mom's not doing well."

"Lynn and Mark are getting married on Saturday, Trudy," Bob interjected. "Could you and I put a rehearsal dinner together at our house Friday evening for Mark's folks and the Pine City people?"

"Would they mind doing low carbohydrates?" Trudy was constantly trying new diets, though she was thin to start with and drank without shame whatever the diet.

"If we throw in dessert and let people drink coffee, I'm sure they'll survive." Bob winked her father's wink at Diane. She turned away.

"I suppose we can put a little oil in the salad dressing, too," Trudy thought out loud. "It wouldn't be fair to impose my vinegar and garlic dressing on the farmers. They like their butter." Trudy's rabid anti-butter views were not popular with her sister-in-law's family.

"How about eight o'clock Friday?" Bob was addressing his niece, but Trudy answered.

"Wonderful. Will you need me at the rehearsal?"

Bob looked at Diane, who wondered if her aunt was hinting at a role in the ceremony. "I don't think so. It's going to be pretty simple."

"I hope I'll see you before Friday." Trudy's tone implied that there was a lot to talk over in private. "Why don't you come over for a drink tomorrow night, say eight o'clock." There was something imperative about the invitation. Diane accepted and while her uncle concluded the conversation with Trudy, she glanced through a *Brides* magazine for ideas. She thought of Bradley suddenly for no particular reason and tried to remember where they had been the week before. Maine. It seemed a lifetime ago. She wondered what Bradley was doing that moment in California.

"I've got the whole menu right here," her uncle said after hanging up.

"I'll have to be surprised—" Diane stood up. "I'm late meeting Lynn. I'll see you tomorrow night." They kissed each other goodbye.

The streets were quiet compared to New York and the crowds light. It was a sunny day, warm by Minnesota standards, though Diane could still see her breath. The streets and sidewalks were clear but wet. Lynn was waiting at the main entrance of the department store.

Neither sister enjoyed shopping, but the desire to make the wedding perfect imbued them with a sense of mission. They were looking for a blue dress for Diane to wear, but fell in love with a peach-colored gown. At Lynn's urging, Diane tried on a dozen spring hats, but they decided against all of them. At the jewelry counter, Diane bought Lynn a string of pearls, at the perfume counter a bottle of *Je reviens*. She talked her sister into buying a fleece-lined aviator's jacket and a pair of baggy beige pants for her honeymoon.

They ate quiche lorraine and salad and drank Perrier water at a stylish café, more quaint than any of the Parisian cafés she and Bradley had been in. Lynn pressed her sister for details about the trip, but Diane changed the subject to her visit with their uncle, and confided that his physical resemblance to their father upset her.

"Sometimes I see Dad in Bob," Lynn agreed. "But I like being reminded of Dad. It's like a part of him is still here."

"Do you see any of *me* in you?"

"I can't imagine being you." Lynn shook her head. "I could never be so much on my own."

"I'm sick of doing things the hard way." Diane was suddenly bitter. "You and I were born into a lot of love. You saved yours and invested it. I've squandered mine on myself. So it's my fault I'm not happy."

"You loved us in a special way," Lynn said, "we know that. You are independent partly because it made Dad happy. I used to get jealous of how proud he was of you. He kept every article you ever wrote.

"Is that true?" Diane colored with pleasure at the idea. "Dad never talked about feelings."

"You had to love him on faith." Lynn smiled.

"I resented that. Maybe there was nothing underneath."

"He had a hard time as a kid," the younger daughter defended him.

"Still"—Diane was not entirely forgiving—"if you don't know your father, who can you know?"

"Very few people. Maybe no one, unless you're lucky."

"Am I lucky?" Diane looked hard at her sister.

"You know me and Mom."

"Do I?"

She nodded, putting a piece of quiche into her mouth. "There's no great mystery to us."

"What about me?" Diane asked. "Do you understand me?"

"You're simpler than you think." Lynn was serenely confident. "You want the people who know you to love you."

Lynn might have begged the question of how they knew her, but Diane found her sister's conviction that she was knowable, and lovable, heartening. This newly noticed sensitivity filled Diane with affection. After dropping her off at the courthouse to meet Mark, she drove home to telephone their relatives about the wedding.

Mrs. Yaeger was humming as she watered plants on the sun porch when Diane came in the front door. In the foyer, the vacuum cleaner stood in a nest of hose. The furniture in the living room had been polished.

"What are you doing up?"

"I don't have to stay in bed you know." Her eyes sparkled. "There's a lot to do."

"Let me take care of that." Diane spoke with authority.

"Trudy's housekeeper can come Friday. You just work on the dress. Lynn is dying to try it on."

"She's an inch and a half taller than I am, but the dress is so long, it doesn't matter."

Diane unpacked her bridesmaid's dress and held it against herself. Her mother liked it.

"It's so wonderful having you both here." She kissed her daughter. "It reminds me of when you dated in high school. I never fell asleep until I heard you come in. You always tiptoed upstairs without turning on the light because you didn't want to wake me up. I'd wait until I heard you asleep, and then lie in bed, listening for the house to be quiet. It was wonderful, being awake with you and Lynn and your father safe and asleep at home. I have never again been as happy as I was those nights. It didn't matter if it was two in the morning, as long as we were all home. Heaven could be waking up every hundred years and knowing everybody is sleeping safe in the next room."

"Did you eat anything today?" Diane asked.

"I had a bowl of oatmeal this morning. It was delicious. I think my body's going to behave for the next couple of days."

Diane had never seen her mother so animated. There was something artificial about her good spirits, and Diane wondered if it was the painkillers.

"I'm going to call the folks up on the farm," she said.

"I already did." Her mother bent down to pick up the vacuum cleaner, but Diane took it from her and put it in the hall closet.

"Were they surprised?" They sat down together on the living room couch.

"Martha started crying." Martha Schmitt was Mrs. Yaeger's younger sister.

"Hadn't Sue told her? I know Lynn talked to Sue."

"I can't believe she kept the secret, but Martha was surprised. Sue's going to be here tomorrow night. Martha and Kate are coming down Friday afternoon to help with the cooking. The men will be down after milking Friday night. I told them to stay here."

Diane was touched by her mother's generosity, but pointed out that it would not be possible to have the house ready Saturday afternoon with that many guests.

"Did you talk to Uncle Mike?" Diane asked. Mike Lindstrom was Mrs. Yaeger's brother.

"He was out at a county board meeting but Kate was thrilled. She and Martha are so different. Martha cried and Kate said 'Isn't that wonderful' and tried to sign me up for their charter to Las Vegas next fall."

They smiled.

"Should we invite any neighbors?" Diane asked.

"You can send an announcement later," Mrs. Yaeger said. "Right now, I've only got time for family. Unless you want to invite John Bradley." She smiled at her daughter, so that the suggestion could be taken as a joke if it was inappropriate.

Diane considered the possibility, but shook her head. "We don't know each other well enough."

"How much better can you know the man?" Her mother was exasperated.

"We haven't known each other long enough, then." Her mother's persistence annoyed her. "There's something bigger than life about Bradley. He wouldn't fit in the house."

"I'm sure the house will be perfectly suitable," her mother sniffed. Diane laughed at her wounded dignity.

"It's not his money. It's his physical presence. I just can't imagine him here."

"Then you lack imagination. I wouldn't be here today if I hadn't imagined myself here," she said.

The vision of her mother as an ambitious woman who had actively shaped the course of her life came as a revelation.

"How far *have* you come?" She was struck by the possibilities of the question.

"From another world."

"Is the new world better?"

"Ask yourself the same question."

"I do."

"I am happy to have experienced both," Mrs. Yaeger considered.

"Did you ever feel rootless?"

"All the time."

Diane could hardly contain her excitement.

"It gets easier, the second generation," her mother said.

"I'm so tired of taking the world on by myself." Diane fought back tears. "I know it's too late to come back, now—" She stopped. Her mother understood what she did not say. "I wish I could have you all with me, all the time."

"I hope you marry someday, Diane, and have a child, so you'll understand how much I love you."

"It couldn't be any more than I love you."

"It must be." There were tears in her mother's eyes. "You can't imagine." They held each other a moment in silence. "The first time my mother came to visit after you were born, I was ashamed of the feelings I had for you. I loved my mother and I was happy to see her, but what was going on between me and the helpless creature I brought into the world took up my whole body and soul. It scared me at first, the way I felt. It was like a hunger, as if I'd been undernourished my whole life up to that moment. I caught Grandma unawares one afternoon, rocking you to sleep on the porch, and I could tell she was remembering her first days with me. She understood. She accepted the fact that life looks forward."

Diane smiled. "It's hard to believe I could feel as close to another person as I feel to you right now."

"There's one thing that worries me." Mrs. Yaeger squinted. The diminishing sunlight made prisms of the water dripping from the eaves. "The closer I get to death, the more I love God the way I loved my parents, and not the way I love my children."

"If your mother understood"—Diane laid her head on her mother's shoulder—"I'm sure God will."

In the twilight, a robin hopped stiff-legged on a bare branch. In that moment of silence, there was time to say everything they needed to say to each other. The sense of time passing too quickly gave way to a calm knowledge outside time, beyond words.

When Lynn got home, shortly after dark, Diane fixed the three women dinner. Her mother's appetite exhilarated Lynn, who watched with delight as she ate. Hope burned in the younger daughter's eyes, and they indulged in an orgy of reminiscence. They argued about which summer

Uncle John had killed the runt pig and Lynn told them for the tenth time a practical joke she had never entirely forgiven him for. There was a heated debate about whether it had been their cousin Tommy or his brother who broke his arm jumping from the hayloft. Mrs. Yaeger reviewed the branches of their family tree, getting by careful exercise of memory back to Europe from each of the girls' grandparents. Several skeletons fell out of closets for the first time: A great-great-uncle hanged himself in the county jail; a second cousin passed out drunk in a snowdrift and froze to death.

They looked through family albums. Diane had a sinking feeling that future attempts to write "creatively" would pale before the multiplicity, orginality, and eccentricity of her family.

They went to bed before midnight, but the pleasant evening tired their mother. She slept until noon on Thursday. Each time Diane broke from polishing floors or washing windows to look in at her, she appeared to be resting peacefully. Diane made her tea and toast when she got up. Diane continued cleaning into the afternoon.

"What is it I like so much about cleaning?" she asked her mother during a break shampooing the carpets.

"A need for order?" She watched her daughter from bed.

"Cleaning gives me an instant sense of accomplishment," Diane said.

"The house looks beautiful."

"Thanks."

"I feel guilty not helping more." Mrs. Yaeger closed her eyes. Diane wondered if she was in pain.

"Think of all the times you cleaned up after Lynn and me."

"You were always good about helping." With difficulty, Mrs. Yaeger shifted her position. "I feel like a baby, sleeping so much."

"You're lucky to be sleeping so well."

"I wish I dreamed more, though. There are so many nice things to remember, and I sleep such a dull sleep. Everything's a blank hum. I try hard to stay awake, to remember. I've been thinking about you."

"What about me?" Diane looked across the room at her

mother as she poured more carpet shampoo into the machine. They had had another sunny day, though the sun was already behind the neighbor's house. The islands of wet soil in the backyard were growing into continents.

"I want you to invite John Bradley to the wedding."

"I already told you, I can't."

"I want to meet him."

"He wouldn't come."

"How do you know?"

"He knows where I am."

"A man needs an invitation to a wedding."

"He wouldn't like it."

There was helplessness and entreaty in her mother's eyes.

"I would," she said.

"I can't." Diane was firm.

"You'll ruin the whole thing with your defenses."

"Mine or his?"

"It doesn't matter whose."

"Please try to see it from my point of view, Mom."

"Your father used to say you can't win a game playing defense."

"I can't risk his saying no."

"You have to take chances."

"I already have. It's his turn."

Sue Schmitt was the herald of festivities. Their cousin's excitement made the wedding real. She demanded to see her bridesmaid's dress before she put her suitcase down. She modeled the gown for them in the living room. Everyone agreed that the color was perfect with her red hair and flattered her thickset but shapely body. She had the garment bag off the wedding gown and held it against herself.

"It's beautiful." Her awe made her seem more than a year younger than Lynn, whose subdued pleasure made her mature by comparison.

"It was Mom's." Lynn smiled.

"Where is she? Where's Emma?" Their cousin suddenly remembered her aunt.

"Asleep," Diane said.

Sue nodded respectfully and replaced both gowns on their hangers. She chattered incessantly. Her brother's wife was pregnant, and not feeling well enough to come down. They had just bought a mobile home, which they parked on their five acres. Her other brother was an automobile mechanic in St. Cloud. He had spent the winter in Las Vegas, hitchhiking back when his motorcycle was stolen. He was getting as bad as their cousin Tommy, who was selling marijuana to students at Pine County High School.

Emma Yaeger woke up as they were finishing dinner, and Sue modeled both dresses again for her. Diane went upstairs to change for Trudy's. She was aware of the care with which she put on makeup and selected her clothes— the spring dress bought on Rue St. Honoré, silk stockings, the Bruno Magli shoes from Saks. Trudy would approve. Diane enjoyed the prosect of her aunt's admiration.

Trudy was Diane's most favorable critic. Yet Trudy strove to be an audience worthy of the drama in her niece's life. She had been Diane's earliest model of independence and originality. Diane acknowledged her influence.

Bob Yaeger's house near Lake of the Isles was of the same vintage as Diane's, but it was larger, on a bigger lot. There was light in almost every window, which gave the house a warm, manorial feeling. A servant might have answered the door, though in fact her Uncle Bob did.

Bob Yaeger was allowed to have one drink with his sister and their niece in the living room before he was expected to leave. It was a pleasant parlor furnished in comfortable Midwestern Victorian.

"Well . . ." Trudy sighed when Bob had said good night and excused himself, pretending to have journals to catch up on in the library. "Can I fix you another drink?" A gold bracelet, laden with charms, souvenirs of ports visited during a generation of winter cruises, glistened and tinkled like wind chimes on her thin wrists. A strand of pearls was draped around her neck in three uneven rows. Diane could not tell whether age or drink was responsible for her shaky steps.

"Scotch and soda." Diane returned her aunt's smile.

"You look lovely, dear."

"Thanks."

Trudy was looking her seventy-plus years. She wore too much makeup; it called attention to circles graven under her eyes. In the same way, the hint of blue in her hair suggested that this gray was not its natural color. She had become too thin for the black sheath dress she wore, but Diane suspected her latest diet rather than a health problem. Trudy handed Diane her drink, and sat down beside her on the tightly upholstered striped couch.

"How's your dear mother?" The old woman sipped her drink. There was duty in the question.

"Pretty bad."

"What can we do for her?"

"Give Lynn a beautiful wedding."

"Yes, of course." Trudy was flustered by Diane's abruptness. "I've got a lovely dinner planned for tomorrow night. I thought we'd serve dinner buffet style. Hilda's coming to help." Hilda had been Trudy's cleaning lady since Diane's childhood. "Is Lynn excited?"

"Incredibly. She's earned a party, these last few months."

"I haven't decided what to wear to the wedding," Trudy said.

"Sue and I are wearing full-length dresses."

"Are you bridesmaids?"

Diane nodded. "The men are wearing tuxes.

"I've got a spring dress that might look good," Trudy deliberated, "if it fits. I've lost fifteen pounds since I bought it."

"I noticed. You're very thin."

"I'm an old mummy." She laughed cheerily and sipped her drink. "You certainly look good, though." She studied her niece as if she were a piece of art. "Bob tells me you have a job with the *Times*. Congratulations."

"Part time. On the business section."

"How exciting."

"It's actually pretty mundane." Diane usually played to her aunt's affection for New York. But tonight the old lady's enthusiasm made her deprecate life there. Trudy resisted realism. "New York" was one of her central myths, a Camelot where style and money and a sense of being in the center of things were part of everyday life. Probably even more than the old late-night movies, more than her father's respect for the Eastern education, her aunt had been responsible for Diane's fierce desire to go to New York.

"Are you still living in the Village?" Her aunt probably remembered that she had moved, but liked using terms like "the Village."

"I live in Brooklyn now."

"Brooklyn Heights, of course," Trudy corrected herself. It had been a severe blow to the old lady when she first learned that her niece had moved to Brooklyn. Once assured that Brooklyn Heights was the home of Truman Capote and Norman Mailer, however, Trudy's imagination annexed Diane's neighborhood to the glamorous "Big Apple."

Diane did not miss New York that evening. The idea of going back filled her with dread. She remembered all the Sunday evenings, coming back late from the Hamptons or the Berkshires, the anxiety she felt crossing into the city, the sinking feeling she would get at the dirt and noise and crowds. For the first time, she realized how deeply afraid she had always been of the city. Her energetic reports back home had been bravado, a play acted for the people who missed her. She did not want to talk about New York.

"How have *you* been, Trudy?"

"Not bad." Diane's aunt took a cigarette from a silver case on the marble-top coffee table and lit it. "There isn't much to tell when you get to my age."

"Are you going out with anyone?" Diane asked the question partly to flatter, partly to discompose her aunt.

"I haven't had a steady boyfriend since Cy Walker, and that was before your father died." Trudy never referred to Bill Yaeger's death without a shadow of annoyance passing over her face. She had doted on her younger brother, spoiling him from childhood. His death had made her certifiably old, had reduced her to living vicariously through her niece. The irony was not lost on Diane that it was only in the past week with Bradley that she had lived in New York in a manner equal to her aunt's imagination.

Trudy was in a hurry to make them a third drink.

"What are you drinking?" Diane hesitated to decline another for fear of inhibiting her aunt's tête-à-tête.

"A stinger."

Her aunt measured brandy into a glass.

"Make my next drink lighter."

Trudy nodded, but Diane was not surprised that it was stronger than the first.

"How's *your* love life?" Trudy sat down beside her again. There was something predatory about the question; it set Diane on edge. She was on the point of lying, when a sudden surge of charity, akin to a woman's giving herself to a man out of pity for his desire, induced Diane to give her aunt some of the details of her week with Bradley. She asked Trudy whether she had heard of Bradley, and was delighted to hear that her aunt had seen him on the "Tonight Show" earlier that week. That her niece had actually gone out with someone who had been on the "Tonight Show" (the closest Trudy had come was a tempestuous affair in her late forties with the weatherman from a local television station) dumbfounded her aunt. Her awe was irresistible. Diane was soon telling Trudy much more than she had intended. The old lady's mouth was slack with suspense as her niece described turning down his first request for a date, and slapped her knee triumphantly when Diane "landed" the dinner invitation for the next night. She followed on a room-by-room tour of Bradley's northern shore mansion.

But Diane had enough self-control to keep from telling her aunt about his proposition. To mention money in a sexual context would disturb her aunt. Perhaps rightly so. The Yaegers were funny about money.

Diane did not allude to the physical dimension of her relationship, either. She was not sure how far Trudy would read into her narrative, but left that element to her imagination. Trudy questioned her at length about her weekend in Paris. She wanted to hear about *Le Café de Flores*, Fauchon, Montmartre. But Diane stopped short of their awkward farewell, and the *Post* photograph with Susan Aldrich.

"How absolutely perfect." Trudy closed her eyes and looked heavenward. "It would almost be better never to see the man again.

"I thought the idea was to live happily ever after." Diane was woozy. Trudy saw that the ice in her glass was gone, and had made another drink and offered it to her guest before she realized why Trudy had gotten up.

"Only in books," Trudy was saying. "In real life, you

can't sustain the excitement of getting to know a man. Eventually they all disappoint you."

"All? Do you think Dad disappointed Mom?" Diane wanted it clear she believed in the possibility of permanence.

"Your father was special," her aunt conceded. "There isn't another man like him."

"Naturally, the one exception to your rule is a man you could never have had. Trudy"—there was a serious note in her playfulness—"you never wanted to live happily ever after. You enjoy falling in love too much."

Trudy shook her head stubbornly."Leave when that first glow begins to fade, and save yourself a lot of heartache."

"You're too cynical."

"Realistic, you mean."

"Are you happy, Trudy?"

"I've had my moments." She gave Diane a coarse wink. "And I haven't let anyone destroy me in the process."

"I'm not sure deep down that you don't dislike men." Trudy recoiled from the suggestion as if stung, and Diane quickly added, "I mean the kind of men who lead you on and then don't follow through."

The third stinger had rendered her aunt incapable of fastening on to an insinuation. Diane smoothed things over by taking the old lady into her confidence. "Mom wanted me to invite Bradley to the wedding. Can you imagine?"

Trudy sniffed; her features rallied to alertness. Diane watched her aunt balance the possibility of appearing inconsistent if she urged her niece to follow her mother's advice against the once-in-a-lifetime opportunity of meeting a celebrity. Diane was not surprised to see her aunt's curiosity and her sense of adventure overcome the distrust of men that had been the unifying theme in her forty years as a divorcee. It was not often that Trudy was called upon to make such a delicate decision, however, and she savored the situation as long as possible before she asked: "Do you think he'd come?" The old lady sat rigidly straight and imposed a parody of calm rationality on her face.

"He *could*, if he wants to." Diane was not sure what she meant.

"Of course he could," Trudy snapped impatiently. "But does he want to?"

"There's only one way to find out." Diane stood up unsteadily and looked around for a telephone.

"Wait, wait. We have to think this out," Trudy insisted. Diane sat back down. "Do you want him to come?"

"I want him to come if he wants to come. But it might be too intense. He's only known me two weeks." Her nose was numb when she exhaled. "Lynn will probably throw me the bouquet." She laughed to herself. "I don't think it's a very good idea."

"Sometimes a wedding precipitates things," Trudy pointed out.

"You would love John Bradley." Diane smiled dreamily.

"Let's call him, then." Trudy stood up and started toward a reading nook where there was a telephone on the window ledge.

"What if he says no?" A shiver ran through Diane.

"Nothing ventured, nothing gained."

"I would like Mom to meet him." Diane did not stop to wonder how her aunt was going to find Bradley's telephone number. "Mom thinks I'm too defensive."

"Defenses have their place," Trudy pronounced. "But Emma might be right in this case. What's his number?"

"He's staying at the Beverly Hills Hotel. The area code's 213. You'll have to get the number from information."

Diane sat down beside her aunt in the cushioned window seat, took the phone from her, and got the number from long-distance information. "It's eight thirty-five there," she calculated from the grandfather clock in the living room. "He's probably out. John Bradley, Jr. please," she told the switchboard operator, who switched her to a male desk clerk who informed her that Mr. Bradley was not taking calls. "He's not taking calls," she whispered to Trudy. "This is his psychic," Diane improvised. "Mr. Bradley wants to speak with me."

After thirty seconds of beautiful music, a woman answered the phone. She was laughing. Diane recognized Susan Aldrich's voice. She considered hanging up, but the moment passed before she could remember if she had given her name to the hotel clerk.

"This is Diane Yaeger," she said in her most professional tone. "Is John Bradley there?"

"Hi, Diane, this is Susan Aldrich. We met last week at Coco's." Susan's friendliness irritated Diane. "Are you in L.A.?"

"No, I'm calling from Minneapolis."

"Brad, it's Diane Yaeger." Though muffled, as if Susan's hand were held over the receiver, the way she called to Bradley was unmistakably familiar.

"Hi. Where are you?" The question was typical. Bradley and his friend assumed she could be in Los Angeles. But there was also an alarming trace of guilt in his tone that told her that what she read in the *Post* was true. The realization that Bradley had lied nauseated her. Bradley and Susan were lovers. She would never need to hear it from him.

Diane had never felt such an intense desire to disappear, to not exist for someone. She tried to think of a way to end the conversation quickly. Her pause must have been as long as she feared.

He repeated the question. "Where are you?"

"At Trudy's house," she said absently. The old lady flushed, shook her head, signaled not to mention her. "In Minneapolis." She knew she had to say something else, but her mind was blank.

"How's Minneapolis?" From the apprehension in his voice, Diane realized that he had picked up on the fact that she had found out about Susan.

'Fine."

"Good."

"The reason I called—" She fought the urge to hang up. Yet as she struggled to find a pretext, a part of her subconscious wondered why she worked so hard to spare Bradley embarrassment and—possibly—guilt. She kept coming back to the word "grown-up" and it made her want to laugh. They were big boys and girls. She had been old enough to know better. Clichés filled her head. The only thing that seemed original and distinctive about her situation was the pain she felt like a blow to her stomach.

"I have one more question before I can finish the article."

She had no idea what she was going to ask him, and there was nothing he could do to help her except reply with painful kindness: "Anything you like." His pleasant manner was a spell that turned them back into reporter and interviewee.

"What's your definition of success?" Diane hardly knew what she was saying, she was so anxious to get off the phone. Her question drove an unbridgeable distance between them. She was not interested in his answer.

"Success is getting what you want." He spoke with something like regret, as if sorry that what he said might hurt her.

"Is that it?"

"I think so."

"Okay. Good luck with the movie."

"Thanks. Let's get together when I get back to New York."

"Goodbye, John."

Diane felt no emotion at his parting remark. It seemed likely enough that she would see Bradley again in New York someday. She was not angry that he left room for his comment to be construed as a promise, but neither did she extract hope from it. She knew finally where she stood and Bradley knew that she knew.

It was almost a relief to know, Diane thought, feeling the numbness in her face as she put the receiver down. Trudy was too intimidated by Diane's silence to ask any questions. She hurried off to make them another drink.

Diane was in such shock at first that it seemed possible she could will the conversation not to have taken place. Objectively, she had not made a fool of herself. To Susan, Diane was a reporter, finishing a story. Surely if Bradley had kept the truth from Diane, he could keep it from his lover. But inwardly, Diane cursed herself for having had the weakness to call. Even if she had not known about Bradley and Susan, it would have been unfair to invite him. She should have had the strength to get through the wedding on her own.

"Not with a bang." Diane lifted the glass Trudy handed her and touched her aunt's.

"What?"

"Nothing. Guess who wants to marry me?"

Trudy shook her head.

"Alan Jennings."

"Such a good dancer. Remember the party we went to near the UN?"

"When he found out about Bradley, he decided we've been more than friends all these years."

"I don't know why he couldn't photograph fashion models."

For Trudy, the fact that he photographed pollution-control equipment and fiberglass bathtub factories disqualified Alan as a serious suitor.

"Mom likes the idea."

"Never compromise," Trudy said, "never. Life will disappoint you enough without disappointing yourself."

"I don't think I want to live alone."

"Better single than unhappily married."

"But don't you have more credibility being divorced than if you'd never been married? No one can call you an old maid."

"I don't care what people call me. Why didn't you ask John Bradley?" The question was too unexpected to be painful.

She's treating me like I blew it, Diane thought. But she was too angry at herself and at Bradley to cry.

"He was there with his girlfriend," she told her aunt.

"So—they aren't married yet." Her aunt's callousness made Diane laugh.

"You should see Susan Aldrich," Diane said. "She exudes class from every pore."

"I won't have self-pity," Trudy chided. "You could have been a debutante. Your father and I had the connections."

"She's beautiful." Diane stated the fact dully.

"No prettier than you are, I'm sure."

"You're so loyal, Trudy. I love you."

"He may not have been a gentleman"—the old lady brushed off her niece's emotion—"but you should have been more direct, too. Life is too short to beat around the bush. If you want him, you should have asked him."

"I don't know why I called." Diane felt like crying, but the frustration within her was a cloud without rain, a cloud that Trudy's reproach failed to seed. "You were right, Trudy. I should have said goodbye in New York. The only thing is"—working the thought out, she forgot about wanting to cry—"how does a woman say 'So long, it's been great' when all the time she's afraid she's been used?"

"Men always make you a fool." Trudy's bitterness sounded rational, but the sequence of her observations belied her seeming sobriety. "Everything's easier for men, even peeing." Diane burst out laughing. Trudy tried unsuccessfully not to smile at the effect she produced on her niece.

Diane had the desire essential to a journalist to get inside the minds of people she met, but she would have refused an invitation to look into the Pandora's box of Trudy's subconscious. There was an abhorrence in Trudy's face when she spoke (as she seemed compelled to do) of bodily functions that made Diane think that it would be frightening to plumb the abysses of her aunt's mind. It was hard to imagine that she had ever made love with a man. Diane suspected that the infatuations since her divorce had been paraded before the public in order to obscure the deeper fact that Trudy was terrified of life, that she saw death—in the guise of germs—lurking in every encounter with another human being.

Diane was still at Trudy's after midnight. She was morosely drunk, listening halfheartedly as her aunt complained about a retired Air Force colonel.

Diane could not stop analyzing how she had bungled the call to Bradley. Bungled was the wrong word, but it recurred. She debated calling Bradley back. *I'm calling to apologize for calling.* She smiled. From his point of view, it suddenly seemed selfish to ask a man she had known so short a time to become involved with a family, a wedding, a dying woman. She loved him, which gave her the right to ask. But not having told him how she felt gave Bradley the right to ignore her needs.

Diane marveled at the quantities of liquor her aunt could drink with no effect more noticeable than garrulousness and a slight slurring of speech. Diane was nauseated, though, and almost too tired to keep her eyes open. She waited five minutes while Trudy described how she got her first job in broadcasting at a local television station before she could tell her aunt that she had to go home.

Diane was lucid enough to know she had drunk too much to drive, but she was desperate to get away from her aunt. She put on her coat, kissed the old lady's flushed face, and got outside as quickly as she could. At the car, fumbling in her coat pocket for the keys, Diane lay an overheated cheek against the cold steel roof. Eyes closed, breathing slowly and deeply, her nausea subsided. The temperature was below freezing, but Diane drove home with all the windows open. It felt good. The wind in her face was liberating. She was alone. She was free. Solitude was freedom, and it seemed to her, as she idled dutifully at stop signs though there was no traffic in either direction and drove with exaggerated caution down deserted streets, that she had never encountered anything as frightening as freedom.

_____ *fourteen*

Before dawn, Diane was aware of her period starting, but she was too nauseated to get out of bed.

The grandfather clock downstairs woke her at nine o'clock. The chiming sounded like metal grating against metal inside her ear. The sunlight made her temples throb; each pulse forced her eyes closed in pain. There was calm between pulses. Then the pain was back. Diane mastered it by thinking about nothing—the blissful absence of feeling, of thought.

Mild cramps in her lower back contributed to her sense of falling apart. Lynn and Sue were laughing in the kitchen. It had never occurred to her that she might be pregnant; she felt no relief, only annoyance at her body's timing.

It was time for Uncle Willie's cure. There were two things she remembered about her late great-uncle: the wicked grin once when he offered her a plug of chewing tobacco, and his surefire hangover cure. Diane went into the bathroom and filled the tub with warm water. The dry blood on the inside of her thighs tinted the water a transparent rose. The water soothed the throbbing in her head, the cramping in her back. The cure consisted of drinking warm water, glass after glass of it, until her body would hold no more. The object: to purge the body of alcohol. Diane gagged and sputtered and choked, and after the third glass of water, she threw up.

Willie had been known to leave the bathroom whistling

afterwards and eat a six-egg breakfast before going to work in the fields. Diane had no desire to eat, and was still shaky on her feet, but her headache and nausea were gone by the time she dried and powdered herself and put on a pair of jeans. She changed the sheets on her bed and went downstairs.

Lynn and Sue were working on Sue's dress at the sewing machine on the dining room table. Mrs. Yaeger appeared to be asleep on the sun porch. The snow was almost gone. Diane said good morning. She felt positively benevolent in the absence of pain. She watched over Lynn's shoulder as Sue put a hem in the dress. She thought of her head only to savor the exquisite cessation of pain. Diane poured herself a cup of coffee. Their aunts were coming at three, Lynn told her. Sue had been shocked when she discovered that Lynn was not planning to wear anything on her head. They were getting ready to see a seamstress about a last-minute veil. Mark was picking up tuxedos and flowers.

There was not much left to do as the wedding approached. The living room furniture was already arranged. The reception would be buffet style, so there was no table to set.

"What time do you think Mom will wake up?" Diane asked as her sister and cousin headed out the front door.

"Not for a while. She was up polishing silver when I got up, but the excitement tires her out. She was sleeping eighteen hours a day before you came home."

Diane poured herself a second cup of coffee and made a piece of toast. The house was quiet. She wanted to talk to her mother, though she had nothing in particular to say. She could not keep Bradley out of her thoughts. He knew why she had called. It upset her that she had shown such weakness. She wondered if she was "getting nervous" about not being married. She *was* almost thirty.

Diane called Alan in New York. He would be there that evening if she asked him. For the first time, Diane realized that she could marry Alan. Suddenly, she doubted the wisdom of being made over by a man, no matter how attractive. To be loved by a man who would allow her to grow in directions mapped out by herself was worthwile.

Diane hung up the phone after the first ring. She could not risk another mistake.

Mrs. Yaeger woke up just before noon, and drank a glass of milk with her daughter in the kitchen.

"How are you feeling?" Diane asked. Her mother sipped the drink thirstily.

"Probably better than you. You look tired."

"I was up late with Trudy."

"I feel fine." The circles under her mother's eyes and the lines in her face undercut her optimistic smile. "It's wonderful really, how much I sleep. And such wonderful dreams last night. I was a girl on the farm again. My mother and I talked all night, only we were the same age. We explained ourselves to each other. I don't remember a word we said, except that by the time we finished we understood each other completely. It was such a nice feeling."

"You're starting your second childhood." Diane smiled.

"You would think I'd fight sleep, with so little time left," her mother mused, not morbid, "but I'm tired all the time. Maybe I'm resting up for tomorrow. How was Trudy?"

"She never changes." The mention of her aunt made Diane frown. "We drank too much and she talked me into doing something stupid."

"You called John Bradley," her mother exclaimed, pleased. Her intuition surprised Diane into telling her about the conversation.

"Don't be sorry you called him," her mother said. "Don't ever be sorry for doing something genuine or telling the truth."

"Even when the other person doesn't want to hear it?" Diane's voice caught with emotion.

"I've never met a man who wasn't a better man knowing someone loves him. Besides"—the sparkle in her mother's eyes was one Diane associated with being given pleasant surprises as a child—"showing Bradley you love him is good practice for when the right man comes along. It's not easy showing someone you love him."

Diane put her arms around her mother. "You're a pretty special lady."

Her mother laughed. "It took you long enough to notice."

Diane described her revelation about Alan, and her decision not to invite him. She wanted to hear what her mother thought of her marrying Alan, but Mrs. Yaeger did not offer an opinion.

"Do you love him?" she asked finally.

Wavering between "I don't know" and "I'm not sure," Diane pondered the question while her mother went to dress.

Emma Yaeger's sister and sister-in-law arrived at two-thirty. Martha Schmitt, Emma's younger sister, and Kate Lindstrom, their brother's wife, might have been psychology textbook studies in the classic ectomorph and endomorph. Martha was tall and thin, with the unmistakable Lindstrom mouth, full but severe, set in a face that was leaner and healthier than her sister's. Kate was short and plump, with playful eyes and an infectious laugh. They were dressed in pants suits and filled the front door, laden with packages and groceries, spilling into the house with enough chatter for a shower of ten women. Kate insisted that she had seen Diane's haircut in *Cosmopolitan*. They interrogated Mrs. Yaeger frankly about her health.

"How are you feeling, Emma?" Kate began unpacking boxes and cans in the kitchen.

"It depends on the day." Mrs. Yaeger was evasive. They knew Kate Lindstrom expected the truth, but Diane's mother would not enlighten her. "Lately I've been feeling pretty good."

Kate dropped the subject tactfully, and the four women threw themselves into preparations. Diane sifted flour for the wedding cake. Her mother greased three enormous pans. Kate mixed ingredients together in an old-fashioned crockery bowl, while Martha peeled ten pounds of potatoes and sliced them into a pot on the stove.

The maxim that life in the country was dull by fastpaced city standards did not stand up to Kate's rundown on the latest Pine City gossip. Most of it centered around her son Tommy, the family's *enfant terrible*.

Tommy Lindstrom had been a hit visiting Diane in New York during a cross-country motorcycle trip. An irresistible combination of good looks, egotism, and generosity, he was the cousin Diane had thought likeliest to leave the farm. He had dated a go-go dancer in Las Vegas, been jailed in Montreal after a barroom brawl, had a rose tatooed on a bicep. He had lived a semester at the Yaegers' house while he studied radio and television repair. However, in the end, Tommy went back to Pine City. Experienced without losing his unaffected innocence, he appealed equally to people with the instinct to corrupt and to nice girls like his cousin Sue, who had had a crush on him from childhood.

They talked about Sue's plans to move down to the Cities. Martha had already served notice that she did not relish the prospect of being left the only woman in the house and was not about to take care of her daughter's three horses. They teased Martha about dying her hair gray because she was due to become the first grandmother among them within the month. Studying the energy in her aunt's smoky blue eyes, Diane felt a pang of sorrow for her mother, who would never know her grandchildren.

Luckily, Kate distracted her from somber thoughts. She regaled them with stories about the odd characters who came into the truck stop where she was a waitress. When they tired of laughing, she outlined the menu planned for an upcoming birthday party.

Diane could not imagine Bradley in her house. He would be hopelessly out of place with these people. At that moment, nothing Bradley offered compared with what she had always had. These people loved her. They accepted her in spite of the fact that she had left them to seek in New York things that did not matter nearly as much, things that seemed as insubstantial now as barely remembered dreams. This is real, she thought—her mother, her aunts, being loved for what she was, for whatever she chose to be. Diane smiled at her mother. She was perfectly happy. This afternoon, in this kitchen, licking beaters, chopping celery, drinking coffee—Diane could feel the vivid moment being transformed into a cherished memory even as she experienced it. In contrast, the week with Bradley was like a game she had forgotten the rules to. She had lost, of course, because it was Bradley's game and Bradley made the rules. But it didn't matter, she reminded herself. What she had was real and it was better.

"Diane's been going out with a writer whose book is being made into a movie." Mrs. Yaeger made the announcement modestly, as if honesty would not allow her to keep the secret any longer. Kate wanted details. Martha took the information in silently, as if it confirmed what she had always assumed were the reasons a young girl went to New York. Neither aunt bothered to hear that she was no longer going out with Bradley. Diane had a hard time convincing them not to call the *Pine City Poker* on the spot.

By five o'clock, the cakes were in the oven, the frosting whipped, the potato and gelatin fruit salads cooling in the refrigerator. The ladies decided to have a drink before starting on the ham, candied yams, and baked beans. Diane fixed her aunts whiskey and Cokes. She and her mother had tea. They sat in the sun porch. The sun was already setting. It was disappointing for Diane to realize she had spent the entire day regaining ground lost the night before.

"I'm going for a walk," she told them.

It was cool outside. The air was humid with melting snow. In the twilight, the neighborhood seemed preternaturally peaceful. As she strolled, she admired the large, comfortable houses full of family histories she would never know. The fences and hedges between them took on symbolic dimensions. She walked for a long time, thinking of Bradley and Alan. It had gotten cold by the time she started back.

Even with three bathrooms, the hour before the rehearsal supper was chaos. Martha and Kate had brought square-dance dresses for the party. Mrs. Yaeger wore a navy-blue sheath, pearls, and dressy black patent-leather heels. Diane had never suspected such elegance. She was proud to be the daughter of such an attractive woman. The older women were amused at how similarly the Yaeger sisters were dressed—they wore long, close-fitting skirts, Diane's black, her sister's navy blue, and elegant white blouses, the older sister's low-cut and long-sleeved, Lynn's frilly at collar and wrists. The only thing that gave away the fact that Sue's floral-print shirtwaist was homemade was its length, to the top of the knee, mere centimeters out of fashion.

They were having too good a time to take two cars, so they piled into the Yaegers' Buick. Diane drove. Silliness prevailed. A good deal of good-natured complaining indicated that Kate had ended up sitting on Martha's narrow lap. Lynn sat beside Diane, looking straight out into the night, smiling.

Bob Yaeger answered the bell. The house sparkled. The living room was dimly lit, and there were candles everywhere. The hors d'oeuvres beside a crystal candelabrum on the dining room buffet were offered with an elegance Trudy probably modeled on the Rose Room, where she had often taken Diane to dinner during stays at the Algonquin Hotel.

Bob Yaeger took their coats. He looked distinguished with his gray hair and finely tailored dark suit. He had always appeared more professional, less the salesman, than her father, Diane reflected. He would look dignified, giving his niece away. Her father would have played to the audience with a wink. Her uncle kissed each of his arriving guests. Diane had never seen him more expansive. He smelled of Scotch and *Kolnwasser* when his lips touched her cheek.

Trudy hurried over to meet them. Formal, she took each woman's hand, reserving her only kiss for Lynn, irresistible with beaming smile and shining blonde hair.

"I hope you plan on being more punctual for the wedding," she reproved her niece. "Everyone else is here already."

"There are the boys." Kate went over to her husband, who still wore the red beard he grew each winter for snow-mobiling and ice fishing. Dressed in a western dress jacket, string tie, and boots, he stood beside Martha's husband, who wore a loose-fitting checked sports jacket, baggy dark pants with cuffs, and black shoes. They were stiff, like young men talked into going to a dance. No one would suspect, Diane thought, crossing the living room to say hello to her uncles, that they were prosperous men, with fifty cows, five hundred acres, and a quarter of a million dollars worth of farm equipment. Their appearances were deceiving. Though reserved, they were not timid men. They were simply waiting for their wives to set the tone for the get-together.

While long hours in all-electric kitchens had given most of the women in Pine City Kate's shape, the men were lean and wiry, with sun or wind-tanned faces and hard, unostentatious muscles.

"Yoohoo!" Kate called to her husband as she approached. The fact that her aunt still used expressions like "yoohoo" delighted Diane with an irrational joy.

"Mike hasn't seen Mom for a month," Lynn whispered to Diane.

"How're you feeling, Emma?" His concern was so restrained that an outsider might have missed it.

"Fine." She gave his arm a squeeze, but they did not kiss.

"Look at all that food." Kate eyed the basket of black and brown and tan and white breads on the buffet. Water was warming under a row of chafing dishes.

"Bob's taking orders for drinks." Trudy spoke graciously as she came up to them. The black dress that hung on her frame sparkled with sequins. As usual, it was difficult to tell if she tottered from drink or because her black heels were precariously high for a woman her age. The Pine City men lifted cans of Hamm's beer. The other guests ordered drinks. Lynn couldn't make up her mind.

"What would you recomrnend?" She smiled sweetly.

"Champagne is always nice." The old lady rifled her repertoire for the right drink. "But we'll be drinking plenty of champagne tomorrow. How about a pink lady? It's one of my specialties."

"It sounds fun," Lynn said agreeably. "What's in it?"

"Gin, grenadine, egg white, and half-and-half."

"It sounds disgusting," Diane said.

"It sounds *wonderful*." Lynn frowned as if her sister wantonly spoiled the party. "I'll try one."

Mark was shepherding his family, the Halvorsons, across the room. They knew Mrs. Yaeger, but not Diane. She had not realized what a big man Mark was until she saw him next to his father, bald, middle-aged, wearing glasses. Diane could imagine him in a green visor, going over figures. Mark's mother was thin, with eyes that darted around the room. She looked high-strung, much more than

Mrs. Yaeger like the type of woman who would be harboring a malignancy. They were an unappealing couple.

"Are Mark and his brothers adopted?" Diane whispered to her sister, who shook her head, smiling conspiratorially.

Lynn had her eye on the middle brother for Sue, and concentrated her efforts on that introduction. The youngest boy had a difficult time concealing his fear of Mrs. Yaeger's disease. He could not look into her eyes, and stood so that his parents were between them.

It was hard to talk to the Halvorsons. The only thing they had in common with the Yaegers was the fact that their children loved each other.

Trudy returned with a tray of drinks.

"Delicious." Lynn complimented her aunt on the pink lady. "Real sweet and creamy."

Diane declined her offer of a sip.

Mrs. Yaeger was left to talk to Mark's father. She had a foolproof system for dispatching bores at parties, one that Diane had put to good use as a reporter. She surrendered to the uninteresting guest. She asked interminable questions about his work, his family, his life, and actually listened to the answers. Bores who were boring because they never talked soon tired of this attention, Diane had discovered. Bores who bored by talking about themselves were used to struggling against the natural resistance of a listener trying to get a word in edgewise, and soon got bored with a passive auditor. Mark's father appeared to belong to the first class of bore.

Trudy had pulled Diane aside. "How's the drink?"

"Fine." In fact, the wine spritzer was surprisingly revivifying. For the first time that day, Diane felt capable of initiating an action.

"I hope you weren't too upset about last night."

Diane shrugged and took a sip of her drink.

"I feel as if it was my fault somehow." Trudy's apology was sincere. "I hope you aren't angry at me."

"Not at all. I wouldn't have done it if I hadn't wanted to."

"Men are like street cars." Trudy sighed. Her breath smelled of *crème de menthe*. "If you miss one, there's always another one around the corner."

Diane could not help laughing. Leave it to Trudy to

expropriate the worn male aphorism and stand it on its head. She was tempted to ask her aunt why she had never caught another one, but said instead:''I never heard a woman say that before.''

''It's one of those universal truths.'' Trudy's eyes glistened playfully.

''I guess I was born on a poorly serviced route.''

Trudy's response to Diane's joke was disproportionately mirthful. They were watching Lynn introduce Mark's brothers to her cousin.

''Tommy's quite the Viking god,'' Trudy said. ''Is he the one who pushes dope?''

Diane smiled at her aunt's jargon and nodded.

''He looks like a boy who's always one step ahead of trouble.''

''When he stayed with me in New York a couple of years ago, I had friends fighting over who got to take him home.''

''Girlfriends?'' Trudy kept a straight, worldly face.

''Some of them,'' Diane laughed.

''He reminds me a little of Chuck Scott. You may have been too young to remember the weatherman on Channel 5 when you were a girl. He and I went out for a while.''

The infamous affair. Diane was silent.

''It's interesting that your mother was the only one who left the farm.'' Kate and Martha and their husbands were talking to Emma across the room.

And now she's dying of cancer, Diane thought. Suddenly, her mother's disease and her father's death epitomized the evils of city life. If all was well only if it ended well, perhaps her mother had made a terrible mistake. Diane had always been able to imagine ''what-if'' situations in which her mother had taken a different road. As a child, she had often wondered what her life would have been like if her mother had married the veterinarian from St. Cloud, or the farmer from Rush City. She had never wondered what life would have been like had her father married a different woman.

Diane wondered if she would inherit the ill effects of her mother's loss, like a genetic original sin. But she was over-emphasizing the difference between city and country life. Her mother had led an exceptionally peaceful existence. There had been only one disappointment and one tragedy: Her elder daughter had left home at the age of eighteen, eager to make her fortune, and her husband had died much too early.

"I've always admired your mother for leaving the farm," Trudy was saying.

"She's become a different person," Diane said.

"A more interesting person—"

"What do you mean by interesting?"

"More complex," Trudy answered without hesitation.

"We make life more difficult for ourselves," Diane said.

"We want more than they do."

"That's too simple," Diane said. "What makes our own lives so difficult?"

"We want things beautiful." Trudy finished her drink decisively.

"Is that good or bad?"

"It depends on how well we do. I have succeeded to a great extent in not compromising my standards," her aunt said proudly, "and I have paid for my integrity with long spells of loneliness." Trudy's eyes were moist with the force of her self-satisfaction. There was fatuity in the rationalization of her fastidiousness, yet Diane was moved by her conviction.

"I'm very lucky to have an aunt like you." She leaned over to kiss Trudy, who shed a tear of pleasure. It was true, Diane thought. Trudy had shown her the importance of being unique. Not that she identified with her aunt. Trudy was a character. Diane enjoyed characters, but for herself, she wanted uniqueness without idiosyncrasy. A character was a lonely person, someone at odds with society. Diane believed that the things she wanted out of life—love, interesting work, travel, marriage, and children—were attainable, and so refused to evolve into a character. Understanding the tragic implications of Trudy's eccentricity for the first time, Diane promised herself to be as realistic as possible about the things she wanted.

Mark's brother seemed to be hitting it off better with Tommy than with Sue. They were all laughing at something Tommy had said.

"I ought to go over and say hello to my cousin," Diane told Trudy.

"Not yet. Come with me to fix another drink first, and then let's go over and rescue your poor mother. She looks exhausted."

Mark's father appeared to have warmed up to Mrs. Yaeger's interrogation. Her face was jowly with fatigue as she forced herself to listen. While Diane made her own spritzer and Trudy added *crème de menthe* to brandy in a glass, Lynn joined them.

"I think he likes her," Lynn whispered.

"What about Sue?" Diane asked. "What does she think?"

"She's interested. Wouldn't it be great if they got together? One couple always gets together at a wedding. Just think—if they got married, Sue would be my sister."

"Isn't one enough?" Trudy was impatient with Lynn's matchmaking. "Throw her your bouquet tomorrow. That's been known to get things going."

"Good idea," Lynn agreed.

"Let me make you another 'lady.' " She took Lynn's empty glass.

"Not so strong," Lynn said. "My nose is already tingling." Trudy took a sip of her drink and assembled the ingredients for her niece's with the ease of a professional.

"The house looks great," Diane told Trudy. "I love the candles everywhere."

"Wait until you see supper." Trudy was flushed with the joys of hostessing.

Lynn thanked Trudy for the drink and headed over to where her cousins and Mark's brothers were standing in front of the fire. Meanwhile, Trudy, with an aplomb and callousness worthy of a Hamptons hostess, informed Mark's father that Mrs. Yaeger was needed in the kitchen.

"Did you see me signaling?" Mrs. Yaeger whispered to Diane.

"We were busy talking," Trudy laughed. "You must have been sending out vibrations."

In the kitchen, the smell of bread being warmed made Diane's mouth water.

"This cake is beautiful," Diane said. "What's in it?"

"It's not a cake." Trudy beamed. "It's the appetizer—a

galantine of turkey. It's a whole boned turkey stuffed with tongue, veal, pork, and pistachio nuts.''

"What's it frosted with?" Diane asked.

"Jellied white sauce."

"God," Diane moaned with anticipation.

"This supper never would have happened if it hadn't been for you," Trudy told her niece. "It's all from *The New York Times Cookbook*."

"What's in the pot?" Diane lifted the cast-iron lid and inhaled a fragrant cloud of steam.

"*Pot-au-feu*. We serve the broth for soup."

"What's for dessert?" Diane asked.

Trudy opened the refrigerator to display two thickly coated chocolate cakes, each almost a foot high. "I couldn't resist a recipe called 'Minnesota Fudge Cake'—not for Lynn's wedding."

Diane saw that her mother was upset. "What's the matter?"

"You look like you're going to be sick," Trudy said.

Diane's mother shook her head. "I'm all right. It's just that I'm not going to be able to eat your dinner, Trudy." She sat down on a kitchen chair. There was pain in her expression.

"Oh dear." Trudy looked distressed as she put the lid back on the pot. Diane was embarrassed that her mother saw her lick the finger that had sampled the frosting on the cake.

"I'm sure everyone will love it," Mrs. Yaeger spoke charitably.

"You've got to eat," Trudy said firmly. "Wait here a minute."

She hurried out of the room, letting the door to the dining room swing shut behind her.

Her mother put a hand to her forehead. "I'm so tired of being sick."

"You'll be fine, Mom. You look beautiful in that dress."

"I'd like to be buried in it. Seriously."

"Come on, Mom." Diane tried to tease her out of her low spirits. "I'll be an orphan if you die."

"You'll get used to it."

"Never." Diane massaged her mother's neck.

"I love you so much, Diane." Mother grasped her

daughter's hand. They had never been physically demonstrative, but Diane felt at perfect peace as her mother held on to her.

"I've got to get through Lynn's wedding," her mother whispered.

"I know. What can I do?"

"What you're doing now is perfect." Diane continued to rub her mother's back.

"I had a massage last week."

"I'd be embarrassed."

"I was too at first. It was a little like losing my virginity."

Trudy burst into the room. Her glass was full again.

"Come with me," she told them peremptorily. "Hurry. It's almost time for supper."

Trudy led them to her bedroom, full of windows with lace curtains, thick Oriental carpets, and heavy Victorian furniture. A long-neglected fire in the marble fireplace produced the only light in the room. Diane did not notice Tommy sitting crosslegged on Trudy's canopied bed until he spoke to her. The air was pungent with marijuana smoke.

"How's life in the Big Apple, Diane?" In the flickering light, he reminded her of the Chesire cat in *Alice in Wonderland*.

Mrs. Yaeger looked inquisitively at her sister-in-law.

"Tommy's got something for your appetite."

"This is too much." Diane was indignant.

"Are you talking about marijuana?" Mrs. Yaeger spoke the last word clinically, taking Trudy's revelation with more equanimity than Diane had expected.

"What else?" Tommy grinned the initiator's grin of relaxed self-confident superiority.

"Have *you* tried it?" Mrs. Yaeger asked Trudy.

"Not this stuff."

Diane repressed a laugh at the not-quite-natural authority with which she said "stuff."

Her cousin struck a match, held it to the bowl of a meerschaum pipe, and inhaled deeply. Diane shook her head when he handed the pipe to her, so he passed it to Trudy. She held the pipe's stem daintily and took a puff.

Diane's first impulse was to take her mother downstairs, but she was amused by the flirtatious way her aunt gave the pipe to Tommy and took it back. Also, there was something soothing about the cocoon of smoke Tommy wove around them. All four sat on the bed.

Mrs. Yaeger had allowed too much time to elapse to be able to leave the room self-righteously. She was fascinated by the ritualistic etiquette with which Tommy and Trudy passed the pipe back and forth. Her nephew let her examine the cellophane bag at close range. He encouraged her to put a piece of grass between her teeth, reasoning perhaps that the harmless action would break down her inhibitions.

"How do you feel?" Mrs. Yaeger spoke to Trudy with an excessive objectivity designed to hide her nervousness.

"Trudy's wrecked." Tommy burst into hearty laughter and clapped the old lady on the shoulder.

"Nonsense, Tommy," she said in her most dignified tone, and then put her fingers to her lips to stifle a girlish giggle. "I suppose I *am* a little stoned," Trudy admitted coyly. "You know, Emma, I read that marijuana's legal in some states for cancer patients." The enticement, and the mention of cancer, made Mrs. Yaeger back off.

"I've never smoked before," she said weakly.

"You'll get high quicker then," Tommy told her. Their eagerness put her mother off, but Diane could see that she was tempted. Tommy and Trudy were poised expectantly. Diane did not care either way. Her mother considered, took a deep breath.

"I don't think I can." Her tone conveyed that she regretted her cowardice.

"Really, Emma," Trudy snapped, disappointed, inhibitions leveled by drink and smoke, "what possible difference can it make?"

"Here, Emma, try it." Tommy offered her the pipe.

"You're right," Mrs. Yaeger said.

They smoked two pipes. Diane joined them. She had rarely been so enjoyably stoned. Trudy was hilarious. Trying to build up the fire, she rolled a burning log onto the carpet. Chaos ensued. Trudy poured a pitcher of ice water on the log and rug. After a tête-à-tête in a window seat, curtains flowing around them like a waterfall of lace, Diane heard Tommy call Trudy a "dirty old lady." He smiled complacently, used to being desired.

"I want to tell you something." Mrs. Yaeger hissed for silence, as if she had heard something. She was smiling broadly, now that she had their attention. Her eyes were puffy underneath, crinkled with amusement.

They waited. She stopped to experience a private sensation.

"Well?" Trudy intruded on her reverie.

"I'm hungry," Mrs. Yaeger announced.

"We did it." Trudy hugged Tommy. "Now let's get downstairs. If Emma's hungry, the rest of us must be starving."

Bob Yaeger met them on the stairs, frowning, puzzled. Trudy signaled to them to halt their conspiratorial laughter, and replied with stiff dignity to her brother's question about their whereabouts that Emma had not felt well. Mrs. Yaeger composed a sober face and told her brother-in-law that she was feeling much better. She put her arm graciously into Bob's and led him downstairs. Sensing they would not be able to look one another in the eye without laughing, the four smokers separated when they got to the foot of the stairs.

The dinner was a great success. Diane ate in the library with her uncles and Tommy. Unconsciously, she slipped into an interview mode. Asking the questions gave her more time to eat, and she could not remember when she had been so hungry. Coming from New York City, Diane was subject to celebrity treatment among the Pine City folks during visits, but she fended off their questions until she had finished a farm-sized piece of Minnesota Fudge Cake.

"Does it always make you this hungry?" Diane whispered to Tommy.

"Yeah," he sighed, grinning wickedly. "How do you think I got this?" He patted his stomach, though Diane saw no excess there.

The women cleaned up when dessert was finished and everyone drank coffee.

"Don't mind if I do." Tommy smirked, taking three cubes of sugar from the silver bowl on the tray Trudy was holding. "Pretty fancy party," he remarked to Diane. Tommy was natural in every situation. Her uncles, on the

other hand, were vaguely uncomfortable in Bob and Trudy's house. They stepped carefully across polished floors,
avoided sitting on "good" sofas, and watched each other
for cues on what silverware to eat with and what to do
with their napkins. Tommy didn't care. He would have
been just as comfortable in Bradley's house as he was in
Trudy's.

After dinner, it was the "boys' " turn to ask her questions about New York. Diane played to her audience. She
told them about going to Coco's, which one of them had
read about in the *Enquirer*. She was surprised they had all
heard of the Concorde. Even Tommy was impressed that
Alan got a thousand dollars a day photographing rats. As
usually happened, Diane got caught up in the myth she
handed down, and it seemed for a fleeting moment that she
missed New York. She could envision life there after
Bradley.

By tacit agreement, the "real party," as Trudy described
it, began at ten-thirty, after Mark's parents left. Bob Yaeger
organized a poker game in the den. Trudy took orders for
refills on coffee or drinks while Diane and her uncles took
places around the table. Lynn wanted to play, too, but
gave in cheerfully when Trudy insisted it was unmaidenly
on the night before her wedding. Trudy made sure that the
card players had drinks, and that Martha, Kate, and Emma
were comfortably installed with coffee and seconds on
dessert at the kitchen table. With deadpan humor, Mike
Lindstrom expressed relief that Kate wasn't playing, de-
ploring as he had for thirty years his wife's beginner's
luck. Trudy wished the players good luck and then she and
Tommy led the young lovers into the library.

Diane was a good poker player. She calculated odds,
knew when to stay in and when to get out, and was adept
at bluffing. She loved playing poker with her family. A
sense of communion came over her as she watched her
uncles: Mike, cigarette dangling from bearded face, squinting to keep smoke out of his eyes as he arranged cards;
John, studying his hand anxiously, as if trying to recall the
rules; Bob, good-naturedly fleeced, sheepish as he lost
game after game. They were so direct and natural. It was
refreshing; she could think of no other word. She thought
of her mother, in the kitchen, and how lucky she was to

have so many good people around as she faced death. In a flash of lucidity, Diane saw that life was too short for sophistication. With so many people who loved her, and took her love in return for something as natural as breathing (though they rarely said the words), she was back in touch with the sense of security that had always been at the core of her being. Her mother might be dying, but playing poker was the right thing to be doing that evening. It was better than conversation, better than silence. Having a good time was a protest against the absurdity of death.

It was after midnight when Diane's aunts emerged from the kitchen to take the boys back to the motel.

"Did you miss me?" Kate winked at Diane as she lay a plump hand on her husband's shoulder, studying his cards as she hugged him.

"Are you kidding?" He squinted. "I won for a change."

Everyone laughed. The often-repeated joke improved with age.

"Good game, gentlemen," Diane said, stacking her chips.

"How much did you win?" Mrs. Yaeger came up behind her daughter and put a hand on her shoulder. She was smiling, relaxed.

"Six dollars." She patted her mother's hand. "Are Sue and Lynn ready to go?"

"I don't know. We figured it would take longer to break up the game, so we came here first."

From the library, they heard the kind of raucous laughter that follows a sexual innuendo. Diane and Mike went to join Trudy's party.

Lynn's face was flushed. There was no trace of shyness in her smile. Sue and Mark's brother were holding hands. Tommy was whispering to Trudy, who broke into forced laughter.

"Hi, Dad." Tommy grinned.

"Hello, Uncle Mike." Lynn ran up to her uncle, threw her arms around his neck, and kissed him. "I'm so glad you're here. Did you know you were my favorite uncle when I was little? You know why?" The question was addressed to everyone in the room. "Because you had horses. Lots of horses. I'm glad you're here, too, Diane. I love you all so much." There were tears in her eyes. She withdrew to Mark, who stood by the fireplace. He put a long arm around her and folded her to him.

"Time to go," Mike told Tommy.

"Mom's ready, too," Diane added, for Lynn.

"But it's so early," Lynn protested.

"It's almost one o'clock," Diane said.

"Trudy wants to stay up all night and get donuts in the morning," Lynn told her. "Doesn't that sound fun?"

"Stay a while longer," Trudy coaxed. "I'll put some coffee on." The mention of coffee was both a concession and an acknowledgment that Lynn ought to stop drinking.

"There's a lot to do in the morning." Diane was sensible.

"You go on then." Lynn resigned herself to her sister's leaving. "We'll just have coffee and be right home. Mark can give me a ride."

Diane had misgivings, but Lynn and Tommy assured her that they wouldn't be long.

There was frost outside. Melting snow had refrozen into thin sheets on the sidewalk, and Diane held her mother's arm as they walked to the car. There was little conversation on the way home. She and her mother had overextended themselves with talk and games, and went to bed as soon as they got back. Diane set her alarm for nine o'clock.

Knocking downstairs woke Diane out of a deep sleep. It took her a long time to open her eyes, longer to find robe and slippers. Bob Yaeger was at the front door.

"Is anything wrong?" She was panic-stricken.

"Nothing serious. But I need help." She followed her uncle to his car. Lynn and Sue were asleep in the backseat. "I did something stupid," he explained. "I left Trudy up with the kids. I woke up because the boys were throwing glasses into the fireplace."

"What time is it?"

"Four o'clock."

It was hard to believe a woman could be as heavy as Lynn asleep. For the first time, Diane understood the concept of dead weight. The strain visible in her uncle's face worried her, but she could not get Lynn up the stairs without his help. They were able to guide Sue's steps to the bedroom.

Once upstairs, Diane assured her uncle that she could

handle the girls. She promised to call in the morning and they said goodnight.

Diane had had her share of hangovers, but her sister's transformation shocked her. Lynn might have been in a coma, it was so difficult to wake her.

"Are you all right?"

Lynn was moaning. "I've got the whirlybeds," she laughed. "When I close my eyes, I go into a spin cycle."

"Here, take these aspirins." Diane propped her up in bed. She was as pale as moonlight. She took a sip of the water and was sick to her stomach. The room filled with the acrid smell.

"Sorry." Her sister sighed and fell back into bed, more unconscious than asleep. Diane cleaned up the floor and went to bed, hoping her sister would be all right now that she had been sick.

_____ *fifteen*

When Diane went into the bathroom in the morning, Sue was sitting on the floor.

"I hope you don't need this right away." She smiled feebly. "I'm going to be here for a while." Her complexion was the color of chalk.

"Want some coffee?" Diane offered.

"I just want to go back to sleep."

Sue was shaky on her feet standing up. She walked on tiptoe back to Lynn's room. Lynn shook her head desperately when Diane tried to wake her. "Go back to sleep then." As if there was any alternative, Diane thought.

Downstairs, Mrs. Yaeger had made coffee in the urn.

"Good morning," she greeted her daughter cheerfully.

"How did you sleep?" Diane asked.

"Like a log. And I woke up starving."

"We'll have to get Tommy to leave you some of his medicine," Diane said.

Her mother smiled. "Want some oatmeal?" Mrs. Yaeger filled her bowl. "I expected Lynn and Sue to be up by now. I was up at the crack of dawn the day Bill and I got married."

"They were at Trudy's until after four," Diane said. "We should probably let them sleep a while longer." Diane empathized with her hungover sister and cousin, but luxuriated in her own sobriety.

The house was ready for guests. Her aunts were on their

way over. The florist was due at eleven, the photographer at noon, Pastor Schulze at one-thirty. When Kate and Martha arrived, Diane went into the library to call Bob Yaeger.

"How are they?" he asked.

"Pretty sick. How are the guys?"

"Mark's fine. He didn't drink much. He was just tired. Tommy's like Trudy—he's immune to alcohol."

"What time are you coming over?"

"Eleven-thirty."

"They'll be up by then. I hope."

"If you need help, ask Kate."

The smell of sauerbraten stung Diane's nostrils when she rejoined the women in the kitchen. Kate's presence, even more than her mother's, evoked the security of childhood. Diane helped them dress a ham, boil and skin sweet potatoes, and clean celery until ten-thirty, when she was forced to agree with her aunts and mother that Sue and Lynn ought to get up.

"Lynn's got to do her hair," Mrs. Yaeger said, "and the photographer will be here in an hour."

There was no sound from Lynn's room as Diane mounted the stairs. Lynn did not respond to Diane's shaking.

"Lynn, are you all right?"

Her sister opened one eye, saw Diane, shut it again. Diane went over and pulled the curtains open.

"Oh, God," Lynn moaned. She put her forearm over her eyes. "Diane, I've never felt this bad in my entire life. I don't ever want to see Trudy again."

"What can I get you?"

"It's hopeless."

"Could you get out of bed?"

"I *could* die, my head hurts so much."

"You're getting married in three hours."

"We have to call it off."

"Here. Try to sit up." Lynn tried, but sank back into her pillow, grimacing.

"I made a fool of myself. I think. I don't even remember what I did. Diane, I'm going to be sick."

Diane got the metal wastepaper basket to the bedside.

"I have to sleep." Lynn lay down. "Wake me up in an hour. Maybe I can get up then."

Diane needed help. She looked over at Sue, who watched silently, afraid of being asked to get involved.

"How do *you* feel?" Diane asked.

"Like my stomach could turn on me any minute."

Her cousin had entered the first stage of recovery—in pain, but capable of imagining a time when she would no longer hurt. The pain could even be the source of humor, like the hangover jokes on neighborhood bar napkins.

"I could use a little more sleep, though," Sue entreated.

Diane went to get Kate.

With *gemütlichkeit* passed down undiluted from Bavarian grandparents, Kate could be depended upon to make the best of the situation.

"Sue's okay," Diane concluded her briefing at the top of the stairs. "We can't expect her to do more than get herself through the day, but if we can get her going, it'll give Lynn moral support."

"Uncle Willie's cure is our only hope," Kate said.

Kate went downstairs with an alibi for her sisters-in-law. The clock struck eleven. Bride and bridesmaid were still asleep. Diane succeeded in getting Sue out of bed and into the shower. She shook her sister.

"My stomach feels awful," Lynn said in a hoarse voice. "I can't get married today."

"Mark's on his way over. You'll feel better after you take a bath." Diane began filling the tub. Dejected, immobilized by pain, Lynn raised her arms meekly so that Diane could take off the slip she had slept in. Diane had not seen her sister naked since childhood. Even with her unhealthy pallor, Lynn was beautiful. She kept her neck and back rigid as she lowered herself into the water, in order, she explained, to keep her headache from touching the side of her head.

"Do you remember Uncle Willie?" Diane asked. Lynn nodded. Diane explained the cure.

"I'll be sick again," Lynn complained.

Diane made her drink a glass of warm water. She was sick immediately. Diane was relentless. Lynn shook her head.

"I can't," she cried. "It's no use. I can't do it."

"Keep drinking water." Diane hooked a rubber hose with shower attachment to the sink.

Kate had come back, and arranged Lynn's clothes. Lynn sputtered and gasped and gagged and moaned while Diane washed her hair. Afterwards, she sat wrapped in a towel, statuesque, leaning forward from the edge of the tub, resting her head on arms folded over her knees, silent while Diane used a blow drier on hair that reached almost to the floor.

Sue was dressed. The front doorbell had rung four different times. Kate managed to slip away and get herself dressed. Sue watched apathetically as Diane put makeup on Lynn. Dusting a rosy blush on her sister's pale face, Diane left her in Sue's care while she ran to get dressed.

There was no time for a shower. Diane had not expected the peach-colored dress to look so good. Already her hair was growing out. She brushed it energetically onto her forehead and over her ears. The look was severe, old-maidish, elegant in spite of itself. She put on a little too much makeup.

Despite Sue's halfhearted exhortations, Lynn was asleep when Diane returned. They woke her up, helped her to her feet, led her to the stairs. Diane went first, in case her sister stumbled. She had the unexplainable sensation that her aunts and uncles were looking at her rather than at the bride. She saw why when she turned at the landing. Alan Jennings stood beside her mother, arms crossed, grin elfin behind his beard. The charcoal gray suit was new, expensively tailored.

"Who invited you?" she spoke softly as she helped her sister past him. She was pleased, not surprised.

"Is that any way to greet a man who's come all the way from New York to see your sister get married?" Trudy was eager to embrace the drama that presented itself. The sunlight accentuated the wrinkles in her old face.

"I invited him," Mrs. Yaeger spoke up meekly. "He called yesterday while you were out, and I couldn't resist telling him." Her eyes implored Diane to let it be the right thing to have done. If that was what her mother wanted, then it *was* the right thing.

"It's nice to see you." She took his hand and kissed him decisively on the cheek. Everyone relaxed. The guests turned their attention to the bride holding onto the bannister, smiling wanly at Alan, and averting her eyes from the flash of the photographer's camera. Lynn was ominously pale.

"Let's take some pictures on the front porch," Diane said to the man with the camera. Someone opened the front door. Outside, it was cool and cloudless.

"Lynn looks nervous, doesn't she?" one of the cousins was saying.

"You remember Alan, don't you, Lynn?" Her mother introduced him as if he were her charge for the day.

Lynn nodded rapidly. "I'll be right back, Mom." Beads of sweat were on her forehead.

"You'd better put your coat on if you're going outside," Mrs. Yaeger called after her. Diane signaled to Alan to follow them outside.

Alan took in Lynn in a wedding gown and veil being supported by her bridesmaid and vanished into the house.

"My head hurts so much, I wish I were dead." Lynn leaned against Diane. "I will never, never, *never* have another drink, as long as I live." Lynn shuddered as she took a breath. When she shut her eyes, the pain appeared to leave her face briefly.

"Not even beer?"

"Don't mention beer, Diane."

Alan returned with a glass of water steaming in the cold air, just as a big black Pontiac pulled into the driveway alongside them. He handed Lynn two aspirins.

Diane waved to Mark's parents.

"Here, drink this." Lynn took the glass from Alan and drank. He took a sister on each arm and advanced toward the future in-laws. Alan introduced himself.

"Doesn't Lynn look beautiful?" Mark's mother said.

"I can't believe there's still snow on the ground." Alan diverted attention from Lynn by being the foreigner.

"Is it spring already in New York?" Mark's father asked.

"It's been cool this week, but there are lots of flowers out."

"I didn't know they had flowers in New York." Mark's father appeared to be making a joke, but no one laughed.

"You have lovely weather for a wedding." Mark's mother looked from Lynn to the sunny sky.

"It *is* pretty out." Lynn mustered a smile. "And not

that cold, really." The observation sounded so natural that for the first time, Diane believed that her sister would make it through the wedding. In the living room, she installed Lynn on a sofa and signaled to Kate that she should come over and sit with her niece.

Diane made the rounds with Alan, reintroducing him to her relatives. Everyone remembered him from the previous visits. They had a moment alone together in the library before the minister arrived.

"You look good." She smiled. "I've never seen you in a suit before."

"You look beautiful." She was afraid he was going to ask to kiss her, but he did it without an invitation, not quite naturally, unused to his tender feelings.

"How come you called Mom?"

"I called you—last night," he corrected her. "Your Mom and I got to talking and she told me about the wedding. I asked her if I could come. I knew you wouldn't want me to, but I wanted to see your mother."

"I thought of inviting you." Diane walked over to a window. Pastor Schulze was getting out of his car. "But I'm like my mother. I don't like being a burden."

"I would like nothing better than to share the unfairness with you.

"Unfairness. That's the right word. When I look at my mother, with so many reasons for living, so many people who love her, so much wisdom—I'm just starting to find out about the wisdom—that's too much unfairness for anyone to take on. I couldn't ask."

"You can, though." Alan's eyes shone kindly. It was still a novelty kissing him, and his thick brown beard—softer than she remembered—tickled her face.

"The pastor's here." She took his hand and led him to the living room. "I've got to see if Lynn's ready."

"The bride's got quite a hangover."

"Trudy got her plastered at a party last night."

"Poor kid."

Diane took Lynn upstairs to lie down until the ceremony. Then Diane brushed Lynn's hair while the bride brushed her teeth.

"Think you can make it?" They started out of the bedroom.

"Pray." Lynn was serious.

The guests in the living room fell silent when they saw Lynn at the top of the stairs. She grasped the bannister like an invalid easing herself down one step at a time. Diane held her breath. Her heart pounded. When Lynn turned on the landing, though, Diane saw her smile, and sighed with relief. Lynn's eyes made no contact with the people who watched her. Gloriously pale, beyond discomforts, she had entered the exalted state of bride.

The ceremony was simple and beautiful. The pastor read the Song of Solomon. Trudy cried. Mrs. Yaeger's eyes filled with tears, but her smile had the radiance of sunshine breaking through clouds before rain has stopped. When the pastor informed Mark that he might kiss the bride, the scene was reassuringly old-fashioned, touching rather than corny. Afterwards, Lynn received well-wishers sitting down on the sofa by the fireplace, too tired from nervousness, Diane explained, to stand up. What little color had returned to her face drained when Tommy offered her champagne. Trudy was making her way toward them.

"I feel the same way about Trudy as I do about split pea soup," Lynn whispered to her sister. "The last thing I ate before I got sick with the flu this winter was pea soup. Now I can't stand the smell of it. And I can't talk to Trudy."

"Just smile and let her kiss you."

Trudy was upon them, pearl necklaces and gold chains knocking against her puffy face as she leaned over to kiss her niece.

"You look lovely, dear." The charm bracelet shimmered loosely on her wrist as she lifted her glass of champagne to her lips. "Lots of happiness to both of you." She toasted the bride.

"Thanks, Trudy," Lynn answered halfheartedly. The girl was becoming dangerously pale in her aunt's presence.

Diane took Trudy to visit with Alan, whom, she suspected, was of greater interest to Trudy than the newlyweds. Alan's arrival had made the old lady forget the disappointment of Bradley's not coming. She flirted shamelessly. They had met twice in New York, and it was tacitly assumed, at least on Trudy's part, that they had arrived at a "special understanding" the evening they had jitterbugged at that party in an apartment overlooking the United Nations. She informed him that he would be expected to dance with her later. In the meantime, she asked him about his strange shooting assignments, and professed not to understand why he chose factories over fashion. Trudy appeared on the verge of alluding to Bradley once, but she made a game of discretion, and only tiptoed around the forbidden territory to titillate herself and alarm her niece.

"Bradshaw couldn't be any better-looking," Trudy announced when Alan had gone off to inspect the serving dishes Martha was setting out on the dining room table. "Though to be perfectly honest, I'm not sure I really saw him on the 'Tonight Show' last week."

"It doesn't matter what Bradley looks like."

"They say looks aren't as important to a woman as to a man"—Trudy finished her champagne reflectively—"but I think a man must have made that up. When I have a choice, I prefer a good-looking man. Your father was a handsome man, wasn't he?"

Diane could not stay mad long at someone who shared such strong partiality for her father. On the mantle above the fireplace was a photograph of Bill Yaeger taken about the time Diane graduated from college. Diane contemplated the source of her high forehead, blue eyes, full Viking mouth.

"Let's go eat," Diane smiled. Trudy promised to join her after getting more champagne.

The Pine City women had outdone themselves. There was sauerbraten and sweet red cabbage, potato dumplings and hot potato salad, ham and "gourmet baked beans," as Diane called them, heavy with bacon and brown sugar. There were bowls of cold potato and macaroni salads, mashed potatoes with creamery butter in craters among the peaks, string beans and green-tomato relish canned from Kate's garden, marshmallow-coconut ambrosia, candied yams, and a venison roast brought back from a winter hunting trip. Centered on the banquet table was the wedding cake, three layers covered with white-butter icing, topped at Mrs. Yeager's suggestion with a soft purple iris.

There was something Old Testament about the abundance of food. It made the wedding guests rejoice at the good fortune of being alive, together.

They were too full for cake until after they had danced.

There was an accordionist, who commenced playing an energetic polka as soon as the living room furniture was pushed to the side of the room and the carpet was rolled up. Kate coaxed Bob Yaeger into dancing. Diane took Tommy for a partner. Diane noticed Lynn disappear unobtrusively up the stairs. When the first dance was over, Diane followed her sister. Asleep, complexion as white as the wedding gown in which she lay as if on a cloud, Lynn reminded Diane of Rosetti's Ophelia. She tiptoed out of the room.

"Know how to polka?" Diane sat down beside Alan on the steps, where he watched. He shook his head. Everyone was flushed and laughing. She preferred this to Coco's any day. It was real. Tommy and his mother ended up on the floor. Everyone hooted and clapped. The accordionist struck up the "Beer Barrel Polka."

"Come on." Diane pulled Alan toward the living room. "I'll show you how."

They spun in a tight circle around the room, clinging to each other to avoid being flung apart. Diane was dizzy, out of breath, Alan's eyes sparkled with exertion. They laughed uncontrollably when their eyes met. The dance was a child's game—aimless, endlessly repeated, intrinsically interesting. Alan was uninhibited on the dance floor, not afraid to experiment or be laughed at. He knew how to lead. It seemed significant that they danced well together. Alan was knowable. He did not bend her to fit a mold. He was comfortable with her people. He was a nice man. At the moment, Diane could not have paid him a higher compliment.

Diane danced with all her uncles, with Mark and his father, surprisingly aggressive on the dance floor, and with her cousins. Alan danced with the aunts. Sue danced every dance with Mark's brother. Mark danced with his mother.

Diane joined her mother on a couch pushed beside the fireplace.

"Is Lynn feeling any better?" Mrs. Yaeger asked.

"She's resting upstairs. The last couple of days have really worn her out."

"Poor girl. We should have taken her home with us last night." Mrs. Yaeger looked preoccupied. The skin was stretched tight across the bones of her face, and the circles under her eyes surfaced through makeup. "Will you still get married in Minneapolis?"

"Let's worry about finding the right guy first." She put her arm affectionately around her mother.

"Alan Jennings is a nice man," her mother observed as they watched the reserve with which he escorted Trudy along the dance floor, careful not to tire her.

"Yes, he is."

"Do you love him?"

"In a way."

"Be open to the possibility." Mrs. Yaeger laid her head on Diane's shoulder.

"There's something missing, Mom."

"There always will be. It's no excuse for not being happy." Her mother swallowed as if choking back emotion. "I worry about you, Diane. You work so hard trying to figure out what you want. Sometimes I'm afraid you'll be too busy looking to recognize it when it comes along."

"If I do find out, though, the hard work will have been worth it."

"You'll never be sure."

"Maybe that's good."

"Did I do that to you? Make you so unsure?" Her mother's brow furrowed.

Diane shook her head. "I've done it to myself."

Kate called to Mrs. Yaeger and pointed to the cake.

"You'd better see if Lynn can get up," her mother said.

It took a long time to wake Lynn up. Then she insisted on splashing cold water on her face, so there was makeup to reapply.

"How are you feeling?" Diane asked as they went downstairs. Lynn walked at a normal pace.

"My headache's gone. But the thought of eating cake makes me sick. The wedding pictures are going to be horrible." Lynn smiled weakly. "Do you think we'll laugh about this someday, Diane?"

"Probably."

"I like Alan."

"So does Mom."

"I'm glad he came."

"Me too."

The cake was positioned on the dining room table for

pictures. The slice Lynn cut was too big to fit into Mark's mouth, which amused the onlookers so much that no one noticed Lynn did not taste her own piece. Lynn was so revived by her nap that she confidently—with a smile Diane knew was relief—put a glass of champagne to her lips.

"Mom, can Mark and I spend the night here?" Lynn called to her mother. "I'm too tired to drive to Bob's cabin tonight."

"Hey, it's our wedding night." Mark was aghast.

"I'll kick the teddy bear out of bed," Lynn teased her husband.

"We could stay at the motel where Martha and Kate are staying," Diane heard him whisper.

"It's too cold out." Lynn put her hand in his and squeezed. "Let's stay here."

"You're certainly welcome." Mrs. Yaeger found her son-in-law's consternation amusing.

"Come upstairs for a minute." Lynn was almost co-quettish. "I want to show you something."

"Let me get a piece of cake first." He followed her upstairs.

Lynn might have gone back to sleep, but she came down at six-thirty to say goodbye to her new in-laws. She stayed downstairs and danced for the first time.

With the exception of Alan, the men had tired of dancing by eight o'clock, so the women danced with one another. Only Diane had a male partner. She kept Alan to herself. She had never enjoyed his company so much. When the musician slowed his tempo, the girls made good-natured jokes about sitting out the dance, and took places on chairs and sofas to watch Diane and Alan dance.

"When are you going back?" she whispered.

"In the morning."

"I'm glad you came." Diane laid her head against his shoulder. The turmoil of recent weeks was stilled for a moment. "Where are you staying?"

"At the Marquette Inn. Want to go for a ride after everyone leaves?"

"I can't leave Mom." Diane could not be alone with Alan that evening.

"She'll be okay with your sister."

"I have to stay." Emma Yaeger sat alone on the couch by the fireplace, too tired to look alert or cheerful. The music, too, had a valedictorian effect on the gathering. Martha and Kate signaled to each other that it was time to go.

"When will you come back to New York?" Alan asked.

"I'm not sure. I have a favor to ask, though." She looked into his eyes. "Will you wait for me to call you?"

"That's hard."

"Promise?"

"All right." He kissed her, almost politely, as if thanking her for the dance. The musician finished the song and everyone clapped. The dishes had been done. Coats were gathered. Alan disappeared up the stairs, and appeared moments later with Lynn on the landing. Kate called for everyone's attention, and summoned Diane and Sue to the foot of the stairs.

"Lynn has to throw the bridal bouquet," she announced.

Sue was blushing. She averted her gaze from Mark's brother and pretended that she did not see in Lynn's playful glance that she would get the bridal bouquet. It turned out to be a ruse, however. Lynn turned suddenly and pitched the flowers directly into her sister's arms. Everyone cheered. Sue's smile became progressively more mechanical as she prepared to leave. Diane heard her aunt telling Sue on their way out that it was only right for Diane to get the bouquet because she was seven years older.

"She almost forgot." Alan smiled mischievously as he took Diane's hand at the front door. The newlyweds said good night to their guests on the porch. Lynn seemed to have gained strength at her mother's expense. Mrs. Yaeger said her goodbyes from the couch where she sat. She seemed frail in her fatigue, but her family did not take leave of her as an invalid.

"We're having a birthday party for Martha two weeks from tonight," Kate told Emma as she leaned over to kiss her. "Lynn's bringing blueberry salad. Mark says he'll drive you up. Will you still be here, Diane?"

"Yes."

"We'll see you at our place then."

"What time?" Emma Yaeger asked.

"Seven o'clock. Any chance you can come up sooner?" Kate asked Diane, who was helping Trudy into her coat.

"If Mom wants to."

"We'll see.

No one mentioned Emma Yaeger's illness as they said goodbye, but they did not ignore it either. It was normalized somehow, relegated to a fact as simple as a new baby or a birthday.

The good nights took a long time. Bob Yaeger explained a shortcut to Mark to get to the cabin. Trudy asked about honeymoon plans, but Lynn cut her off with a dutiful kiss. Alan promised Tommy copies of the photographs he had taken from an Iowa crop duster. When Alan leaned over to kiss Mrs. Yaeger goodbye, she took his hand and held it for a moment in hers.

"I'm so glad you could come." Her voice was hardly more than a whisper. Alan kissed Lynn, too, a kiss that told them all he had won her over. Last, Alan kissed Diane. Though he kissed her on the lips, it was a public kiss, familiar but not possessive.

"Call soon," he whispered. Goodbye kisses from Trudy, Martha, Kate, and Sue indicated that his conquest of the family was complete.

Lynn and Mark and Diane walked the wedding guests to their cars, where the goodbyes started all over again. The slam of car doors thumped in the clear, cold air. Emma Yaeger was asleep when they went back inside. Her mouth was open in exhaustion, her head tilted backwards, her neck arched forward. She was so silent, so pale, that the fire-light reflected on her closed lids was the only suggestion of life in her face.

_____ ***sixteen***

They slept late Sunday morning and spent the early afternoon getting Lynn and Mark off on their honeymoon.
Diane and her mother waved goodbye to them from the
front porch. It had gotten warm overnight. The only snow
left was in the shade of the evergreen shrubbery. Thick,
puffy southern clouds had replaced the impersonal cirrus
clouds of winter. The new clouds had character. They
were friendly.

"I made it." Mrs. Yaeger inhaled the warm air and
offered her face to the April sun. Mark honked. Everybody
waved a final wave.

"You were magnificent." Diane put her arm around her
mother's shoulder. A surprisingly fat robin hopped on the
front lawn.

"It was beautiful, wasn't it?"

"Yes. Did you sleep enough last night?"

"You would think twelve hours would be enough,"
Mrs. Yaeger said, smiling, "but that's the awful thing
about cancer. You do things that are good for you—eat
good food, take a pleasant walk, get a good night's sleep—
and your body still runs a deficit."

"Come inside." Diane took her mother's elbow. "I'll
make you toast and tea."

"No thanks. I'm still full from yesterday."

Mrs. Yaeger slept all afternoon. Diane cleaned the house.
Her mother woke up for a couple of hours in the evening

and they had a cup of tea together. However, the emotional intensity of the wedding had exhausted them both and they went to bed early.

When Diane woke up Monday morning, she heard activity in the master bedroom.

"What are you doing up so early?" Diane greeted her mother, who was pushing hangers aside one by one in the closet.

"Packing."

"Packing?" Diane's stomach knotted in alarm.

"It's time to go to the hospital."

"But I thought—" Diane choked on her words.

"It's time." Her mother was resigned.

"Wait—let me help you," Diane said.

"I can do it." In the room she had shared with her husband for almost thirty years, Diane's mother put clothes into an overnight bag.

"This reminds me of going to the hospital to have you." She folded a nightgown and put it into the bag. "I never packed ahead of time. I was afraid if I did, something would happen and I wouldn't get to go. It's funny. I never was afraid. I never *am* afraid of things once I realize I can't do anything about them. I let God take over."

"I love you, Mom."

"You make me feel so lucky." Her mother stopped, smiled at her. "I wonder if God intended people to be this happy." Diane marveled at her mother's sincerity. Mrs. Yaeger became progressively more excited as she packed.

"I don't think this will need cleaning." She left the dress she had worn two days earlier hanging on the closet door. "Do you think it looked all right? I've lost a lot of weight."

"You looked beautiful."

When the suitcase was packed, Emma Yaegar asked her daughter to carry it downstairs. Diane took the bag but remained with her mother, who appeared to be having a stomach pain. Her lips were compressed to white lines, her jaw clenched. When her face relaxed, she inhaled gratefully.

"There," she sighed. "We spent twenty-seven years together in this room." She spoke respectfully. "So many nights in bed, huddled under Pine City quilts—remember? They gave us a new one every Christmas. We used to lie in the dark, listening to the clock downstairs, and imagine growing old together. In our daydreams, we were eighty and had a houseful of grandchildren. I still don't entirely understand why things have ended so early." She paused, surveying the room. "I suppose life wouldn't be very interesting if God explained all his moves." Mrs. Yaeger walked slowly around the sunny room, opening dressers, peeking into closets. "I should have given away Bill's suits when he died. But I never touched a thing. He died so suddenly, sometimes even now it's as if he's just away on a long business trip and he'll be home next week. Look at these shoes, Diane. They're so heavy. He paid over a hundred dollars for these. I said it was a sin, paying that much for a pair of shoes, but he said they'd last forever. Here they are." Her laugh was not bitter.

Mrs. Yaeger shut the bedroom door behind her as if closing a book at the end of a chapter.

"If you felt that way about Dad's things, why were you in such a hurry to pack my things away?" They were passing the "guest room" on their way to Lynn's room. Diane had never realized that she resented what her mother had done.

"I don't know exactly—" Mrs. Yaeger searched for a clue to the contradiction. "It was very painful for me, your leaving. I cried every time I walked past this room. The poster of the Eiffel Tower, the sailboats you and your father built, the shelves of books—it all reminded me that you were never coming back. Maybe putting your things away was my way of getting back at you for how much it hurt when you left."

Diane put her arm around her mother and held her for a moment.

They walked into Lynn's room. The wedding gown hung from the closet door, the only evidence of the recent ceremony. Mrs. Yaeger fingered the lace of the dress, *her* wedding gown.

"I hope Lynn will be happy," she said.

"She will."

"Good. Will you stay close?"

"Of course we will."

"If I could only be sure you'll be happy, too."

"Happy." Diane spoke the word thoughtfully. "Marriage and children."

"I won't apologize for wanting for you what every woman wants. You can have the other things, too." She dismissed the "other things" with a wave of her hand.

"I haven't thought about the 'other things' for a week now," Diane said. "They don't seem so important now."

Diane helped her mother downstairs. Each step was a painful effort for the older woman.

"I want to have a look around downstairs, too," her mother whispered. The pain passed. Her eyes grew soft. Diane followed her mother into the library.

"Remember watching 'Felix the Cat' with Lynn here Saturday mornings?" Her mother's face relaxed into a smile. "You made your father and me stay in bed, even though we were awake, so you could babysit. You were always in a hurry to grow up."

"I would fix Lynn cereal and cinnamon toast and then we watched what I wanted because I could read the *TV Guide*."

The room was a catalog of memories, histories, associations. Mother and daughter browsed there long into the afternoon. Attempting to translate inscriptions in Swedish on the yellowing pages of the Lindstrom family bible, they came across the family tree, brought up to date by Emma Yaeger with the birthdays of both her daughters and the date of her husband's death. Diane wondered if her mother was thinking about the next date to be added. They turned the page in silence.

They rummaged through a deep desk drawer filled with old letters. "I thought about sorting through all these papers," Mrs. Yaeger said, "but I'm afraid you and Lynn are stuck with the cleanup." She smiled enigmatically.

"I'm not throwing anything out," Diane warned her. "I've thrown away too much already."

"You won't have time to go through it all. Life goes on."

"I'll make time."

They walked onto the sun porch. It was bright with afternoon light. The air was humid and smelled of peat moss. Mrs. Yaeger picked a yellowing leaf from a plant Diane did not recognize. She squeezed water from an atomizer onto the frond of a fern, and turned a tropical plant almost as tall as she was so that the other half of its leaves were exposed to the sun.

"Lynn will try to take care of them," Mrs. Yaeger said, "but she's like her father. She thinks God didn't intend plants to live through a Minnesota winter."

"I'm worse," Diane laughed. "I'm the only person I know who can kill a philodendron."

"That takes work." Her mother stroked the waxy leaves of a small tree. "I'm a lot like these plants. We're both uprooted from the land, transplanted into a house, loved. The best years of my life have taken place in this house. You're too much like your father to understand how I love this place."

"Stay, then." Diane saw with sudden insight that her mother belonged in the house. "Stay here. I'll talk to the doctor. I'm sure it can be done. We'll get a nurse."

Mrs. Yaeger stroked her daughter's cheek affectionately and looked into her eyes.

"Lynn and I talked about that. But I could no more die here than I could have given birth at home. I understand why people invented a separate place for giving birth and dying. I want to leave the house peaceful, the way it is now."

Mrs. Yaeger went into the kitchen.

"Are you hungry?" Diane was hopeful.

"No, but you haven't eaten yet."

"I'm not—"

"Let me make you a sandwich—one of my special ones."

"Do you suppose every mother has a special touch with sandwiches?" Diane watched her mother pile cold cuts onto bread.

"It's part of the job." Her mother cut the sandwich in half and poured her daughter a glass of milk. It tasted creamy. The sandwich was superb, but it was difficult to eat with her mother watching.

Diane thought about all the times her mother had watched: from a bench at a playground; on a towel, with all her clothes on, at the beach; in an audience while her daughter delivered a prize-winning speech on good citizenship. Diane knew that her mother was too ill to eat, but she rebelled suddenly at this vicarious maternal pleasure. She wanted to put the sandwich aside, to demand angrily to know why her mother had never gone down a slide or worn a bathing suit or told her she was "full of shit" as her father had for the editorial in the paper. But it was too late to teach her mother assertiveness. Her mother was who she was—a woman who made great sandwiches and enjoyed watching her daughter eat them.

Diane carried her mother's suitcase out to the car.

"I feel the way I used to feel before leaving on vacation," her mother said as Diane locked the front door. "Like I ought to check the stove one more time to make sure it's turned off and all the windows are locked."

She took her daughter's arm and they walked in silence out to the car.

_____ *seventeen*

Diane was disconcerted by how eagerly her mother embraced the role of patient. Shown into her private room, Emma Yaeger was impatient to climb into the high metal bed.

"Everything is so clean and white," she sighed.

She was only too willing to surrender to the reassuring routine and got increasing pleasure each day out of being a "good patient."

Diane had never spent time in a hospital before. It amazed her that her mother was able to sleep amid such ceaseless activity. There were clocks in every room, corridor, and hallway, and day and night a continuous parade of hospital staff moved in and out of Mrs. Yaeger's room. They took her pulse, probed her abdomen, adjusted the intravenous or changed the bottle of glucose, administered injections, gave her pills, read charts, took her temperature, changed her sheets, delivered flowers, and took her in a wheelchair to rooms where she was examined, questioned, studied, lectured to, tested, x-rayed, and, once, operated on to alleviate pressure on her stomach. It seemed a new shift was always coming on; the staff called cheerfully to one another in the halls; patients were continually wheeled past Mrs. Yaeger's room.

Diane did not like Dr. Martin. She was suspicious of a man who would devote his life to the terminally ill. He used his jargon too freely, and was too ready to admit his helplessness. She felt hatred and rage for this man who used Latin and Greek words to describe the progress of a disease he could not control. She especially disliked his manner of explaining in exact but simplistic detail what he was doing while he examined her mother and attempted to deaden her pain. For Emma Yaeger, the flood of senseless words was soothing, but they infuriated Diane. She avoided the doctor whenever she could.

Lynn and Mark returned home Thursday. Diane met them in the hospital lobby. Lynn was upset that Diane had not called.

"How is she?" Lynn asked. Diane had lost track of the weather beyond her mother's drawn blinds, but her sister's ruddy cheeks suggested that it was cold again.

"Not very good." Their mother had eaten no solid food since the wedding. The operation had weakened her. She resisted heavy sedatives, insisting that they interfered with her visit with her daughter.

It struck Diane as she accompanied the newlyweds to her mother's room that the worst thing about the hospital was the absence of privacy. Conversation was invariably interrupted by a doctor or nurse. Diane had already given up hope of further talks like the ones of the week before. However, her mother did not seem to mind. Pain made her self-centered, and when she was awake, which was not often, she talked almost entirely about what was happening to her body. Watching her sleep, hour after hour, Diane had the sense that her mother was weaning herself from life. It was a peaceful process. It would have been horrible if her mother had fought it, but if anything, Emma Yaeger accepted it too easily. Diane resented her ready submission.

Mrs. Yaeger was asleep, but she opened her eyes a moment after they entered the room.

"Hello, Martha," she whispered to Lynn.

"I'm Lynn." She leaned over and kissed her mother's cheek.

"You looked like my sister just then." She smiled wanly, not embarrassed by the mistake. "She was your age when she got married. I've been dreaming about her. We were young again. It was very pleasant."

"How do you feel, Mom?" Lynn took her hand and caressed it with her cheek.

"Not so good. Except when I sleep. I have wonderful dreams. It must be the medicine. This morning I dreamed about *my* wedding. Your father wore tails. He had all his hair then. It was wavy brown. He was what we called an Arrow shirt man."

It surprised Diane that her mother talked about her own wedding without asking about Lynn's honeymoon.

"Lynn says the ice is all broken up on Lake Superior," Diane told her.

"Diane, do you remember the time you pushed Lynn in the water up at Bob's? It was August," Mrs. Yaeger told Mark, "but the water was so cold Lynn couldn't breathe. I never could enjoy the cabin when the girls were young. Diane jumped from rock to rock on the shore like a crazy mountain goat."

"There was too much ice to walk along the shore," Mark said. He was polite but diffident, as if fearing that recognizing his mother-in-law's diminished condition would make it worse.

All that afternoon, Mrs. Yaeger talked feverishly about Lynn's wedding, Diane's job in New York, the difficult adjustment to her husband's death, which she seemed on an unconscious level to think had caused her own illness. Like jewelry she was weary of, Emma Yaeger divested herself of her memories, happy to hand them to her daughters. Diane imagined an elderly woman, trapped in a burning house, throwing her favorite things to onlookers out windows that are too high to afford escape. The ultimate effect of this piling up of reminiscenses was to reduce memory to a mechanical act. Her absorption in the past set a barrier between mother and daughters rather than bringing them closer together.

Diane and Lynn took turns sitting with their mother. The few hours she was awake, Mrs. Yaeger talked mainly to herself or addressed people from her past in snatches of dialogue that sounded as if they surfaced verbatim from memory. She traveled backward through her life. She spoke to her truant brother about a chore he had not finished, scolded her sister for letting a horse out of the pen, remonstrated with her mother that she didn't want to go to church. Her brow was furrowed with anxiety as she told someone, firmly, that she could not marry him. She

hummed nursery rhymes, old polkas, hymns that epitomized the staunch Protestantism Diane's father had saved
his daughter from. Yet Diane learned little new about her
mother. There was no pattern to the fragments. Her mother's dreams, too, had to be jettisoned before the ship went
under.

There were things Diane wanted to say, though she was
silent during the periods when her mother ascended from
her isolation and recognized her. What was there to say,
after all, even to someone she loved as much as her
mother? Did her presence make it any easier for her mother
to face death? Mrs. Yaeger implied that it did once, when
she woke from a troubled sleep.

"Hi." Diane put *Better Homes and Gardens* down.
(She had been through every magazine in the newsstand by
Friday.) "How'd you sleep?"

"I dreamed about the pony again."

Diane had been haunted as a child by the story of her
mother being carried far from home on a pony she was
riding at the Pine County Fair.

"How far did the pony run?"

"Over a mile into the woods."

"Why didn't you pull in on the reins?"

"I was five years old. I was lucky to keep my grip on
the saddle horn. When he stopped, I was afraid to get off
for fear the horse would bite or kick me. I just sat there
crying while the horse ate grass. It was almost dark before
they found me. It's funny to think the past can be more
frightening than the future." She rang a bell beside her
bed and spoke into the intercom. "I'd like a painkiller,
please."

When a young nurse they had not seen before arrived
with a pill and a glass of water, Mrs. Yaeger explained: "I
can't swallow that. They've been giving me injections."
The nurse apologized and returned to administer an injection.

"That's better." Mrs. Yaeger's sigh indicated immedi-
ate relief. "Will I get addicted to that stuff?" She smiled
benevolently at the nurse.

"It *is* habit-forming," the nurse informed her. "But you
can't think of it that way. It's good for you because it
controls the pain."

"This medicine does funny things to me," she told her

daughter when the nurse left. "Sometimes I'm awake, but I'm dreaming. Sometimes I'm asleep, but I hear you turning a page or feel you watching me. I'm so glad you're here."

"Mom—" Diane saw her mother's face through tears. Emma Yaeger folded her daughter's hands into her own.

"We face God alone when we die. That's the way God wants it, and I accept that. But thank God you're here. As long as I'm not lonely, I'm not afraid, Diane. I'm not afraid."

Her voice faded. Emma Yaeger closed her eyes and was soon asleep. She slept all afternoon, waking briefly after dark for a visit with Bob and Trudy Yaeger.

"You looked just like Bill when you came in," she said, smiling. "It gave me a start." Her voice was hardly more than a whisper.

Trudy had been crying. Diane was afraid that the distress on her aunt's face would alarm her mother. But Emma Yaeger was oblivious to the gravity of her situation. She was too weak to talk much during their visit, and fell asleep while Trudy asked Lynn about the honeymoon.

Bob and Trudy went home at nine. Lynn left an hour later, promising to return early in the morning. Shortly before midnight, Diane noticed a change in her mother's breathing. Doctors were called, injections given, readings taken. Mrs. Yaeger had lapsed into a coma.

"How long?" Diane asked.

"An hour, a week." The doctor shrugged. He advised her not to call her sister.

Diane determined to watch her mother all night, but sometime before dawn she dozed off. She woke up because the room was too quiet. In the dim light, Diane bent over her mother. Pain no longer circled her closed eyes. The triumph of solitude was peaceful.

An unearthly stillness reigned, a silence death did not entirely explain. Outside, snow fell thick, straight, on a street unlined by tires.

_____ *eighteen*

Diane had been prepared for the food and drink after the wake, but not for the gaiety. She tried unsuccessfully to recall Hamlet's observation about the meats of his father's funeral furnishing the cold cuts at his mother's wedding.

Maybe it was living around animals, Diane reflected.

Huddled under a pile of quilts in an unheated upstairs bedroom at Martha's, she lay awake long into the night watching the moon. It was almost full. Life and death were everyday currency on the farm. Nurturing and harvesting, maybe farmers arrived at a vision of the cycles of life, beginnings and ends, in which death lost its unique terror. Only Lynn and Trudy, raised in the city, had cried at the wake. Martha and Mike accepted condolences about their sister with the grim matter-of-factness with which they might have discussed a disastrous harvest or a neighbor's barn fire. Diane resented her aunt's and uncle's acceptance of her mother's death.

It had stayed cold all weekend. There would be snow on the ground for the funeral. Diane could not sleep. She was thinking about Bradley's flowers again. Addressed to Mrs. Yaeger with a note that read simply "John E. Bradley, Jr.," the pink roses, clearly a get-well offering, had arrived as Diane packed up her mother's belongings the morning after her death. She was neither angry nor grateful about the flowers. The gesture seemed ill-timed, cowardly, but somehow characteristic of Bradley. It made her

a little less sorry that they would never see each other
again.

Someone was snoring down the hall. Lynn, sleeping
with Mark in the room next to hers, sighed and turned over
in her sleep. A dog barked in the courtyard and was quiet.
The Schmitts' two-story white-wood farmhouse was richer
in associations of her past than Diane's Minneapolis home.
There, her life was recorded in pictures and documents, as
in a history. Here, childhood memories arose unbidden in
the moonlight, taking on mythic proportions.

Diane had no sense of having slept. It seemed only
minutes before she heard her uncle downstairs listening to
the radio. It must be lonely, going out into the cold and
dark to milk cows. The moon had set. The night was dilute
with dawn. A screen door slammed, footsteps crunched ice
and gravel as John Schmitt walked out to the barn.

Putting on jeans and a sweater, Diane went downstairs.
A fire was burning in the cast-iron kitchen stove that had
belonged to Grandma Lindstrom. Shivering, Diane put her
feet up on a pile of dry wood and poured herself coffee.
The quiet, cozy kitchen justified winter. She tried to imagine growing up in her aunt's house, but the distance between her world and this was perhaps greater than that
between her world and Bradley's. Still, it was nice knowing this world was here when she needed it.

When she heard the truck leaving for the creamery,
Diane put on coat and boots and went outside. A cold
white winter sun rose between the slats of an empty corn
crib. A horse neighed. A sow squealed. A thin layer of
floury snow lay on frozen ground. Diane hurried across the
courtyard and let herself into the barn. It was dark inside.
The fetid warmth of the cows was overpowering, the
stench breathtaking. The cows had been standing at their
stanchions all winter now.

Looking down the aisle at the thirty black and white
Holsteins nudging languidly at hay, nostrils billowing steam
as they scattered the oats thrown down before them, thirty
udders relentlessly replenishing themselves with milk, thirty
backsides, intermittently emptying gallons of urine and
sweet rotten dung into the gutter—looking at all of this,
Diane was repulsed by life. If this was life—the mechanical inexorability of the body's functions, waiting, pas-

sively used and using—she wanted no part of it. For a moment, she envied her mother the dignity of no longer taking part in the cycle. What was frightening about the cows was that they existed simply to need. They were no more than the sum of their phlegmatic appetites. The sight of all this animal hunger suddenly horrified Diane. She let herself out a back door into a pasture.

After cows, the solitary trees in the overgrazed field were the essence of dignity. Plants were reassuringly simple. She understood now why her mother had felt such kinship with them. Diane was thankful for the inanimate world too: the sky—almost purple blue, covered with a transparent veil of cirrus clouds, miles high; the sun— more orange now, moistening the snow; the clear air and the firm, flat earth. The world became more beautiful as it descended from animal. It was consoling that her mother would be consigned to that beauty that afternoon. It was better than life. Her mother had escaped.

Diane took a walk. She felt conspicuous, walking along country roads. The few cars that passed stopped to see if she was in trouble. No one walked in the country; things were too far apart. The sun had gotten warm. The snow was dry, so it evaporated rather than melted, exposing stubble in the cornfields. The open space excited Diane. She did not want to think about going back to New York as she approached the farmhouse built in a grove of oaks—an island of dormant trees in an undulating sea of fallow cornfields.

Everybody was up when Diane got back. Martha, Sue, and Lynn were preparing breakfast. John was back from the creamery.

Trudy called from Kate's, where she and Bob were staying, to see if anyone needed a ride to church. Like a visiting relative showing off a different accent, Trudy had a good time in Pine City, exaggerating her sophistication. She would tiptoe into the barn in heels, remove a glove to pet a cow. She always rode in a pickup truck to a dance or picnic. Diane reminded her that they had Mark's car, and promised to meet her at church shortly before noon.

It was remarkable how routinely Martha orchestrated the huge country breakfast. There were fresh eggs from their own hens, scrambled in butter from their own cows. She broiled thick-sliced bacon from the hog they had butchered, and prepared cornbread, home-fried potatoes, and oatmeal. There was toast from homemade bread, orange juice, coffee, and a pitcher of milk pasteurized that morning. Where did the women find the energy to keep putting the meals together? Diane would rather have milked cows or worked in the fields. At least there there was sky, sun, fresh air. But someone had to feed the men who produced the food.

Diane stopped being hungry halfway through breakfast. She was surfeited with food and family.

"I want to go home right after the funeral," she told her sister as they were getting dressed.

"Is anything wrong?"

"Too much togetherness, I guess. They keep this merry-go-round of get-togethers going so they won't have to think about the things there are to be afraid of."

"They're doing it for us," Lynn defended them.

"I know. And I appreciate it. But I'd like to be home before dark."

"We'll go home with you, then."

"You don't have to."

"I want to."

The austere, underheated church was on a tree-lined street in Pine City. Emma Yaeger's family filled only the first few rows of the mercilessly hard pews.

The service was the antithesis of Bill Yaeger's funeral. Diane's father had remained a public person to the end. His obituary appeared in both Minneapolis papers, and a smaller version even ran in St. Paul. Hundreds of co-workers, business associates, and local government officials had come to the Yaegers' parish church. Her mother had been awkward, accepting condolences from strangers, letting them shake her hand or kiss her. At the time, Diane had been impressed by the turnout. It had seemed to her that the success of one's life could be measured by the impact one had had on the world left behind.

Emma Yaeger's funeral showed Diane how much she had grown up in the past three years. In retrospect, the "successful" people gathered about her father's body should have shown her the limitations of ambition. Who thought much about her father today, beside the people gathered in this church? For the first time, her mother appeared the wiser of Diane's parents: She had known all along that the only people who mattered were the ones who loved her.

The service was beautiful. Diane cried when Pastor Schulze read the Twenty-Third Psalm as if he believed what he read. His eulogy touched her.

"Though we were not far apart in age," he told the congregation, "Emma reminded me very much of my mother. I envy them their faith, those two women. It was so deeply imbedded that it seemed a part of their natures, like kindness or generosity. If I could learn the secret of that faith, and share if with just one of you today, I would consider my ministry a success. Perhaps God makes it easier for some people—" The pastor reconsidered his words, aware that he had bared personal doubts. "Praise God we have such examples of faith to inspire us. We are lucky to have known a woman as good as Emma Yaeger."

He maintained his composure, though his final words released silent tears among the congregation.

Diane cried for a lifetime of misunderstandings and disappointments, for all the things she would never be able to tell her mother and father. She cried because she could not remember faith, could not even imagine it. Unbelieving, she prayed that it would overpower her some day, without warning, like love, that she might be the one to be touched by her mother's faith.

The cemetery was muddy. The afternoon sun had thawed the black topsoil on the way to the gravesite, though the ground dug that morning had been frozen. The graveyard was situated on a knoll shaded by a grove of oaks. There was no fence separating the plot from the cornfields it overlooked.

It was almost a family cemetery. The first generation of Lindstroms buried there had spoken Swedish. The Lindstroms and Schmitts who watched the pine coffin set over the open pit owned a corner of the field for their own family plot. Emma Yaeger was buried next to her husband.

The pastor's words evaporated into the air, like the snow. Diane contemplated last fall's stubble, crushed by six months of winter. The bare branches of the oaks clacked in the breeze. It might be the last snow of the season disappearing. Diane looked skyward to avoid thinking about her father underground and her mother soon to be lowered beside him. She could not suppress the image of decay. She closed her eyes to the sun. She had not been out in the open since returning home. The quickening of her pulse, her joy in the fresh air and sunshine, were a betrayal of her mother, acceptable, Diane decided, only if she did not take life for granted. It can all end at any moment, she thought. She and Lynn stayed to watch the gravedigger lower the coffin and cover it with mud and ice. Diane took her arm, and they joined their uncle, who waited for them under a nearby tree.

"How soon do you start ploughing?" Diane asked.

"About two weeks. If it dries up some."

They talked of acres of corn and oats on the way back, of cows calving and horses foaling, of combines and cornpickers. At the Schmitts', Diane went upstairs to put her things together. She was closing her bag when Martha came into the room.

"You're staying for supper, aren't you?" She watched her anxiously. Beneath her taciturn manner, Martha grappled with the loss of her sister.

"I need to get home, Martha."

"The Cities?"

"For a while."

"Listen." Diane saw a spark of humor in her aunt's eyes. "If you stay for supper, I won't let anyone polka."

Diane could not help smiling. It pleased her that her aunt understood her so well.

"It's a deal." She embraced her aunt. "You are all so wonderful."

"I better get down and see to the roast." Martha had no intention of giving way to her emotions. She squeezed her niece's shoulder. "Don't worry, we'll get you on the road before dark."

PART THREE

_____ *nineteen*

Diane took an extended leave of absence from the paper. She stayed in Minneapolis several weeks, cleaning the house, storing or giving away her parents' possessions, sorting through records, documents, and business papers.

Lynn inherited the house, the car, and enough money for veterinary school. Diane received stocks, bonds, and insurance policies. The first thing she did with the money was repay Bradley. She sent no note with her check; she did not thank him for the flowers.

Alan kept his promise not to call, but sent two framed photographs of Mrs. Yaeger and her daughters at the wedding. Diane did not remember Alan taking the pictures. She was touched by how well he had captured the beauty of each of them.

Spring came, cold at first and rainy. It took Diane a while to get used to living with Mark and Lynn in their parents' house. Diane convinced them to move into the master bedroom once the closets and drawers were empty, but it seemed at times that the newlyweds were playing at grown-up, that Bill and Emma Yaeger would return home and surprise this invasion of privacy. Lynn and Mark tried to talk Diane into spending the summer in Minnesota.

She was tempted. In the first weeks after her mother's death, Diane actually considered staying permanently. But gradually she began to see that learning to appreciate her family was not the same thing as choosing to live again in their midst. Few women were as loveable as Lynn, but her innocence often irritated Diane. Lynn's unshakeably inborn optimism was Emma Yaeger's most useful heritage. Lynn mourned, but their mother's death did not shake her fundamental sense of rootedness, which marriage only deepened. They were very different women.

Staying in Minneapolis several weeks showed Diane how completely the city had changed in the ten years since she had lived there. She knew that with time she would learn her way to the new suburban shopping malls, but familiarity with the city was not hers just for claiming. She would have to work at it. To her surprise, Diane discovered that she had actually grown comfortable with the uprootedness she cultivated in New York. For the first time Diane saw the positive sides of alienation, the most important of which was mobility. She would come home more often, but she would never come home to stay. The truth of her mother's death was either that she had no home, or that whatever home she had was within her.

Pine City, too, lost its mystique now that it was an hour away. A trip to the farm was no longer one long party for the visiting celebrity, but rather immersion in the ceaseless comings and goings of busy farmers engaged in a symbiotic relationship with the "cities" nearby. She had always regarded the farm as a calm retreat from the vicissitudes of metropolitan life, more "real" than the world she had emigrated to. Her relatives wanted her to use part of her inheritance to buy a small farmhouse near them and come up there to write. However, the Pine City folks still had the social traditions of pioneers. Life was a constant exchange of shopping, farm work, and chores. It was a far more social existence than any Diane encountered in New York and she doubted that she could get any serious work done.

She also saw for the first time how much extra work it was for her family when she visited.

"We won't have time for the red-carpet treatment all the time when you buy Olaf's farm," Kate had warned her, laughing but serious. "You'll be one of us."

Her warning did not offend Diane, but made her conscious of the possibility that she preferred to romanticize the country and impose on her loved ones once or twice a year. The red-carpet treatment was part of the mystique.

Diane needed to be alone. When the house was clean and their affairs in order, she left for a cottage she rented in Nantucket. It was good to be by herself. The weather was cool and sunny. She slept late every morning and took long walks along the beach.

Diane expected solitude to soothe her sense of loss and help her accept it. Instead, the dreams she dreamed and the thoughts she thought, walking mile after mile along the beach, were filled with anger.

She was surprised at how much she resented her mother for dying. It had been easy to accept her father's death. He was a high-powered businessman; a heart attack was part of the stereotype. But her mother's mother had died at the age of eighty-three, not so many years earlier. Emma Yaeger was the shield that had protected Diane from a direct confrontation with the reality of her own death so that she could focus on developing her career. Diane was shocked at first at the selfishness of her grief and the extent to which it was caused by the fear of coming face to face with her own mortality. Her grief was not only self-ish, it was also self-centered. Her mother was no longer suffering. Diane grieved for her own certain death.

There were times when she felt near almost petulant tears, as if she were a child again and her mother had left her to get lost in a crowded department store. Irrationally, she felt that her mother had allowed herself to develop cancer, that it was a decision she could have avoided. At the funeral Diane envied her mother's faith. In retrospect she saw it as misguided, enabling her mother to accept what she should have resisted. In the end, it seemed a passive death, in keeping with the passivity that character-ized her life.

One of the most damaging emotions brought on by her mother's death was a never-before-experienced sense of being unlucky. None of Diane's friends her age had lost both their parents. She had said jokingly to her mother that she and Lynn would be orphans if she died. Perhaps what made it so difficult for Diane to stay home with Lynn and Mark was the fact that Lynn, flushed with the excitement of a new marriage, could not share Diane's sense of being orphaned. It was odd, but Diane felt embarrassed that both her parents were dead. Death was, after all, the ultimate weakness. She was surprised how deeply the death of her parents assailed her image of herself as a strong woman.

Her mother would have loved the saltbox cottage where she stayed. The low ceilings, rickety furniture, and bottle-glass windows were of colonial vintage. Seasoned kitchen utensils turned out perfect omelettes and flapjacks that should have been impossible without her mother's advice. She made Indian pudding from a recipe in a well-thumbed book on New England cooking and then got too upset to eat it, thinking how much fun it would have been to share it with her mother.

Diane often tried to make her mind blank, but silence or serenity too reminded her of her mother and the dull ache would return. Diane never doubted she would survive her grief. The poignancy with which she welcomed spring on that windswept island—as beautiful lashed by driving cold rain as when the breezes shimmered ripples in patches on a sunlit pond, the music of an aeolian harp made visible—gave ample evidence of recovery. But in the meantime, thoughts of her mother and Bradley and Alan succeeded each other so rapidly, they defied her efforts to order and classify them.

There was no telephone in Diane's cottage. At night, walking along island roads, her fear of solitude mitigated by the friendly clouds of stars, she often found herself headed to a phone booth on the edge of town. Its light was as disembodied as that of a light-house. Like a captain of the whaleboats that once frequented the island, Diane was equally drawn to and repelled by the loneliness of its light.

The phone booth gradually took on the quality of a destination. Diane would end up there on her late-night walks the way an old man might stroll to the post office each morning to inquire about mail, though perfectly aware that no one knows where he is. Once she tried to charge a call to Alan to *The New York Times*, but it was after midnight and there was no one on the switchboard to accept the charge.

The phone booth had the concrete arbitrariness of the object that a medium uses to summon the dead. Without thinking, one night Diane put the receiver to her ear. She realized with a start only after the operator had interrupted her reverie that her mother was no longer on the other end of the line to accept a collect call. Another night she lost track of time contemplating the phone booth. It was not until she was home in bed that she realized she had been trying to make the phone ring out into the night with a call from Bradley. Alone in bed in the cottage, however, Bradley was as dead to Diane as her mother.

Alan still did not try to contact her. It seemed typical that he would not know when it was time to break his promise, though he could have gotten her address from Lynn. She thought a lot about Alan, and her thoughts were confused. Again, Diane was surprised by how intensely she resented Alan. It seemed significant that he had been a pre-medical student when she met him. A college friend of Diane's had been engaged to a medical student, but broke up with him after a year because he insisted on them waiting six years until he finished his internship before they could get married. Diane felt contempt that a man could "put life on hold" in such a calculated manner while he carried out a rational life plan.

Perhaps Alan had more of that personality than she cared to admit. His sudden declaration after Bradley and the urgency with which he made love to her on the couch had been exciting. His arrival at Lynn's wedding seemed masterful. But these actions did not compensate for Diane's feeling that Alan had taken her for granted all the years of their friendship.

But perhaps he had not so much taken her far granted as he had hoped in his absentminded affection that she would change slowly and gradually enough to allow him to realize his own ambitions before settling into a relationship that would change him in ways he could not control. In one frame of mind, she could look at his detachment as a rare and admirable male tolerance that allowed her to develop and find herself. But on a deeper level, she suspected that while Alan had always cared strongly about her, his failure to declare his feelings sooner had not come from concern for her development but rather from absorption in his own career.

If she were to continue their relationship on this heightened plane, her biggest problem would not be believing that Alan had finally fallen in love with her. The challenge in loving Alan would be to forgive him for having taken so long.

Diane's desire to marry and have children had intensified since the trip home; it seemed to her to have almost a developmental quality. It never occurred to her that this would involve any compromise. Men didn't choose between career and family, and neither would she.

But was Alan the right man? He had a lot going for him. He loved her. It had finally fit into his plans to inform her of that fact. Or was it rather that she had forced his hand? He had known her parents. It was funny how important this now seemed. It linked him with her past, providing continuity farther back than their own friendship. Her family liked him too. That meant a lot. Most important, Diane loved Alan. She had no trouble admitting that she loved him. The question was whether she loved Alan the way she had always expected to love a husband or was what she called love merely the strong affection she would always feel for a friend who had shared with her so many important stages of her life.

They would have to spend time together when she got back to New York. The beauty of Alan was that he was familiar. She was comfortable with him. He was also a fast learner, and could probably be taught to love her the right way. It was hard to imagine having the time or the energy to get to know another man that well.

Yet she was not sure she could forgive Alan for his control. She would not marry a man, even a man she loved, because it was time or because she no longer had the patience to look. She would not be able to marry Alan until she was absolutely certain that the act was not a compromise. She did not allow herself to dwell on the fact that the question of compromise had never come up during her week with Bradley.

Alan sent her a copy of the *Rolling Stone* article when it was published. Diane half expected to hear from Bradley. She could not help wondering what he thought of the article. Everything about Nantucket reminded her of him. Eating chowder in a cozy inn, she wondered whether he had ever tasted better. The harbor recalled their day in

Maine. One golden afternoon Diane had the heart-stopping sensation of thinking she saw his boat.

Diane had worked for months engineering a move to the "Arts and Leisure" section. The article on Bradley convinced the editor there that Diane was qualified. Even more exciting, Diane was invited to fill a position as a full-time reporter. Diane's tremendous personal satisfaction was balanced by the prospect of New York without Bradley. She expected to see him again. She tried often to explain to her incredulous family that New York was a small town in many ways. She constantly ran into friends and celebrities on the street. Knowing that someday she would see him was almost as agitating as actually seeing him. Forgetting Bradley would be difficult.

Diane spent a lot of her time alone trying to assess Bradley's impact on her life. In many ways it was positive. She learned a lot from him about what she didn't want. The fact that he had lied to her about Susan Aldrich now colored Diane's initial envy of his money and his renown. She wanted neither at the price of personal dishonesty. His "immorality"—and she saw his act in that light despite her own lack of religious faith—made it easier for her to give him up.

Diane was hard on herself about Bradley. She could not have been lied to so easily, she decided, if she had not been so willing to believe. She could not have fallen in love so quickly if she had not needed to be in love. She never denied that she had been in love. She was not sure that she wasn't still in love. But no one bears a grudge as fervently as a moral person, she knew from personal experience, and she found it impossible to forgive his lie.

The question that intrigued Diane was what she would have thought of his values if he had not lied. There was not anything intrinsically wrong with having money or a reputation. She still wanted both for herself. The immorality came from striving for them or using them at the expense of another person. Taking Bradley up on his proposition had in no way diminished his being. Her ambition had done him no harm. But it might have hurt her, so perhaps it was excessive after all. You had to use gifts like Bradley had wisely. The more power you had to hurt others, the more careful you had to be.

The advantage of this line of thinking was that while it made Diane feel like a better, wiser person, it also allowed her to give full reign to the resurgence of ambition that followed the news of her new job. She did not leave for New York until she was impatient to get back.

The more interesting question Diane asked herself was how she might have changed had she come home without having known Bradley. After all, the most important thing Diane learned from her mother before she died was that the kind of success that Bradley epitomized (but which Diane has aspired to long before meeting him) existed on a distinctly inferior plane.

Face to face with death now that her parents were gone, the love she felt for her family, living and dead, assuaged her dread of life and death in a way that she had never experienced in her work. Freud had said love *and* work, but once acknowledged and enjoyed, the satisfaction of her promotion paled before the idea of loving a man sincerely, of spending her life with him and beginning with him a new network of love relationships. She had hoped that that man would be Bradley. Only time could cure her of that dream.

Perhaps Bradley's ultimate value lay in his having been a case history. Without him, it was possible that the residual rebelliousness in Diane's relationship with her parents would have prevented her from absorbing so completely her mother's wisdom. "Maybe things do work out for the best" was the message she might have left for her mother from the phone booth in Nantucket.

twenty

Diane was not happy with the article on an Off-Off-Broadway revival of _Ubu Roi_. Squinting at the words on the screen of her word processor, she felt a twinge of nostalgia for pen, legal pad, and manual typewriter. She was running out of time. The phone rang. It was Alan.

"I've got a story due in forty-five mintues."

"Take a two-minute break," he said. "I'm leaving for Houston in an hour."

"What are you doing in Houston?"

"We'll be shooting that offshore oil drilling platform in the Gulf of Mexico I was telling you about. It's being completed two weeks ahead of schedule."

"At least you'll be warm. I was on the phone three times this morning trying to get the super to turn the heat on."

"Why don't you stay at my place while I'm gone? My heat's already on."

"I may if it stays this cold."

"I saw a nice apartment this morning," Alan told her. "Two bedrooms and a view of the harbor. It's only thirty thousand more than the one we looked at on Sunday."

"I don't know, Alan. That's an awful lot of money. Maybe this isn't a good time to look."

"I've got to make the plunge sometime. Will you have a look this weekend?"

"Okay."

"Will you miss me?" Alan lowered his voice, as if someone might overhear him.

"Are you kidding?" She teased him out of intimacy. Even after six months, Diane was still not accustomed to their being lovers. "I'm going to stop at B. Dalton on the way home and buy a pile of books. I haven't read anything heavier than *Time* magazine since your trip to Québec last month."

"Well, I'll be thinking of you, while perched on an oil derrick over the high seas."

"Don't do anything stupid," she said. "I'll get tired of great literature. When do you get back?"

"Friday evening."

"Come to dinner?"

"Great. I'll bring a six-pack of Lone Star."

"See you Friday, then."

He hung up.

Forty minutes later, her editor buzzed.

"I need the *Ubu* piece."

"I'll be right in." She pushed a button. The machine began printing a corrected draft of the story. When it stopped, Diane ripped the paper out of the printer and wound through a labyrinth of open office toward her boss's desk.

"Thanks." After a brief glance at the article, he put it aside without corrections. "Put it through," he told her. Diane felt a spasm of pride. "Sit down." The abrupt invitation surprised her. She was annoyed that she had forgotten a pad and pencil.

"Are you and John Bradley personal friends?"

"No." The abrupt question made the color drain from her face. She had eaten breakfast, but a nervous tremor, as if from hunger, passed through her body. She compressed her lips tightly together and waited for him to explain the question.

"At our last editorial meeting, we decided to do an interview with Mr. Bradley on the making of the movie version of *The Great Thaw*. It's a colorful story—literary chap on location in the Mexican desert, on a glacier in Alaska—" He pressed hands together and moistened his lips. "When we approached his agent for an interview, we got a strange request."

His pause was so long that Diane finally said: "A request?"

"He said he'd give us an exclusive if *you* do the interview."

"He must have liked the *Rolling Stone* piece," Diane ventured.

"It wasn't *that* good." He probed her face for the deeper significance of request.

"True." Diane was sincere. The idea of seeing Bradley face to face filled her with panic. She knew from a newspaper article that he was back in town, but he had not called.

"I don't think you're ready for a major feature yet," her boss said.

"I agree," Diane said wholeheartedly.

He had expected a protest. He was puzzled; he tried to understand. 'You don't want to do the story?'

"No."

"This isn't a 'Brer Rabbit' scheme?" His face lit up at his solution to her reaction. She shook her head. Diane did not have a personal relationship with her boss. Since she could not level with him, she tried to evade the interview as rationally as possible.

"No." She answered with a hard-fought evenness of tone. "I exhausted the subject the first time around. Besides, the *Times* magazine did a story on him last spring."

He nodded. "But the movie's coming out right before Thanksgiving and it's going to be big box office. I'd really like the story."

"Wouldn't it establish a dangerous precedent, letting this man do your job for you?" The question was provocative, but Diane was determined not to do the interview.

"It's happened before."

Her voice fell. "But surely he doesn't have the right to pick one reporter over another. Discrimination is against the law."

Her boss's smile was amused and condescending. "Luckily, we're still free in this country to refuse an interview. You really don't want to do it, do you?"

"I really don't. He's a rude, overbearing man. It was extremely difficult interviewing him. I don't think I can do it again." Her voice betrayed emotion against her will.

"Would you do it as a favor, for me?"

Diane's heart sank. She expected to see Bradley again one day, but not alone, face to face. The prospect nauseated her. She considered telling her boss what had passed between them, but could not bring herself to mix personal problems with business. Her self-image as a professional won out over her fear of seeing Bradley.

"When?"

"This afternoon at two o'clock."

"Where?" Diane felt sick. Her bowels tingled with dread.

"At his apartment. I'll have my secretary confirm the appointment. We need the story by six tonight. Thanks, Diane."

"Thank you." Diane was too intent on getting out of the office to wonder why she was thanking him.

Back at her desk, she picked up the telephone to call Alan. She almost wept with frustration when she remembered his trip to Houston. The lack of his moral support was almost worse than having to see Bradley. She had never needed Alan so much. She closed her eyes in anger when the answering service picked up his line. Diane felt an irrational desire to punish Alan for his absence.

It took a good quarter hour for Diane to compose herself. Gradually she saw that she had no right to be angry with Alan. She had told him all about Bradley, but the needs that led her to that relationship were essentially outside Alan's emotional field. She could be angry with Alan for not being there when she needed him, but it was no more fair to blame him for not being able to understand what she had felt for Bradley than to blame him for not being able to sing. It was simply a question of incapacity.

Alan had not had time for unsensible passions. He would not have allowed himself to make Diane's mistakes with Bradley. It was not so much strength of character on

Alan's part as it was a too ready acceptance of limitations. The reason he was instantly comfortable with high-level executives as well as celebrities (she remembered how nonchalantly he shook hands with Bradley) was that he did not compete with them. Perhaps what bothered her most that moment about Alan was how comfortable he was with himself. Diane's frequent discomfort, psychologically, stemmed from her desire to be like so many different people. Alan would never understand the restlessness that made her susceptible to Bradley's glamour. There were days when she saw Alan's stability as a virtue, something to be envied, even emulated. But this afternoon, she resented his plodding energy. He had an immense capacity for love, now that it was time to turn his mind to it, but he lacked the element of passion that allowed him to lose control.

By the time Diane left for Bradley's, she was glad she had not been able to reach Alan. Seeing Bradley was taking on the inevitability of death. Like death, it was something she must undergo on her own.

Diane sat down on a bench inside the East 72nd Street entrance to Central Park. She needed the fifteen minutes to reach Bradley's by two o'clock, but she was not ready. She could not bring herself to surrender the tranquility of the day for the chaos of life beyond Fifth Avenue.

She would be able to handle the interview, to ask questions, to write down answers. He would probably make an allusion to their week together. She rehearsed the possibilities, but she could not figure out Bradley's motive for seeing her. It was like him, but what did he want out of it? He would hardly be sardonic, not after the phone call she'd made from Minneapolis. It was equally difficult to imagine an apology—not after six months. Too much had happened to her, too much had changed. She had assumed he was sensitive enough to understand that, but now she was not so sure.

Bradley was tan, trim—and tired. Diane managed a cool "hello." She did not take the hand he proffered. His apartment was cold. There were boxes everywhere, some filled, some empty. There was an echo in the hallway as she followed him into the living room.

It would not have been accurate to say Bradley seemed like a stranger, but he was transformed. The tension between them was a steady reminder of what had been. But the energy was debilitating, like a persistent mild electric shock dulling her emotions.

"Would you like a drink?"

She shook her head, unable to look into his eyes. He poured Scotch into a tumbler for himself. It was the gesture of a man who had gotten into the habit of needing a drink. He sat down on the wing chair opposite her.

"This is very difficult," he said.

"Yes, it is." She took a steno pad and pen out of her purse.

"No tape recorder?" His allusion to the previous interview did not affect her.

"There isn't time. The story's due this afternoon."

"Congratulations on your new job." He took a sip of his drink. "I enjoyed the article. It was nicely done."

"Thank you." Pleasure competed with resentment at his compliment, but she fought to make her words indifferent. He must not affect me, she thought. "When's the movie going to be released?" She sat with pen on paper. "And who's releasing it?"

"I didn't ask you here to talk about the movie."

"That's the reason I came."

"There were things I wanted to tell you after you called from Minneapolis" he began. "But when I found out your mother died, I knew I'd waited too long. Did the flowers—?"

"They were late."

"I am terribly sorry about your mother. Terribly. I had to tell you that in person."

Diane was trembling. "I have to do this story. But I won't talk to you about my mother."

"Still, I'm sorry."

Bradley walked over to the fireplace, took some paper off the mantel, and handed it to her. "Here's the press release on the movie. It will answer your questions."

"It won't describe your experiences on the filming."

"I spent most of my time in Los Angeles rewriting the script." Bradley's impatient tone made it clear that the subject did not interest him.

"Why was some of the movie filmed in Mexico?" she asked.

"We were allowed to dam up a small river in lower California and film the desert being flooded. It's supposed to be Palm Springs. The effect is spectacular, but it's hard to believe the time and expense that went into building a set and then destroying it in thirty seconds. It was incredible." Bradley got excited, remembering.

"You went to Alaska, too, didn't you?"

Bradley nodded. "It wasn't at all what I expected. It was hotter than hell. On the way back from the glacier before shooting, the Indian guides would pick handfuls of mosquitoes off their faces, the way you brush hair away from your eyes. They won't use repellents."

"What did you do in Mexico and Alaska?" She jotted down his observation about the guides.

"Once in a while we rewrote dialogue. But it was tedious. I don't know why anyone would choose to become a director. Diane—" He broke off suddenly. "I want to talk about what happened."

"I'm here to talk about the movie." Diane's smile was contrived; it did not cover up her resentment. She didn't care. Bradley studied her as she wrote. He was not nervous. The word she settled on was *subdued*. He did not dominate the conversation. He did not show off. Diane had the impression that he was watching her, waiting for the right moment for a speech he had rehearsed. But Diane wanted no explanations. Everything with Bradley had been false. She was not sorry to have known Bradley; people learned from mistakes. It was some consolation to her that so far, at least, she had always become a better person for her mistakes.

"Didn't seeing me have anything to do with your coming?" he asked.

"I wanted to see you six months ago." It was futile, supposing they could meet again and not talk about what had happened. "I spent six weeks alone in Nantucket. It was so quiet at night, the silence rang in my ears. More than anything in the world, I wanted you to call and apologize. I also wished I'd never met you. I have never experienced such a strong desire to undo something."

"Paying me back didn't undo anything."

"I cringe every time I think about taking your check." For the first time, Diane was able to look into his face. "It's taken me a while to regain my self-respect."

Bradley shook his head. "You still take money too seriously."

"If you don't understand why I shouldn't have taken the money, you're more insensitive than I thought."

"What does that make me for offering?" They might have been discussing situation ethics.

"Nobody blames the tempter," she said. "He's just testing the person, or satisfying his curiosity. He's got nothing to lose. It's a game."

"It was more than a game," Bradley insisted. "I was fascinated from the beginning with your sense of what you deserved."

"I deserved better than I got from you." Diane's eyes blurred with tears, but she managed to keep the choking out of her voice.

Bradley stood up and walked to the window. In the autumn sunlight, he looked older than she remembered. His face was grave, with deep circles under his eyes and skin soft with fatigue. He had not finished his drink.

"Susan and I broke up the night you called."

"I'm not talking about you and Susan."

"I'm sorry I lied, Diane. But I knew you wouldn't be interested in me if you knew that Susan and I were engaged, and I couldn't wait. I never wanted anyone the way I wanted you."

Her face flushed with his profession of desire. "I can accept the fact that you lied," Diane blurted out. "But what I really resent was all your talk about time and money and how it would improve me."

Bradley frowned. "All I did was offer you the opportunity to live out your own fictions. I tried several times to tell you I was unhappy, but you didn't want to hear it. My unhappiness didn't fit in with your conception of life among the rich and famous. You were seduced by *your* false values, Diane, not mine."

She acknowledged the possible truth in his observation by casting her eyes down.

"Susan must have been as mad as I was when she found out."

"The problem was, she wasn't. I left Susan because she was too ready to forgive me, too ready to believe it was just a casual fling. She acted as if I'd committed an indiscretion with the help. I am sick to death of arrogance and nonchalance."

"I called to invite you to the wedding," Diane said, staring doggedly at the lighter squares on the walls where Bradley had taken down paintings.

"I knew that."

"I was afraid. I didn't think I could face my mother's death alone. But I did. And here I am, I've lived to tell about it."

"I wanted to call you back that night and thank you for having had the courage to call."

"I was so embarrassed when you didn't." Her observation was uttered with a choked whisper.

"I hope someday you'll forgive me for not coming." Bradley was solemn.

Diane felt flat, dull. She wanted to leave. "Alan came."

"Smart man. Will you marry him?"

"Probably."

"That's the beauty of a back-up."

"You have no right to say that." The words burst forth so angrily from between her compressed lips that they startled Bradley.

"You're right," he said. "I just get bitter when I realize that I may have blown everything because I lacked the imagination to believe that you might forgive me. If I had had the courage to call."

"Did I make it that hard?" The fact that she no longer cared enabled her to restrain tears.

"I knew if I met your mother I would tell her I wanted to marry you. But I was afraid to make the commitment. When I found out she had died, I wanted to marry you more than ever. But I felt like I'd waited too long. Not seizing the opportunity was the unforgivable sin."

Bradley's declaration was not real. It belonged to the

realm of the might-have-been like a conversation about the South winning the Civil War. Diane was surprised, but more than anything she felt immense relief. She had been closer to his feelings than she realized. She frowned. This sense of justification was not the right note at all, but she could not help it. Bradley had loved her. It mitigated the suffering. It made her feel less foolish.

"I don't know which of us is the bigger egotist," she said. "You left because your timing got screwed up. I sit here thinking it doesn't matter anymore how much it hurt because knowing you cared means I didn't make a total fool of myself." She looked up at him. "Your experiment has blown up in our faces."

"But you at least emerged a better person," he said. "You learned something."

"I learned that dreams are disappointing when they come true."

"You were too old to believe in fairy tales." His stare fixed her.

"Yours were so entertaining, I could hardly wait to suspend disbelief."

"You're mad because they didn't come true."

"You're pretending you never believed what you said," she protested. "But you offered your creed like a missionary preaching gospel."

"To a receptive heathen," he smiled. "Diane, you were happy with me and I was happy with you. For one week, the dream was true."

She shook her head; the distance between them was too great for regret. When he approached, she raised her hand as if fending off a blow. He dropped into the chair across from her. "You can't marry Alan because of what I did."

"He loves me."

"You don't have to do penance for dreaming."

"It's—" The telephone interrupted her. Bradley sprang up, expecting the call, and went into the kitchen. Alone, Diane saw everything in an altered light—cold, stark white. Bradley's voice, her footsteps on the parquet floor pacing from window to window, echoed hollow. She could not remember the atmosphere of rootedness, of success, that had pervaded the apartment during their first dinner together. She recalled falling asleep in front of the fireplace, waking up in love, but these events were remembered from a former life.

She was not sorry it had happened. She retained the habit of her old values, and felt pride remembering. That he had been falling in love with her, too, overjoyed her. She was tempted to agree with Trudy that their sudden ending was better than the slow death of her relationship with Bradley. It was almost enough to revive her sense of adventure.

Diane thought of all her friends for whom New York had yet to live up to its promise—actors who waited tables, composers who played piano bars by night, abstract photographers shooting catalogues for Montgomery Ward. She was on her way. The article that had come from her interview with Bradley was the foundation on which she launched her entry into the entertainment world. She learned that its values were false, but it would be fascinating, documenting the lie firsthand. This new perspective might even work to her advantage, enabling her to keep her bearings in a crazy world. Diane knew what was important now. Going home had enabled her to emerge from Bradley's experiment not only intact, but with a stronger sense of herself.

Agitated, her mind racing, Diane walked over to the fireplace. She was no longer nervous. The dull throb of memory was subsiding. She opened herself tentatively to the associations of the apartment. She felt clearheaded. It was as if a migraine sufferer opened her eyes suddenly and discovered that the pain was gone. Completely. She would write another good article. Something positive would come of all this pain.

A Jiffy bag on the mantel spilled stuffing from a jagged tear. It was from Bradley's publisher. There was a set of galleys inside. Diane pulled them out and read the title page:

Propositions
(Working Title)
A novel by John Bradley

Diane decided not to read the brief description that followed, and was putting the galleys back in the packet when Bradley got off the phone. He came into the room with a bottle of Scotch, a bottle of soda, and two glasses filled with ice.

"Sorry about the interruption."

He had not seen her put the galleys back. She was sitting again when he set the glasses on the table between them.

"Are you sure you won't have a drink?"

"Some soda, maybe." She smiled for the first time. She felt better. "I've got to write the article this afternoon."

"That was my agent." He poured her drink. "I owe Hartley-Bennett a final chapter on the new novel. They want the book out by spring. It's getting tight."

"That's the novel you gave me the advance for, isn't it?" He was no longer intimidating. It was not hard to ask the question.

He nodded.

"Why don't you cash my checks?" she said, indifferent to his uneasiness. "It's hard to balance my checkbook with fifty thousand dollars outstanding."

"I have no intention of cashing them." He was firm. "You may not keep your end of the bargain, but I'm keeping mine. Besides, I owe it to you. You gave me the idea for the second novel."

Diane had not intended to discuss the book, but hearing this, she could not pretend to herself that she was not curious.

"I saw the manuscript on the mantel. You're not a 'Junior' anymore."

"I've dropped the suffix." He smiled. "It's part of the new me—a redefined relationship with my father."

"I hope you've decided to be nice." Diane regretted the familiar tone of the observation. Bradley smiled.

"I did a lot of thinking after I found out your mother died. One of the things I like most about you, Diane, is how genuinely you loved your parents. It seems one of life's typical ironies that you lost both your parents while mine lived, unappreciated and—yes—unloved. I had a long talk with my father about us. I had to tell someone exactly how I felt about you. Never in our life together had we attempted a conversation of that magnitude. And I discovered something: Asking my father what I should do about you was a way of asking him what we should do about ourselves. We could never have discussed it directly. But he responded enthusiastically to my question."

"What did you ask him?" Diane said.

"If I ought to marry you. He said yes. I told him it was too late. He offered to call you himself." They both smiled. Bradley's eyes were moist. "It was like being a child again, bringing an insoluble problem to an all-knowing father, except that I never had that experience as a child. The strain in our relationship goes back as far as I can remember. And then to have him offer to call you—it touched me. I've no doubt Dad would have been as overbearing as ever on the phone with you. But the fact that he offered to help changed everything. He's still a pompous ass. But one of the things you taught me, Diane, is that I don't have to like my parents to love them. They have their weaknesses, and God knows I've got mine. But when my father offered to help, I discovered the link between us." Despite the tenderness with which Bradley watched her, Diane felt like crying not because Bradley had become closer to his parents, but rather because what he said reminded her how much she missed her own mother and father.

"There is so little time," she said, reaching over to look for a tissue in her purse, "and so few people who matter."

It was becoming clear to her as she returned his concerned gaze that despite everything she had tried to tell herself, she still cared about Bradley.

"I want to tell you about the novel," he said.

"Go ahead." She wiped her eyes. "You've been trying to tell me about it ever since I got here."

"It's a love story," he began. "Max Henley is a forty-two-year-old millionaire with a novel on the best-seller list. He's in New York, working on the film version of his book. He meets Kathryn Bergman, the film's promotion manager. Kathryn is young, beautiful, and"—Bradley looked at Diane meaningfully—"ambitious. Henley's seen the type, but he's attracted in spite of himself. They go out, get drunk together. Kathryn talks about the things she might have been, the things she might have done, if she'd been born into Henley's world of money, family, and connections."

"Sounds vaguely autobiographical." The observation was easy to make. Diane even managed a smile as she wrote down the names of the book's hero and heroine.

"Based on fact." The mischievousness in his smile was premature. She could have listened to the actual history of their affair without flinching. "Max and Kathryn do a seventy-two-hour version of the week you and I spent together."

"Just the way it happened?"

"The parts in New York and Paris. I made some of it up, of course. We—Max and Kathryn—go for a moonlight skinnydip in St. Tropez, and pick strawberries outside a chateau on the Loire. If we did it over again," Bradley reflected, "I'd leave New York and Paris. The big cities make people false. That's the only way I can explain not going to see you in Minneapolis. Our best day together was in Maine. We were ourselves there."

"I don't see what living in New York or Los Angeles had to do with your not coming to Minneapolis." Diane found the trace of self-pity in Bradley's voice irritating. "I'd rather have you say you didn't want to take responsibility for my life because it was an unreasonable request on my part than because you live in New York. Where are you moving?"

"I bought an old farmhouse in the Berkshires." Diane thought about the six weeks in Nantucket, the peace and solitude. Perhaps there was some truth after all in what he said about cities. Yet they were sweet-tasting potions that intoxicated before they poisoned. Now that she knew her limits, Diane was not afraid to indulge occasionally in the delusions of big cities.

"I wouldn't be back in New York if it were as simple as you pretend," she said.

"I have to try something." Bradley was morose. His eyes moved restlessly around the room. "I have grown intolerably dissatisfied with myself."

"What happens to Max?"

"Max's first wife left him for another man, and he won't risk being hurt again. Kathryn feels compromised by their affair. At the same time, she's grown comfortable with the chip on her shoulder. Their defenses appear insurmountable. Or it may be that Kathryn just prefers to see them that way. Then Kathryn's mother dies suddenly and she asks Max to go home with her. But Max is afraid—" Bradley cleared his throat. "He cannot accept his share of the responsibility for their feelings. He allows them to drift apart."

"Max is not a coward." Diane's observation was explosively detached. "He's just mature enough to be a realist."

By talking about Bradley's fictional characters, they could talk about themselves. It was the final level of irony in their relationship.

"I want to read you something." He got up, took a sheet of paper out of the Jiffy bag, and read standing at the fireplace.

"In *Propositions*," he began in a dramatic voice. (Was anything *real* in Bradley's world?)"A man and a woman experience a happiness for three short days that most people only dream of, a happiness they lose because they cease to believe that the moment can be recaptured. It's a real-life love story, a bittersweet reminder that true love demands a never-ending faith in all its possibilities."

"That's pretty melodramatic." The excesses of style protected her from an emotional reaction.

Bradley was undaunted. "That's what the phone call was about just now. We're debating whether to insert an 'almost' before the word 'lose.' "

"How would it read then?"

" 'A happiness they *almost* lose because they cease to believe that the moment can be recaptured.' "

"They want to give the story a happy ending?" Diane felt utterly detached from the novel.

"I want to." Bradley was precise.

"Why?"

"Two reasons." He had presented his argument before. "First, because romance is in, and it will sell a lot of books. But more important—" His eyes met hers. He was earnest. "Because that's the way the story ought to end. Our lives have a natural rhythm. You and I violated that rhythm when we drifted apart."

Bradley's "you and I" hit Diane's ears like an explosion. Literature became life. Interview became explanation. She could not speak. She was not elated, not dejected, not angry. She felt empty. She had not expected to hear what she had heard. She could not take it in.

"You and I have something in common." Another assault on her senses. "You've always believed that you could get where you wanted to go. It took me longer to accept the possibility of success. But here we are, Diane. You and I are successful people. We were meant to be happy."

"It's taken you a long time to let me in on the secret," she said bitterly.

"After I didn't go to Minneapolis, I was certain of failure. I knew that you would never forgive me for letting you down. Later, when it occurred to me that you might forgive me, I was afraid of success. Success is much more frightening. If I tell you what a terrible mistake I've made and ask you to forgive me and you decide not to, all we have to do is say goodbye. Failure is very straightforward. But success is an ongoing thing. You have to work at it. Once boy gets girl, he has to keep her. There are very few things I've worked hard for, Diane. The most important thing I learned from you is that there *are* things worth working hard for. You're one of them."

"It's too late." Head lowered, signaling with a shake of her head that he was not to comfort her, Diane wept silently. She cried all the tears she had not cried at her sister's wedding and her mother's funeral. She cried for the life she would lead far from her family, describing a culture that offered no lasting cure for emptiness. Like a desert traveler dying of thirst who stumbles into an oasis but who is too weak to lower a bucket into a well, Diane arrived too late at Bradley's revelation.

"I won't believe that." There was stubbornness in his denial. Bradley would always expect to get his way, however else he changed.

Diane stopped crying and rubbed her eyes on the sleeve

of her blouse. "I have to get back. This article is due at
six o'clock."

"I need your help on the last chapter." Bradley handed
her the manuscript.

"I'm sorry." Diane stood up and prepared to leave. "I
can't."

"Take this with you." He handed her the manuscript.
"Start reading after you finish the article."

"I can't, John."

"I'll meet you in front of the *Times* building at
seven-thirty."

Diane consulted her watch, calculated, accepted his
invitation.

Diane had spent six months building a geometry of
axioms proving that it was impossible for them to get back
together. She had invested too much psychic energy in the
system to unlearn it. Bradley had been dishonest. It made
everything that happened between them false. They had
become different people. It was too late.

Again, she felt the pain of his lies; the aching lump in
her throat hurt the same way as the realization that her
mother was dead.

Among Diane's friends, it was not uncommon for lovers
to end up friends after they separated. But she was not sure
that she had the strength to see Bradley again. It seemed
foolish that she had agreed to read the book, insane that
she considered forcing herself to work with him on the
project. Diane was saddened, suddenly, to feel herself
falling into the old trap of considering not just the emotional
aspects of working with Bradley but also the ways it might
advance her career. Clearly, the lesson she'd learned because of Bradley was to have the maturity to pass up this
kind of opportunity. Yet here she sat in the cab, on her
way back to the paper, with a manuscript on her lap
written by a man with whom she had fallen in love, a man
who had hurt her deeply.

She didn't have to be around Bradley long, she reflected, smiling to herself, to be filled with contradictory
emotions. In the next moment she was grateful for his
callousness, which led her, after all, to Alan, her friend for
as long as she had been away from home. Alan had known
her mother and her father. In a moment when Diane felt

the familiar urge to call her mother from work—since coming back to New York it often seemed that she and her mother were merely separated by fifteen hundred miles again—it meant a lot that Alan had shaken her father's hand at graduation and kissed her mother goodbye after Lynn's wedding. A part of Diane had died with her parents. Bradley had chosen not to know that part of her. Feeling again the pain of Bradley's rejection, Diane *knew* for the first time what she had only realized before: Her mother was dead. Diane would have to get through life without her.

I am alone, she thought.

I am on my own.

I am free, Diane said to herself.

Each thought circled the same disturbing reality.

Pondering the gigantic map of the world in the *Times* lobby, Diane was frightened and exhilarated by the roads before her. She was just embarking on the journey of her life. There were countless lands still to see. Bradley's declaration of love was indirect, which kept it unreal. The one thing that was certain was that Diane would read Bradley's book as soon and as quickly as possible. That she worried whether Alan would be angry that she met with Bradley again was an indication of how serious their relationship had become. Her mother had said that Alan would allow her freedom. Her meeting that night would be his first test.

Impatient to start Bradley's book, she finished the article on his movie quickly. Though not inspired, by sticking to the straight-forward and factual, it was interesting. Her editor's revisions were minor. Neither alluded to her earlier reluctance to interview Bradley.

After filing the story, Diane got a cup of coffee. It was quieting down in her area. The next morning's paper and most of Sunday's were written. She sat back, put her feet up on her desk, and began thumbing through the manuscript. She took notes on a pad of yellow legal paper as she read.

It was difficult at first to accept the female protagonist. Bradley's Kathryn was brash, sexually aggressive, single-minded about her career. To meet Kathryn Bergman was a chastening experience. The character had some of Diane's worst flaws. She found herself writing comments such as "Not true" or "She *never* would have done that" on the pad. Bradley's apparent perception of her made it difficult to believe that he could have fallen in love with such a woman.

The book showed Diane the tremendous transformation that had taken place within her since the trip home. She wanted to take Bradley through the book page by page to show him how much she had grown. Because these changes were partly due to her relationship with Bradley, there was gratitude intermingled with the pain of growth. It was ironic, she thought, that the pain of her relationship with Bradley had imparted a knowledge more profound than he had promised. Equally impressive, he was able to chart the development of his characters from a self-centered man and woman concerned only with their own ambitions into decent human beings whose tragedy was their inability to be honest with each other. Diane found she cared enough about Max and Kathryn to hope that they would be able to let down their defenses.

Diane would have disavowed the portrayal altogether if it had not been for the honest depiction of Bradley as Max Henley. The author did not spare himself. He came across with all his vanity, arrogance, and aimlessness.

In the early chapters, Max and Kathryn were busy exploiting each other. At first, they were barely nice enough to interest the reader in their fates, but as the book progressed, they outgrew their selfishness. Gradually, Max made up for his earlier callousness, so that when he begged Kathryn to forgive him for not going home with her after her mother's death, the reader was set up to feel that the heroine ought to forgive him. However, forgiveness did not come so easily to Diane in the real world.

By the time Diane finished the book, her instincts as a writer were taking over. She had distanced herself from the story's autobiographical roots and was absorbed in how it ought to end. She ignored parallels between what Bradley had called the "rhythm" of their lives and those of his characters. Yet with a book based so much on her own personal experience, Diane found it difficult to be objective. Bradley had clearly written a good novel. However, with a residue of her ingrown puritanism, Diane was not sure that it was fair to write a book so close to the "real story." As a mirror of reality the book could never do justice to the pain of her growth. Perhaps it was unfair for Diane to feel a vague dissatisfaction with the novel. It was not the book she would have written. Possibly it was better.

Signing out of the building and putting on her raincoat, Diane was not nervous about seeing Bradley. If anything, she was excited. Whatever the book's sales, it was more important than his first book. She was proud to have inspired the book, but her personal evolution justified the honor. She was a worthy model. The opportunity to renew her relationship with Bradley, however altered the circumstances, was too important to dismiss categorically. So much would depend on what she said about his book, and how he reacted. However, she was learning that beneath an appearance of fragility relationships rarely hang in a balance. Like children, they were deceptively resilient.

Forty-third Street was jammed with taxis returning from the theaters. Her shoulder bag bulged with the manuscript as Diane surveyed the crowded street. She wanted to see Bradley before he saw her, but she heard him call her name before her eyes found his.

He was sitting in the back of a horse-drawn hansom cab, which pulled up to the curb where she stood. She could not repress a smile.

"Hello," he called to her. The driver, dressed in a top hat, got down to open the door of the hack and help her up. Bradley was in a tuxedo. He offered her a dozen roses as she sat down beside him. "Champagne?" He poured wine to the brim of a crystal glass. Diane shook her head at his incorrigibility. She took the glass, spilling it on both of them.

"What do you think?" Bradley nodded toward the manuscript.

"It's good." She took a sip of her drink.

"What about the last chapter?"

She considered her words carefully. The driver was looking toward them for instructions, but Bradley, eager to read the message in Diane's eyes, did not see him. "I think''—she paused, considered—''I think your publisher's right. People won't buy a happy ending.''

''You're wrong.'' Bradley was disappointed and hurt. ''You underestimate the imagination of the average reader.'' He looked up into the tall buildings or the sky, as if searching for additional evidence that would show her she was wrong.

''It doesn't happen that way in real life, John.''

''It can. I'll give you an example. Suppose I ask you to marry me and you accept?''

His words burst upon her. Could she ever consider marrying a man who had hurt her so much? Suddenly, despite all her sensible arguments to the contrary, she realized that she could. Then she thought of Alan, and the words ''kindness'' and ''friendship'' came to mind. It was painfully clear to her that she loved both men—deeply, with different parts of herself. Her friendship with Alan and her passion for Bradley were equal in intensity. However, though her feelings of friendship came from a part of her that she had learned to value during the trip home, Bradley's passion spoke to her heart. Diane had not expected the painful luxury of having to make this choice. She needed time.

''What did you say?'' Diane looked into Bradley's eyes.

''I asked you to marry me.''

''You want to marry me?'' Diane smiled with disbelief. ''Why?''

''Because I love you. I've loved you since the night at Coco's, when I realized you wouldn't use me to meet famous people.''

Satisfaction made her smile. ''That was earlier than I fell in love with you.''

He laughed. ''I would marry you just to make you stop keeping score. How about it, Diane. Will you marry me?''

''I don't know, John. I'm afraid . . .''

Time and place dropped away. Diane was slipping over the precipice. Alan reached out for her but it was too late. She was falling. His face receded to a point of light. At the moment it vanished, she was flying. Diane was torn between the desire to close her eyes and fly and the desire to look at Bradley. She kept them open.

''Diane.'' Bradley's voice recalled her tenderly.

"I'll marry you on one condition," she said.

"Anything." It was the most romantic thing she had ever heard him say. His urgency almost made her lose her concentration.

"Cash my checks."

She would not have imagined Bradley capable of a whoop. Several passersby stopped to stare. He grinned.

"Have some champagne." He handed the driver both their glasses. "We're going back to my place." He turned to Diane. "The bank opens at nine o'clock," he said.

"There's a cash machine down the street from you," she said, smiling.

He was laughing as he took Diane into his arms and kissed her. She met his lips eagerly. When she closed her eyes, there was nothing in the world except Bradley's touch, and the music of the horse's hooves on the asphalt, like the sound of bricks falling one by one from the walls around them.

ABOUT THE AUTHOR

Tim Paulson works as an advertising sales executive in Los Angeles, where he lives with his wife, Jane, also a writer, and their three sons. This is his first novel.

FROM THE BESTSELLING AUTHOR OF

F A M E & F O R T U N E

—A NOVEL OF THREE BEAUTIFUL WOMEN,
RISKING EVERYTHING TO HAVE IT ALL . . .

PERFECT ORDER
KATE COSCARELLI

A fast-paced luscious page turner that pulls out all the
stops to tell it as it really is for the super-rich, the
super-powerful, and the super-sexy. Glamorous Manhattan, with its whirlwind of social, political, and romantic intrigues, sets the stage for the story of Trish,
Ann, and Millie—three women who share a passionate interest in the handsome senator and presidential
hopeful Red O'Shea, and are soon swept into the
exciting millionaire's world of Fifth Avenue condos,
appointment-only luxury shopping, and high-level political game playing.